A MIGHTY FORTRESS

BEING AN ANTHOLOGY

OF

MORMON STEAMPUNK

EDITED BY

HOLLI ANDERSON

CONTENTS

INTRODUCTION

To be honest, I wasn't much into Steampunk before this series of Mormon Steampunk anthologies was suggested by D.J. Butler. In fact, the only Steampunk book I'd ever read was The Extraordinary Journeys of Clockwork Charlie: The Kidnap Plot by Dave Butler (the aforementioned D.J.). So, this has been a great opportunity to open up a new genre to add to my ever growing list of "books I like to read."

I'm still astounded at the number of submissions we've received in these last couple of years – who would have thought that combining two unlikely concepts such as Mormon and Steampunk would evolve into *four* anthologies full of stories as different from each other as we humans are.

I'm thrilled to have been asked to edit this edition. It was genuinely a pleasure to work with these amazing authors – both well-known and new to me. The vast array of stories shows that the imagination is as immeasurable as the cosmos.

Holli Anderson

Marvelous Works, and Wonders

Michaelbrent Collings

It was my mother who got me into this, I was sure—she was the one who insisted we go to the "Mormonite" church in the first place.

"Brother Josiah."

Either her or the Book of Mormon.

"Brother Josiah?"

Or maybe the Legend of Joseph Smith, or perhaps Brother Brigham himself.

"Brother *Josiah!*"

The shout finally penetrated the tangled skein of my thoughts. I'd been wondering more and more if I really wanted to be here, and one of the chief reasons for my doubt now stared at me with concern in his eyes. The eyes were huge, just like everything else about Brother Ezekiel. Well over six feet tall, with hands big enough to crush stone, feet that looked like paddles on one of the Ute steam warships, and muscles that would give a Clockwork Brave pause.

Of course, that last would only hold true if the Brave knew nothing of Ezekiel's spirit, which was also huge. Too huge. My missionary companion was a weeper. At first I loved that; such a tender heart, so much love! But the morning I found him weeping over oatmeal, muttering about the goodness of the Lord in each water-logged oat, I knew two things:

The first was that Brother Ezekiel was very likely going to Heaven. He was just that good a man.

The second was that I would very likely be the one who sent him there.

He was a good man, that much was true. I had no illusions about that, or about the sincerity of his belief. But he was so utterly *boring*. Everything was a miracle of some kind or other; a manifestation of the Spirit and the Lord's Arm Made Flesh. But here's the thing about everything being a miracle: if everything is a miracle, then you soon realize how boring miracles really are.

"How are you, Brother Josiah?" Ezekiel asked now.

"I am well enough, I suppose," I replied, fumbling with my purse for the only thing I really thought of as salvation these days: my Monica. I had bought the novelty from a traveling merchant named Hohner six months ago, and it had become my wont to fill the air with music whenever Ezekiel opened his mouth.

Well, perhaps "music" was a generous turn of phrase. But the sound *did* fill the air—at least enough that I could pretend not to hear Ezekiel. For that reason if for no other, I would always view that merchant with kindness and would give him the shirt off my back should he ever conspire to find me and should the request ever be made.

Not that he would need my shirt—he had not even needed my custom, and had "sold" me the amazing Monica for nothing at all after listening to Ezekiel drone about the marvels of clockwork the man had stuffed into his wagon along with instruments, elixirs, and everything else found in such traveling stores.

"You need this mouth harp more than do I," said Hohner, handing over the miraculous little instrument. He glanced at Ezekiel, who had moved into a full speech on the Miracles of Heaven which, I knew, would last another hour or so before finally moving onto the topic of Restored Gospel Things and Messages from Heaven.

"But I don't know how to play any Monica," I protested.

"Then learn, boy," he answered, with a dark, fearful glance in Ezekiel's direction. "For the love of the God you serve, *learn*."

Ezekiel saw me patting my pockets now, looking for the diversion my Monica presented. He was big and slow, but evidently he had finally figured out what my motions meant, for he began speaking in a rush:

"Walking along like this gives me pause and reminds me of the goodness of the Lord A'mighty and his wondrous ways—a marvel!—so many things a marvel and a miracle, a marvelous work and a wonder, isn't that right, Brother Josiah, and no, don't answer, I see you agree with me and would you please put your Monica back because you don't really know many songs in fact all you know I think is the opening notes to 'Airship to Kolob' and that is a lovely song though I wish you would let me sing along when you play your notes which though few are quite good and you really have come along nicely in your playing since –"

"Brother Ezekiel, do you have a point?" I heard the words come from my mouth as from a great distance. Had I taken full and final leave of my senses? I *knew* what his point was—that God is Good and the Lord Jesus Loves Us, for that was the point with *everything* where Ezekiel was concerned—and had no desire to hear it yet again.

Ezekiel blinked his big eyes. Shut... open. It took three seconds for the flap of skin to travel the vast distance over his massive eyeball, and I reflected that "in the twinkling of an eye," as it says in the scripture, might in truth mean "rather slow, all things considered," depending upon whether the apostle Paul was speaking of a normal twinkling or a huge, languid, Brother Ezekiel-style twinkling.

Even so, when the blink finished neither my right hand nor my left had managed to locate the Monica.

Ezekiel began speaking again. "No point, other than it is a marvelous, bright day, and gives me mind of marvelous, bright things as we continue upon our marvelous, bright mission to proclaim a marvelous work and a wonder."

I wasn't sure why I did what I did next. Perhaps it was a remaining shadow of the testimony that we are all children of God— the very thing that had inclined me to accept this mission call in the first place. Perhaps it was a hope that Ezekiel might say *something* I could like and so give me an anchor to love the ox-like creature.

Perhaps I had simply gone mad. No matter the reason, I again answered. "What kind of marvelous, bright thoughts are you having, Brother Ezekiel?"

Ezekiel seemed quite as caught off guard to hear the first question—and then its following inquiry—as I was myself. I kept searching my person for my Monica, but did not find the small box with its reeds that might save me as they had once saved Moses. Not from drowning in the Nile, but from suffocating under the weight of Ezekiel's tearful, fearful *sincerity*.

There! I found the instrument. I raised it to my lips.

Again, Ezekiel spoke, his words tumbling over themselves as he sought to interpose his thoughts betwixt me and the instrument of my salvation.

"Well, what kind of marvelous thing you ask and a good question, it is well I am minded of a story my Pa told me once—a great man, my Pa!, but of course you already know that—and it was about when he and Ma were first married (this was before the sealing was revealed of course but of course they were sealed as soon as feasible, sealed to the Prophet himself as their Spiritual Father!)—and they were eating the first meal together as man and wife and Pa—great man, Pa, a true marvel and a miracle, and so bright and witty of speech, that's where I got it from you know—and I guess Ma made chicken and I suppose it wasn't quite cooked and Pa—what a marvel, is my Pa!—said the most marvelous-amazing-wonderful-surprising thing."

I blinked. Ezekiel had stopped for breath, and to my surprise the story had actually *engaged* me. "What did he say?" I asked. I spoke in a whisper of near-reverence. Perhaps this was the answer to my prayer. Perhaps what Ezekiel said next would actually make me laugh, or give me pause to thought, or make me cry, and I would finally *understand* my companion and so would remember the belief in human kindness I had once possessed.

"What?" Ezekiel finally said.

I tamped down my irritation, pushing it deep as a ball in a musket, hoping I wouldn't explode. "What marvelous, amazing, wonderful, surprising thing did your Pa say, Ezekiel, when his new wife's chicken was not quite cooked?"

Another agonizingly-slow eye twinkle occurred. Then Ezekiel smiled a smile as big as the rest of him and said, with a look that would have told any onlooker that he was in the process of being caught up to Heaven, "Pa... he said the most marvelous thing. He's witty, my Pa. So smart. I love him. He's a *miracle*, and he said... he said..." And here Ezekiel put on an expression I supposed must have been an impression of his wise Pa's saintly features, though it mostly put me to mind of the face he had made when we ate a bit of bad meat and suffered internal distress for three days. "He said... 'I don't think this meat is quite cooked, my dear.'" Ezekiel had been walking throughout the course of his "story," but now paused. He shook his head in Rapturous wonder. "Amazing. A great, wise, witty man, is Pa."

I answered the only way one *could* answer such as this: I brought the Monica to my lips and blew as hard as I could.

Ezekiel usually fell silent at this point. But not today. Today he must have determined to no longer be junior companion to a mouth harp. He walked closer, and raised his voice, saying, "Isn't Pa a marvel? Isn't he witty and wise and –"

"*NO!*" I shrieked.

Ezekiel jumped back. My shout was the loudest sound either of us had heard in days, and it took us both by surprise. We'd been told the Indians didn't like loud noises, and to walk quietly when we reached their lands. We took that to heart. I even played my Monica quieter once we passed the Mizzy River. The Indians were the dominant power in the Promised Land, after all, with their Real Clockwork airships and paddle-boats, and any White crossing the Mizzy Line took his life in his hands.

But Brother Brigham had told us to go, and go we did. Things were looking worse and worse for the Saints, and he called us on a mission to preach the Gospel to the Indians in the southern part of America. "The Saints need help, boys," he said. "And I can think of no better way to help ourselves than to enlist the aid of a powerful nation like the Mapuche or even the Guaraní."

"We'll convert them all, Brother Brigham!" shouted Ezekiel—and bless me but I loved him for it at the time!

"Do that," said Brother Brigham. He stared at me as he then added, "But convert them or not, make sure to bring back some of the treasures of Heaven."

"What —" I began.

"Knowledge, Brother Josiah!" shouted the prophet. Or perhaps he whispered it; 'twas oft hard to tell one from the other with Brother Brigham. He clapped a hand on my shoulder. "We would love a great nation to join us in the Gospel. But if not, then perhaps they will take pity on us and lay bare some of their secrets to you. Knowing how to make Real Clockworks would certainly give the government pause next time they came for us."

That was true enough. Real Clockworks weren't things like the Monica or even the clockworks you found in the biggest stores at the Fort of Boton or Fort Plymouth. Real Clockworks were the reason the Indians had spread through the territories of North and South America, and tamed the wild places throughout. When the first pilgrims landed at Plymouth, expecting empty wilderness, instead they found the lands populated by cities with buildings that near to scraped the sky, the fields tilled by machines the like of which no White had ever seen or of which we had ever even dreamed.

The first Whites figured they were entitled to the secrets of Real Clockworks. The Indians said, politely enough, "No." The early settlers persisted. This time the "No" came in the form of the first Clockwork Braves, who trod out of the forest on steel legs, bladed arms flashing in the light.

The arms did not flash after a few scalps had been taken. They dripped with red and gore, and the scalps the Clockwork Braves took were then delivered to the folk at the forts along the coast where some Whites had somehow managed to maintain a toehold in this land.

The Indians sent actual people to deliver the scalps, and that, it is said, was the touch of hubris that gave Whites their chance. Within three months the Indian Nations were reeling—not under the might of the White Man's arms, but under the weight of the White Man's *diseases*. The Indian Nations caught twin blasts of pox and the French Disease, and it decimated them to the point they withdrew from the eastern half of North America, then set checkpoints beyond which Whites were forbidden, and withdrew behind them.

The Whites who dared live closest to the Indian Nations' lands said they heard loud thunders, and clanks and whirs as the Reds worked their arts of Real Clockwork. People were curious—people always are—but not many dared cross the Mizzy River, which marked the line between White and Red.

But Brother Brigham dared. Or at least, dared send *us*.

We had crossed the Mizzy three days ago. We walked quiet, for silence was the only thing every traveler said might give us a chance at survival.

So, of course, now I was shouting. But I couldn't help it. It all came bubbling up, and I shrieked at Ezekiel, again and again: "No, no, *no, no, NO!* I do *not* find your Pa to be a marvel, I do *not* think calling undercooked chicken 'undercooked chicken' is in any way a sign of wit or wisdom, and most of all *I hate every weepy, Spirit-touched word you speak!* Say one more thing today, Ezekiel—one thing at all!—and I swear to Heaven I will yank your tongue out by the root and then you'll never have to hear me play again because I'll never have need because you'll no longer be able to aggrieve me with your speech!"

"Brother Josiah," said Ezekiel quietly.

I growled—I do attest and swear, I actually *growled*—and started toward Ezekiel. "Open wide, Ezekiel. Speak what last words you –"

I stopped my march toward my missionary companion, halted by the look that had come over him. He pointed over my shoulder with a shaking finger, and I turned and looked—but I knew what I would see.

Three Clockwork Braves stood nearby. I probably would have heard them—they moved in clouds of steam, the whirr of their gears foretelling the doom that always accompanied them—had I not been yelling so loudly. Now it was too late.

Not that we could have run even had we heard them coming. A Clockwork Brave could run down a full-growed grizzly and beat it to death, then chase a mountain lion right up a tree, knock the tree down, and then beat the mountain lion to death as well.

Ezekiel fell to his knees, and I thought it was in fear, but then he said, "Oh, great one. We are missionaries who have brought the word of the Great Spirit to the Indian Nations."

I couldn't reckon at first why he was talking to Clockwork Braves, then I heard the laughter and realized that an honest-to-goodness Indian was standing just behind one of the behemoths.

It was a girl. Deep brown eyes, high cheekbones, hair that dangled in a long plait down her back. I had never seen an Indian—you could tell that just by looking at the hair that still sat firm on my skull—but I had heard tales of their beauty. Any White Man would sell his soul to simply see a Red Woman, it was said.

If anything, the stories understated it. The girl smiled as she laughed, and I had never seen teeth so white or straight. Looked like she had them all, too, which I had never seen to be the case in any White. My own mother had a full set of steel dentures she bought off a man who claimed to have gotten them from his great-great-great-granddaddy back when the Reds didn't completely despise the Whites and would actually give them bits of their miraculous inventions.

But the girl's teeth—so white! So straight! They stood out beautifully against the deep tones of her skin, and somehow those teeth became in that instant my idea of perfect beauty. "A marvel," whispered Ezekiel, and for once I agreed with him.

The girl touched the leg of one of the Clockwork Braves, and they moved toward us and I forgot about the Red Woman's beauty in that moment. I steeled myself, forcing myself not to run.

We were here for the Saints. We were their only hope.

The girl and her Braves stopped twenty paces from us. "You are missionaries?" she asked, and this story turned out true as well: she spoke perfect English, in tones so lovely and cultured that they would have made the King of England ask for lessons. She sounded amused.

Ezekiel, still kneeling, nodded. His head whipped up and down in the fastest movements I'd ever seen from him. "Yes, ma'am. We desire to stay among you for a time, to be your teachers if you wish or to be your slaves if you prefer."

I tried to tell Ezekiel to shut up, but not fast enough. The beautiful girl's features hardened when Ezekiel had the gall to suggest a White could teach a Red. But they softened fast enough when he suggested slavery. Not that she looked like she was considering the proposition—she was just laughing. "Slaves?" she managed between gasping laughs. "*White* slaves?" She wiped a tear from her eye. One of the Clockwork Braves vented, the steam sounding like he was laughing with his mistress. "What on earth could a White do for a Red?"

"Uh... we could tell you stories?" said Ezekiel.

The girl shook her head. "We have heard your stories, Ezekiel. For three days we have listened to them."

It did not surprise me that she knew Ezekiel's name. Or that she had heard his stories. Clockwork Braves, warships, and flying machines were not all the wonders the Indian Nations possessed. I had known they had machines that could listen to things a great distance away, and there were even stories of a thing called the Face Book that let the Reds talk to their friends and families even when they were miles apart.

So yes, they had been listening.

And yes, they knew our names.

And yes... that meant they also knew what kind of value Ezekiel's stories held.

We were in deeper trouble than I had thought.

"We don't have to be slaves," I said. "Or teachers. Just... just..." I tried to remember the reasons I had come. The Gospel. Enlisting the Indian Nations' aid for the Saints. Finding bits of technology Brother Brigham could use to trade for goodwill or just threaten off the mobbers that came upon the Saints nightly.

None of it came out of my mouth. I acted automatically, doing the thing I had trained myself to do whenever faced with discomfort. I put my Monica to my mouth and wheezed out the opening bars of "Airship to Kolob."

The girl turned her gaze upon me, and I still saw beauty, but woven with rage. "And we have heard your music, as we have heard your good brother's stories."

She gestured, and the last thing I saw was the Clockwork Brave's bladed arm coming at me, and the last thing I thought was if my mother would still love me even if I had no scalp.

The Brave must not have hit me with the edge of his blade, though, because I didn't fade into complete darkness. Nor did I ascend to the Bosom of Abraham or lose myself utterly in the destruction that awaits the faithless.

I experienced time as a jittering, quivering thing. Things grew light, then dark, then light again before settling into a murky haze. I thought I heard voices several times. Mostly Ezekiel's, and that was when I thought I *must* be in Hell, because he was always telling one of his boring, terrible stories... and worse, people were laughing and shouting as though in glee.

Then brightness came again. I saw white at the edges of my sight, with a dark smudge in the middle that gradually became the smiling face of Ezekiel. I groaned.

Well, I *tried* to. No sound came. Not a wheeze.

Ezekiel's smile drooped a bit. But only for a moment. "I have wonderful, marvelous news, Brother Josiah!" he shouted.

"What?" I asked. Or, again, *tried* to ask. Something was wrong with my throat.

I became vaguely aware that I was in a strange kind of bed, in a white room full of whistles and pops and odd, mechanical tones. One of the sounds was jittering regularly, a sound that I realized coincided with my heartbeat.

I reached for my throat, and saw that my hand had been swaddled in bandages. A tube of some kind had been inserted in the back of my hand, and I cried out—silently—at the sight of the thing burrowing into my flesh.

Ezekiel caught my hand. He pushed it down, gently but firmly. "Easy," he whispered. "You've been through a lot."

I shook my hand free, looking down at it and catching sight of my chest and belly. They were covered by a colorful blanket, but something about the shapes beneath was off. I shook my head in fear, trying to talk, to speak, to shout, to make *any noise at all!*

That semi-sad look reappeared in Ezekiel's eyes, and once again fled behind the ever-brightness that was his only real state of being. Going to Heaven, for sure.

"It's okay," he said. "I talked to them while you were asleep. They..." he hitched in a huge breath. "They *love* me here, Brother Josiah! Can you believe it? They say I'm the first White they've ever met who has anything sensible to say!"

I still couldn't speak, so made jittery motions with my hands. Ezekiel was slow, but he figured this out quick enough, and disappeared from the room for a moment, reappearing with a piece of paper and what looked a bit like a pencil but when I pressed it down on the paper a fine, even stream of ink trailed behind it.

"They call it a 'pen,' ain't it a marvel?" asked Ezekiel. Then he turned his head to read what I had written. "We're in a hospital," he answered. He looked around in wonder. "Lordy—oh, sorry, didn't mean to take His name in vain, but... well, have you ever seen a place like this?"

I scratched out another question. Ezekiel read it. He shook his head. "No, they ain't going to kill us."

Then what? I wrote.

"That's the best part, Brother Josiah!" he nearly shouted. "They love me, I told you that, didn't I?" My expression must have darkened a bit, and Ezekiel nearly cringed away. Then he brightened—always bright, always a bit of sunshine, my companion!—and said, "So they said that I was the first and only White they would ever let leave, and they would grant me a boon!"

Boon?

"A wish! Anything at all, they said they'd give it to me! Called me a great storyteller, and named me a Friend to the Indian!"

All my fear, all my dread—even the staggering memory of months on end with only Ezekiel's wit for company—all of it left in an instant. We could ask for *anything? ANYTHING!* That meant...

We can save the Saints, I wrote.

"Oh, I did better," he said. As he spoke, the door to the strange room opened and in walked a Clockwork. Not a Brave, this one was smaller, and had a thousand little arms that twisted and clicked as the thing adjusted various machines that ran to tubes that ran under the blanket that covered my body. Ezekiel watched it for a moment, and breathed, "What a marvelous work and a wonder!" He turned back to me and said, "I call it a Clock-doc!"

I ignored that, pointing at the question I had written: *When do you get to ask your wish?*

"I already did!" crowed Ezekiel. He beamed. "And they said *yes!* They agreed to take a copy of a Book of Mormon, and even to pay the printing cost! Not just in dollars, either—they gave us these!" He reached into his pocket and pulled out a handful of beads. He waited, then frowned. "Why are you crying, Brother Josiah?" Then he snapped his fingers and said, "Oh, I near forgot the best part!"

He turned to the Clock-doc that was still whirring around the room and said, "Can you show my good brother his gift?"

The thing twisted, clanked over to me, and threw aside my blankets. I was going to look down, but couldn't, because Ezekiel's face filled my vision again, this time haloed in brightness caused by a mixture of sunlight and the tears flooding my eyes. "I didn't want to accept their boon at first," he said. "'I couldn't think of it,' I said. 'Not unless good brother Josiah gets one, too.'" He grew pensive. "They didn't like that too much. Not at first. They said you were noisy and they didn't like you. But..." He brightened again. "I insisted! They wanted to know what you would like, but of course you had that hit on the head and couldn't talk much."

The hit on the head they *gave me!* I wanted to scream. And, of course, I could not.

Ezekiel continued, "So I had to tell them what you wanted. Of course, I *knew* what you wanted, since that's been the whole focus of our time together!"

I felt a ray of sunshine in my soul. We were here for the Saints. We were going to save the –

The Clock-doc made a sound like a knife scratching flint. It had no mouth to speak of, but there was a slit in its face area, and out came a sheet of paper. It was covered in markings—odd shapes that made me wonder if this was the Reformed Egyptian that the Nephites had no doubt passed on to their children and which perhaps even existed today in this place! After a moment of the sound, the Clock-doc tore the sheet of paper away, then leaned in close and...

I wanted to scream. But I couldn't. So I screamed in my mind as I watched the Clock-doc feed the paper into a slit in the mechanized monstrosity that had once been my body. I still saw bits of myself here and there—a patch of skin with the thick black hair that had always covered my chest. A line of muscles that had once sat firmly inside my body. My belly button was even there, suspended in the middle of a stretch of what looked like woven steel.

And the center of it all was a breathing bellows, covered in ribs of metal. The bellows moved in and out, and I felt myself breathing through them.

The paper the Clock-doc had been shoving into the hole in my chest suddenly jittered as though it had caught on something. The Clock-doc let go, and the page kept reeling into the thing that had been my chest, drawn in by some strange mechanism. The "lungs" inside me billowed, then squeezed, and a strange-but-familiar sound rang through the air.

Ezekiel fumbled around on a nearby table, and when he turned back to me he held up a mirror, showing me what he had given me. Showing me my wish.

I wanted to scream. Of course, I couldn't. That noise was forever forbidden me.

Ezekiel grinned, apparently not able to tell ecstasy from horror. "I knew you'd like it. You love your Monica so, and I told them all you ever desired was to play. And they did it. They made *you* a marvelous work, and a wonder indeed." He pointed to the paper still reeling into me. "It's the music, you see. It tells your Monica what to play."

My Monica.

The Monica that I had held to my lips a thousand thousand times.

The Monica that was now a *part* of me, the holes like a terrible grimace where my mouth had once been.

The sheet of paper entered.

The notes played through me.

"It's all you've focused on, all you've wanted. Your favorite song," whispered Ezekiel. "And now you play it... so... *beautifully*."

ABOUT THE AUTHOR

MICHAELBRENT COLLINGS IS AN INTERNATIONALLY-BESTSELLING AUTHOR, produced screenwriter, and multiple Bram Stoker Award finalist. Best known for horror, he has also written bestsellers in fantasy, science fiction, thriller, suspense, mystery, YA, and middle grad works, and even romance. More about him at his website, WrittenInsomnia.com.

Beautiful Zion, Built Above

Bryce Beattie

Seth Nickerson stayed late to polish the cylinders and scrub the rubber tubing that made up the bulk of his lakesuit. If he wanted to get that recommendation and become an engineer's apprentice, he'd need to demonstrate his commitment to stewardship.

"Nickerson? You still back there?" The booming voice of repair boss Levitt Felthouser filled the equipment locker.

"Yes, sir." Seth walked around the rack. "Just cleaning up my suit."

"Atta boy." Levitt motioned from the doorway. "There's a policeman here to talk about what's been happening with the pistons."

A man stood in the corner of Mr. Felthouser's office, dressed too fashionably to be this far west. He extended a hand. His handshake was as crisp as his suit.

"My name is Inspector Cochran. Might I have a word?"

Seth looked to his boss. "I guess?"

Mr. Felthouser nodded. "Just tell him everything you've seen down below, son."

Inspector Cochran pursed his lips. "And what exactly have you seen... down below?"

"Well, sir, I work on pistons 41, 57, and 58 for shaft five. And the last few times I've checked, 41 has had some unusual damage."

Cochran flipped open a journal. "What kind of damage?"

"It's all on the regenerant line." He paused to think of the least crazy manner of describing it. "There's a number of deep divots, in haphazard rows, right up next to the transfer fins."

"In a row?"

"In rows. Three or four marks together in a line, and dozens of lines all around the outside."

"And what do you think is the cause?"

"I honestly don't know. That steel is pretty thick. I'd have to use a torqued hammer to dent it like that."

"Torqued hammer?"

Mr. Felthouser nodded and pointed a meaty finger nowhere in particular. "One on a bench that's been geared up to the workshop's shaft."

Inspector Cochran nodded and wrote. "I see. And you really have no idea what is causing it?"

Seth opened his mouth but didn't want to say anything to the stiff interloper. Truth sounded too crazy. "No. Sir."

Inspector Cochran's expression didn't change. "No signs of a man or a crew other than yourself around the piston? Broken tools?"

"I've looked around, but haven't seen any tracks that I didn't make."

An uncomfortable silence hung in the air as the inspector wrote in his journal. Once finished, he looked straight into Seth's eyes with a careful, cold, and perceptive gaze.

Seth couldn't help but feel as if the inspector was memorizing everything about him.

"Anything else you think I should know?"

Seth shook his head.

"Very well. Thank you." The inspector placed his journal into his bag and pulled free a small card which he handed to Mr. Felthouser. "If any of your workers see anything, please send a messenger down to the central station to let me know."

"Of course, Inspector." He tossed the card on his cluttered desk.

The inspector turned and saw himself out.

As soon as the door shut, the beefy Leavitt Felthauser came around the desk and put a hand on Seth's shoulder. "Tell me what you didn't tell him."

Seth shook his head. "I don't even know how to say this, but lately the damage looks like..."

"Bite marks?"

Seth recoiled. "How did you know?"

"You'd better sit down for a moment."

Leavitt stared off into nowhere for a minute. When he finally began talking, his voice was low and gravelly. "This may sound like a jest, but it is not." He messed with one of the stacks of paper on his desk. "Everybody who works under the lake surface for long enough knows it. We just don't talk about it."

Seth shifted in his chair and could hardly squeak out a response. "What?"

"There's a beast, an enormous lizard, or something akin to it, that lives down there. Janson on two says its called an allie-gater."

Seth's stomach buzzed. "But it-"

"The boys who've seen it say its something out of Greek myth. Its head is as tall as a man, and its body is that length at least six times over."

"That's impossible." Seth shook his head. "How is it nobody knows? How does it survive winter?"

"We think it lives in caves heated by the same type of hot springs that drive the pistons. And really, nobody knows, because it ain't never touched a human, and we that keep the pistons pumping don't want to scare the folk of the city." His frown deepened. "Or scare new repairists."

Mr. Felthouser had to be making sport. Seth refused to believe an animal like that could exist. But what else could make those marks?

Mr. Felthouser turned around and walked back to his side of the desk. "Sometimes it'll take an elk or a bison from the shore. But the herds are so large, nobody notices."

Seth's mind raced. Could it be possible? A giant lizard? Those marks on the regenerant line... They looked for all the world like teeth marks.

"Try not to think on it too much, son." Leavitt clapped him on the back. "Me and the other repair bosses will come up with something."

Try not to think on it? Seth would be hard pressed to think of anything else.

Leavitt nodded to the door. "I'll see you tomorrow. And Nickerson, don't be telling that business to anyone."

"Yes, sir."

Seth Nickerson walked out of the building onto the pier and looked at his city.

Yellowstone Lake City, the beautiful Zion built above the lake, stretched out before him. Of course, the city had spread onto the shore two decades prior and now was half on land and half on stilts. The city bustled, with cable cars and rail trucks moving people and commerce.

Out of the city ran five long piers which jutted into the lake one hundred yards or more. Alongside the piers ran the shafts with their supports, cranks, and pistons.

The countless machinations of the city all drew torque via chain or gear from one of these five shafts. The shafts turned day and night, powered by the swarm of pistons, designed by Brother Sterling himself. The pistons were embedded into the lake bed atop underwater hot springs and geysers.

This city itself was one giant machine, beautiful and constant. The motion of the pistons reaching from the water was a clockwork poetry.

It was Seth's job to help keep the engineering marvel running. He was awestruck at the ingenuity and the hard labor that had turned wilderness to promised land.

Because they were able to harvest the earth's heat, Yellowstone Lake City didn't have the blanket of dirty smoke produced by the coal-fired steam engines that powered most cities. It was clean and it was beautiful.

Seth was grateful Brother Brigham had turned north instead of building a city on the ill-smelling shores of the Great Salt Lake down in the Utah territory. That would have been pitiable.

So whether the cause of the mysterious damage was beast or misguided man, Seth Nickerson promised himself he'd do anything to keep the pistons pumping.

As he walked down the pier onto the boardwalk of the city proper, a figure approached him from the lengthening shadows.

Seth recoiled before realizing it was the entirely too-well-dressed Inspector Cochran.

"So sorry to startle you, Mr. Nickerson. I thought it best to interview you briefly outside Mr. Felthouser's watchful eye."

"What?"

"I will be swift. Have you seen the beast?"

"What? No. I told you everything I saw."

"Ah." Cochran nodded. "But Mr. Felthouser told you about the beast?"

Seth's mind raced. He hated the thought of bearing false witness, but there was something about this Cochran fellow he didn't trust. "I'm sorry, sir. I don't know about this beast you've mentioned."

"Really? I've spoken to several repairists on other shafts who seemed quite comfortable discussing it."

Seth's fingers jittered and his voice wavered. "Really?" He was a horrible liar and he knew it.

Cochran's eyebrows pointed upward. "No matter. Wanting to protect someone you work for and respect is admirable, but there's much more at stake here than one man's reputation. That beast could mean the end of this city's power, and Leavitt Felthouser is doing nothing to stop it. If you decide you wish to speak, ask for me at the central station."

∞

Seth was the first one inside the repair station in the morning, besides Mr. Felthouser, of course.

The two other repairists on shift arrived just in time to see him in full gear, air pumps running, halfway descended in the aqualift.

His standard repair round went quickly and uneventfully. Nothing was amiss, except for even more damage on piston 41's regenerant line. If he hurried, he could do what he needed to do topside and have one more dive before the end of his shift. And maybe Mr. Felthouser would let him stay under until after dark.

Long before quitting time, Seth found himself in the workroom tying a net out of the thickest rope he could find.

After the other repairists had gone home, Mr. Felthouser stuck his head in the room. "What are you still doing here, Nickerson?"

Seth looked up from his work. He hadn't gotten anywhere near as far as he thought. "Tying a net, sir. I want to try to catch the beast."

"You think we haven't tried?"

"I figured, sir. I still want to give it a go."

"You're a good repairist, son. I'd hate to see you get hurt." He off-handedly slapped the door frame. "But, I'd wager you'd try even if I said no."

"Is that a yes?"

"Keep up on your rounds. And let me know when you are going to set up whatever your trap is."

"Of course, sir."

It took Seth the better part of a week to finish tying the net. His repairist brethren thought he was crazy, but they didn't know about the beast yet. Their lines hadn't been chewed on.

Thrice more, Inspector Cochran approached him on the boardwalk. Each time, Seth politely refused to say anything about the beast.

After that third try, Seth spoke to Mr. Felthouser.

"Well, I'm glad you haven't said anything to him." Mr. Felthouser put his feet on his desk. "I'm starting to think he might be working for one of the big steam engine companies back east."

"How so?"

"Big steam wants nothing more than for those pistons to fail.

Because if any of the main shafts go down, the city will have to replace the lost torque somehow, and you can bet they've got several factory-sized engines ready to load on the rails the day we ask for them."

Seth swallowed hard. "Really?"

"You have no idea how far big steam will go. No idea. I guarantee they have more than one spy in Yellowstone Lake City. Maybe they even know what the beast is doing and they want it to succeed. And they have enough money to buy anybody, even the inspector." He pulled his feet off the desk, scattering papers everywhere. "So you'd better pray that net of yours works. When will it be ready?"

"I think the net is big enough now. I just need a pulley. I could try this evening, sir."

"Good man, good man. I'll find you a pulley. After your rounds, get your tools back up into the locker, then get back down there. Stay down as long as you need. And good luck."

Seth's chest swelled with pride as he walked from the office. Mr. Felthouser was already treating him like a man. Like an equal.

∞

His underwater rounds went by quickly and uneventfully. Before he knew it, he was prepping and donning his suit once again, then lumbering back onto the aqualift.

Seth pushed the lever, and the aqualift began its slow descent.

The suit was bulky and made movements slow, but Seth loved wearing it underwater. He loved the way the sunlight danced in the waves and reflected off the brass plating. He loved looking through the half-dome glass helmet and seeing moss, fish, and lake bottom.

The part he didn't like was managing the air hoses. Two for intake, and one for exhaust. They kept him breathing fresh air, but were a bit cumbersome. This problem was compounded by the fact that he needed to drag the bundle that held his home-made heavy duty net. Seth smiled in spite of the difficulty.

The aqualift jarred into place at lake bottom. A swirl of silt rolled outward.

This was a good plan and he knew it. It was simple and direct. Made possible by the fact that he knew exactly where the allie-gater would be. The same spot had been damaged every night for the last several days. Seth couldn't figure why an animal would do such a thing, if there was indeed a beast. And his net would catch a person just as well even if Mr. Felthouser was wrong about there being a creature.

A pathway of water-logged railroad ties had been laid in a path running alongside the pier. Bisected ties made up the branching paths which ran out to the piston installations.

Seth checked the air lines and ropes to make sure there were no tangles, then set off down the path.

The swaying motion of the lake made it feel alive and breathing. And in some respects, it was. All around this area were steam vents, hot springs, and even underwater geysers. Some of the learned folk said there was more heat coming up from underneath the lake than from all the geysers and such on land.

Piston 41 was the closest installation to the pier. Looking along the surface, it was a mere stone's throw away from the repair station and pier to where the piston protruded from the water. It felt much longer while walking underwater.

When he reached his branch, he dropped the pulling end of the rope. The catching end went with him.

The incessant motion of the colossal piston was always a bit more impressive to watch from below than above the surface.

Seth reached the cement foundation and worked his way around the side to where the thick regenerant line stuck out and fed into the cluster of transfer fins.

Even with this thick rubber lining, Seth could feel the elevated temperature immediately surrounding the fins. They were doing their job, rapidly cooling the air in the line and pulling the piston back down.

Seth fumbled with the net until it lay perfectly near the regenerant line. He looped some rope over the top of a fin to give a good angle for the corners of the net. When he finished, he walked back to the main pathway.

He tugged on the end of the rope until he had removed most of the slack. All that remained now was the waiting.

Now and again an uncovered steam vent would erupt and release a mad flurry of shimmering, scalding-hot bubbles.

Seth always felt an outpouring of gratitude when he was witness to such a display. Thousands every year came to visit the Mormon-settled Yellowstone Lake City. Thousands continued northward to see Continued Faith, that famous geyser, erupt. But he was one of a handful of people who would ever see the majesty and the beauty of such powerful natural phenomena under the waves.

Seth stood next to one of the pier's support columns and waited as patiently as he could.

When the reds of the sunset skies appeared, the lake water became an enormous, gyrating shadow.

Seth squinted against the growing darkness and decided to head back to the aqualift empty handed. He took one final look toward the piston.

A shadowy form sped out from around the massive installation. Seth had never seen an animal so large, or so terrifying. It was every bit the size Mr. Felthouser had described.

Its hide was covered in patches of moss, with glittering scales showing through in places. Short legs lay against the powerful torso. An immense tail swished behind it, propelling it through the water. The worst part was the creature's long snout with its jagged teeth protruding alternately top and bottom.

Seth gasped. He hadn't been prepared to see anything that monstrous in size or appearance. Or anything that moved so quickly.

He could have sworn he heard a reverberating clang as the form closed the distance and attacked the regenerant line. For a moment, sheer terror washed over him and he dropped the rope. After the third strike from the beast, he regained his wits and fumbled for a new grip on it.

Seth was no longer sure that either the net or rope would hold, but what options did he have? Hand over hand, as swiftly as the lakesuit and water would allow, he pulled on the rope.

At first there wasn't much resistance. But after he had reeled in a couple of yards there was a tug, then a mighty jerk on the line.

Seth was lifted clean off his feet by the strong pull.

In a panic, he let go again and fell to the lake bottom. All of the rope he had pulled down zipped back up, then slacked.

A chill shot down his spine. He had thought the weight of his lakesuit would certainly be enough to hold and reel in the beast. He was woefully unprepared, and this wasn't going to work after all.

The silt kicked up by his fall wafted away, revealing the fearsome hulk of the allie-gater speeding straight for him.

Seth pulled and pulled and pulled on the rope, trying in vain to take up the slack. His arms burned from the effort, and his hot breath fogged up the front of his glass helmet.

The beast veered away just before reaching him.

Wide eyes straining to see sideways through the unfogged portion of helmet, he caught a full view of the allie-gater up close. Thank goodness the net was tangled around its snout and neck.

Seth's arms screamed in pain as he continued to pull the rope. He couldn't keep up. He worked as fast as he could, straining against water and lakesuit.

The creature swam underneath the boardwalk, circling wide. Every few yards it shook its head, trying to remove the thick net.

Seth wrapped as much of the rope as he could manage around the support pillar, then flopped it over the top of the portion leading back to the pulley. It wasn't exactly a great knot, but at least it made some kind of anchor.

The allie-gater veered sharply and raced back toward the center of the lake.

Seth gripped the rope and leaned back.

The creature ran out of slack. The rope went taut for one heartbeat, then snapped and drifted toward lake bottom. The beast swam by the piston and out into open lake.

Seth stared off into the distance, angry that his trap had failed. The creature was gone, and he might never see it again.

The beast whipped out from around the piston installation.

Anger pivoted into a gut-wrenching fear. Seth flung his body to the side, hoping to dodge the charge.

It was no use, the creature was too fast. Its mouth opened and chomped down on his left leg.

Pain and pressure tore through his leg, then he sunk again toward the lake bottom. The cylindrical brass armor had held, but bent under the strain.

He fell onto his back just to the side of the marked path. A cloud of silt erupted around him.

Seth whipped his head all around, searching for the terrible beast. He caught a glimpse—a close one. It zipped by so fast, he couldn't tell whether he had seen tail or trunk.

And then it was out of view again.

Seth held his breath, waiting for the creature to kill him. Another jolt and he spun on the lake floor, kicking up even more muck. Water jetted in at his neck. He reached up and grabbed at his air lines. When he pulled them close, he stared at three torn, ragged ends. Some part of the allie-gater's hide must have snagged the lines and ripped right through.

Seth's heart pounded and his gasping breaths intensified. Cold water filled his helmet.

He pushed up on his torso, allowing the water to pour down into the body of his suit. More continued to flow in. He jammed the gloved fingers of his left hand one at a time into the ends of the broken supply lines. The torrent slowed to a dribble. If he kept the hand low, he might still take on some water due to pressure, but at least it would stop the rest of his air from leaking.

The lake swept away the surrounding cloud of silt. The sunset reds deepened past violets and purples and faded into grays. Daylight was almost gone.

With his right arm and the help of a support pillar, Seth managed to get to his feet.

He turned left and right. He couldn't sight the beast. With every footstep, he was certain it would swim out of nowhere and bite him clean in half. He found himself flinching at the same gentle lake motions that had been comforting before.

But the strike never came. The beast had moved on.

Seth moved along the path, slowly and surely. With every step, he used a bit more of his oxygen. The bent cylinder on his left leg made it even harder.

It was a cruel and slow race, but Seth Nickerson pushed on, unwilling to surrender. Each breath felt like it might be his last. The remaining air inside his suit warmed.

Still, while there was any strength left in his limbs at all, he would keep moving.

He managed to pull the lever as he collapsed onto the aqualift.

Gears above turned and hefted the platform toward the repair station.

As his body broke the surface of the water, his elation turned to horror. No fresh air rushed in. A trickle may have entered through the severed lines, but it was too little, too late. There was nothing to force enough new air into the line. He could still suffocate inside his suit.

Not yet to the platform level, Seth fumbled desperately with the latches that would release his helmet.

Darkness crowded at the edge of his vision. His arms and fingers, not nimble in the suit anyway, now seemed even more like sausages glued to the end of logs.

Just as Seth was about to surrender himself to death, he managed to hook his thumbs on the flanged latches. They clicked open.

A surge of air rushed in and a stream of water leaked out.

Seth knew he should get out of his lakesuit, get dry and get to a doctor. But he was too tired to stand, let alone take off the suit. So, instead of doing anything useful, he lost consciousness.

❦

SETH WOKE UP COUGHING, and not on the aqualift. He was still wet, but no longer in his suit. Someone had wrapped him in a couple of wool blankets. The young repairist was not dripping wet, but still more than merely damp.

Light crept in under the door.

He rolled onto his side, noticing exactly how stiff a night of fighting a monster and sleeping on the floor could make him. His mind tried to process the situation. How did he get here? Where was he?

As stupor receded from his mind, he realized he was back in the equipment locker.

Standing up was something of a painful chore. But after some grunting and wincing, Seth was back on his feet and limping.

The more he moved around, the better his joints felt.

He stumbled out the door, down the repair station's hallway, and in front of Mr. Felthouser's office. It was unlocked, which was always the case while the boss was around.

Seth pushed open the door. "Mr. Felthouser?"

No answer came from the cluttered office, or anywhere else in the building. Morning light from an open shutter filled the room and called to him.

Seth stepped in and walked to the window. Outside he saw main shaft number five, cranking along, providing torque to the many gears and drive chains of the west stake of the city.

The sight was a comfort. As badly as he had failed last night, at least the city kept turning.

Something caught his eye off in the distance, on the next maintenance pier to the east—shaft number four. Most of the pistons pumped just fine, but one did not crank at all. It jutted from the water, as motionless as one of the supports. A broken connection dangled from the still-rotating shaft.

Seth knew what must have happened, at least mechanically speaking. Something had gummed up the piston, but the others kept cranking. The immense combined torque from the others on that shaft snapped the stuck piston at its weakest point.

Seth's stomach twisted into a knot. How well would that section of the city even be able to operate while missing so much torque? Would they stop the cable cars, or shut down the factories?

The worst part about all of this was that it didn't make any sense. There was no reason whatsoever for an animal to attack machinery. None. The machinery didn't look like food, nor a predator.

Had someone trained the creature? It seemed impossible. No one could teach a beast of that size in secret.

And what of Inspector Cochran? Was he really on the take?

Seth spun around and started looking through Mr. Felthouser's papers. Maybe he had useful notes somewhere.

On the desk were maintenance logs, written and rewritten safety checklists, a dog eared copy of the schematics for the enormous Stirling Engines that powered the city, various personal letters, an untouched Book of Commandments, a couple of candles, and some waste papers.

There, left among a loose smattering of unreviewed daily reports, was the calling card of Inspector Cochran.

Seth found it odd that Felthouser would hang on to it, seeing how much he distrusted the man. Of course, looking at the rest of his desk, perhaps it had simply been tossed and forgotten.

He instinctively picked up the card to get a better look.

Underneath it was a paper that had obviously been written by somebody other than the workers or even Felthouser himself. The workers' papers were water stained with messy handwriting. This letter was written on the whitest paper he had ever seen and had been penned with a smooth and steady hand.

The visible words read, "...consideration of our offer. Sincerely, Heath Glenbury, Northeastern Steam and Steel."

Seth yanked the letter from the bottom of the pile. It was addressed to Leavitt Felthouser. Seth almost couldn't focus enough to read it, so swam his head with new questions.

Seth slid the paper back as best he could, then went around to the far side of the desk, looking for any sort of further evidence.

He refused to believe Felthouser had fallen to such a temptation.

Of course, the letter didn't mean Felthouser was actually a traitor to his people and his city. Didn't he say that big steam would do anything? It was entirely possible that Felthouser had responded in the negative, or hadn't dignified the dirty offer with a response at all.

That had to be it.

The desk had only one drawer. It was filled with plans and designs.

As he rifled through the stack, a drawing about halfway through caught his eye. It was glued to the cover of a folder.

The picture was of a series of tightly wound springs connected one to the other by small gearing assemblies. It was labeled "Mechanical Spring Battery, version 2." In the bottom right corner it had been signed, Leavitt Felthouser.

He opened the folder. Drawing after drawing described the ingenious device which stored a surprising amount of mechanical energy. It was similar to the concept of a pocket watch spring, only it could drive a large machine a long distance.

The design was brilliant. Seth wondered how the man was still only a repair boss.

The last few pages were drawings of a large mechanical creature. With a long tail. And a snout. Exactly like the allie-gater he had escaped only one night prior. The drawings were labeled "Yellowstone Dragon."

Seth's stomach and the folder hit the floor at about the same time. His mouth hung open. Could the beast that was slowly tearing apart the city's power supply be man made? Fashioned from brass, steel, and rubber, like his lakesuit?

It would explain much about the attacks. How a creature could chew through steel. Why it would continue to do so.

Seth suddenly became aware of how precarious his position was. He couldn't get caught in Felthouser's office like this. He swiftly picked everything up and put it away. He ran out of the office and back into the equipment locker.

He couldn't think straight. He needed to be doing something with his hands. And he needed to not look guilty.

The misfortune of his damaged suit was the excuse he needed.

Seth dragged the heavy suit back to its storage compartment, then went to work with a couple of wrenches to pull off the bite-damaged plating.

As he worked, he wondered if there was any way that Mr. Felthouser could be innocent. The answer was yes. If it was true that Cochran was a spy for a big steam company back east, then he would have both reason and resources to implicate Mr. Felthouser.

Either way, someone was lying, and that didn't sit right with him. He was used to putting his shoulder to the wheel with the salt of the earth folk who always shot straight with him. He didn't care much for falsehood.

He had just tossed the various mangled pieces of plating onto the bench in the workshop when Leavitt Felthouser burst through the door.

"There you are, my boy. Thank goodness you're alive!" He strode across the room and embraced Seth. "Last night I was more than a little worried you wouldn't make it."

"What happened?"

"I waited next to the aqualift for some time. Around dark I thought I heard somebody creeping around the station, so I went out to chase them off. I never saw them, but by the time I came back you were coming up, half dead."

He made a few wild motions with his hands as he spoke. "I

dragged you into the equipment locker where I had tools to get you out of your suit. By the time I got you wrapped up, wouldn't you know it? That Cochran feller starts beating on the door. I figured it was him before, sneaking around. I had to go back with him all the way to the city so he didn't know what we were doing. It was only safe to come back just now."

"I can not even-" Seth sat his work down. "I honestly thought I was about to see the spirit world."

"What happened down there?"

"I saw it. The beast. Tore right through my net," he pointed to his damaged gear, "then it tried to take a piece out of me."

"What did it look like?"

"Like you said, the biggest lizard ever, with a long snout. And teeth to match. Parts of it glittered like fish scales do in shallow water. Others were covered in moss and such. It moved so fast, I couldn't see much else."

Felthouser nodded. "All right. Go ahead and go home, get some rest. I'll warn everybody before they head down. Get back here tomorrow and we'll make a plan."

⚯

As Seth stepped off the cable car near his boarding house in the land side of the city, he heard a familiar voice.

"You saw it last night, didn't you?"

Seth spun around and came face to face with Inspector Cochran. Cochran's eyes were red and decorated with heavy bags like he hadn't slept a wink. But his suit was still immaculate.

Seth couldn't think of anything to say, so he shut his mouth and set his jaw.

"Did you hear about what happened on pier four yet? Something took down piston 35. How long are you going to let this go on?"

"Yeah, I saw the broken piston."

"Next time someone could get hurt or killed." Cochran poked his bony finger into Seth's chest. "I have reason to believe Felthouser has built some kind of contraption, which, believe it or not, is the very beast I'm sure you saw yesterday. And I'm almost certain he will use it again this afternoon or evening to wreak havoc on one of your crew's pistons. He probably sent you home because he wants you out of the way."

Seth shook his head and looked down, eyes darting about, looking for explanations that weren't written on the ground. He made a lot of sense, but did the inspector know a little too much? "I simply can not believe he would do that."

"Yeah? How many times has he sent you home early before?"

The answer was none, but he didn't want the inspector to have the satisfaction. "What do you want from me?"

"I just want you to do what's right. Help protect your city."

Seth very nearly broke down to tell him everything. But, he simply could not be sure about the inspector's motives. Cochran said all the right words, but he was too perfect for his own good. And Felthouser had warned him about the inspector, hadn't he?

So Seth did the only thing he could. He straightened his back, looked Inspector Cochran in the eye, and returned to saying nothing.

The inspector threw up his hands. "Find me if you decide to choose the right." He turned and walked away.

The fact of the matter was that Seth had already decided what to do. His new plan just didn't involve trusting anyone.

ॐ

THAT AFTERNOON, and on his way back to the pier, Seth saw something strange. Two of the repairists on his crew rode the cable car going the opposite direction.

There was no way Felthouser would have sent that many away under normal circumstances. Was he trying to protect them, or was he trying to avoid witnesses?

It didn't really matter; Seth's actions would be the same either way. It would be nice to know, though.

He walked out from the portion of the city built on supports above the lake and onto pier five. Normally, Seth loved the fresh smell that took over after he left the busy wooden streets. Today, he was too jittery to even notice.

A few fishermen came and went, and further past the repair station a crowd of gawkers stared and pointed across the water at the broken piston.

The repair station was locked when Seth arrived. His breath quickened and his heart pounded in his ears. The station was never locked during the day.

He didn't want to look like a burglar, but he needed to prepare for the allie-gater.

Every window on the walking side of the pier was locked.

Seth swallowed his pride and shuffled sideways on the tiny ledge the ran along the water side of the repair station.

If anybody noticed him, they didn't call out.

As he carefully approached Felthouser's window, he slowed down and listened.

He couldn't hear any movement in the office.

Of course, the splashing water and the drifting murmur of the crowd made it hard to tell for sure.

Seth spared a quick glance into the room. Nobody.

He pulled on the window frame. It opened with a creak.

Hands grasping the window sill, Seth jumped and flopped onto the floor of his boss's office.

From his ground level vantage point, he caught sight of a reddish pile of cloth on the other side of the desk.

He leapt to his feet and ran to investigate.

It was a set of Leavitt Felthouser's clothes. They had been ripped up and thrown in a pile. They also appeared to be soaked in blood.

Seth gagged down the urge to vomit. It's one thing to see gore while you're gutting a fish or cleaning a jackrabbit. It's quite another when the blood might belong to another human being.

As soon as the nausea passed, he started to wonder why there would possibly be a set of bloody clothes in the middle of an office. Before he could form a theory, a massive, splintering crack rocked the building.

A chorus of screams invaded through the open window.

Seth ran down the hall, unlocked the door, and jumped out onto the street. The crowd to his left had now turned away from the far off piston, and toward him. Some of them were even sprinting his way.

He turned to his right.

A fifteen-foot chunk of boardwalk was simply gone. The heavy rails that had supported the planks now hung ragged, having been snapped off on either side. No immediate help from the city could be expected.

Seth's eyes widened and he froze.

Before he could even process what had happened, a jolt rocked the pier, followed closely by a scraping vibration. Every few seconds, another lurch, followed by shaking.

Seth doubled back and looked over the edge at the supports that bore the weight of the repair station.

An immense shadow backed away from one then struck it again, locking into place. There was no doubt, this was Felthouser's mechanical dragon. With a heave of its tail it rotated around the support, splintering away wood with its metal teeth. Before too long, it would saw clean through. And if the station didn't immediately collapse, Felthouser's beast could always chew through another.

The ramifications hit Seth like a bison stampede. If the station collapsed, the pumps would be gone. The tools would be gone. There would be no way to keep the pistons on this shaft pumping. And worse yet, people might die.

There was no time to plan, to build, to prepare. Seth had to act quickly, and with whatever was available.

He took a sharp breath through his nose and forced himself to regain calm and focus. He took no further notice of the crowd or their screaming. He bolted back inside to the equipment room.

The lakesuit was heavy and awkward, but Seth refused to let that matter, even though the suit worked so much better when he could just climb in and walk. He grunted as he lugged the dead weight over his shoulder.

As he left the locker and turned down the central hall, a silhouette stood in the doorway to the pier.

He couldn't tell who the stranger was at first glance. It didn't matter, anyway, the backlit personage was merely an obstacle needing to be removed. Seth lumbered faster, attempting to reach a more suitable ramming speed. "Move!"

A familiar voice shouted, "Whulp!" as its owner leaped out of the way.

Seth took a sidelong glance at Inspector Cochran lying on the deck as he passed. He prayed Felthouser had lied about the persistent inspector. He didn't have time to deal with yet another problem.

He dragged the brass and rubber suit up to the edge of the pier and let it drop. It clunked down onto the wood.

Seth ran back past the inspector, who was straightening and brushing off his suit coat.

A moment later, Seth reappeared in the doorway carrying a four-foot pipe and a length of rope.

The inspector reached out. "How can I help?"

Another jolt shook the pier.

Seth blinked. He didn't have time to waste. He needed to take a leap of faith. "Tie this to the hand of the suit, so it looks like it's holding a weapon."

"Right." Cochran grabbed the pipe and rope and set to work.

Seth ran back and fetched a coil of cable, straining under its weight.

The pier shook again. The support had to be getting close to failing.

Seth dropped the cable next to the torque housing where a giant drive chain ran from shaft number five to the repair station.

He pulled two bands and a crimper from his pocket, and hurriedly used them to make a loop in one end of the cable. He used both bands to secure the loop. His whole makeshift plan depended on it holding. He pulled a much larger length of cable through the loop, fashioning a steel cable lasso.

The inspector looked up from his work a few feet away. "Done. Now what?"

"When I tell you, push the suit into the water."

Another jolt, followed by scraping.

Cochran stood. "How is that going to help?"

Seth jammed the untied end of the cable into one of the holes of the station's main gear. Shaft number five continued to rotate, pulling the chain, which in turn rotated the gear. As the enormous gear turned, it wound the cable around the shaft that led inside the repair station.

The mechanical reel wound in steel cable at a steady pace. All Seth needed to do now was catch a dragon before he ran out of cable.

The station's support groaned and creaked and threatened to snap.

"Ok, push it in."

The inspector bent down and hefted. It looked like the thin man's arms might shake clean off, but he got it over the edge.

The suit hit the water with a tremendous splash.

The Yellowstone Dragon took the bait. Seth bet there was no way Felthouser could run the risk of allowing a repairist to stop him. With a twist of its tail, the beast turned and snapped its powerful jaws on the brass and rubber suit.

Seth grabbed and extended the cable lasso opening, then held it with one hand. "Last thing. There's an emergency lever in the shop on the other side of this wall. Once the beast is out of the water, you run in there and pull it. It will disengage the drive chain."

The inspector's sweaty brow rose—he did not look confident. "Right. But what if-"

"Figure it out." There was no time for second guessing. Seth sucked in a deep breath and jumped from the pier.

On his way toward the water, he discovered that the pier was much higher than he had supposed and now he had plenty of time to second guess the quality of his plan.

Seth splashed into the cold mountain water. The sudden chill shocked his system, and he stifled a scream.

A flurry of deadly teeth and glittering scales thrashed not far below. The monstrous clockwork dragon tore into the decoy suit, shaking, whirling, and biting.

If it wasn't so dangerous, Seth would have marveled at the beauty of the construction. Thousands of tiny parts interlocked and moved, giving the impression of a solid skin, of musculature, of life. Felthouser was a genius.

Seth kicked and descended toward the commotion. He didn't try to be fancy, he just held his arm out, extending the loop as far down as he could.

Water pressure pushed painfully against Seth's ears as he neared the thrashing beast.

In that moment, Seth Nickerson almost abandoned his task. But he remembered the people on the pier above. If the repair station collapsed, it could easily pull that whole section of walkway down. In the chaos of collapse, how many would be caught and killed in the wreckage? No, there was no way he could quit now.

Seth kicked and plunged that last ten feet.

The clockwork monster rolled over, grinding the empty suit on a support pillar. As it did, the beast's brass leg snagged inside the cable loop, pulling it tight and ripping it from Seth's grasp.

The giant body took up slack quickly and the cable whizzed through the water. It struck Seth across the torso, forcing what little air he had out.

The brave repairist now kicked lamely toward the surface. His lungs burned and his limbs shook. For the second time in two days, he nearly starved for air.

But his head finally popped from the surface and he gulped in a breath of fresh air. His strength gone, he struggled to keep his face above water.

The shaft kept turning, reeling in the great beast.

A rope dropped into the water from the pier above. Seth looked up and saw several of the crowd, shouting. Cochran was at the front of the crowd, frantically pointing somewhere else entirely.

Seth's cold hands managed to tie a bowline around his torso.

The crowd above heaved as one, and Seth shot up.

Half a second later, the Yellowstone Dragon exploded from the water, gleaming jaws agape. The massive beast narrowly missed its target and splashed down—Sethless—into the lake.

The mechanical dragon turned for another pass then jerked to one side. It had run out of cable.

In no time, its massive form was pulled, thrashing, from the water. It shook and slammed against one of the repair station's supports. Once the beast was fully out of the water, Seth and Cochran pulled the emergency shut off lever.

Out of the water, it was much easier to tell the beast was mechanical, and merely disguised with clumps of moss. Nobody had ever seen a machine like it—terrible, powerful, and intricate.

It took another thirty minutes before the beast's ingenious mechanical batteries spun down and the creature went still. Leavitt Felthouser gave himself up shortly thereafter.

In the days that followed, Inspector Cochran scoured Felthouser's office, piecing together how he was able to construct such a massive machination in secret. The repairists worked day and night with city engineers to fix the damage to the boardwalk and supports.

"I'm afraid he has been in the secret employ of big steam for several months," Cochran told Seth one afternoon. "Promises of wealth and power, and a comfortable life back east."

"But what about the clothes?" Seth asked.

"Oh, they were a decoy. If his plan had worked and the station collapsed, we would have eventually found them and counted him among the dead."

Two months later, Seth took his final underwater walk as a repairist. Due to his valorous actions and sharp thinking, he had been granted an apprenticeship to a city engineer and would begin in the next few days.

As he looked out across the untapped underwater geyser basin, one of the steam vents erupted in a dazzling display of silvery steam bubbles.

He waved goodbye to nature's send off.

As he did, he noticed something that hadn't been lying on the lake bed before. Was it a log? A capsized canoe? He couldn't quite tell.

Just before the brave repairist was about name it a mystery and turn away, the log wriggled and came off the warm stretch of lake bed. As it did, the object became clear.

An enormous, green-skinned, toothy, long-snouted creature swam off toward deeper water, leaving behind a cloud of silt.

ABOUT THE AUTHOR

Sometimes I feel like I was born 70 years too late. I love big band jazz and swing dancing. I read pulp novels written by folks like Robert E. Howard, Edgar Rice Burroughs, & Lester Dent. I often listen to old time radio programs. I dig the style of the '30s and '40s. But then again, I also love my Kindle, air conditioning, and YouTube, so maybe I'm lucky to be right where I am.

Other stuff: I'm very religious (LDS). Politically, I am libertarian. I love my family (a wife, three little girls, and a son). I love old pulp novels, radio theater, swing dancing, jazz and blues music, firearms, writing, reading, and I believe in being prepared, laughing often, and showing respect to people around me.

Metal Marshal:
Whole in the Wall
Berin L. Stephens

The steam buggy bounced high as it hit a large bump in the "road" leading north out of Oakland, Utah. If Deputy Marshal James Caldwell hadn't been strapped into his seat, he would have been bounced out to the hard, sagebrush-covered ground.

"Whoopee! That was a good one," Doctor Matt Solomon said, smiling at James from under his dust-covered driving goggles.

"If ya say so," James said in his Georgia drawl. He double-checked to make sure the wires that recharged his mechanical arm were still plugged in. He currently wore his wooden leg since his metal leg had been damaged in his fight with the Andersen gang. At least his arm still worked after Matt reattached it. It just had a few dings in it from when it fell off. "Ya sure you can git my leg fixed in Salt Lake City?"

Matt nodded, then shrugged. "I think so. They should have the right tools. Unlike that cesspit of a town we just left."

"I don't know why ya couldn't just throw in some bailing wire and chewing gum and get my leg as good as new."

"Don't laugh. I *did* use bailing wire to *try* and put it back together. It's all I could find there. But they didn't have the right materials to reconnect the acid battery to the motor."

"Wait. What? Are ya tellin' me that I've been runnin' around with acid in my leg? Why didn't you warn me?"

"I did. It's what holds the electricity that powers your arm and leg."

"But it's acid. I may only be a gunfighter, but even I know that acid is dangerous."

Matt shook his head. "Oh, don't worry, I keep it in a tight container inside the limbs. It's perfectly safe. I think. Just don't go sticking your cigarette matches inside the storage compartment. If the sulfuric acid reacted with the potassium chlorate, it would create an enormous exothermic reaction."

"I see your lips moving but only nonsense is coming out of 'em." James decided to change the subject. "That Mormon girl, Esther, she sure took a shine to ya."

"Oh, please," Matt replied with a grimace. "Can you imagine *me* settling down in a place like *this?*" He gestured at the blandness around him. "There's no theater, no universities, no apothecaries. I would be miserable."

James noticed the redness spreading up Matt's neck. *Yup. Got him on that one.* James's smile evaporated. Where the single women of Oakland found Matt attractive, they thought of James as ugly, hideous even. The cannonball that struck him at the Battle of Atlanta not only took his arm and leg, but scarred the right half of his face.

Matt looked at him, concern showing on his face as if reading his mind. "Don't worry my friend, we'll find you that perfect woman."

"The last thing I need is a woman in my life," James muttered. "It's a good thing I'm uglier than sin because I wouldn't wish the curse of being married to a lawman on any woman." At least it sounded good, but it didn't help fill the hole James felt in his soul.

They bounced along the wagon tracks in silence for the next several miles. As it drew near sunset, they saw three riders approaching. James removed the thong from off the hammer of his Colt just in case. They were probably only locals passing through, but James had learned he could never be too sure.

As they drew closer, the three horsemen stopped. One of them gave a friendly smile and wave. They each had rifles on their saddles and pistols at their hips, but their hands weren't anywhere near them. These three seemed safe enough.

The man who waved pointed a gloved hand at the boiler on the back of the buggy. "What in tarnation is that thing? Is that a trackless locomotive?"

James groaned as Matt pushed in the knob that controlled speed and pulled back on the hand brake, bringing their steam carriage to a stop. Matt, with his three doctorates, could never resist the temptation to talk about his infernal inventions. James leaned back in his seat, pulled his hat over his eyes, and figured he might as well get a good nap in while Matt gave them his lecture. *Poor souls*, James thought.

A moment later, James felt cold steel against his neck. He pushed his hat up and found himself looking along the barrel of a shotgun. One of the horsemen frowned down at him, all friendliness gone. "Get out!" the man ordered.

James debated as to whether he could draw his Colt fast enough. Despite the speed he could move his mechanical arm, it was still wired into the steam buggy and if the man squeezed a little harder on that trigger, the shot gun would messily remove his head from his shoulders. "What do ya'll want with me?"

The man who had waved at them had his pistol trained on Matt. He replied, "Oh, we don't want *you*. We want your friend and his machine, here. Just do as we say and you won't be harmed. Miss Cassi don't like needless killin'."

James reached over to unplug his arm.

"Slowly!" the man next to him barked, pressing the shotgun harder into his throat.

James glared at him as he removed the wires and then undid the leather straps that held him in his seat. Once free, he again calculated his odds of drawing and shooting in time. The number he came up with was "zero."

He stood and stepped out of the buggy, his arms in the air. The horseman backed off and started dismounting, his shotgun still aimed at James.

The man's head turned away for a split second. James sent the mental command and his arm moved in a blur, drawing the pistol out and firing at the shotgun man. The bullet struck the man square in the chest and knocked him out of the saddle.

"Hey!" shouted the third man who had been disconnecting the supply cart attached behind the steam buggy. He drew and fired at James.

James didn't turn in time and the bullet struck him in the right knee, shattering the wood and sending him falling to the ground. Two more shots rang out as James fell into a dry gully next to the road. His head struck a rock as he landed, and the sky went black.

James awoke with a splitting headache. *That's funny. I don't remember getting drunk.* It took his foggy mind a moment to remember what had happened. He pushed himself up and looked around. The lower half of his leg was gone and his hat lay a few feet away with a hole in the top. His Colt was nowhere in sight. He grabbed his hat, shoved it on his head, and crawled out of the gully.

The steam buggy and Matt were gone. The cart with all of Matt's scientific equipment still sat there. James's non-functioning metal leg would be in there, though, so he could at least use that to replace his shattered wooden one. He made it to the cart and pulled himself up to stand on his real leg. As he rummaged through, he found the leg and replaced the remains of the wooden one with it. He could stand once again.

As he searched through the cart, he found his double-action Colt, the Thunderer. It had jammed the last time he had used it and he had asked Matt to fix it. James doubted he did, though, since as much as Matt denied it, he did enjoy spending time with that Mormon girl.

James pulled Thunderer out and tested it. To his surprise, it worked. *So, Matt did find time between his flirtations to get it fixed.* James tucked it into his holster before grabbing a saddle bag stuffed with a few supplies. He didn't know where the next town was, he just hoped he wouldn't have to walk far and that he could find a horse big enough to carry his half-metal body.

After finding his spare cane, James limped off into the sunset. He couldn't see any sign of life within several miles. A few minutes into his walk, he realized that he didn't have a way to recharge the battery in his arm. He switched it off and used a strip of cloth from the saddlebags to make a sling for it to rest in before resuming his journey.

At least two miles later, and well after ten o'clock, James finally saw a light. It appeared to be a ranch. James trudged toward the light, out of breath and exhausted from slinging his heavy leg along with his opposite hip. Without the electrical battery to help it move, it ended up being almost more of a burden than a help.

James clumped up the steps and onto the front porch, taking a moment to catch his breath before knocking on the door. He didn't want to gasp for air between every word.

Before he recovered, the door opened and a young man, about seventeen, stood there. "Can I help you, sir?"

James took a deep breath before speaking. "I hope so. I am Deputy Marshal James Caldwell and I need to borrow a horse from you. Is your father around?"

The boy looked out into the dark night. "No. Pa's in England serving a mission. And it's awfully late to be out riding."

"Is your mother here, then?"

"No. Ma's in town getting some supplies and gossiping with her sister. She should be back in a day or two."

James stood there thinking and trying to breathe so it didn't sound like he was about to die.

"You're welcome to stay here tonight," the boy said as he opened the door wider. "You sound exhausted."

"I really should be goin' before I lose the trail."

The boy perked up. "Are you on a manhunt? Tell me about it!"

"There isn't much to tell. It's just the longer I wait, the behinder I get."

"Well, you're not going to see much tonight. There's no moon. Please, come on in. I can get you some water and food."

"No, please, just loan me a horse. Preferably a big one that can handle a lot of weight. I'll bring it back in a few days and pay you for the time."

The boy shook his head. "Uh, that's the other thing. Ma took the horses with her. All I have here are the Sons of Zebedee and the old wagon."

"Sons of Zebedee?"

"Yeah, our oxen, James and John."

James mentally chewed on that information. No moon. No horses. And a couple of oxen that he could more than likely outrun with just one leg. "Anyone else have horses around here?"

The boy shook his head. "Sorry, sir. Town is about ten miles up the road that way. That would be your best bet."

James knew he couldn't walk that far, even if he went all night. And there was no guarantee there would be anything there he could ride. He started to fall over from the mixture of exhaustion and disappointment.

The boy stepped forward and caught James before he fell. He put his arm around him and helped him inside the cabin made mostly of mud with a few logs mixed in. The inside felt cozy, though. The boy helped James sit in a rocking chair. James's metal leg let out a loud shriek as it bent.

"What was that?" the boy asked, surprise showing in his eyes.

"That was my leg. It's fake."

"Oh. Did you fight in the war?"

"Yeah. Cannonball took it."

The boy winced. "Sorry to hear that."

"What's your name, son?" James asked.

"I'm Moroni, but my friends call me Rone. You just relax, sir, and I'll fetch you some water and bread." Rone smiled at him before heading to the cupboard and pulling out a tin cup.

James didn't get the water or the bread that night since he fell asleep before Rone could make it back across the room.

When James awoke, he found himself lying on a mat next to the stone fireplace with a blanket over him. The sun streamed in through the front window. There was no sign of Rone, but a pitcher, cup, a small loaf of bread, and some bacon sat on the table. James used his cane to help him stand before limping to the table and sitting down. The bread was harder than a Yankee's head but the water helped soften it up enough so he could chew it. At least the bacon tasted delicious.

Five minutes later, Rone returned. He smiled when he saw James sitting at the table. "Morning, Marshal. You must have been pretty tuckered because you were sound asleep. And I know what you mean by needing a big horse. You're heavier than you look."

"Did ya happen to find a horse?"

"No, sir. But I have the Sons of Zebedee all yoked up and ready to take you to town. We should be able to find you something there."

"Much obliged." James tore off a chunk of the bread and followed Rone out of the house. A large cart, used for hauling hay, sat there with two of the largest oxen James had ever seen. They looked strong, but at the same time, they looked even slower than he feared. *At least I won't be out of breath when I reach town today. Or tomorrow.*

James remembered something the bandit had said. He had mentioned Miss Cassi. That could only mean Cassi Butcher, one of the most notorious cattle rustlers in Utah. *Except why would she need our steam buggy?*

"Maroney," James asked, "do you know the whereabouts of the gang leader, Cassi Butcher?"

"Moroni, but again, just call me Rone. It's easier for you non-members to remember." Rone's face grew serious. "And, yeah, I do. It's called Liars' Lair."

"Could you take me there?"

Rone frowned. "Well, see sir, my pa taught me to obey the law. And I do try, but those outlaws there have built themselves a mighty fortress up in the hills. They can see anyone coming at them for miles."

"My friend's life is in danger. I need to rescue him before they kill him."

"Oh, my." Rone pursed his lips and tapped his fingers along the side of the wagon. He closed his eyes for a moment, almost as if he were praying. When he opened them, he said, "Okay, it feels like the right thing to do. I'll help you."

James smiled at him, with the half of his face that could still smile.

Rone nodded and smiled back, sending his long brown hair waving. He snapped his fingers. "I got an idea." He led the oxen and the wagon around to the back of the cabin to a supply shed. Rone entered and started taking barrels and flour sacks out to load them into the back of the wagon.

"What are ya doin' there, son?" James asked.

"I figure that if we take a bunch of supplies to Liars' Lair, they'll let us in."

James nodded. "Good thinkin'." He realized, though, that it wouldn't work. "I'm afraid, though, most of the outlaws in these parts know of me. Someone will recognize me."

Rone stopped. "Oh." He looked around the shed and spotted an empty barrel. "What if you hid in that as I take you in?"

James studied the barrel. It was a little small, but he supposed he could fit in if he removed his leg and arm. He didn't think it would be very comfortable, but he had to get into that hideout and he couldn't think of any other options. "That might work."

Rone took the barrel and tossed it into the wagon.

"Need a hand with anything?" James asked.

"No, sir. I got this."

When he finished, Rone climbed up onto the seat, slapped a floppy hat onto his head, and reached down to help James up. Rone had to strain a bit, but between the two of them, James made it to the seat. Once he settled in, Rone flicked the reins, and the Sons of Zebedee started off.

A few miles up the road, James slapped at his pocket and swore.

The word made Rone jump. "You okay there, Marshal?"

"Yeah. I just realized I left my cigarette tin back at the cart. I don't s'pose ya have some tobacco in the wagon?"

"No. Afraid not."

"An' I s'pose it's out of the question for a bottle of whiskey."

"Yes, sir. Our prophet, Joseph Smith, received a revelation about how those things are bad for us. If you want, I could tell you all about him."

"No thanks. Already had an earful." James smiled to himself at the memory of all the preaching he'd received from Bishop Rigby. He was a good man who loved his religion, but there was no way James could give up his creature comforts.

Rone looked ahead. "But it would have been real nice if we had some tobacco and liquor, along with some coffee. The outlaws up there love that stuff. We'll just have to make due with what we have: flour, beans, bacon, matches, and kerosene."

James watched the slow plodding of the oxen. "How long will it take the Sons of Zippity, here, to get us to Liars' Lair?"

Rone smiled and laughed. "About two days. And I know they aren't very fast most of the time, but these two can move pretty quick when they have the right motivation. One time, we came across a snake and these two suddenly decided they were race horses. It was all I could do to keep from falling out the back of the wagon."

They spent the day riding over more flat sagebrush land. By nightfall, they reached the mountains and camped for the night near a canyon entrance. The next morning, they followed a road that twisted and weaved its way up into the hills.

After a while, James felt like he was in some kind of stone maze. Rone kept stopping and studying the landmarks and features around him. Everything looked the same to James.

By late afternoon, Rone led the oxen to a side trail that went up into a ravine with steep sides. "This is the area they keep lookouts. It's why no lawmen have ever been able to get up here."

"Alright, then." James said. "Stop the wagon."

While they had traveled, the two of them discussed their plan.

James would hide in the barrel with a sack of beans on top of him. He had carved a little hole for air and to help him see his surroundings. Rone would also hide James's metal arm and leg under the flour sacks. With luck, the outlaws would let them in with their cover story which Rone had thought up. Then, Rone would drop off James with the supplies and leave, allowing James to sneak out and search for Matt. They hadn't quite figured out how to get James back out of there, but he hoped an opportunity would arise.

Once inside the barrel, it grew hot and stifling. James soon had sweat oozing out of every pore in his body. At least the hills were a little cooler, but not enough, especially with the late afternoon sun beating down on the barrel's lid. He wondered how long it would be until they reached Liars' Lair and if there would be anything left of him other than a puddle of sweat by then.

James startled awake when the wagon stopped. He couldn't see out so he drew Thunderer and placed it on his lap. "What's going on?" he whispered.

"Some riders are approaching with rifles," Rone whispered back. "Stay quiet."

A minute passed. "Who are you and what do you want?" sounded a rough voice.

"My name is Rone. I was asked to bring some supplies to you folks."

"Who sent ya?"

"Bert told me to bring these supplies to you. I got some flour and beans and—"

"I don't know no one name Bert," the man interrupted. "Are you the law?"

"Now, why would I be with the law? I'm here unarmed and with a bunch of supplies in the middle of nowhere. Bert paid me to bring them to you, so that's what I'm doing."

"I still don't know anyone named Bert. Do you?"

The other outlaw grunted something that James couldn't quite hear.

Rone said, "He said he was with the Simpson gang and they were coming up here to hide out for a bit. Are they here yet?"

"Never heard of a Simpson gang," the outlaw replied.

"Oh. Well, I guess I'll just take all these supplies back to town if you don't want them. It doesn't matter to me since I've already been paid." The wagon creaked as Rone shifted his weight to turn it around.

"Wait. Let's see what ya have." The wagon shook as someone climbed into it.

James heard crates and barrels being opened and bags being moved around. He hoped Rone hid his arm and leg well. The barrel James hid in wobbled as someone pried the lid off.

"What do we have here?" the bandit asked.

"Beans," Rone answered, maybe a little too loudly. Nervousness filled his voice.

James still gripped Thunderer, his finger on the trigger. He didn't want to shoot his way out of this, but he would if he had to. The man poked at the bag of beans wedged above James's head.

The lid closed again. "Well, those smell terrible. I think they've gone bad."

James slowly and silently let out the breath he held, though he kept his finger on the trigger.

The man climbed out of the back of the wagon. "We'll take 'em. Go on up to the wall and tell 'em Dain sent ya. They'll let ya in."

"Thank you, sir," Rone said. The wagon resumed moving forward.

After ten minutes, the wagon slowed down and Rone whispered, "Okay, Marshal, we're coming up to the wall. It blocks off the entire ravine so it's the only way in or out. I have to admit, sir, that I'm a little nervous."

"Just act all natural-like. You'll do fine, son. Unload the supplies and me and then head back out."

"Okay, sir, but I don't feel good about leaving you behind. I don't know how you'll get out."

James grunted. "Me neither."

After a minute of silence, Rone said, "I just offered up a silent prayer that we'll all get out of there safely, if that's okay."

"Much obliged." James figured it at least couldn't hurt.

The wagon sped back up and a few minutes later, James heard shouting. He couldn't quite make out what they were saying.

"Dain sent me!" Rone shouted back. "I have some supplies for you."

There were more voices James couldn't make out followed by a loud clanking sound, like the unlocking of a steel door in a bank vault. *Where would they get something like that?* James wondered. A loud squeal sounded and the wagon jerked forward again. After fifteen seconds, the door squealed and closed with a clang.

"Where do you want me to unload?" Rone asked someone.

"Over there," a woman's voice answered. "Next to the other supplies."

"Yes, ma'am," Rone said. The wagon shook as he jumped down and started unloading.

Several minutes later, James's barrel scooted across the wagon bed. Rone whispered, "This don't look good. There are more than just a few outlaws here. There's a small army."

"This sounds like a li'l more than a rustlin' job."

"Yeah. I can look around if you want, before I leave."

"No. Don't risk it. Just finish unloading and git outta here. The last thing I want is yer ma stringin' me up fer gettin' ya killed."

"Just hold still, I'm moving your barrel now so don't be alarmed." The barrel shook as Rone slid it to the end of the wagon and then picked it up. James got bounced around a bit but Rone was a big enough boy that he seemed to handle it fine. He put the barrel down and positioned the hole so James could see out.

"Your arm and leg are under the flour sacks behind you. I'll be heading out now."

"Thanks, Rone. Yer a good lad."

"Good luck, sir." Rone's footsteps retreated.

James peeked out the air hole. He saw Rone climb into the wagon. As he did, a woman with long, brown hair and wearing two bandoleers loaded with rifle ammunition, stepped out of a shack. She wore a sombrero and had a scar across her face. Even with it, James found her strikingly pretty. It was none other than Cassi Butcher.

"Where do you think you're going, young man?" she asked Rone.

"I delivered my supplies and was heading back for more."

Cassi shook her head. "No one leaves. Not now."

"But my ma will be waiting for me. She'll get nervous and call the sheriff if I'm not back soon."

Cassi raised a brow. "Does she know where you are?"

"Of course not, ma'am. It's just that she'll worry, you know, since she's a mother and all."

Cassi shook her head again. "I can't risk it. There's too much at stake. You'll have to stay here with us for the next few months until the hornets' nest has settled down. Know anything about cattle?"

"I *am* a rancher, ma'am."

"I have a sick calf back at the rear pasture. See what you can do to help it. Take your wagon with you since I need this area kept clear."

Rone's jaw worked as he tried to think of something to say.

"Go. Now. Before I throw you in with the other miscreant." She glanced back at the shack.

"Yes, ma'am," Rone said before snapping the reins and sending the Sons of Zebedee deeper into the ravine.

James leaned back in his barrel. Now he not only had to worry about getting Matt out of there, but Rone, too. *He's a good kid and doesn't deserve to be mixed up in this mess.*

James had to wait until well after midnight to make his move. There were always outlaws roaming around. It also sounded like they were having a good party back deeper in the canyon. Once things settled, James risked pushing the barrel lid off and poking his head out. No one was around for the moment, so he leaned back and let the barrel fall over onto the flour sacks. From there, he crawled out, set the barrel back up with the lid on it, and dug through the sacks until he found his arm and leg. He hopped as quietly as he could to a dark corner at the base of the metal wall and put his leg on. The wall wasn't made of solid metal, like he originally thought, but appeared to be metal sheets bolted to large posts. James reattached his arm and turned it on. He hoped it still held enough of a charge for it to work. He flexed it, hearing the motors and rods move inside, and felt relieved when the gloved fingers moved.

He limped as quietly as he could across the ravine. James examined the metal wall as he did. A large, steel door sat in the middle, big enough for a wagon to pass through. It was now closed and locked and a rifleman sat atop the wall, his head bowed from dozing off.

On the opposite side, James saw the shack Cassi had come out of. It looked like a good kick would knock it over, but the door had a chain and padlock keeping it locked. Since knocking the building over would make too much noise, James elected to try opening the links in the chain with his metal hand. With a mental command, the metal fingers squeezed the chain links, bending them out of shape and allowing them to be taken apart. He then pulled the chain through the padlock and gently placed them on the ground without a sound.

Opening the door made the most noise as the old, rusty hinges let out their disagreement. James couldn't see anything in the dark interior.

"James?" sounded a weak voice from inside.

James let out a sigh of relief. "Matt. You okay?" He slowly closed the door again, though it still let out more noise than he wanted.

"Just fine. What took you so long?"

"Well, ya know me, had to check out every gin joint and saloon from here to Mexico first. Then I thought I'd mosey on over and check on ya." He crept forward to where Matt lay on the floor. "Did they hurt ya?"

"Oh, they beat me over a time or two when I tried to be altruistic and tell them I wouldn't help. They finally convinced me to get the buggy ready for them."

James could hear the pain in his voice. He had a feeling Matt received a pretty good thrashing. "What do they plan to do with it?"

"A train heist. A huge, and I mean huge, shipment of gold is coming up from San Francisco and heading to Chicago. They plan to use my buggy, *my buggy*, to chase down the train along the Salt Flats and stop it so the rest of the gangs can catch up and rob it." As he spoke, James drew his knife from his gun belt and cut the ropes from Matt's hands and feet.

When he finished, James asked, "Ya ready?"

"Yeah, sure. Maybe."

James helped Matt to his feet and used his metal arm to hold up his friend. They went to the door and opened it.

Cassi stood there, holding a rifle on them, along with six others who stood behind her. "Well, what do we have here? Who's stealing my mechanic? Virgil?"

One of the bandits, the one who had originally abducted Matt, turned up the kerosene lantern he held, illuminating the area.

Cassi raised a brow as she studied James. "Well, I'll be. It looks like we're getting a visit from the Metal Marshal himself. I should have figured you'd show up."

James had his metal arm around Matt so he couldn't reach for Thunderer. Even if he could, though, he knew he couldn't take out all those gunmen—and woman—in time before they filled him with lead. "So, all ya'll got me," he said.

Cassi motioned with her rifle toward the ground. "Now, put your friend down and drop your gun, nice and easy."

James first lowered Matt back to the floor before pulling out Thunderer. It clattered on the wood floor of the shack. One of the bandits stepped forward and picked it up, smiling greedily.

Cassi continued studying James. "Virgil told me you was an ugly one. Get that in the war?"

James nodded.

"Nasty business, that war was. Lost too many good folk."

Virgil chuckled. "Yeah, Miss Cassi has a soft spot fer you veterans."

Cassi's brow furrowed as she thought of something. "We could use a man like you. You're good in a fight, I hear." She took a step closer to him. "And the part of your face that wasn't burned is pretty nice to look upon." She came even closer until her nose almost touched his.

James raised his brow. "What is it ya want, ma'am?"

"I don't know. There's just something about you. I can't bring myself to have you killed, though I know I should if you don't join me. I'll have to think about it." She turned and said to her men. "Lock them both back in. Keep three guards on them at all times. No one goes in or out of this shack without me. Got it?"

Her men nodded, though a few grumbled about not getting to shoot the marshal. James was happy to disappoint them.

Cassi backed away to let her men tie James and Matt up and lock them back in the shack.

Once the outlaws' footsteps retreated, James muttered, "Well, that didn't work. Ya have any brilliant ideas?"

"No, that's your department," Matt answered. "I'm just your doctor."

"I can't believe they let me live." James tested the ropes behind his back. They were too tight to break with his hand but he started working the leather glove off the metal fingers. The edge of his index finger should be sharp enough to saw through the ropes.

"I think that woman has taken a shine to you," Matt said.

James almost burst out laughing. "Nah. She's just playin' head games." His glove came off, and he started sawing the rope.

"No, I think she is attracted to your rugged masculinity."

"Yer imaginin' things." The metal edge on the finger cut through the rope fast. James soon had the coils away from his wrists and went to work untying his legs. Once finished, he untied Matt.

Matt whispered, "Now what? Do you have a plan besides

bursting open that door and punching out all three of the well-armed bad guys?"

"Nope. That's perty much it." James rolled up his pant leg and opened the secret compartment in the calf of his metal leg. It held his Derringer. "Where's the steam buggy at?"

"It's only a hundred yards up the ravine. Didn't you see it?"

"No. I was too busy tryin' to rescue yer sorry hide. Anyway, once I burst this door open and start shootin', I need ya to run to the buggy and start 'er up."

Matt snorted. "First of all, I'm in no condition to run. I *might* be able to aggressively limp. Second of all, I can't just 'start it up.' It takes time for the boiler to heat up and create enough steam for the buggy to move. I've told you this before."

"Oh. I keep forgettin'." James stood and straightened out his leg since it no longer did it on its own. It let out a small squeak.

"What are you going to do about that metal door between us and freedom? Even if the buggy were warmed up, there's nowhere for it to go."

"Don't worry about that. I have an idea."

Matt sighed. "I was afraid of that."

"Ready?" James asked.

"No."

James put the Derringer in his left hand and pulled his mechanical arm back to punch the rickety shack door from its hinges.

A wagon approached from outside, causing James to pause and listen. A moment later, the rumbling stopped and a voice said, "I'm here to help watch the prisoners." It was Rone's voice.

"Ain't youse that new kid?" one of the ruffians asked.

James peeked through a crack between the boards. In the lantern light, he could see Rone sitting on his wagon with the Sons of Zebedee out front.

"Yeah. Cassi sent me to relieve you," Rone told the gunmen.

"I've ridden with Miss Cassi for three years now. An' she just barely trusts me. I don't think she be up to trustin' you yet." This outlaw wore a beat-up straw hat and had his rifle pointed at Rone's chest.

Rone just smiled and shrugged. "What can I say? I guess I'm just better looking than the rest of you."

"Git down from there and put your hands up," the outlaw said. By this time two others came out of the shadows to join him with pistols aimed at Rone.

Rone didn't move. If he felt nervous, he didn't show it. "Well, gee. I just thought I'd help you fellas out but I guess if you don't want me, I'll go back to watching the cattle." He flicked the reins to turn the wagon around.

The outlaws started to step out of the way.

Rone flicked the reins hard and shouted, "Ha!" The Sons of Zebedee burst into a gallop faster than James thought possible. The three outlaws tried to jump out of the way. One of them got an ox horn right in the gut. The other two dodged out of the way and aimed their weapons at Rone.

James took his cue and smashed his arm into the shack door. It exploded outward with a loud crunch, distracting the two outlaws before they fired.

James slapped the Derringer into his right arm. For some reason, he had always been a better shot with his mechanical arm, probably since he had been right-handed before he lost his real arm. He fired, the bullet striking the outlaw who had taken Thunderer in the forehead.

The rifleman brought his gun around but not before James fired his last shot into the man's chest. His eyes went wide and the rifle slipped out of his limp fingers before he slumped to the ground.

A gun fired from above, the bullet whizzing past James's ear. He dove and rolled to where Thunderer had been dropped. He snatched it up and rolled again just as another bullet struck where he had been. He whipped Thunderer up and fired three quick shots up to the top of the wall where the guard stood. One of them struck true and the man fell backward to the other side.

James pushed himself up and looked at Rone. "Nice timin'. How'd ya know to come?"

Rone smiled and shrugged. "It just felt like the right time."

"Except now the whole camp knows about it." James could hear shouting coming from up the ravine. He turned and looked up at the wall. He didn't see any quick way through.

Matt came stumbling out of the shed and headed toward where the steam buggy sat beside one of the steep ravine walls.

James shook his head. There wasn't enough time. "Did you see any keys to unlock that door?" he asked Rone.

"No, Marshal. Shall I search?"

The shouting drew nearer and James could see kerosene lamps and candles bobbing toward them. "No time. Undo your oxen from the wagon."

"Why?"

"Just do it. Hurry!"

The wagon was parked lengthwise across the ravine. Rone hopped down and pulled the peg that held the yoke to the wagon. Once it came loose, James went over and planted his metal leg into the ground before reaching under the wagon with his mechanical arm and lifting up. The wagon fell on its side, blocking most of the ravine.

"What are you doing?" Rone asked.

"Buying us some time. Hook your oxen to the steam buggy."

Rone shrugged but obeyed. He led the Sons of Zebedee over and tied them to the buggy as Matt worked frantically to get the boiler started.

There isn't time. James looked down and saw the dropped rifle. He picked it up and hid behind the wagon as he shot at any shadows that moved. That at least forced the outlaws who were closest to dive for cover.

Rone soon had the oxen tied to the buggy. "Now what?"

Gunmen fired back, blowing out chunks of wood from the wagon. James aimed for the muzzle flashes. They stopped firing and he thought he even heard someone cry out as if they'd been hit.

James handed Rone the rifle. "Here, keep them busy."

Rone held his mouth open as he took it. "But Marshal, I've never shot a man before."

"Just keep them ducking for cover." James turned and limped his way toward the supply pile. Once there, he rummaged through the items he and Rone had brought. When he found what he needed, he commenced removing his metal leg. Once off, he opened the thigh compartment just as a bullet pinged into the wall above his head. He grabbed his knife and used it to pry open the acid container inside his leg. He next grabbed a handful of matches and thrust them into the acid. James had no idea how much time he had so he shoved the whole leg into the wall between a couple of the wooden posts supporting the steel door, and then hopped as fast as he could back toward the wagon. Rone stood there, firing up the ravine but aiming too high to hit anything.

"What's going on?" Matt asked as he continued stoking the boiler. "Where's your leg?"

"Let's just say that it will be a lot harder fer ya to fix, now."

The wall exploded, sending flames and twisted metal up into the air. A shock wave slammed into them and knocked James down.

Matt recovered from the shock. "Oh. But this boiler isn't hot enough yet. I need at least another ten minutes."

Rone came over and helped James stand on his remaining leg. James took the rifle from him. "Go with Matt, git him and the buggy outta here. I'll hold 'em off."

Matt looked up. "No, James, I won't leave you behind."

"Just do it." James looked up the ravine to see if the outlaws were closing in. To his surprise, they weren't. Instead, a lone female figure approached. A very attractive figure.

Cassi had her hands up as she came closer. "Marshal, it doesn't have to end like this."

"Stop right there or I'll shoot," James said, though he wasn't sure if he could do it. *Shoot a woman? What would Gramms say?*

"I'm unarmed. I just wanna talk."

James nodded. Talking was good. It would give Matt and Rone more time to get away. "About what?"

"My offer still stands. I think we could work well together."

James let out a short laugh. "I don't think so. We have completely different views about life."

"Do we?"

"Yer a cattle rustler, Miss Butcher. I'm a lawman."

Her voice went softer. "Call me Cassidy." She paused for a second before staring deeply into James's eyes. "Do you believe in love at first sight?"

James's mind went into a whirl. *What's happening?* He shook his head. "I don't believe you. What do you *really* want?"

Cassi came around the wagon and stopped in front of James, her hands still raised. "I guess nothing. I just thought there was something between us. Didn't you feel anything?"

"No, ma'am." As James said it, he knew it was a lie.

Cassi sighed and turned to head back up the ravine. "Very well."

She might be our best way out of here. James reached out and grabbed her, pulling her toward where Matt, Rone, and the steam buggy still sat. "You are under arrest fer cattle rustlin' and anythin' else I can think of." She resisted some but not much as he guided her into the buggy's passenger seat. Rone snapped the reins and the Sons of Zebedee sent the buggy forward and through the flaming hole in the wall.

James kept an eye out behind them, expecting to see several horsemen galloping in pursuit. Nobody came.

Cassi said, "They won't come after us unless I give the signal."

"Then don't give the signal." James drew Thunderer out and held it with his left hand. The battery had finally died in his right arm and he couldn't let go of the rifle.

They reached the spot where the ravine entered a wider valley and turned back toward civilization. The sun peaked up above the hills and the boiler started spewing steam. "It's ready," Matt said. "Should I destroy it or race out of here? We don't want those outlaws getting a hold of this thing."

James looked behind them again. There was still no sign of pursuit. "Let's just skedaddle. If they come after us, we'll blow it then."

To James's surprise, Cassi stood, kissed James on the lips, and leaped out of the buggy.

James tried to grab her but he didn't have a free hand. She rolled on the ground before jumping up and running back toward Liar's Lair. James aimed Thunderer at her but couldn't bring himself to squeeze the trigger.

Rone pulled on the reins. "Should we go get her?"

James watched her lithe figure weave around the boulders. "No. Her gang can't be far behind." To his surprise, his next thought was, *Will I ever see her again?*

They continued on until they were out of the mountains. Since the buggy now moved on its own power, Rone and the oxen trotted alongside.

"So, what *did* you do back there to cause that explosion?" Matt asked James.

"I did what ya told me to never do. I stashed some matches into the acid compartment."

Matt smiled as he nodded. "Ah, I see. I didn't know you were listening."

"I wasn't."

"Well, it was good thinking, anyway."

"I just used what was available." James's thoughts went back to Cassi and the relationship that could never be.

ABOUT THE AUTHOR

Berin Stephens was born and raised in the magical kingdom of Alaska in the area known as Chugiak. He earned a master's degree in music performance and pedagogy and is now a saxophone and clarinet teacher and performer. When he's not laying down some groovy jazz or teaching, he writes novels. He currently lives in Orem, Utah with his wife and several others who keep raiding his refrigerator. For more information, you can visit www.berinstephens.com.

Eternal Round

Elizabeth Mueller

CHAPTER 1: PRIZED POSSESSION

Her heels tapped loudly through the empty Museum of Ancient History, Cumorah. Sariah had always loved visiting here ever since she was a little girl, her father having been the curator during his days. Though the position had been passed to her, she felt it best for her brother to take it. She rather enjoyed exploring than running the place.

"Sariah!" A tall man in a suit and tie fast-walked toward her. "Welcome." He turned and matched her pace. "What brings you to Cumorah so early?"

"The relics the archeologists discovered," she said, breathless. Her heart pounded. "Where are they?"

Her companion paused, a secret smile sparking his gaze. "Over here, if you will."

Sariah bowed her head and followed at once. Their dual heels tapped sharply, the echoes bouncing off the glass displays. They owned many curious collections from the Nephite Age—from the broken steel bow that started a battle between brothers, to an old sheep's bladder canteen from the ancient Holy City believed to belong to that of Father Lehi. She especially loved the brass ball, called Liahona. Gears and spindles and fine lattice work—the museum's most prized possession next to Laban's sword and brass plates and Joseph Smith's spectacles he wore during translation. How could she resist not admiring the historical remnants?

"Sariah?" her companion asked, his brow lifted in question.

She shook her head with a dismissive chuckle. Cumorah was blessed indeed. "Please forgive me, Jacob, but I just love your collection."

"Our collection," Jacob corrected.

She glanced at him. "Very well."

Jacob side-stepped so he could pass her, as she'd stopped to study a piece of bark from the ship Nephi had built many centuries before.

"Yes, the shipment." A sheepish smile crept across her face. "I apologize."

Jacob laughed. "No harm done. What's a visit from the great Sariah without her appreciative eye?"

She threw her head back with a loud bark of a laugh. "I wholeheartedly agree."

"You're afraid," he said.

Sariah swallowed. "As equally as I am thrilled. Yes, I am."

He reached out his hands and held hers. She giggled and tugged against his hold but he didn't let go. "I promise, little sister, that you will love it."

She nodded with bated breath and followed more slowly this time. After crossing several doors and a few flights of steps and into a dim room, she paused at the threshold. The telltale of the ticking wall clock announced their arrival. There, upon the large, oblong table, resided their findings beneath a cloth.

"Are those—?" she asked, unable to speak the words.

Jacob nodded, his eyes closing. "Take a look." He signaled to his assistant who pulled back the cloth.

"Careful," Sariah whispered more to herself, her throat dry and tight. But she kept her eyes closed as she stepped closer. The powerful lure of its call rippled across the room, gripping her like a vice in its grasp. Could all the anguish of centuries of waiting finally be defined into one single moment in time? Was she prepared to handle the answer?

"Breathe, little sister, breathe." Jacob stood beside her, his hand clasping hers as he led her forward.

Her breath quivered and she opened her eyes. It was an arrow. Rusted with time. Copper riveted together along the lengthy shaft. The feathers were as fine as she'd always imagined them—undulating and soft in the stillness. She blinked, her breath a shot of swift air.

"How is this possible?" She dropped to her knees, her fingertips aching to graze along the surface.

"With lots of money." She heard the satire in Jacob's tone. "And love."

"I-I don't know what to say," she said, choked.

"Thank you?" Jacob responded.

All she could do was nod, her lips forming the words, her voice forgotten. All her life she'd dreamed of this arrow. Its significance a profound emotion without words. It had been sought by archeologists from all over the world and none had ever come close to its discovery. Tears glossed over the visage of the arrow.

"Samuel," Sariah whispered, reaching out a hand. She was afraid to ask the next question.

"It tested positive. The blood, though fossilized, is his."

She knew how ludicrous she must've looked to Jacob and his assistant, but at that moment, nothing mattered. Could it be? Her hand curled into a quivering fist before she splayed her fingers wide and moved her hand toward the arrow.

CHAPTER 2: THE TREE

As Sariah touched the arrow, a blast of wind buffeted her face. The power sucked her breath away and her hair flung from its chignon into a banner behind her. Dirt whipped across her eyelashes. The orange sky filled with billowing towers of smoke. An angry whining sound vibrated in the air and she looked up to locate its source.

She yanked her hand back to her side with a cry. The lighting surrounding her fluctuated to the dimness of the museum's collection room with the incessant ticking of the wall clock.

"Sariah!" Jacob steadied her. "Are you alright?"

Her breaths heaved as she gathered her wits. "I-I, I touched it and I wasn't here, but I am." She swung her eyes to him. Worry creased his brow. "I am here but…" She forced down a swallow. "What happened?"

His wide gaze revealed he was just as concerned, just as surprised as she. "Nothing happened. You reached out, touched it, screamed, and fell back, but I caught you. Are you feeling well?"

Unable to fathom how to explain what she'd experienced, she thinned her lips. She longed to touch it again, but fear kept her at bay. "I don't know."

"Here, let me call Mom. You aren't well enough to fly back home."

"No!" she shouted, shocking even herself. At his surprised expression, she lowered her voice. "No. I'm alright. It's all the excitement. I forgot to eat this morning. Came straightaway, you know." She chuckled as she tried to convince herself. At her brother's hesitation, she waved him off, irritated. "I'm a grown woman. I can handle myself."

"Grown or not, we're fallible as human beings, Sariah."

Wanting to sort this out without him or his ogling assistant, she dismissed him. "Tell you what, I'll feel better if you fetch me a donut with milk." He looked doubtful. "Go on." She waved him off again. "I'll wait here for you." She leaned against the table, vigilant with how close the artifact was to her.

"Okay, sis. I'll be right back."

As he spun to exit, she called out, "Take Orville with you. His stares give me the creeps." This elicited a gale of chuckles from the man. "There you go. Get yourself some while you're at it." She waited a few good minutes before turning back to the table, her hands shaking.

Without further ado, she shot her hand out and gripped the arrow. Resounding booms drew her attention to the heavens. Several crude dirigibles floated high in the air, tiny ships dangled below with what appeared to be cannons pointing at her.

A strong grip laced through her hand and wrenched her forward. She lost her footing but caught herself as she stumbled into a clumsy run. A man. A man with flowing black hair, clad in dark leather from head to foot, pulled her along. His billowing red cape trailed behind them both, his muscular arm extending toward her as he faced the direction they headed.

"We must hurry!" He whipped his face at her, his hazel eyes wide with fear.

"Samuel?" Sariah heard herself whisper his name. Her heart broke and tears ran. This was the man who'd haunted her since childhood. In her youth, she'd fallen in love with him, but the dreams stopped the day her father died. She decided against questioning the improbability of ever dreaming of her beloved again. Her heart soared with the simple fact that she was with him—she'd willingly live out this dream until she awakened. Before her brain could process anymore, a loud explosion sounded at her right. Shards of debris rocketed into the air, and she shrieked.

"Sorai!" Samuel bellowed.

He flung his cape around her as he tackled her to the ground. They rolled to the dirt, large rocks slashing her knees with their descent. They didn't stop there. The incline moved them faster and faster until they collided into a solid object below.

"Sorai." The desperation in Samuel's voice brought her back. "Are you hurt?"

"My legs hurt." She ground her teeth, but being in his presence healed all wounds. She stared at him in stunned silence. Every last detail the same as she remembered him. From his impressive muscular form to his bronze, statuesque face.

He hissed, and under the cover of surrounding brush, he examined her. "They are bloodied but not broken. Can you stand?"

Still in a trance, she nodded and moved to her feet with his assistance. Only then did she turn to regard what had stopped their descent. A looming copper wall of riveted plates soared high overhead. She pressed her palm to it, surprised at the depth of its chill.

"Zarahemla," he said with bitterness in his voice. "A city once filled with joy and goodness, now dark and corrupted."

She stared at him, dumbfounded. "Zarahemla? As in the city that existed in 6 B.C.?"

"Exists, and yes. Are you well, Sorai? You are disoriented." His expression sobered. "I should have left you home. Being big with child does not make our task any easier." He nodded, his eyes at her belly.

Big with child? She followed his glance and gasped at the size of her tummy. She was pregnant? Her gaze shot to his and found fear there.

"Please forgive me." Samuel crumpled to his knees. "I should have listened to Mother." He rose with a finality that sunk her heart.

"No. Being pregnant won't hinder me. I'm just as limber."

An explosion resounded nearby, sending debris their direction. Again, Samuel hid her with his cape but most of the surrounding trees had deflected the blast. To show that she was no feeble thing, she pushed him aside. Her hands touched the warmth of his skin where his leather armor did not cover and a shock connected them.

She gasped, looked up at him, and sobbed at the loving caress of his eyes. "Can it really be you?" she whispered to herself. She lifted her hand and stroked his smooth face. He closed his dark lashes and leaned into her touch. "I've missed you. I can't bear another second without you, and I won't go even if you send me away."

His lips pulled into a brilliant smile and his eyes fluttered open. "Sorai. Stubborn as she is sweet." He nodded. "This is no easy task, my love. We must practice caution. The Lord has urged me that these people are in need of His counsel and I can no longer procrastinate the day." He regarded her as though seeking permission.

She nodded. "Okay."

"I will ask of you later what that word means but now is not the time." He laced his hands with hers and tugged her along. "As goes with every walled city, therein lies a culvert. With the famine, it will be fairly easy to traverse."

She stopped, not understanding why he'd want to go under the wall when he was supposed to go over. "What about climbing the wall? They'll kill us if we enter the city."

He paused, his brow furrowed.

Comprehension dawned, and it infuriated her. "I'll have you know, buster brown, that I was an expert tree climber in my younger days. Being 'big with child,' as you say, will not inhibit me!" She jumped around, touched her knees to her chest as best as she could, and bent down to touch her toes with her fingertips. Slightly out of breath, she crossed her arms with a defiant lift of her chin.

Samuel stared at her until he burst into clear, beautiful laughter. "Very well, my sweet Sorai, you have convinced me. It is no easy task, but I do recall your climbing days and you have always impressed me. Now to seek the tree that grows into the wall. We shall start there."

CHAPTER 3: BATTLE ZONE

By the time Samuel found the tree, the flying cannons had cleared the skies. Sariah supposed the enemy had thought them dead. Shouts and cheers like faint whispers floated in the wind, sailing high above the copper wall.

They traveled along the barrier in the event the armed airships returned. A rhythmic thud vibrated within the wall, and she found it odd how certain parts of it was warm. They came to a stop when Samuel announced their arrival to where they'd climb.

"What's that noise?" She tapped the wall as she watched Samuel secure his cape at his waist.

"That is how they warm their homes. With great boilers."

"And power their dirigibles and cannons?"

"War is not a beautiful thing." He closed his eyes. "It is my deepest regret that you saw that."

She drew in a breath. "You can't protect me from everything,

Samuel." With his cape tied up and away from his legs, she was surprised to see that he didn't have his bow or quiver full of arrows. He wore no weaponry. "You came here without protection?" She was incredulous.

He paused in his preparation for the climb and offered her a devastating smile. "What more can I ask from the Lord when He will shield me?"

She drew in a patient breath and held it for a second or two before releasing it.

"You, my love, on the other hand, must not present yourself. Stay in the branches." His eyes caressed her face, and he snickered. "I would ask you to stay here but we both know that is a futile thing."

"Believe it!" She snapped at him with her teeth, trying to bite the tip of his nose, but he ducked his head away.

"Ah, Sorai, how I love you." He brought her into a fierce embrace. "I shall survive this day. They may shoot their bombs and arrows and fireballs and everything which they possess, but nothing will come to harm me this day."

"I believe it," she muttered as he motioned her to follow.

The climb wasn't as easy as she thought nor was it as difficult. There were a steady amount of hand and foot holds and with the way the goliath tree grew into the wall—half submerged either by choice of the tree or hunger of the wall, Sariah couldn't tell which—served their purpose famously.

As they crested the wall, a fierce wind whipped her hair from her face, carrying with it cries and cheers of the people who lived there. The treetop continued upward for a good few yards, offering them needed protection.

"This is where I will declare the Lord's word, sweet one." Samuel placed firm hands on either of her shoulders, his gaze deep and searching.

She understood his meaning and nodded once. "I know you'll be protected, but I can't help but ask that you be careful anyway."

He chuckled softly, brought her close to his heart, and pressed warm lips to her forehead. They lingered for a few minutes before parting. "The words of your lullaby to our little one, sing those while I speak."

Ready tears pressed behind her eyelashes. She knew no harm would befall him but it still worried her. The people were vicious. They weren't shy to the ways of killing, and though she knew of Samuel's enduring faith, she worried anyway.

With one last kiss to her head, Samuel squeezed her and turned aside. He leaped the remaining five feet, leaving her below within the safety of the wall and tree. She watched him as his hair and cape pitched behind him with the buffeting wind. He dropped to one knee, his fist steadying him as he bowed his head in prayer.

Within the arbor of the treetop and against the wall, she lowered to her heels, folded her arms, and watched him in awe. The longer he prayed, the stronger the peace burgeoned within her heart. So much so, that she felt if she looked up from him, she'd see concourses of surrounding angels.

Samuel stood, lifted his head, and opened his mouth to speak. His voice carried loud and strong over the barrier. The people far below, Sariah observed through the knotted branches as she climbed a few inches higher, stopped their revelry and turned to face him. A shock of silence ensued, punctuated with Samuel's words of authority.

He spoke with such moving power, her heart burned. She felt as if fire had descended upon her, setting her alight with its truth. On and on he spoke as the sun set. Lingering to listen, the populace lit their bonfires. Soon, some protested against his words, demanding to bring down the pretender from the top of the walls. Others, she noted with horror, brought out their slings and arrows, their rocks and javelins and crossbows.

Along with the people's cries of outrage, the sound of gears turning and clicking into place filled the air, followed by piercing whistles.

Sariah craned her neck. Through the branches, she spied

crossbows with arrows burning with brilliant fire tips, shooting high, all taking aim at Samuel.

"Samuel!" she shrieked as they flew in masses toward him. She dropped below the wall and curled into a ball. He didn't flinch or duck or cower. He remained in his regal posture, unaffected by the whistling weapons of death. She blinked, tears leaking down her face. How was this possible? She thought of the masses below, their aim perfect for Samuel, yet, every one missed.

Livid curses wafted upward in maddening spirals, and yet more weapons took aim but fell impotently at Samuel's feet. Movement within Sariah's peripheral vision caught her attention and she turned. The night sky filled with heaving airships of all sizes. The cranking of cannons taking their aim, the engines shooting out puffs of black exhaust behind them.

Terror paralyzed her. "Samuel!" She tried to call out again, but her voice was lost in the pollution of war. Despite the clamor, she could still hear the sound of Samuel's thundering voice. Her heart took to fear regardless of his faith. She thought of how lousy the people's shots were from far below in the gathering darkness and attributed his survival to that, but what of the big guns pointing at him?

An explosive report ricocheted from the airship, shaking the wall where he stood. She screamed, ducked her head, and held still. And she prayed. She couldn't remember the last time she'd prayed, but she prayed with every fiber of her being. Heat blasted behind her where the ball had shot past. She whipped around and stared at a roaring fire that consumed the surrounding jungle. Impossible. She'd seen the cannon focus on him!

Another cannon exploded and again, she covered her face, but only for a moment. Amazingly so, Samuel remained unaffected. His cape and hair fluttered in the fantastic backdrop of explosions, fiery arrows, and whistling balls. She took heart and rose to her feet, her stomach a wild flutter.

His godly declaration warmed her soul and gave her hope and

courage. She became confused as to why these people were so against him, and she frowned. A new sound soon joined the cacophony as some airships drew closer while others retreated. She gazed down the wall into the city and spied a gathering of soldiers shouting. They pointed up where Samuel stood. They gathered rope and shackles and began their ascent within the cranking crudity of an elevator.

She panicked and searched for a way to jamb the gears that were within her grasp. She reached for a branch and pulled. With much effort, it broke off and she thrust it into the gears. It ground to a halt. The machine screeched and smoked until the branch shattered into slivers. Again, she searched for something significant to destroy the system. More branches. It would do nothing to stop their eventual arrival. There were no convenient rocks or debris, either. Where did all the arrows go?

It wasn't until the men were only a few yards away that she decided to interfere with Samuel's sermon. "Samuel!" Sariah shouted above the din as she clutched the hem of her tunic. "They are coming!"

He turned to her, tears glistening within his brilliant eyes. They streamed down his cheeks when he blinked, and he ran toward her. His entire body trembled as he pulled her into his embrace, his lips finding her hair. Without a word, they scrambled down the gnarled branches of the goliath tree.

Voices high above resounded, shouting and cursing. The tree shuddered as they pursued. She kept her lips tight, refusing to cry out in dismay. She didn't want to prove Samuel right by showing her fear. A sharp whistling pierced the air and she paused to look up just as a fiery glint came fast at her. Before she knew it, debilitating pain exploded in her chest, and she wailed.

"Sorai!" Samuel screamed.

CHAPTER 4: ETERNAL ROUND

Sariah cried out, released the copper arrow with the fossilized blood, and crashed into the hard, cement floor. There were no surrounding jungles or floating dirigibles with cannons or an imposing copper wall. The goliath tree was gone. The pursuing soldiers were gone. Even her beloved Samuel was gone.

"Sariah!" a man shouted, followed by many footfalls. His pale face peered over her, his blond hair framing his blinking blue eyes. "What happened? Where did all this blood come from? Orville, call 9-1-1!"

Voices faded in and out and Sariah lay there in her brother's arms, benumbed. She didn't feel any pain in her chest as she'd expected, other than the cold realization that Samuel was yet again a mere dream. Her body convulsed, she flipped to her side, curled her legs to her chest, and screamed.

The hospital was a blur. The flight home was a blur. Jacob wheeling her into her home was a blur. For the past several days all she could think about was the life she never had with the man she loved, surely her husband. She was to have his baby.

She remembered his amazing faith. How she could see his love for her with a simple glance. He was the most amazing person ever to live, she knew that much from reading the scriptures, but to know he was only a dream to her, killed her.

Sariah picked at her food as her brother rattled about in the kitchen. She felt his worry from the other room but was too dazed to respond to his attempts. She stood from the sofa, walked to the huge glass sliding door, and continued onto the patio. The swimming pool glimmered in the weakening light of day, the reflection of passing airships drifted lazily about for their nightly cruises.

She strolled to the edge of her yard—right up to the railing—and gazed over into the city far below her air-domicile. The lights blinked on like miniature Christmas lights. With a sigh, she rested her elbow along the top and gazed further at the pumping engines of her home.

They were not a barbaric grinding of gears or hisses as she'd heard while with Samuel. It was amazing to see how far technology had improved since 6 B.C. Again, the hollow cramp in her chest crushed her and she clutched her hand to the pain with a whimper.

"To never see you again, Samuel, is death." A tear slid down her cheek and she pushed off the railing and trudged her way back into the house. She gave her brother a weak smile.

"Where're you going?" he asked as he stirred something on the stove.

The mouth-watering aroma tickled her, but she ignored it. "I'm going to bed. Please don't let anyone bother me." She took the curved stairs to her room slowly. She dragged herself onward to her bedroom and, leaving the lights off, she threw herself onto the bed.

The doctors found nothing wrong with her. The blood was hers, but there were no wounds to be found. They had demanded her brother to keep a close watch over her. She sighed, turned to her back, and closed her eyes.

A soft hum of an engine outside her window begged her attention that a visitor had arrived. She kept her eyes closed. Jacob would take care of it. As a protective brother, he'd make sure to see to her wishes. The soft vibrations of him climbing the staircase to the upper level alerted her of his impending visit.

"Jacob," she said, too weak to be angry. She flopped to her side, giving her back to the door. She heard his heavy footfalls upon the lush carpet, his breathing soft. "Jacob, what're you doing?" But she was too down to look. "Go away."

He sat on her bed, ignoring her pleas. She sprang upward, full and ready to launch into him for not respecting her need for solitude. Her mood swiftly changed from floundering sorrow to livid fury and she hurled her fist into his chest.

His powerful hands stopped her attack and her eyes lost their sleepiness. Within the dimly lit room, her gaze snapped up to his eyes and she stared at him in stunned silence. Rather than seeing amused blue eyes, she fell into deep hazel ones. Every last detail was how she remembered him. From his impressive muscular form to his bronze, statuesque face. An involuntary sob slipped from her throat and she covered her mouth.

"Samuel?" She reached out to him but hesitated. Her chin quivered, confounded as to what her heart felt. She shook her head. "This can't be." He grabbed her hand and she cried out with his palpable touch. He was solid, warm, and oh so alive! Her tears ran faster. "But how?"

He glided his thumb across her cheek, wiping off her tears. His tender smile brightened the room as well as her heart. "I brought you a gift," he whispered, presenting her with a long and narrow box.

Sariah sniffed and gazed at him questioningly.

"Open it." He nodded as he pulled her into his arms.

From the trauma of loss and shock of the impossibility of his presence, her fingers became clumsy. After a few attempts, she laughed, he along with her.

"There is no rush, my sweet Sorai," he murmured into her ear.

"But I want to see." She smiled, finally pulling the ribbon free. Next came the lid. She held her breath and looked at him instead of into the box. He gave her an encouraging smile. She returned to her gift. Upon fine wood shavings lay the copper arrow with fossilized blood that Jacob had brought to the museum. She blinked as it came into clearer focus. It was the very one which had struck her.

She set it down and pulled her shirt aside, gazing at the scar where it had hit. "Samuel, how is this possible?"

He smiled, adoration filling his tear-filled gaze. "Love and time knows no bounds—they are one eternal round."

She burst out laughing and threw herself into him. His lips captured hers, filling her fallible soul with eternal promises. How his presence healed all wounds.

ABOUT THE AUTHOR

Award-winning author Elizabeth Mueller lives in Texas with her husband, five lively children, five indoor kitties, a few outdoor kitties, and a whole lot of tumbleweeds. While she enjoys homeschooling the kidlets, she thrives as a full-time writer of any genre that captures her heart. Say hi www.facebook.com/ElizabethMueller Author or visit her website www.elizabethmueller.com.

I Stand at the Door

Roy Hayward

The girl barely ran fast enough to stay ahead of the metal man that chased her. I knew that soon the relentless pace of the machine would wear her down. And he would catch her.

The metal monsters had started to attack people three days ago. Now the streets were clear. Deserted. Silent. Everyone that had avoided them was behind locked doors or had fled the city.

The look of the girl told me she had been running too long and would not make it much farther. If I didn't help, he would have her in a block or two. So I opened the door wider and stepped out into the open.

"This way!" I waved one hand so she could see me and not waste any steps. My other hand held onto the door to keep it from swinging shut. She didn't have much time. I couldn't hold the door open long. If she wasn't to me soon. The metal man would have us both.

She increased the speed of her pace for a few strides, but then she stumbled and almost fell. I wanted to go to her. But if I let go of the door it would close and lock behind me and we would both be trapped out on the streets.

So, I just gritted my teeth and waited for her to get to me. I prayed that she would make it before it caught up to her.

With only a yard to spare, she rushed through the doorway. I slammed the door and lowered the bar to brace it shut and keep him out.

I turned and looked at the girl. Woman really. She leaned on the wall of the entryway, panting. She had clearly been running near the end of her endurance.

"Hi, I'm Elder Ricks." My hand moved to the black name tag on the pocket of my white shirt. I stopped myself from continuing with the next sentence on my lips that would lead into an introduction of the Church. Instead, I followed with, "And you are?"

"Maria. Maria Sullivan." She stood straighter, still breathing hard, and ran her hand through her tangled red hair. It got caught, and she ended up pulling it out without helping her hair to regain any sense of order.

"I'm glad to meet you." I cleared my throat. I was breaking the rules by talking to her alone. If I hadn't been emptying our bins I wouldn't have even seen her. And I would have had Elder Macomb with me, and he would have never let her in.

The door shook and the metal man pounded and clanged against it. She jumped.

"Let's go on upstairs and see what's happening."

She nodded and followed me. I knew this was not going to end well, but I needed to return to my companion before he thought something had happened to me.

"Hey Elder, couldn't even empty a bin without attracting the chrome domes, I see," Elder Bailey said. He turned around, looked past me to where Maria stood, and took a step back as if I had just let the enemy into the apartment.

"Oh, this is just too much," Elder Macomb said when he entered the room. "You are in so much trouble, they are going to send you home."

"That doesn't sound so bad you know," I said. Then I turned to our guest. "Can I get you some water?"

"Yes. And may I sit."

"Yes," I said.

"No!" Said Elder Macomb at the same time. "She can't stay here."

"How do you suggest we get her out? Open the door and hand her to our metal friend?" I pushed past the still immobile Elder Bailey, filled a plastic cup, and took it to Maria.

Her shoulders drooped and she stared at the floor. When I stopped in front of her she looked up. Her eyes focused past me for a moment before landing on my face and then falling to the plastic cup in my hand. I handed it to her.

"I just need to rest a bit," she said.

"Don't worry, you're safe here." I tried to reassure her, which wasn't easy with Elder Macomb shaking his head and digging for his white rule book in the breast pocket of his white shirt that was too full with a planner, a note-pad, and several highlighters.

"Elder, it says right here that members of the opposite sex are not allowed in missionaries' apartments."

"I know the rules, Elder." I turned on him, snatching the rule book and stuffing it back in the breast pocket of his shirt. "But we are helping her. We are not doing anything stupid. And if there is trouble for it, I will take the blame."

"I'm calling the president as soon as the phones are working again." He turned and stormed into our room, shutting the door behind him.

"A girl." Elder Bailey stood there with a piece of bread in one hand and the butter knife in the other.

"I thought I heard a woman's voice." Elder Kim entered from the other bedroom. He looked at her sitting on our couch, t-shirt twisted, jeans dirty, and flame-like hair looking like she had held it outside of a speeding trolley. "Well, this certainly explains why Macomb was making so much noise."

Maria screamed and threw her cup of water at Elder Kim. "He's one of them!" She scrambled backward, trying to climb over the couch. There was nowhere to go. The room was small for just the four of us Elders and didn't get any bigger for her being there.

"Fetch," Elder Kim said with resignation as he wiped the water from his face and looked down at his soggy tie.

"Watch your language Elder Kim! Put a dollar in the jar," Elder Macomb yelled through the closed door of our room.

"Sorry, Macomb, won't happen again."

"You mean *Elder* Macomb, don't you Elder Kim? That's another dollar, Elder."

Kim shook his head.

"Are you trying to drive him into a seizure or something?" I asked.

"A girl," Elder Bailey said.

"He is not with them. He's with us." I grabbed Maria by the shoulders and stopped her from scrambling out a window or attacking Elder Kim again. "He is not the enemy."

"They brought the auto-men," Maria insisted. She stopped trying to get away as she stared at Elder Kim standing there, pressing the water out of his necktie.

"He was here before they came. And he didn't have anything to do with them."

"But he may know a way to stop them," Elder Kim said, speaking of himself in the third person. He walked over to our small balcony and looked down. The auto-man still banged away on the downstairs door.

"I don't think telling them about the Book of Mormon will get them to run away as it does most people you talk to," I said.

"A girl in our apartment." Elder Bailey tried to put his hand in his pants' pocket, but he was still holding the slice of bread and it didn't fit.

"What is wrong with him?" Maria asked, her voice returning down to a normal pitch.

"He's been out for a while now. I think this is his final transfer before going home," I replied.

"What?"

"Never mind." I shook my head. "He isn't used to being around girls anymore."

She looked at the four of us. We all clearly lived here. "Are you guys... "

"No," I said. "We are just serving as missionaries. Teaching about Jesus. We don't date or hang out with girls for two years."

"I'm sorry to intrude," she said slowly, shaking her head in confusion.

"It's a Mormon thing." At the word "Mormon" her eyes widened and she swallowed hard. She pulled away from me a bit, but I ignored it. I was used to what mentioning my religion did to people.

"I think I need to take apart the washing machine," Elder Kim said, still standing on the balcony.

"Why?" I stepped away from Maria and joined him at the railing. The auto-man stopped banging on our door and whirred and clicked as it adjusted its head to look up at us.

"I need the wire and electromagnets from the motor," Elder Kim said. "I have an idea, and I think we are not going to have much time before we will see if it works."

The auto-man made a pumping motion with his arms. I didn't think you could see a metal pressure tank fill up but I could have sworn his metal chest was getting tighter.

Maria pushed between the two of us and looked down. "Why did it stop?"

As if to answer her, a small pipe popped out of the top of the auto-man's conical head and a shrill whistle sounded, followed by a series of sharp bursts. The three of us clapped our hands on our ears until he stopped.

"What was that?" I asked.

"If my guess is right, he is calling for help," Elder Kim responded.

"So, tell me about your idea."

"Have you ever played with magnets?" Elder Kim asked.

"Sure."

"If there is enough iron in our metal friend, we should be able to hold him still with magnetic force long enough for me to turn him."

"I don't understand what you're thinking, exactly, but it sounds like a better plan than just waiting for the AP's to send a trolley for us."

We had to disassemble the washing machine, the oven, and Elder Bailey's toaster that he brought from home to get all the parts we needed for our electromagnet contraption. By that time there were a dozen auto-men in the street in front of our apartment. They banged on the door in turns, then milled about, ruining the flower garden and landscaping our downstairs landlady spent so much time on.

"Are you sure this will work?" I asked.

"No, but we won't have time for another try if it doesn't."

"What are you two doing out here?" Elder Macomb emerged from the bedroom.

"We are going to try and stop the auto-men," I said.

"I think this is a bad idea. We were told to stay inside until help came," Elder Macomb said.

"And we will stay inside." Elder Kim's smile told me that what he was going to do would not make my companion happy. So, I played along.

"Can you stay here with Elder Bailey while I help Elder Kim with his cables?"

He looked at me with suspicion. He was always suspicious whenever we swapped companions. I guessed he felt that it was close to breaking a rule but he hadn't quite figured out which one. I took that as a yes, and Maria, Elder Kim, and I grabbed the various parts of the appliances we had dismembered and headed downstairs into the narrow entrance hall of our apartment.

"Okay, put one of these on either side of the hall here," Elder Kim instructed Maria and me. "Tie them down as firmly as you can. There should be a lot of force and we don't want them to come free."

Boy Scouts came in handy now. I synched the metal bar coiled in wire to the water pipe on my side of the hall and then checked on Maria. She wasn't doing as well. The rope she had been using was wrapped in a big tangle that might not come untied but was certainly not very tight.

"So, can you let me try that?"

She looked at the bindings I had completed on my side. "I give up. It's all yours."

I untangled and retied the rope, securing the bar to the ventilation grate on that side of the hall.

"Sister Sullivan, would you be so kind as to stand behind me on the stairs," I said motioning for her to move up and behind me.

"I'm not a member of your church and if you think..."

"Just get on the stairs, already," I said, nudging her in the general direction.

"Okay, Mat, when I tell you, lift the bar on the door and then get behind me as fast as you can," Elder Kim said.

"Mat?" I raised an eyebrow.

He grinned. "I was just checking to see if Macomb could hear us."

"If this doesn't work, we might not all get upstairs in time."

"If this doesn't work, you are gonna have to think of something else, because I won't be having more ideas."

"Okay." I grabbed the bar on the door. "I'm ready."

"Do it!"

I pulled up on the bar and took it with me down the hall and up the stairs. Behind me, the door opened. I heard the whirring and clicking of the auto-men and the clank of their feet on the tile of the hallway.

As I passed Elder Kim he pressed down on the toaster levers and all the hair on my body stood on end. I halted and turned to look, forgetting about the plan to flee.

The metal men moved jerkily, but they made no progress towards us. They'd just lift up a hand and then put it back down. They also shuddered a bit as if something inside them was stuck.

"Hold these down." Elder Kim shoved the toaster parts into my hands and I struggled to grab them before he let go.

Maria came down and watched with me as Elder Kim approached the first metal man in the hall, careful but confident.

He popped open a small door on the chest of the metal man and reached inside. I couldn't see what he did next, but the auto-man stopped moving and froze in place.

Elder Kim moved to the second and repeated the process with the same results.

"Okay, Mat," he said over his shoulder. "Let go of the levers."

"But... the auto-men," Maria said.

"They won't hurt us now. And we don't want to burn out the toaster."

I let go of the toaster levers and the auto-men shifted and assumed a passive stance.

Elder Kim shut the door. "Now give me that bar."

I squeezed past the metal men blocking the hallway. Even though they stood frozen in place, my hands shook just being that close to them. I handed Elder Kim the bar and he shoved it down into place to hold the door shut.

"There are more out there, but they didn't try to enter with these two," he said. "Now the real work begins. I need to take a look at what is making these fellows so angry."

"You know how they work?" I was starting to worry about how familiar he was with the inner workings of the auto-men.

"Where I am from, these are not uncommon. And I may know enough to get them to switch sides. But it will take me some time."

"This is just too much," Elder Macomb said from the bottom of the stairs. He stood behind Maria, fishing in his shirt pocket for the rule book again.

"I don't think there is anything in there about automatons in our apartments," I said.

"Why did you have to let them in?"

"Let's just call it a teaching moment," Elder Kim said. "We are hoping for a true conversion."

"You shouldn't mock sacred things." Elder Macomb scowled.

"I'm not. I'm just mocking you."

Elder Macomb retreated up the stairs. Elder Kim turned to the first of the auto-men and pulled off the panels of his chest and torso.

Underneath the panels was a maze of gears, wires, and switches. "You understand all of this?" I asked.

Elder Kim shook his head. "This is more complicated than anything I worked on before my mission."

"I have faith in you, Elder." I placed a hand on his shoulder.

"Hoon."

"What?"

"My name is Hoon," Elder Kim said.

"Okay, Hoon, I have faith in you. But let's pray for help and then try the best we can."

I forgot that Maria was even there until we finished our prayer and stood up from our knees. She looked at us as if we had just grown horns and wings and flown around the room.

I'm sure that if the auto-men hadn't been outside, she would have bolted.

"I may need a second set of hands," Elder Kim said.

"I don't think Elder Macomb would want me to leave you alone with these fellows any more than he would want me to leave you with our guest."

"Is she still down here?" Elder Kim looked back to the stairs. "I'm sorry. I didn't mean to be rude."

"I'm still keeping an eye on you. But I think I'm going to be able to trust you," she said.

"Well, that is something, then." Elder Kim smiled.

"Now, Mat, I want you to hold these toggles open for me while I slide this panel out."

"Like this?"

"Yes, just hold those."

I helped Elder Kim pull out a bunch of parts from the first metal man. After we had so much of his workings out that I had no idea how we would ever get him back together, Elder Kim held up a disk. "This is it."

"Great! What is it?"

"This is in backward."

"That seems too simple."

"Like it says in James, 'the tongue is a little member,

and boasteth great things,' so is this disk small but will change the entire purpose of our friend here."

"Shhh. Elder Macomb will hear you and accuse you of misusing scripture." The three of us laughed. We got to work putting the tin man back together.

The second one went faster. Elder Kim popped open a couple of toggles and ejected the disk. Then he just flipped it over and put it back.

"Who would do this?" Maria asked when Elder Kim reactivated one of the auto-men and he didn't attack but just started cleaning up.

"I'm not sure this was sabotage. I think it is more likely a factory mistake. A batch of these were assembled wrong and didn't go on their rampage until they got here and were activated."

"So what do we do now?" I asked.

"Well, I'm gonna try and program these two to go out and be our first auto-man missionaries."

"Say that again?" Maria shook her head, looking confused.

But I had followed Elder Kim's humor. "The auto-men will be able to get close to others without raising alarm. If he can teach them to eject and flip the disk on the mis-assembled fellows, then they will, in effect, be spreading the gospel to the automatons."

"You guys are really strange, you know?" Maria had been stepping closer and closer to us and was now trying to get a look past Elder Kim's hands inside the chest of the automaton he was working on.

"Is that a good strange or a creepy strange?" Elder Kim asked.

"Definitely creepy strange."

"Okay, let's get this done," I said, shrugging.

It took hours before we were ready to release them. It would either work or at least we would have two metal men that would not continue the rampage. We opened the door and they shuffled with the whirs and the clicks and the clanks on the tiles of the hallway and out into the street.

The three of us went up to the balcony to watch. I held my

breath, worried they would be seen as a threat, and all our hard work would be smashed on the paving stones.

The two metal missionaries sidled up on either side of one of the metal men on the street. One of them popped open the panel, the other ejected his disk, flipped it over, and put it back. Then they released him.

The new convert switched tasks and began cleaning up the mess he had been making of the flower garden. It had worked.

"Congratulations," I said. "Elder Kim, I believe you have your first conversion."

"First two," he corrected.

"Both of you are in big trouble as soon as I can call the president." Macomb picked up the phone again, listened, and slammed it back down.

Maria watched the auto-men in our street. "This is going to take a while."

"Hours just to clear our street," Elder Kim said.

Maria looked back and forth between all of us. She shook her head and tried to run her hand through her hair again. Then she looked directly at me. "Fine."

"What?" I asked.

"Tell me what you guys are doing here, again?"

ABOUT THE AUTHOR

Roy spent much of his years growing up holed up in well-lit corners of libraries reading all of the fiction that he could find. Now he enjoys writing science fiction and urban fantasy to share with friends, family, and random people on and off of the internet. Find him at royhayward.me.

Crossroads of the Sky

Jenna Eatough

"Annabelle Mable Jean Wheeler," a voice boomed behind me, taking full advantage of my Pa's Catholic bent when it came to names. Odd, since that hadn't been the religion he professed believing before dying or, more important, before me being born. "A lady your age shouldn't be working on a fueling platform." I groaned. Was it already time for that conversation again?

Turning, I crossed my arms, eyeing Mr. Jones. "And just what would you have me doing? Ain't none family or person to take me in below."

He looked me over like I was some riddle to be solved. Either that or a particularly funny bone the hounds had decided to fight over. "I'm sure I could convince Miss Hardy to take you into her circle." His voice rumbled as slowly as a passenger train pulling into station. Wasn't me he was thinking of helping when he thought of Miss Hardy. He was just thinking of an excuse to see her sister.

"Oh, I'm sure you could," I said, all sweetness and smiles. "But whatever would I do there? Quilting and praying?" I tapped my lips with one finger. "Supposed I could add in storytelling. Like that one time the Dart passed through..."

Jones gawked at me, the languid smile slipping off his face to be replaced with a scowl. "You wouldn't."

I gave him my most mischievous smile in reply. "Try me."

Grumbling, Mr. Jones turned away. After a brief search of the deck, he decided on someone a bit easier to pick on. Muttering, he strode away. Good. Turning back to the rail, I looked over it to the Vista with a sigh. This conversation was beyond tiring. When would

Jones realize I wasn't about to get grounded and was his best motor hand besides?

I glanced over to where Archie was working—more like barely not destroying. He struck station one with his wrench and I rolled my eyes. No, I didn't have much competition in him. Besides, with three stations, three capable of motors were best. Archie was first motor, Irving was chief, and I was the second. Though honest, I should have been first. Shoving away from the rail, I walked over. I caught his wrist on a backswing. "Here, let me."

Archie shrugged and handed me the wrench then stood. He swung his arms as I crouched, like some crazed windmill. "It ain't gonna give easily." Leaning over, I grunted in response and tucked my disagreeable red hair behind my ear, wishing again Irving would let me crop it. "I've been trying to get the valve open for hours. It just ain't gonna give. Irving will have to..." He trailed off.

I glanced over my shoulder as I yanked on the wrench. A hunk of a ship drifted into view. The rusty metal sides had definitely seen better days, as had the cannon. The balloon holding it up was more patches than material, and she belched steam like Irving after bean night. But she was ours, the Nauvoo Legion still working to protect, and that was supposed to be proud or something.

A couple of the roughnecks emerged from the cover, swarming toward the dock the ship headed for. Of course, they'd pick the one close to where I was working. Mr. Jones wasn't far behind the boys. He glanced at me, and I hunched over, pressing my shoulder against the wrench. I watched his nose twitch, knowing he was thinking of at least sending me inside.

The valve finally gave before he could say anything. I yanked more tools from the pack Archie had left, and Mr. Jones snorted and turned away. "Greetings," he called out when the ship came in range. "What's the word?" I scoffed. The roughnecks hadn't even caught the lines yet and he was already demanding news.

"Not good," a voice called back from the ship, only slightly damped by the ropes whizzing through the air. No more was offered until the boys finished hauling the lines taut and tied them off. The man stepped off the ship, pulling off his gloves. Irving was already moving to connect the pumps to the ship's tanks. "They're sending an army."

Mr. Jones' brows rose to hide in his bangs. "They?"

"The US, President Buchanan in particular." The man shook his head sadly.

"Ain't they already done enough? I mean, after trying to get requisitions out of us. Who're they sending?" Mr. Jones turned the man away as he spoke. *Probably trying to corral him and pump info out while we pumped supplies in.*

"Johnston," the man said as they neared the door. "I've got orders straight from Daniel Wells." They disappeared inside before I could hear anymore. Archie came shuffling back. I blew out a breath trying to get my hair out of my eyes again. "Here," I said, standing. I shoved the tool back in his hands. "Think you can handle the ship alone?"

"Of course," Archie protested as I hurried away in the opposite direction of Mr. Jones and his guest. I wasn't daft enough to try eavesdropping. Not when I had a better, easier solution.

Reaching the back of the station, I hauled the hatch open and slid down the ladder. "Irving." I rubbed my eyes to try adjusting them to the dim light quicker. He was in the back next to the porthole. That was the only natural light in the place, and it faced the wrong direction this time of day with the platform's positioning. "Irving." I hurried to the edge of his table.

The man in question held up a finger, motioning me to silence. Skidding to a stop, I hopped onto the stool next to the table and watched him. His hair was graying and shaggy, hiding his expression as he leaned over the table. He was surrounded by an oddity of equipment with no distinction between what was broke, working, or experimental. I had the feeling experimental held his attention today.

Irving reached to pick up his blowtorch, the fuel sloshing in the reservoir. Pumping the tank, he frowned and lowered his goggles over his eyes. I grabbed mine as well, settling them in place before he could start the blaze. I didn't need to be told twice anymore. Or once even. Blue flame shot out of the mouth of the torch as he twisted the valve open. Must have heated it before I showed up. As he lowered the flame to his project a white light flared, blinding me. I cried out and turned away, eyes watering.

Irving did more than cry. A string of cusses filled the room followed by the blowtorch's rumble cutting off. "It's ruined," he said.

I hopped off my bench and put a hand on his shoulder. "You'll get it." I grinned at the man reassuringly. He'd cared for me since my parents' deaths crossing the plains. I knew better what he was capable of than anyone. He turned toward me and pressed his forehead against mine for a moment.

"Course I will." He replaced the blowtorch and pulled his goggles off. Grabbing a cloth, he rubbed at the soot covering them. "I'm sure you didn't come down to watch that. Who're our guests?"

"Some legion people, I think." I leaned closer to his project as he spoke, but it really was a charred mess.

"Ah, no wonder Jones sent you down." Irving said. "Not a proper crowd for a young lady." I glanced up to see him grinning. Jones might want me gone, but Irving sure didn't.

"He didn't send me down."

Irving nodded his head once. "So, what's the news distracting him from protecting your virtue?"

"Please, he ain't worried about my virtue. He's looking for..." I cut off, ducking my head as Irving scowled at me. "Well, he ain't," I muttered sullenly.

"The news, Annabelle."

I shrugged. "Something about Johnston bringing an army here."

Irving cleared his throat and rose before I could say anything else. "Stay here until I return." He darted up the ladder before I could protest. Not that I would've. Irving would tell me everything he learned soon enough.

War. For a week, all anyone could mutter about on the platform was war. The government was sending Johnston, and we were all in danger. The messenger said we were to do what we could to bedevil the army, but not to fight 'em direct. News of their invasion had come with a mail run not because the Easterners had bothered talking to us. Why would they when they could just fight us? Wasn't honorable to me, sending an army after those just trying to survive.

When I complained while fetching Irving parts, he tried to sit me down and explain it some, blathering on about religion, politics, more sides than one. At first I fidgeted on the stool, trying to follow, but it just seemed a confusing mess. I decided such things weren't for me to worry about and let my eyes glaze over.

Jones ordered the roughnecks to drift the station off by way of the Bear River. Rumor was the army was coming by way of Echo, but Mr. Jones figured there were enough men headed that way to slow them. Us, we'd check out this-a-way. Fool that he was, Mr. Jones had tried putting me off again over Centerville. Even me threatening to tell tales to Miss Hardy hadn't stopped him. Irving had. Jones wasn't about to risk losing Irving with me, and Irving said he'd have gone.

Weeks of staring at the browning landscape followed. Mountains stuck up to either side of where we'd anchored with the Bear River looking a trickle of water below and not much else. What spring rains there had been were long past, summer had scorched, fall was dry, and winter... Eh, they said it was coming.

Just like the army.

But all I saw was a spattering of beleaguered airships drifting through. They'd stopped for fuel but had no news to share, and kept westward with their loads of weary people. They'd have spent their last coins on berths. Still, those people were lucky compared to those that trekked by foot. I'd done that.

If we were supposed to be annoying anything, we were failing. Eh, forget that. We were successfully annoying each other.

Archie claimed a spot on the rail next to me. I twitched, taking a step to the side and scrunching my nose. "Ain't you supposed to be going on a water run?" I glanced pointedly at the raft being readied to be lowered. Hopefully one of the boys could dunk him in the river while they were grounded.

"Naw," Archie said. "That's roughneck work." He didn't say more, and he didn't move away.

I glanced at him. He gnawed on his lip as if he was trying to break answers free. "What you thinking, Archie?" I asked, more to break the monotony than because I cared to know the answer.

The man froze, his lip caught so deep between his teeth that his face looked like it was clay someone had smacked out of order from frustration. "I was thinking," he paused, scowling. "I'm thinking we might be wasting our time, but Mr. Jones says we plant ourselves here." Archie shrugged, a slow roll of his shoulders which carried partway down his back. "He reads the air well."

"Yeah," I said grudgingly. Jones did read the air well. A fact that kept his position as station boss. He knew where to plant the platform to hit travelers drifting through and sell them on fuel and supplies. Well, that and him being smart enough to bring Irving on and keep him happy. I slouched further over the rail.

I blinked. Was that movement on the horizon? I grabbed Archie's sleeve and tugged as I pointed. He followed my direction and muttered. That was definitely movement on the horizon. A trio of blue ballooned ships that resembled cook's coffee pot more than anything else wafted our way. Blue—the army had arrived.

"I got's to tell Mr. Jones," Archie rumbled and lumbered away.

Good, I didn't have to.

The three balloons drifted closer, angling towards us. Not that they needed to move quick to hit us. Platforms didn't move quick, especially when anchored. I moved to the first station before Jones hit the deck. He looked at me wrapping the hoses around my body, prepping for arrival. His nostrils flared and he turned away. Three stations, three hands. Being needed was grand.

"Greetings," Mr. Jones called, much later than he had with our own ship.

"Hail," a man called back from the quarter deck of the lead ship. Hair covered the man's ears and a mustache drooped over his mouth. He stood in the blues and brass of the army. Trim enough. I could believe he'd seen some fighting. Not like the man next to him. That man was pudgy at best. Pudgy and posh. I didn't like him already. "We're looking for fuel."

"Eh, we've got enough for your ships," Jones called back. "Though our lines are running low. Meant to have them checked next time we landed. Oh, and we're low on roughnecks at the moment." He gestured to the raft now most of the way to the ground. "Dock and we'll get you taken care of as quick as possible." He glanced at me, eyes wide, daring me to challenge him. As if I would. I knew the orders, bedevil the invaders.

"Understood," the man called back as I turned away to close the valve near tight before stomping on it and bending the metal. Irving emerged from his shop. Someone must have warned him there were three ships since he took position at second station. Archie waited ready at the far station. I turned back to see the first ship headed straight for me while the others circled around picking opposite spots to dock and not knock us akilter.

I wondered where Jones had stashed the other roughnecks. Normally there were two per station and I knew only three had gone for water. Only one was about on the deck and it was Gerry. I dodged the line that was tossed, narrowly missing me head. "Hey!" I glowered at the soldier who'd thrown.

The man retorted, "Help your roughneck."

"You help him," I shot back. "It ain't my job, nor my skills."

The soldier appraised me for a moment before taking to the winch on his ship, helping haul them in. Good, he'd taken me for a boy, a small one, with the hoses wrapped about me. Not that the roughneck was much bigger. Gerry was the runt of the group. Small and always wearing clothes three sizes too big for him, he never looked like he could move a full jug, forget secure a ship to dock. Which meant he was still bigger than me.

I leaned sideways against the rail, watching as the roughneck hauled the ship in, huffing like a locomotive. I almost felt sorry for Gerry. At least until he winked at me one time with his back to the soldiers. Took him a good twenty minutes to finish securing the ship. Impressive, since normally they did it in two flat.

I shoved off the rail and rambled over. Taking my cue from Gerry, I landed on my butt, much to the soldiers' amusement. At least I didn't have to fake my ears turning red. How had Gerry made incompetency so natural looking? "Get up, whelp," Mr. Jones said from where he stood on the deck, fists planted on his hips. He enjoyed insulting me far too much. I bit my tongue, though, and bobbed my head as I struggled to my feet.

The head solider glanced at me as he walked to the gangway. I stumbled, bending over and dropping the hoses about me. When I looked back again, he was on the platform. I slung the hoses back over my shoulder and headed to the front of the ship. "Back there," a soldier said, grabbing my shoulder and turning me around.

I squinted in the direction he pointed, knowing full well where their tank's access was located. "Oh, right," I squeaked and moved away.

Dropping my hoses unceremoniously on the deck, I pried the cap off the tank as I listened to Mr. Jones greeting the army. "Welcome, sirs," his voice rumbled without a hint of sneer. "I'm station boss Jones."

"Colonel Johnston," a voice replied, carrying over the general din easily. "And this is Mr. Alfred Cumming." That must have been the pudgy one.

"A pleasure, a pleasure." I could imagine Jones engulfing their hands and shaking them rambunctiously.

"Is there any way to hurry the docking process?" Mr. Cumming asked. "That was dreadfully slow."

"Oh," Mr. Jones drawled, "normally it wouldn't take any more than ten minutes, but we're slow due to the water run. Can't have thirsty roughnecks." His voice faded as he talked, and I had to suppress a laugh as I finished prying the tank lid off. I looked at the man standing over me and showed him the cap. He looked at it briefly before nodding. I slipped the nozzle tightly into the tank. I wasn't dumb enough to actually damage their equipment.

Pulling out my book, I noted the current reading on the tank and held it out for the soldier to inspect. He compared the numbers to the tank and nodded. I could only pretend to be so incompetent. Motors went through training, unlike roughnecks. Beginning to pump hydrogen over, I made a show of sitting on the deck and gnawing on my thumb nail. The numbers ticked slowly upwards. Very slowly. The solider watching me muttered something and moved away. I wished I could join him. Instead I kept on sitting until I was numb.

Shifting, a glimmer hit my eyes making me drop my head. Looking up, I gawked at the gleaming monstrosity hanging from the quarter deck of the army ship. The thing looked like a dragon cast in gold and polished, as it sparkled in the sun. I glanced around, no one was near. Most had wandered off to the platform's deck. I didn't blame them. Their ship was smaller than I'd thought from a distance. The few who remained were at the railing watching those on deck, including the one that was supposed to be watching me.

Freeing myself from the tangle of hoses, I bounded silently up the stairs. Yep, it was a mechanical dragon of some kind hanging from chains attached to the partially spread wings. In the center was a disc. I squeezed between the wheel and rail to get a better look. The thing could fold up. The gears on the wings were tiny, much better than anything machined out here. How had they gotten the bands in the gold coloring?

Curiosity Irving had taught me driving me, I braced my foot between the rails and pushed upward trying to get a look at the disc. A compass maybe? I grabbed hold of one of the wings and screeched as I lurched forward. A bit of chain struck my temple as I tumbled over the rail to land on the hoses.

The air whooshed out of me, and I stared at the dragon teetering precariously from a single chain. Took me a minute before I realized the buzzing in my ears wasn't just in my head, but a whistle belting out. Screaming voices converged on me.

Hands grasped me, pulling me roughly to my feet. My head refused to translate the riot of voices until one voice cut through, a bit on the shrill side. "He's a girl!" Great, they'd noticed.

Raising my head, I saw a bunch of soldiers gaping at me, with Colonel Johnston and Mr. Cumming at their center. Jones hovered at their shoulders. Archie hopped at the back of the crowd behind the soldiers. He was probably trying for a better view. "She's my crew," Mr. Jones bellowed.

"She destroyed our ship key." Mr. Cummings pointed at the compass. Huh, ship key. I've heard of those. Something which was supposed to help lock a military ship down when not deployed. If that was a key, the durability was lacking.

"A slim thing like her? How could she have done it?" Mr. Jones scoffed, and I peered at him, confused. Was he defending me? "She had no tools and certainly not the weight to pry apart a sound chain on her own."

"Would someone silence that whistle and let her go. She's not running." Colonel Johnston stood with his head tilted up. His men dropped their grips on me, and the bleating faded away to a hiss as the last steam emptied from the pipe. He was right. There wasn't a chance of me running. Not being this high and the raft being down. "It was damaged in the storms over Kansas," he said grudgingly. His gaze turned back to me and I shrunk backward. "What I want to know is what she was doing there."

"I... I," I forced myself to stammer, "I was curious how it was made."

"Curious how it was made?" Mr. Cumming snorted in derision. "Preposterous. She's a spy no doubt. A temptress." I rolled my eyes at that notion. Jones glowered at me.

"Not so," a quiet voice said from the back of the crowd. There was a quick reshuffling and I saw Irving standing on the gangway,

Archie next to him. "She is mine and curiosity is a trait I instilled in her."

Johnston regarded him. "Irving Gibbs." He walked toward the man and extended his hand. "I hadn't heard you'd married, let alone had a child."

Irving closed his hand around the colonel's and shook his head. "She is my ward, not my daughter. Her father was Maxwell Wheeler. He and Ida died crossing the plains. They were caught in a stampede. I promised Maxwell I'd look after her and have for seven years now."

"A terrible ordeal," Johnston said, shaking his head. Was the ordeal caring for me or losing my kin? Either way I didn't know which to be more shocked about, Irving talking about my past so open or Johnston seeming familiar with it. Parts of it anyway.

Irving grunted his agreement and lowered his head. "I'm sorry she caused a ruckus. She helps me out, and her curiosity gets away from her."

Colonel Johnston looked over at me. "Are you sure that a platform is the best environment for a young lady?" Jones looked pointedly at Irving, and I scowled. Just what I needed, an authority suggesting I ought to be elsewhere as well.

"Oh no, as I said she's my ward. There's nowhere else I'd have her be." Irving lowered his head, shoulders hunching as if he bore a weight. I wasn't no burden on him. "It would comfort me if you allowed me to take her back to the platform. I promise she won't be of further trouble."

Johnston paused, looking at the dragon again. His nose twitched before he nodded. "Take her, and see that she stays out of trouble and sight. Our stay will be longer than I planned."

Irving nodded once, holding out his arm for me. I moved toward him, taking it and feeling completely awkward as he led me away. Only partially because of the unfamiliar grasp. The other part was the eyes I could feel watching me until I slid down the hatch.

SUNSET and still no one came for me. I kept on pacing in the oil lamps' light, glancing up whenever I heard muted footsteps on the boards above. They came close, but never to the hatch. I cussed Irving for insisting on good walls. I could only hear muffled voices. Even they'd been reciting a soliloquy, I doubted I'd have caught anything. Keeping the noise of his experiments occasionally exploding mostly contained was keeping me in the dark. There wasn't nothing at the door to below decks at the far end of Irving's room either. I'd have gone there but didn't want to risk breaking Irving's word. Sighing, I slumped into a chair.

The door creaked open, followed by a lengthy silence. Finally, the door slammed shut again. "Where is she," Jones bellowed. I sprung from my chair and was halfway to the ladder before I stopped myself. Up wasn't a retreat. I turned as footsteps thudded into the room. Jones looked about for a second before spotting me and stalking my way. Gulping, I looked for a place to hide, but my will to move came too late.

I started as he loomed over me, reaching out to grab me and... lift me into a hug. "I couldn't have done it more brilliantly myself!" Jones laughed and my jaw dropped open at the delight in his eyes. Couldn't say I'd ever seen that outside of the presence of Ms. Hardy's sister. He let go of me while I was still a foot above the ground. Stumbling, I staggered back from Mr. Jones to brace myself against the wall.

"You ain't angry?" I asked, gripping a beam for balance.

"Angry?" Mr. Jones threw his head back laughing. Huh, I'd never actually seen a belly shake from laughter before. Didn't aim to repeat the sight soon. "You took out a ship, their flagship even, all while looking completely innocent." My eyes widened as Jones leaned close. "That leaves only two," his voice rumbled as he tried to keep it low and failed.

"Two for which we have a plan." Irving appeared around Mr. Jones' girth. He seated himself in a chair with a contented sigh. "Though I admit I missed your aid on deck today. It has been too long since I did that much hauling of pipes and hoses."

"Excellent work on the valve, by the way. That ship is still trying to finish filling." Archie trundled into the room claiming another chair, only to be shooed out of it again by Mr. Jones.

I blushed, ducking my head. "Hadn't been trying to sabotage no ship," I muttered.

"That's what made it so perfect!" Mr. Jones looked at me intently, still grinning like a man at... well I wasn't supposed to know what.

"Umm, you're welcome," I said lamely, climbing onto my usual stool.

"Praise aside, there is still work to be done," Irving said. His voice at least retained its usual calm.

"Yes." Mr. Jones slapped his knee. "We're going to ground the other two ships as well before they can depart. Tonight."

I gaped at Mr. Jones. "You're telling me this why?" Suspicions formed in my head as I asked. Jones would only tell me if–

"Because we need your help, of course." Yep, that explained his sudden willingness to include me in any conversation.

"But I'm supposed to stay out of sight." I crossed my arms. "You trying to get me in trouble with the military?" I didn't particularly feel like dying today.

"Out of sight is exactly what we want," Archie said. "If I moved like you, I'd do it myself." His shoulders slumped.

"And I am far too old for such shenanigans," Irving said. He placed a hand reassuringly on Archie's arm.

"So, what's the plan?" I asked. Listening to the answer, I decided that could go on the list of questions I wish I'd never asked. Mr. Jones kept interrupting Irving as they explained the plan. Not that I believed for a moment Jones had come up with any of it. To sum it up quick, they needed small, agile, quiet, and quick for sabotage.

"I'm still only one." I shook my head. "This whole mess depends on taking out both the other ships nearly at the same time. Archie and Irving can't help me. You going to hit the other ship, Mr. Jones?"

Mr. Jones scoffed, his face transforming back to the scowl I was used to. "Of course not. I'm far too prominent. I'll be hosting the dinner."

"I'm going," another voice chimed in. Gerry sat in the door's frame. Huh, he did have a voice. I'd never heard him speak before. "I'm small, strong, and ain't afraid of heights. Can you say the same?"

I tilted my head in irritation and snorted at him. That didn't deserve a response. Instead I turned to Irving. "You okay with this?" His voice had stayed flat while he was explaining. "I saw you have history with Johnston. I'm out if you've got qualms."

I folded my arms stubbornly, ignoring Mr. Jones' glower. "But your duty. Our duty. You can't just ignore–" I raised my hand to silence him, surprised when it worked.

Irving sighed, resting his arms on the table. "You're correct, there is history there, but I can't afford to allow that to stop me from protecting lives."

I nodded and turned back to Mr. Jones. His face was breaking out with that strange grin again. "I want a promise from you before I agree." He blinked and the grin disappeared as quickly as it had been born.

"What?" I could hear the suspicion in his voice.

"I ain't gonna risk my life without a promise." Irving grinned as I spoke. Grinning so that Jones couldn't see him. Good, I didn't need him calling my bluff. "I pull this off, and you never try putting me off the platform again. If I'm working so others can keep their homes, I get to keep mine." I nodded my head for emphasis.

"Fine," Mr. Jones said. "You've got my word."

"Good." I doubted he meant it, but I had witnesses. "When do we go?"

❧

GERRY SNAKED out the porthole ahead of me. I waited the ten seconds he'd asked for and followed, grabbing blindly for the promised ropes. I wasn't no roughneck to go swinging about the ship willy-nilly. A hand grabbed mine, directing me. Archie leaned out once I was secure, holding out a couple of kits. Gerry and I each took one.

Gerry nodded at me before disappearing to the right. I felt Archie's hand on my arm before I could move. He gave a quick squeeze and released me. I turned left heading for station three. Nope, he wasn't going to get to me now. Even if I could still feel the pressure from his grip.

From above came an undecipherable jumble of voices and the clatter of dinnerware. Well, undecipherable except for the extra loud voices of roughnecks. No wonder they'd been able to convince the soldiers more had come up on the raft than had. They sounded near like an army themselves.

Working my way around the hull, I found the white paint of the army ship brilliant against our dark wood. I listened for footfalls above. Someone would've been left aboard. There. The soldier's steady pace approached, stopped, and then retreated. I switched over to the army's rigging as he moved. I pulled the rope chair out of my pack, hooked it to their rigging, and straddled it.

I pressed my forehead against the wood and panted. I was in good shape, but unlike Gerry, this wasn't my habit. I didn't climb around like a crazed monkey whenever Mr. Jones wasn't looking.

Gerry. Gritting my teeth, I shifted my way along the hull. I wasn't going to let him beat me. Reaching the back of the ship, I positioned the chair again and took a secure seat as I pulled a screwdriver out. Holding my breath, I listened to the noise on deck, waiting. Again, the soldier paced by above, and I waited until he was well away.

I pressed the tool into the joint of wood in front of me and rapped the handle lightly with a hammer. A dull, hollow metallic sound echoed off in both directions. Yep, this was where the tanks butted. The weakest spot on the ship. I pulled out Irving's blowtorch and a small tin of oil and settled them securely in my lap. I was ready. I just needed Jones to give the signal already.

Leaning backward, I wrapped my arm around one of the chair's ropes and stared into the sky. Stars looked back at me, brilliant in the dark night. I couldn't even see the platform's lights down here. They were somewhere beyond the curve of both hulls.

A boom shuddered through the timbers, shaking me moments before color blossomed in the sky. There was my cue. I lowered the goggles over my eyes and, taking the screwdriver, I pried at the planks. I constantly checked above, sure someone would hear, that the fireworks wouldn't mask the sound. Still, I got a space above the left tank cleared without incident.

Opening the tin with one hand, I poured the contents into the flash pan. Pulling out my flint, I ignited the fuel and watched it burn. "Come on," I whispered, willing the flame to heat the blowtorch faster. Finally, the oil burned out and I twisted the valve, primed the pump, and ignited the main flame. It burned orange for a moment before the fire settled into a brilliant blue. Tucking the flint back into the pack, I turned the torch and seared at the bare metal patch I'd cleared above the oil tank.

"Who's there," a voice cried from above. Looking up, a dark form was silhouetted against the night sky. I could see him easy. My light would have been a beacon in the dark. Why'd I get the soldier who didn't stare up like a normal person during the fireworks? These were Irving's best. Unappreciative mongrel.

Grabbing the hull rope, I cussed and pulled myself out of sight using the hull's curve. "I know you're there," the voice demanded, and I heard the grind of metal against metal as he readied his musket. "I won't ask again."

A shot fired at the same moment another firework went off. I only heard it because I was close. Too close. Wood splintered to my left. The splinters bounced off my goggles and a few even bit into my flesh.

Well, whoever the soldier was, he was at least inventive. Those were cuss words I hadn't even heard the roughnecks use. Metal and wood rattled as the musket hit the deck followed quickly by the rail groaning above. A boot appeared over the rail.

I grit my teeth against a swear and concentrated on the tank. I had to break through and set the oil ablaze. If the ships caught fire, we'd have to set them loose and they'd have to take to ground.

The nearing foot struck my head, and I swung away unable to keep my grip on the torch. The blue flame extinguished as it fell, and I spun dizzily, barely keeping my seat. A hand grabbed my shoulder, and I looked up. He was close enough to make out his features in the darkness. Huh, it was the one that had been supposed to be watching me before. Guess he was doing a better job of it now.

He swore again, adding my name into the mix. Who'd told him that? Grabbing my shirt, he started to haul me up. I grabbed his arm and pulled myself close enough to bite. His scream was muffled by another firework. The show had to be nearing its end by now.

Metal flashed in the darkness, and I screamed. The man had drawn his dagger and struck, glancing off my bracer and nipping my wrist. I reached blindly, clawing at him with one hand as I grabbed at the knife.

I'm not certain what happened, but my finger sunk in something gooey, and he screamed, releasing the knife to tear at my hand with both of his. And letting go. The note of pain changed to terror in his scream as he fell, the sound fading quick.

Wide-eyed, I watched him twisting in the air as if searching for something substantial to grab. Every scary story Mr. Jones told me about those who fell off a platform came back. I didn't even hear the thud and crunch when the man hit the ground. He was just a dark spot among many.

Gulping air, I grabbed a hold of my seat. I closed my eyes tight, but I could see him falling again clearly then. Fallen, because of me.

Opening my eyes, I rubbed furiously at the tears lining my face. Nope. I wasn't gonna cry. I was a platform worker. A motor. Heights and falling was part of the work. Besides, I had a job to finish and no blowtorch to do it with. The screwdriver had fallen as well.

I stared at the knife I still clutched. The thing was well made and had a sturdy point. The hull's metal was close to breaking already and still glowed a bit. Bracing my feet against the hull, I slammed the knife hard enough against the metal that I bounced. Landing, I repeated as screams sounded from across the platform. Gerry must've been done already.

Scowling I slammed the knife again and again. My hand slipped, and I sliced my palm on the blade. Finally though, the blade broke through and a tiny bit of oil gushed out.

I shook my hand, trying to rid it of the liquid, and stared at the hole. If I'd been using the torch the oil would've been burning already. Instead I had to ignite it somehow.

The flint! I still had that. Reaching into the pack I pulled it out, striking it against the knife's blade. Sparks sizzled in the darkness, too far from the hole to do good. I was shaking too much. That was it. I pushed the knife back against the hole, steadying it, and struck it again. The oil blazed with light, scorching my face. Crying out, I shoved off the hull and away.

Landing, I looked at the black smoke billowing to the sky. I'd done it. The knife slipped from my grip and fell into the darkness. I raised my right hand and stared at it in the fire's light. Red trickled between the slices in my glove and the thing screaming hurt. I bit back a scream and closed my eyes.

I have to move, some part of my brain informed me. How I'd do that, the rest of me didn't know. I slid my sling along the rigging until I hit a cross section of ropes. Reaching, I grabbed a hold of the merging ropes with my left hand. My right hand followed it, but pain blinded me. Self-preservation alone kept a scream in. I could hear the boots above now.

I stared dumbly. Guess that soldier wouldn't be the only one falling tonight.

I looked over to the platform and safety. And Gerry. He moved toward me swinging on the ropes. "Gerry," I said unable to even workup indignation at the tremble in my voice when he stopped next to me.

"This ain't no place to rest," Gerry said, grabbing hold of my chair. "Let's get before Irving skins me for letting you get in trouble."

"Irving?" I asked. "Don't you mean Jones."

"Nah," Gerry said, grinning. "Irving is the scary one. You just never see it. Now let's get."

"I can't," I held up my hand covered with blood. "I can't grip the ropes with this."

Gerry shifted, holding himself with one arm, and wrapped the other under my armpit. "Guess I got to be your other hand then. Now come." He nudged me out of the chair, and I grabbed the rigging, half leaning on him. Slowly, we crawled back toward the platform, Gerry giving me encouragement all the way.

Moving backward, he reached for the platform's rigging. I screamed as we fell, echoed moments later by Gerry's scream and us jerking to a halt.

Looking, I saw him gripping the platform's rigging, the bottom most rigging, with one hand and me with the other. Tears and snot ran down his face. Such a heroic sight.

"Annabelle," he said, my name more a wheeze than a word. "You gotta..." He tried again, repeating the words, but got no further. Not that he needed to. I had to get a hold before we both fell. Twisting, I reached for the rigging or his vest. Anything, but it was all out of reach.

The platform rocked drunkenly as the flaming ship fell away, illuminating the darkness below and slamming Gerry and me against the hull. I scrambled, reaching for a rope before the ship righted itself. Grabbing, I got the rope wrapped around my arm.

Gerry held me still, pulling me close as he grunted into my shoulder. My muscles screamed. Even with my weight distributed over my whole arm, I knew I couldn't take it much longer. I looked up. The top of the platform was too far away. I could see under the thing now, not over. "Now what?" I asked glancing around. Neither of us could climb now.

"Now," Gerry grunted, having regained his breath a bit. "Now I think is a good time for praying."

"As if I were any good at praying," I retorted automatically. Then gulped.

"Eh, there's a first time for everything." Gerry tried a grin.

A final shudder ran through the platform as the third ship, the one where I'd broke the key, was cut free. With the platform reeling they couldn't afford to keep their docking or risk tearing both apart. Instead, the ship sunk toward the ground. I watched as the platform's anchor lines went slack, followed by the army ship.

The three ships floundered in the air, but each managed to slow their fall enough to hit the ground with a grinding noise instead of a crunch. Men carrying torches poured out of the ships and scurried across the ground. Not that I got to watch much longer. The night had a breeze and the platform was drifting away, freed from its tethers.

The rope slid against my arm, burning my skin. Gerry grabbed a hold of me, steadying me even as I watched his grip weaken. I looked at him wide-eyed and nodded, hoping he could see my respect. We'd done what we set out to do.

Water hit my face, chilling my heated flesh. Great. I didn't want to go out crying. I rubbed my injured hand across my face and felt more cold strike. The specks were barely visible in my vision, but that was tiny flakes glittering and melting on my hand. Guess I got to see the start of winter.

A hatch fell open in the bottom of the platform. Archie's head stuck out as he looked around. "Found them!" he screamed, and I caught sight of hands hauling him back in. Moments later the other roughnecks spilled out of the hatch, moving across the ship's belly like it was nothing. I felt myself moved to someone's back and tied there. Felt the jerks of their quick retreat into the ship. Felt it, but I couldn't believe it. My legs refused to hold when they freed me and tried setting me down. I sunk to the floor and threw up. The last thing I really knew was Irving wrapping his arms around me as I blacked out.

og

WINTER HAD STRUCK with a vengeance that night and Johnston and his men had been left to camp the best they could. I'd call that adequate bedeviling. That night, the ships falling, and the platform damage was remembered as a horrible tragedy. One in which, thankfully, only one soldier lost his life, allegedly trying to save the ships. At least that is what the report said when Irving showed me, but I knew different. Or maybe it was right enough. He had been trying to stop me after all. I still wake at night, my screams echoing his when he fell.

Mr. Jones had been certain I'd ask to be put off when we landed in Salt Lake for repairs, but I hadn't, and winter gave way to spring. Spring found me at the railing of the platform, looking over the vista.

"Annabelle Mable Jean Wheeler," a voice boomed behind me. Turning slightly, I watched Mr. Jones. He stalked toward me with a determined set to his shoulders. I braced myself against the railing when he reached me, and I looked Mr. Jones in the eye, frowning. He spoke first. "Ain't you ready for civilization yet? Ms. Hardy keeps asking when I'm going to drop you."

Yep, time for that conversation again. I'd known his promise wouldn't last. "You ain't," I said flatly. "We're fighting to have homes and you ain't taking mine away."

Mr. Jones raised his finger. "Listen here, young lady..." He stopped as all the roughnecks, Archie, and Gerry dropped whatever they were doing to turn and watch. I also knew word of his promise had spread through them. Gulping, Mr. Jones spun and stalked away. "Get back to work," he hollered over his shoulder, and he stomped into his office. Gerry winked at me before returning his attention to Archie and his training to become a motor.

Irving said he could use a third assistant and Gerry hadn't been quite as eager to climb the riggings even once his shoulder mostly healed up. He was a bright one though. He'd learn quick enough. If Archie didn't ruin him first. Pushing off the railing, I ambled over to the pair before any bad habits could be set.

ABOUT THE AUTHOR

JENNA EATOUGH IS AN AWARD WINNING, best-selling author of short stories, poetry, and flash fiction. She has managed a 100-250-word flash fiction group for five years, posting weekly. When not dreaming of other worlds, she works as a librarian helping students grasp their futures and as an organizer of an SF&F non-profit writing, art, and game development conference. More of her work can be viewed at her blog, www.mistglenmoon.net.

Mekanikers

Kevin Folkman

The sun was setting, the Gulf of Mexico in reflection as gold and red as the sky, when the boat bearing Arthur Kessler pulled alongside the steam sailing vessel *Northumberland*. After an exchange between the boat's pilot and an officer aboard the larger vessel, Kessler was invited on board, and met by the *Northumberland's* first mate at the top of the ladder. Kessler asked about the Danish emigrants, and the mate pointed towards a crowd on the foredeck. Men, women, and children were singing a melody familiar to Kessler, but the hymn's words were foreign. He paused long enough for the hymn to end, and then pressed forward.

"I'm looking for Elder Swenson," Kessler said. Most of the group were dressed in the kind of clothing Kessler had seen all too often. They were farmers, hired tradesmen, and other poor working folk, their worn clothing evidence of their humble origins. They also smelled of a few weeks at sea, with little water for more than a cursory wash of their hands and face, and none for their clothing. As one of the State of Deseret's immigration agents dedicated to helping these foreign families find their way to a new Zion, Kessler no longer found it unpleasant. To him, it looked and smelled like hope. *They will need more than hope*, Kessler thought, as he contemplated what waited for them in New Orleans the next morning.

"Swenson?" Kessler asked again. He knew no Danish himself. If he were to help these people on their way, he needed Elder Swenson, the Danish-born returning missionary responsible for this group on their journey. Most of the crowd looked at him without responding, but one older man nodded his head and pointed.

"Swenson." The old man smiled, pointing to a red-haired man near the center of the group. Kessler worked his way through the crowd, as the mix of men, women, and children moved aside to let him pass. The men mostly smiled, the women looked at him blankly, and the children stared curiously.

"Elder Swenson," Kessler said as he extended his hand in greeting. "I'm Arthur Kessler, one of Deseret's immigration agents."

"Ah, Brother Kessler." The red-haired man took Kessler's hand in an enthusiastic grip. "Most happy to see you," he said in his accented English. "I've been trying to reassure these people that they would be well cared for on the journey to the Valley."

"As best I can, Elder," Kessler replied. "But the journey, as you well know, will be long and hard. I am sure you have had hardship on the crossing. But the next hardship will likely come in the morning when we dock in New Orleans."

Kessler lowered his voice. "I've come to warn you of the violence that awaits you tomorrow. We have been having problems with gangs of ruffians, land pirates, if you will, who are planning to meet the ship as it docks. Before you have time to acquaint yourselves with the best of this new country, I am afraid you will meet some of its worst."

"I have heard of such things," Swenson replied, no longer smiling. "When I first came through New York City four years ago, we had problems with men who tried to take advantage of our company, taking our luggage with promises to deliver it to the rail station, but stealing it for themselves instead. We learned to avoid them. Is it worse here in New Orleans?"

"Much worse, I'm afraid," Kessler said. "These men won't pretend to help you at all. A gang of thugs will rush the ship as soon as the gangplank touches the dock, thirty or forty at a time, armed with clubs and knives. They will take all of your possessions they can grab or threaten you out of. They will beat or stab anyone who fights back. And no one will help you, not the crew, not the police. It seems that the men behind these gangs have paid off both the police, and the ships' captains.

The ship's cargo remains untouched, but anything your people have, these mobs will steal. I'm here to give you as much warning as I can, so that you can organize such protection as is possible."

Swenson slowly shook his head. "We will try, but all of us are weakened from the weeks at sea. Some have never overcome their illness from the movement of the ship, and the food has not been plentiful or very good." Swenson glanced about at the men, women, and children that were his charges, and then nodded to Kessler. "Many have already endured beatings at the hands of our countrymen when they were baptized. They are brave, but they are not strong. I will explain this problem, and see what we can do."

Swenson raised his hands to get the attention of the crowd on the foredeck. As he began speaking in Danish, Kessler could see the smiles and anticipation turn to frowns and looks of fear. As Swenson finished speaking, a few men stepped forward, apparently offering their help. Two men in particular seemed the most animated, Kessler noticed, and after a few questions back and forth, Swenson smiled and gestured back to Kessler.

"These two men," Swenson said, "are brothers, Jens and Christoffer Olsen, and *mekanikers* by trade. They think they can be of the most help."

Kessler smiled at the two brothers and shook their hands. They seemed strong and healthy enough, but he doubted that the two of them would be a match for forty mobbers with clubs.

"Blacksmiths?" Kessler asked.

Swenson shook his head, but still smiled.

"They were blacksmiths once, but they have learned some new skills, and practice a different trade now. They build marvelous machines, they say, and they have one on board that may help us, if we have time."

"Time?" Kessler asked.

"Yes, time to put it together. And they think that it may also do us some good with the captain."

One of the brothers said something to Swenson, who nodded again.

"We will need some light, and a few helpers," Swenson said. "If I explain this to you, do you think you could speak to the captain for us?"

"I should think it must be an extraordinary story," Kessler said, "if I have any hopes of influencing the captain. What are we talking about?"

With that, Swenson and the brothers exchanged a few more words in Danish, and then began talking to others in the crowd. Men nodded, and then moved off purposely. One of the brothers disappeared below deck to where the steerage passengers had traveled, and returned with several rolls of large paper drawings. Others returned with lamps, and within minutes, the majority of the crowd streamed below deck to where the other brother was prying open a few large crates. As Swenson translated, Kessler began to see the vision of what the brothers had in mind. Reassured, he began to compose his story to tell the captain.

⚭

WHEN KESSLER RETURNED to the hold after speaking with a somewhat skeptical captain, lamps were being hung to light the work area. Tools had been produced, and metal parts laid out. Jens, the younger of the two brothers, did most of the hands-on work, while Christoffer, the elder, directed the work in Danish, consulting his drawings and also using some kind of a brass, glass, and silver circular tool. About ten inches in diameter, Kessler could see fine lines etched around the edges of concentric bands of metal. A glass and metal bar, attached at the hub of the device, could be moved about the circle seemingly at random, and the concentric bands each moved independently. Christoffer referred to it as a *lommeregner*. Kessler assumed it to be some kind of calculating device, and was struck by the thought that perhaps Father Lehi's Liahona had been of similar construction.

Kessler had been of a mind to help, but quickly realized he was out of his depth. He was skilled at selecting ox teams, purchasing sturdy wagons, and avoiding the kind of cheap tinware that would melt or burn through the first time someone tried to cook a meal over an open fire. This night's work was something different, unlike anything he had ever seen before. He quickly ascertained that the Olsen brothers were indeed very skilled in their trade. It was just a trade that he never before had imagined. He started taking some notes and drawing a few pencil sketches in the worn leather-covered notebook in his coat pocket.

The work continued throughout the night. The men, led by the brothers Olsen, worked steadily. Occasionally, someone would bring drinking water and some bread and cheese to refresh the workers. Kessler himself began to feel the late hour and lack of sleep, but could not pull himself away from the work unfolding before his eyes. In his mind, he was already drafting a letter describing the scene, to be included in his annual report to President Young. He only subconsciously noted that in the dark hours, the *Northumberland* began to move towards the river delta and the docks of New Orleans.

As dawn approached, lamps began to be extinguished. A couple of sailors arrived with a bag of coal, "compliments of the captain." Kessler wearily climbed the stairs to the main deck. The hours had passed more quickly than he realized, and the *Northumberland* was approaching the docks. More of the Danish saints climbed up to witness the sunrise and the events of this first day in their new country. Kessler glanced up to the platform at middeck, just before the ship's large smokestack. The captain looked down at him and nodded slightly. Kessler smiled and waved in return.

As Elder Swenson came up beside him, Kessler pointed to the dock, now only yards away. "Look, Swenson, there they are."

Swenson took in the crowd of rough-looking men waiting patiently, cudgels and axe handles in hand. "I believe many things,

Brother Kessler," he said. "I believe God has brought these people from my homeland for a purpose. I believe He brought you here to warn us of this trouble. And I also believe that these men," Swenson indicated the stirring mob with a sweep of his arm, "are about to be very surprised."

Swenson barked a short laugh and turned to his charges to give instruction.

The women and children were directed below decks, and the strongest of the men lined up on the side of the ship away from the docks, opening up the space around the hatch to the hold. Some of the men were armed with prybars, an axe handle, or a sturdy piece of wood from one of the crates. The open hatch gaped between them and the side of the ship where the crew was making the steamer fast to the docks. The crew secured the gangplank and then quietly disappeared.

Kessler climbed up to the elevated foredeck for a better view, followed by Elder Swenson. A puff of smoke emerged from the hatch, bringing a smile to both their faces. They turned and saw the mob of thugs swarm up the gangplank.

Swenson shouted something in Danish that sounded to Kessler like an ancient Viking war cry. In reply, the blast of a steam whistle came up out of the hold, followed by the Olsen brothers' fantastic machine.

In the morning light, Kessler could see the machine clearly for the first time. Jens Olsen had referred to it as a *løftemaskine*. The metal contraption erupted from the hatch in a flurry of spinning gears, pulleys, and taut cables. It had four massive legs fabricated from girders on which it moved about, and two arms, with a span of about twelve feet, ending in vise-like appendages that opened and closed quickly with a clanking sound. At its center, Jens Olsen sat in what looked like a tractor seat, rapidly moving levers with his hands and pushing pedals with his feet. Behind him, the miniature steam engine smoked and puffed, and Kessler thought it had the look of a dragon with its head on backwards.

With another blast from the whistle, Jens snatched up an empty crate in one of the machine's terrible hands, and flung it at the gangplank. Half a dozen of the pirates leaped from the gangplank into the muddy Mississippi, and a few others were thrown back to the docks. A handful of thugs made it to the deck of the *Northumberland,* but immediately backed up to the ship's railing as they caught sight of the mechanical monster bearing down on them. On Swenson's signal, the group of Danes on deck rushed forward, brandishing their makeshift weapons. A few of the mob appeared ready to fight, but many chose the river as their means of escape.

Jens Olsen rushed his mechanical mount across the deck, whistle blaring and steel hands clanking, with arms spread wide to push the ruffians away. Each step boomed on the wooden deck like a war drum. It stomped across the deck and down the gangplank, confronting the larger group of men on the dock. Some tried to duck the swinging arms and took some hard blows despite their effort. Most took one look at it and fled back across the dock, over the levee, and back down into town. Kessler smiled at the bruising the mob was taking.

It was over in a matter of minutes. The mob scattered, and the Danish Saints offered up a shout of triumph and broke into a series of songs. At least one of them resembled a familiar hymn, Kessler thought. The *Northumberland* crew members on deck, witnessing the scene, broke into shouts of "Hurrah!"

The rest of the day passed quietly enough. Tired as he felt, Kessler was able to quickly assemble the previously arranged transportation for the emigrants and their baggage to the steamboat farther up the river. Swenson and the Olsen brothers set the steam-belching mechanical monster to work, unloading the rest of the ship's cargo in record time. Once completed, the brothers disassembled their fantastic creation, and returned it to the crates from where it had emerged.

As Kessler prepared to leave the ship, the captain stopped him.

"I owe you an apology, Mister Kessler," the captain said. "I assumed that you had made up some sort of fabulous story, hoping to extract some sympathy from me and my crew. I couldn't believe your story. I would not have believed it had I not witnessed it myself."

Kessler smiled and offered his hand to the captain.

"No apology necessary, Captain. If I had not seen it coming together myself during the night, I would have doubted my story as well."

The captain shook Kessler's hand and smiled.

"I will also forget the charge for that bag of coal," the captain said. "I fully intended to extract a dear payment from you in exchange. I would also offer those two young men my recommendation to several individuals here in the city who would be most interested in acquiring their labor."

Kessler smiled and glanced down the gangplank where Elder Swenson and the Olsen brothers waited. He looked back to the captain.

"Captain, I am certain that they will have no trouble, even without a command of our language, finding all that on their own. But they already have a destination set, and a long journey ahead of them. Their skills are unique, very different from my own. But who knows, they may end up needing the kind of help that I can offer. Perhaps, if we meet again, I may even be in their employ. Good day, sir."

And with that, Kessler strode down the gangplank to join the brothers and Elder Swenson, their heavy wagons waiting to give him a ride to the riverboat. As he sat on the wagon seat, Kessler began to imagine a train of wagons pulled by the *mekanikers'* curious inventions, not bound to rails like a steam locomotive, but able to traverse the countryside at will. *Perhaps*, he thought, *I may need to be as accomplished at appraising steam engines as I am at ox teams, and metal alloys beyond just cheap tinware.*

As the wagons started to move, Kessler began to sing William Clayton's hymn of the crossing of the plains. "Come, come, ye Saints, no toil nor labor fear!" Swenson and the brothers joined him joyfully in Danish. Kessler couldn't understand their words, but he certainly understood their sentiment.

ABOUT THE AUTHOR

Kevin Folkman is an insatiable reader, occasional writer, and independent historian. He has published articles on Mormon history in the Journal of Mormon History, Pioneer Magazine, and guest posts at Ardis Parshall's Keepapitchinin.org Mormon history blog. He also reviews religious non-fiction books for the Association of Mormon Letters. After graduating from Weber State University in English and Journalism, he worked as a janitor, radio DJ, high tech sales guy, computer network engineer, and currently is employed in IT for the Issaquah School district in Washington state. He and his wife Katie live in Redmond, Washington, and have six children and ten grandchildren. In his spare time, Kevin is learning the finer points of bird and nature photography and how to play blues guitar.

AUTHOR'S NOTE: I first learned of the dock pirates of New Orleans and the role of emigration agents from Keepapitchinin.org, the church history blog of Ardis Parshall. See "We Have Left No One Behind: Agents for Ourselves and for Others," keepapitchinin.org, July 30, 2010.

The Deseret War

James Pyles

Ute Tribal Lands, Utah, July 1857

"It is not right that you do this, Quray. Speak with Walkara. The Ute must not make war on the Mormons. I have met with their Brigham Young and he is a peaceful man." Kanosh was not yet forty, but the other Ute chiefs would listen to him, or so he hoped. He sat on the dirt floor of Quray's wickiup in the center of this small village. Outside were his men and their women and children, leading their lives at the edge of Ute territory, just fifty miles east of the Mormon settlement of Fort Utah.

"You speak to Brigham Young and tell him to stop his Mormons from raiding our livestock and hunting our wildlife..." The even younger Quray of the Timpanogots band stopped speaking as an unfamiliar humming invaded the air. Jumping to their feet, they could also hear people outside, at first murmuring in low tones, and then, as the buzzing became a series of loud whines and the first gunshots sounded, angry yelling and screams of terror.

Quray, long braided hair trailing behind him as he flung the wickiup's grass-woven door aside, rushed out with Kanosh following, his large mustache obscuring downturned, grimacing lips. The gunfire continued, but strangely, the shots came from up in the sky along with the screeching of a vast swarm of locusts, only what they saw attacking from above were not insects, but men.

Kanosh grabbed Quray's arm and pulled him backward as bullets pelted the ground, throwing up puffs of yellow earth. The sound of a ricochet rang in his ears and Quray's body jerked and went limp.

Lying on the ground, halfway back inside the wickiup, Kanosh wiped blood from his face and stared at a small hole in the young chief's forehead above his right eye. The back of his skull had exploded—spewing bone, blood, and brains across his bedroll and the loose dirt.

Struggling from beneath the corpse, on his hands and knees, he looked out again at what his mind told him was impossible. Men, a dozen men in the sky riding saddles suspended by cords under round balls, and driven by strange, spinning motors mounted on metal tails behind them. Attached to the spinning fans were what looked like cans or jars of blue-glowing metal trailing billows of steam, painting the air like a quilt. Each craft had a rifle mounted on a metal framework in front of the pilots, swinging with the motion of these air soldiers. They chased running, frantic people on the ground, frenzied Ute men shooting back with their own rifles and pistols.

These sky men crisscrossed the background of tall, verdant Elm, Maple, and Pine, which the Timpanogots thought would shelter their encampment, showcased against the sentinels of the snowless summer mountains to the west.

The women and children had disappeared, but as the men fell to the bare ground one by one, other sky men aimed at the flimsy wickiups, the rifle slugs splintering wood and straw roofs. The guns of the air riders missed often, but not always, as Kanosh heard the death cries of his people.

Grabbing Quray's bolt-action rifle, he slid a shell into the chamber and ran back out, preparing to die along with the others—but the firing stopped. The sky warriors retreated, the ground littered with the dead of the Ute men, their blood seeping into the dirt, scattered amid the uneven grouping of wickiups. He and four or five others, his friend Guera among them, gazed at the departing figures. One of the sky soldiers was slumped down in his saddle, held up by leather straps lashing him to thin, metal poles, his strange riding balloon making lazy circles in the air as it drifted downward to the south.

The air riders were nearly out of sight and a new humming arose, getting louder with each passing moment. The vibration became a roar, and the ground trembled beneath Kanosh.

"More of them?" Guera, a young man who had only earned the right to join the hunters one year past, staggered toward Kanosh, not injured but eyes wide with terror.

The fragile-seeming shelters shook, and an aberrant wind surged over the treetops. Kanosh yelled to be heard. "No, not many men in the sky. Something much worse."

He had seen pictures of balloons, great bags filled with heated air that lifted baskets attached by ropes, and containing one or a few men. They looked vaguely like what the sky men rode, but had been at the mercy of the wind, without the spinning fans that let the sky saddles change direction.

Emerging from over the canopy, this thing, this vast airborne monster, was hundreds of feet long. An enormous wooden lodge hung from beneath an almost equally large platform above, interwoven with rope or metal cable, spun as if by a gigantic spider. Within that dizzying network, four round bags spanned the length of the airship. Either side held fans like those of the sky men, but so much larger, each fully half the size of one of the balloons. On the upper hull, between the two great whirlwind makers, was something even stranger than the ship itself, a sort of monstrously large canister of black iron, engulfed by clouds of steam, with places where it glowed bluer than what the white men called Utah lake.

It soared with majestic slowness, a fearsome apparition against the pale azure above, casting a malignant shadow across the entire village, eclipsing the astonished Ute below. The old people, women, and children, overcome by curiosity and the fear of not seeing what was killing them, straggled from their shelters. Some speckled with blood, some limping, they all stared in amazement at this leviathan of the clouds, as if the Mormon Jesus had finally come, but not to save them.

Some of the survivors tried to flee on foot or jumped upon the horses that hadn't stampeded. Kanosh squinted at the tree line surrounding the small village. The Nauvoo Legion, militiamen of the Mormons, hemmed them in. With their rifles, they cut down anyone approaching them, driving back those who still stood.

Gazing skyward again, he saw sections of the lower part of the great airship's hull on both sides open up and cannons emerged.

"Run!" Kanosh scrambled toward Guera, whose eyes were still riveted upon the sinister specter, and grabbed him. "We've got to get..."

The cannons fired. An explosion of unnatural blue lightning propelled Kanosh and Guera through space and slammed them to the ground. The young chief wailed, everything below his waist in blinding pain. His legs had disappeared into a mass of blood and pulped meat. He held Guera's upper torso in his arms, which was all that was left of him.

More lightning cannons fired at the chaotic melee of people who vanished in the flames, smoke, and dust. Kanosh's ears rang as he witnessed clouds of earth thrown up and people running in panic, their screams like a distant whistle of wind. His sight dimmed, and Kanosh lay on his side, no longer feeling pain, his life oozing from him. He had come to plead with the Timpanogots for peace, but instead, became one of the first of many to fall, a victim of the coming war.

∞

"Mr. Eddington, your creation continues to perform with impressive precision." Daniel H. Wells stood on the sky craft's bridge forward of the helm, gripping a brass railing at the level of his waist. He looked outward through the panorama of windows encircling the pilot's cabin of the airship, *Joseph Smith*, as it wrought absolute devastation upon the small Ute community two-hundred feet below.

To Stephen Isaac Eddington, the subject of such admiration, Wells reminded him of a great bear of the polar north, his white beard extending downward across his tie and suit jacket, while snowy locks flowed like water over his ears and across the back of his neck. He knew he should show at least some deference to the General of the Nauvoo Legion and member of the LDS Church's First Presidency, though at the moment, he felt loathe to do so.

"Science demands its sacrifices, I suppose, just as God demands His." Stephen kept his voice flat and stoic, but as with the Atkins Campaign, as Wells called it, and Mountain Meadows before that, he was appalled that servants of the Lord Jesus Christ could massacre their fellow human beings in such a savage, violent manner. He had meant his martial creations to be used against the U.S. Army, and only for the defense of the Church. Yet, here he was watching helpless men and women cut down with no possible chance to respond or escape.

His thoughts drifted back in time. In his native England, having discovered the plight of the Church and the murder of the saints in Illinois that caused them to flee into the Utah Territories, he brought his plans and inventions across the Atlantic, and then by wagon train across a nation, finally placing them and himself under Governor Brigham Young's authority. Now, having witnessed yet another bloody atrocity, grief and remorse clutched his chest like an unrelenting fist.

The bustle of activity behind them concealed their softly spoken words, so Wells was free to express himself to the young Englishman. Unlike the old soldier, the scientist had no beard, instead effecting dark brown, scraggly sideburns down to his jaw line, shadowed under an unruly mane poorly hidden beneath a stovepipe hat.

"No need to conceal your thoughts. Your eyes and mannerisms betray you."

"I did offer to make weapons of war, and of course, weapons kill." He turned from the dire scene he had caused and faced the general. "But I meant for my ship only to engage the Army, to prevent them from slaughtering innocents and destroying the Church. This..."

The bombardment abruptly ceased and Lieutenant Phillip Myers, standing at a megaphone beside the helmsman, reported,

"General. There's no movement in the enemy camp. Gunners believe the target has been eliminated. Confirm the order to cease fire."

"The order is confirmed, Lieutenant. Carry on," Wells uttered in a casual tone that belied the horrors they had just committed.

"Aye sir." The youthful, thinly mustached officer cried into the wide mouth of the rubber tube that pierced the deck and traveled down to where a sergeant stood waiting. "Order to cease fire confirmed."

Wells added, "Oh, and verify that the ground militiamen have retrieved the fallen Aero-Saddle Soldier. No sense having either him or his equipment taken by the enemy."

"Very good, sir." Myers put his face back into the communication piping and started barking orders.

Wells turned to the young helmsman at the vessel's sailing ship-style wooden wheel. "Return to base, Mr. Rasmussen."

"Acknowledged, sir. Returning to base." The clean shaven man of no more than twenty, dressed in a close copy of a crisp Naval uniform, swung the wheel about in a leisurely fashion, having been well trained for the position. The mighty airship responded, turning to port, its starboard fan becoming louder as it picked up speed for the maneuver.

Wells circled back to face Eddington, leaning in toward the man's ear. "I believe you were saying something about how weapons kill."

The British convert to Mormonism caught sight of the smoking ruins of what was once a thriving village as the ship passed overhead. Nothing below moved, and the burnt remains of the mutilated bodies no longer looked human. Every structure, every cooking pot, bedroll, and children's plaything had been wiped away, and what had been a living Ute community nestled in idyllic forested foothills, was now the gateway to Hell.

"We'll settle with the rest of the tribe in the coming days. In a week, the offending Indians will either have fled or be beyond saving." Wells basked in his own satisfaction.

"'*Now, if these men do not die well, it will be a black matter for the King that led them to it.*'"

"Shakespeare, dear Eddington? Do you cast Brigham Young in the role of Henry, or do you fancy yourself as King?"

"More a merchant of death, I fear."

"If you are to blame yourself, then this is hardly your first crime. Are you telling me, Mr. Eddington, that your own acts of betrayal and theft against your benefactors in England weren't as grossly heinous?"

"Westcott meant to cheat me, even implicate me in Rolf's death, of which I had no involvement, all in order to force me to give up my share of the Westcott-Liechtenstein Engine."

"A share this Rolf Liechtenstein promised you before his untimely demise."

"The three of us worked on the engine together, although I was only brought in during the final year of development as a student of Liechtenstein's. He took a fancy to me, and I knew I could trust him."

"But this other man, Carson Westcott..."

"He never kept his prejudice for me a secret, especially after he learned of my conversion."

"So you can justify those acts but not this?"

"On behalf of the Church. I do nothing for myself and have no interest in fame nor wealth. I live and work only for the glory of God."

Wells strolled to the starboard side of the bridge, stood near the lookout who focused his telescope aft, and peered behind just as the remains of the Ute village vanished from view, the last rays of a dying sun extinguished, as was every person in the smoldering ruins.

Returning to Eddington, Wells uttered, "It is sometimes peculiar what the glory of God requires of man." He watched as the weight of his words finally broke through the Briton's resolve. "Fear not, your secrets are mine to keep. Governor Young will never know how you acquired your wondrous technology. He will continue to believe that all this..." he waved his arm around the cabin "...is the product of your individual genius. And, you are correct, after what the Church has suffered, we will not be intimidated by President James Buchanan nor the United States Army. If he, or any Gentile, believes he can defeat and subjugate the Church of Jesus Christ of Latter Day Saints, he will discover our Lord has provided us with a mighty sword to serve in our defense. You are that sword."

Daniel Wells clasped Eddington on the shoulder as both men watched the lights of Great Salt Lake City glittering like diamonds in the dark distance. "I do have one complaint, though. The Aero-Saddle Soldiers, their flight seems unstable, and every time they fire their rifles, the recoil jostles their vessels, ruining their aim. Is there something to be done?"

"Yes." Eddington's palms sweat as he grasped the railing in front of him. "I've put into production a more advanced design. These first saddles were prototypes. I'd already recognized their shortcomings."

"Very good. I trust they'll be ready by the time the Army arrives at our borders. The Governor will want to have every advantage in the coming conflict."

"It will be close, since the craft must be completely retooled, but I believe my construction team will have them ready." Eddington regarded the approaching lights of the capitol as if they were pyres burning for the dead.

Echo Canyon, Utah, September 1857

"In his hand are the deep places of the earth; the strength of the hills is his also."

"Taking to quoting scripture, Major Cooper?" Colonel Albert Johnston pondered his orders as he rode at the head of the advancing Utah Expedition, the Army unit assigned to reinforce stability and sovereignty of the United States in the Utah Territory and facilitate the peaceful transfer of authority from Brigham Young to a new Governor, Alfred Cumming. The Colonel was thankful that

Cumming wouldn't make the trip out west until his men secured the Great Salt Lake City. The last thing he needed was a civilian to nursemaid.

Johnston's demeanor and bearing showed him every inch a career military man. Having enlisted as a private in the Texian Army during the Texas War for Independence, he eventually rose to the rank of colonel. President Zachary Taylor himself appointed Johnston as a major in the U.S. Army with the subsequent President Pierce making him a colonel of the new 2nd U.S Cavalry.

"I was taken by the beauty of this land." Jonathan Cooper, five years Johnston's junior, rode his pinto next to the colonel, gazing at the twisted, winding sandstone formations as Echo Canyon's entrance beckoned the advancing company.

Both men slowed their mounts as they entered the canyon. Even the ground beneath them gave the impression of an amber and ruddy river that had been recast as stone by the hand of the Almighty. Ridges beneath their horses' hooves haphazardly curved and layered, providing for uneven footing. Metal horseshoes struck the wind carved surface, clattering and then echoing across the ravine.

The canyon walls narrowed as the company proceeded, and offered the same etched and painted landscape, though some few pines managed an unlikely purchase, growing upward out of nearly vertical walls.

"Admittedly, an impressive sight after the uncomfortably flat and open grasslands we were forced to traverse to arrive at this juncture." Cooper spoke while gazing ahead.

"You're speaking of our being harassed by the Mormon militiamen, Colonel."

"They set the grass aflame to inhibit our advancing, stampeded our cattle, and delayed our resupply. Guerrilla tactics can be traced back to 7th century B.C. China, and its use tells me that General Wells and his Nauvoo Legion are unprepared to engage us directly."

"Is that why you chose to disregard Captain Stewart Van Vliet's recommendation to not pass through Echo Canyon due to possible militia fortifications?"

"That's why I was given command of the Utah Expedition in place of 'old granny'." Johnston expressed uncharacteristic mirth in that last statement.

"I'm sure Colonel Alexander wouldn't appreciate such an appellation, and these men might not either."

"Edmund Alexander's reputation for being overly cautious earned him that appellation, and every man in this unit is well aware of it, Major. It is good that he was sent back to quell the uprisings in Kansas."

Cooper's chest rose and fell, his expression one of concern. "Bleeding Kansas. Another territory vying for statehood while dancing on the razor's edge of whether or not to welcome slavery."

"It is not generally known, Cooper, but one of our tasks in the current endeavor is to make sure the pro-slavery states do not expand into this territory."

"The Mormon Church is not known to be in favor of slavery, Colonel."

"They are not known to be against it either. We're here to stack the deck in President Buchanan's favor, though I fear it may not be enough." Johnston grimaced at the thought.

"You mean the rumors of a Southern secession from the Union."

"Yes, but the less you say about that, at least in front of the men, the better. No one wants to face the possibility of a war with brother fighting against brother." The colonel lowered his voice a bit as if participating in a conspiracy.

A grim silence hung between the two officers as they continued to penetrate deeper into the malformed, multi-hued gorge.

"What of the other matter we were sent to investigate?" Cooper hoped changing the subject would lighten Johnston's grim mood.

"You mean of this lime-juicer, what's his name—Eddington? Bah. Wild rumors, nothing more. How could the man be the author of even half of what he has been reputed to have accomplished?"

The major straightened in his saddle as if attempting to appear taller."Stephen Isaac Eddington. I've seen our orders, too. According to the English government, Mr. Eddington made off with a rather large amount of materials and the plans for constructing devices of a significantly fantastic sort. England's Prime Minister personally appealed to Buchanan that Mr. Eddington be detained and deported back to his country in irons and whatever he was to have stolen returned unexamined by our military and scientific authorities."

"Should we encounter this Eddington, it will be mere icing on the cake. Our primary goal is to establish military control over the territory pending the transition of governorship to Cumming."

"Then you discount the reports that have been coming out of England this past half-decade, of experiments on astonishing technologies, self-driving carriages, medical miracles that could double human life spans, incredible airships that harness energies to propel them against the wind, cannons with the destructive force of..."

The edge returned to Johnston's voice, signaling his annoyance. "If this Eddington really is the source of such tools, then it is good we have him on our side of the Atlantic. And if all these rumors are just that, then we will send him on his way and concentrate on matters vital and substantial to our nation."

"Yes, sir. I must admit that your decision to proceed by Echo Canyon was a sound one. In spite of Captain Van Vliet's misgivings, we haven't seen any indication of militia activity since..."

"A moment, Major. What do you make of that sound?"

Cooper turned to see the company hesitating, the first faint sign of a coming panic at facing the unknown, as the distant low hum from above the canyon wall to the left became a deep, ominous rumbling. "Sergeant Duffy," he yelled behind him over the growing cacophony. "Maintain formation." He could barely hear the aging non-comm's acknowledgment, but then he swiveled his mount, and the men and horses resumed their discipline, though fear was plainly written on their faces.

Cooper turned forward again to see the colonel's gaze fixed on the top of the now quaking canyon wall. Loose rocks and dirt fell down onto the stony floor, raising clouds of dust around the entire party, while tall pines shuddered like wraiths of impending doom.

A great bulk emerged over the gorge's rim, preceded by what Johnston thought to be an observation balloon with a sailing ship's forepart suspended beneath. It continued to expand over the canyon's lip, revealing a much greater hull, and finally the four mammoth balloons firmly and intricately bound to an aircraft fully three-hundred feet in length bow to stern, driven forward by twin, rotating fans. Just as with a sea-going ship, cannon ports had been raised, and what looked like the barrels of long nines menaced the terrified Union troops.

Cooper was speechless as Johnston quickly glanced back at the horse soldiers he was leading. So far Duffy and the other sergeants were maintaining order, but just barely.

Yet another set of alien noises arose, and from behind the behemoth of the air, a dozen or more much smaller craft appeared, like flies buzzing around a vulture. Each tiny vessel contained a man sitting in a saddle, with a single balloon lifting it from above, and a fan mounted in the rear, driving the small aircraft, trailing billows of steam, as did the much larger ship. They aimed their rifles at Colonel Johnston's men but, like the mighty skyship, refrained from firing.

"Colonel Johnston. Colonel Albert Johnston." A baritone voice boomed from the ship, sounding loud enough to be the utterance of the Almighty. "This is your opponent, General Daniel Wells of the Nauvoo Legion aboard the warship *Joseph Smith*. On behalf of Governor Brigham Young and the Church of Jesus Christ of Latter Day Saints, I order you to surrender or face destruction."

Johnston looked around and then back upward, recalling how he had scoffed when Major Cooper had related the reports of Mr. Eddington's crimes and what he considered technological fantasies.

"How can I respond, General?" He doubted very much that he

could be heard over the roar of the *Smith's* engines and the whining of the one-pilot flyers.

"I understand your being dumbfounded, as would any reasonable man faced with such incredible armament. You may signal your surrender by riding several yards forward away from your complement and raising both hands. That is, after ordering your men to dismount and lay down their arms. Oh, don't bother to attempt retreat. My ground forces have blocked both ends of the canyon. Alone they could not hold you for long, but all they have to do now is delay your escape for a few moments."

"Sir, should we surrender?" Cooper's face had gone pale and his voice cracked like an adolescent's.

"This..." Johnston continued to look heavenward toward the origin of Wells' voice. "This is madness. I am a soldier, and I am fully capable of leading men into battle, but not to the slaughter like sheep."

He could just make out Cooper's voice. "Old granny will never let us live it down."

"Probably true, assuming we survive this catastrophe."

Johnston's and Cooper's horses whinnied, stomped, and pulled at their bits as did each of the other mounts behind, loudly protesting the unnatural apparitions above them.

"I can see you are reluctant to comply with my commands. Perhaps a demonstration of the *Joseph Smith's* might will convince you that surrender is your only hope."

Colonel Johnston watched in helpless horror as the *Smith* rotated to port putting its starboard cannon array to bear on his men. One cannon was raised higher than the others, and a bluish glow shone from its maw just before a deafening explosion. The top of the canyon wall to the right vaporized in a column of flame, then smoking debris plummeted down upon the first two columns of the troops.

"No! Don't do..." Johnston held up both hands, crying impotently, as if beseeching the gods of the air, before hearing rifle shots. The colonel wheeled his skittish steed about and witnessed a terrible tableau; an instant frozen in time that wrote the epitaph for his command.

An individual skyman had steered his diminutive vessel a mere fifteen feet above his soldiers, far below his companions, as if taunting his dread-filled prey. A few soldiers at first, and then many more, raised their Springfields and fired, a hail of bullets raining death upward. Sergeant Duffy was in the midst of them, attempting to halt the chaos as Major Cooper, having pivoted his horse, galloped at the men, ordering them to cease fire.

Like a man submerged underwater, Johnston reached out, trying to stop the impending carnage with force of will, just as the sky soldier's balloon was pierced by the rifle volley and then detonated, hailing down flaming debris in a cloud of incendiary gas.

Men and horses were set on fire, writhing in burning agony, and Wells' voice boomed again from above. "Very well, Colonel." His next words were fainter as he gave a command to his gunners. "Open fire."

Johnston retreated back toward his men, trying to shield them, crying out for Wells to stop the ungodly bloodbath, as the landscape before him erupted like the volcano Vesuvius.

The world of Colonel Johnston went from gray to black, as it did for the men of 2nd Cavalry.

⚥

Albert Johnston regained consciousness again, this time realizing he wasn't dreaming. He had felt the effects of morphine before, but the pain in his face and right leg continued to protest some undetermined bodily insult.

"Who's there?" He couldn't open his right eye and, reaching up, gingerly touched gauze padding. His voice was hardly audible to his ears and his lips were chapped and dry.

"I'm glad to see you awake, Colonel. Doctor, nurse, you may leave us now."

Blurred shadows of a man and woman briefly crossed his field of vision, then what remained of his eyesight focused on the face he recognized as belonging to Daniel Wells.

"Do not struggle. You are in a hospital receiving the best care we can provide. Just lie back and try to relax."

"My men?" He sounded as if a frog was speaking.

"Those who survived are being attended to. They are our honored guests, as are you. When you are well enough, we will have a more formal conversation, Colonel."

Johnston pressed his hands against the mattress, trying to push himself up. Perspiration beaded across his forehead and ran down his face, a wave of nausea accompanied by dizziness consumed him, and once again the light faded to darkness.

Hours before, Johnston had been escorted to an antechamber in the Great Salt Lake City's Mormon Tabernacle, a small, bare room with numerous low wooden seats arranged around a conference table he guessed was used for informal or private meetings. The Colonel was accustoming himself to the patch over his blind right eye, but the loss of his right leg below the knee continued to vex him. Crutches rested against the back of his seat. He was alone save for the two armed militiamen at the single entrance, and he kept drifting in and out of consciousness. In his nightmares, he continued to hear the relentless hum of Eddington's abominable engines; his airships of destruction.

"Are you well enough for this?" Wells had just entered, trailing Stephen Eddington—a man who looked too young to have authored an atrocity—numerous high ranking Nauvoo officers, and finally Governor Young, or President as Johnston was told he should address the man. The portly supreme leader of the Mormon Church stood just over five feet tall. He wore his dark hair similarly to Wells, but his beard seemed to grow straight downward rather than encompassing his face, terminating below his tie. His suit was a severe black, the only break from this being a gold watch chain that hung from his vest pocket. He assumed a position at the head of the table, flanked by four armed escorts. Wells and Eddington took their places opposite Johnston, as did their small company, while several more armed men remained standing behind Johnston.

"I regret that we meet like this, Colonel," Young began. "Unfortunately, your assault upon our territory forced us to take drastic defensive measures."

"Mr. President, I promise you that our intent was never to initiate hostilities. We were ordered to establish authority and to keep the peace pending the arrival of Mr. Alfred Cumming who was to assume the role of governor of this territory at the order of President Buchanan."

"That was what Captain Stewart Van Vliet had assured me of some time ago, though I have since received conflicting reports."

"I did not give the order to open fire. Some of my men panicked at the sight of your incredible weaponry. We had no possible defense and no reason to initiate an assault."

Young briefly glared at Wells, who remained stone-faced. "I understand that mistakes were made on both sides, Colonel. However, the damage is done. I have been told that you have seen your men."

"What's left of them. Barely a quarter of my original complement."

"I am deeply concerned over the loss of life. I assure you that the dead were provided with an honorable burial."

Johnston closed his eyes and witnessed a vision of the last time he had seen Cooper, Duffy, and so many of his other men still alive, their final moments a testimony to man's futility against what he considered nothing short of demonic power.

"I accept your assurances, sir. However, should their families wish the return of..."

"We will accommodate, of course."

"With your permission, Mr. President." Wells rose.

"By all means, General."

"Colonel Johnston, I formally request that you surrender your command to the Nauvoo Legion on behalf of the Church of Jesus Christ of Latter Day Saints and the State of Deseret." He reached inside his military jacket and produced papers which, when presented, the Union officer saw to be the legal niceties of such an act. For the first time, Johnston noticed a quill and ink fountain on the table.

"For the sake of my men, I have little choice, General Wells. In any event, we are your prisoners. I do hereby offer my surrender and will apply my signature and my word of honor."

He quickly took pen in hand, hastily dipped it in the well, scribbled his name on the bottom of the document, and then shoved it back toward Wells.

"Thank you, sir. We will see that you are repatriated with all due haste."

"My men?"

"We have a proposal."

Johnston sat back in his seat, wincing at a dull ache behind his right eye, and listened.

"President Young graciously proposes a treaty between the State of Deseret and the United States government, a non-aggression pact that will assure mutual survival and cooperation in common interests."

"I do not believe my government recognizes the sovereign State of Deseret as encompassing the Utah Territory, thus how can a treaty be made?" Johnston rubbed his temple, attempting to quell the headache, his hearing dominated by an incessant buzzing.

"Our state is indeed a good deal larger, extending the full length and breadth of Utah Territory, up through portions of the Oregon and Nebraska Territories, as far south as areas of the New Mexico Territory and into the lower arm of California."

Shock pulled Johnston upright in his chair. "Are you mad?" He immediately regretted his choice of words, given his vulnerable position and the thinly veiled malevolence of the general towering over him.

Wells scowled, raising a hand at the colonel, but Young cleared his throat, and the general regained his composure. "Have a care, Colonel. These are the lands claimed for our new state, California being key, since it provides our nascent country not only with a seaport, but rich gold deposits. Oh, nothing like Sutter's Mill, but sufficient to provide for our national defense."

"You may have a formidable airship, accompanied by your numerous sky raiders, but it is still only one ship. While you can return me to Washington with a proposed treaty, President Buchanan may select a military solution. Can your redoubtable but small number of forces hope to combat the full might the Union can bring to bear?"

"About that, Colonel." Wells nodded and two men came forward, flanking Johnston. "Please accompany us, sir." Wells motioned to Eddington, who had been silent throughout the exchange, but who, Johnston noticed, seemed decidedly uncomfortable by the entire affair.

As the colonel struggled to rise, the men beside him—strong, well-muscled, the epitome of Wells' Nauvoo militia—gently assisted him and provided him with his crutches. He looked at each of the figures, and without a word, communicated that he could manage himself. He saw respect in their eyes and returned it, for in them there was no taint of the aversive ambition that he saw on the general's visage.

He followed Young, Wells, Eddington, and their men with his own guard surrounding him, out of the isolated room and into the Tabernacle's main corridors, the thumping sound of his crutches out of time with the other men's footsteps. As they approached an exit, the ringing in Johnston's ears became impossibly intense, replaced by something far more sinister.

The doorway they had taken outside faced south toward an open field in the lowlands below the city. There, Colonel Johnston witnessed a dread far worse than he had ever experienced, even in the depths of Echo Canyon.

"As you can see, Colonel, we have more than a single airship and, indeed, the Nauvoo have now become legion." Wells placed a hand on Johnston's shoulder in false camaraderie while waving with dramatic flourish at the military of the State of Deseret. The Texan counted at least six airships to rival the *Joseph Smith* idling on the ground. Rising in waves nearby were an adaptation of the one-man craft he had witnessed before. These were longer, with wings like bats, though they did not flutter, a larger fanned engine at the rear, and a complement of two soldiers each, a pilot and a gunner, though the weapon with which they were equipped boasted of multiple barrels. When several were test fired, brilliant shards of blue emerged faster than the beat of a hummingbird's wings and more numerous than a swarm of bees.

Nearer to them on the ground were some number of self-propelled carriages, armored plates extending around their entire frames, and a small cannon mounted on each of their fronts.

Foot solders followed the armored carriages, every man hoisting a smaller version of the many-barreled guns he had already seen, no doubt also with a capacity of firing faster than any infantryman's rifle.

"How have you accomplished this?" Johnston kept his lips thin and tight.

"I mentioned our acquisition of gold mines, Colonel. We also have sources of iron and copper, which Mr. Eddington can convert into more exotic materials, plus he has devised a process of extracting hydrogen for our big ships from the waters of the Great Salt Lake. Do you still think us helpless before the United States Army?"

Wells abruptly stiffened and stepped back as Brigham Young approached.

"Colonel, we have arranged this demonstration to impress you, not to intimidate you. I very much desire a peaceful relationship with your government as an alternative to a gory Civil War."

Johnston turned a bit too quickly to face the President, recalling his last conversation with Major Cooper about the threat of the same with the southern states. Then Young nearly proved himself a mind reader.

"I know of the bloody engagements in Kansas and the threat of a Southern secession. If President Buchanan and Congress are agreeable, they would have the State of Deseret's full support in quelling any such insurrection. What we ask in return is that we be allowed to rule our own lands in peace in accordance with our faith in the Lord Jesus Christ."

"President Young, I will take your proposal to Washington with your promise of continued good treatment of my men and their eventual safe return to their families."

"You have my solemn word, sir."

Awkwardly on his crutches, Colonel Johnston shook Brigham Young's hand with a sideways glance at Daniel Wells, who he did not trust at all, and who he believed Young should not trust either.

Colonel Johnston was provided with the documents he was to present to the Union government and began his long journey east in the company of Nauvoo security men. The diplomatic pouch contained one sealed envelope not sanctioned either by Brigham Young or Daniel Wells.

Fort Bridger, Nebraska Territory, May 1858

A TALL, solitary man in a trapper's buckskins, hat pulled low over his eyes and a full, brown beard obscuring his features, stood at the bar of the only saloon in Fort Bridger, a border town on the edge of Deseret, gateway to the still untamed Nebraska Territory. To any casual observer, of which there were few on the late-spring afternoon, he could have been sipping whiskey, but he had quietly insisted on being served only water.

Stephen Eddington was holding the glass, still sitting on the bar, when he heard the doors swing open behind him. Slow, booted footfalls approached before another man leaned against the counter to his right.

"Whiskey," he grunted at the barkeep, a fat man sporting a stained cotton apron, thinning hair slicked back, and a full three-day growth on his jowls.

The bartender silently set a glass in front of the newcomer, and when the stranger put a coin down, filled it from a bottle and moved on.

"Eddington?" He spoke in a whisper and with an accent clearly indicating a native of Massachusetts, hardly what he would have expected, but then again, an Englishman was equally out of place.

"What do I call you?"

"Caldwell, George Caldwell. You are Stephen Eddington, aren't you?"

"How do you know that name?"

"Your message to President Buchanan last autumn, sent in the care of Colonel Alfred Johnston. We've been exchanging covert communiqués for months."

"Very well, but keep your voice low. I'm sure the proprietor is harmless, but you never know who else is listening."

Caldwell looked around. By his appearance, he could have been anything from another trapper to an Indian agent, but like Eddington, he was something else entirely.

"I was in London before returning to the United States last year and was amazed at the work being done by Carson Westcott at the Royal College of Chemistry. Those inventions have put England on the cusp of the greatest revolution in technology the world has ever seen."

"Except for the State of Deseret." Eddington's voice carried the weight of guilt and bitterness.

"You know I'm a chemist. I've come to verify that you have the documents you promised. There's a small band of men five miles east who are prepared to take us back to Union territory. May I see them?"

Eddington tapped a finger against his temple. "I was barely able to elude observation and escape across the border, but I would never have been able to do so if I had absconded with any vital materials. You shall have to trust the knowledge I innately possess. I will happily answer any questions you have, but not here."

Caldwell, who had ignored his drink up until that moment, swallowed the contents in a single gulp and then coughed and wheezed, enough for the barkeep to look up from wiping the other end of the counter and chuckle.

"Let's get out of here." Eddington gripped Caldwell's arm and helped the latter stagger outside. The wind from the north was cold in spite of the brilliantly blue sky. He saw another horse tied up next to his.

"Wait a moment. I do have one more question. Why?" Caldwell took a deep breath.

"Why? You mean leave the church, betray Daniel Wells, help your Gentile government?"

"Something like that. You said Wells. What about Brigham Young?"

"You probably haven't heard yet. Young has fallen ill since winter, deathly ill. Wells has assumed the Presidency. The so-called treaty is in peril. I have no proof, but I strongly suspect the general misused the life sustaining medicines developed from my various formulae to overdose President Young, placing him in a coma."

"What does this mean for our governments?"

"Wells has no intention of honoring Young's promises. In any war between the North and South, he'll play both sides against each other, and the State of Deseret will consume the loser, adding their lands to his own. The only way to stop him is to make sure the Union is equipped to defend itself against this merciless despot, because, failing that, I fear nothing can stop him."

"Then there is a way to balance the scales."

"In a year, and with my knowledge and the Union's resources, the

United States Army will become the most formidable military force in the world, and may God have mercy on my soul."

ABOUT THE AUTHOR

JAMES PYLES IS A PUBLISHED science fiction and fantasy writer as well as a freelance Information Technology textbook author and editor. A growing number of his short stories are appeared in anthologies and periodicals in 2019. He also has a passion for reading the genres he writes and is currently working on his first full-length novel.

You can find him at https://poweredbyrobots.com/ or on Facebook at https://www.facebook.com/jamespylesauthor/.

Follow the Temple

Nate Givens

Bennie Browning caught up with the Nauvoo Striding Temple as it meandered southwards along the east bank of the Mississippi. She gripped the controls of her clockwork ornithopter and pulled back, bringing the 'thopter into a gently bobbing hover. She worked the pedals to keep the machine from rotating and leaned over the encasement protecting the mainspring like a rider leaning over the neck of her horse.

The mighty Mississippi River lay directly beneath her. Moonlight glinting off the water made Bennie think of glistening scales. If she turned her head to look north or south, she saw the mighty river stretching to either horizon. She imagined it circling the entire globe like a massive serpent, just waiting to squeeze. Bennie did not belong out east.

She couldn't see the temple clearly at first. It was obscured by the flapping wings that stretched out for more than a dozen feet on either side of her, mechanically pounding the night air into submission to keep the 'thopter aloft. She worked the pedals again, this time to carefully spin the 'thopter for a better view of the temple.

Unlike the flashy gleam of the water, the pale walls of the temple reflected the moonlight with subtle grace. Bennie took in the familiar arched windows; the octagonal, dome-topped tower; and the familiar sunstones. Her throat ached. She'd found Nauvoo at last. Now she just had to convince the temple to come back home to the Salt Lake Valley.

Bennie swooped lower and flew a narrow circle around the temple. It was propelled by eight massive legs. The heavy legs shook the branches and leaves of trees for hundreds of feet around the temple with every ponderous step. They were splayed out from the bottom of the main temple as though a monstrous, mechanical hermit crab had decided to use it for a home.

The legs held the floor of the temple so high off the ground that Bennie easily flew through the space between the muddy riverbank and the temple's pale underside. It was hard to tell in the dark, even with a full moon, but she saw no sign of damage.

Bennie engaged the flapping wings again and coaxed her 'thopter back into the sky. When she looked back, she saw that Nauvoo had stopped. The temple scuttled in a slow, 90-degre turn that left it facing the Mississippi.

Come on, Nauvoo, thought Bennie. *You can't cross here.*

The temple started forward again, picking up a little speed as it entered the water. Bennie worked the controls to pace Nauvoo's progress. Streams of water cascaded down from the legs as they lifted out of the water. When they plunged back down, they sent foam-capped waves racing out across the river's surface.

Please, Nauvoo, go back.

The temple kept going until the water threatened to swamp the building perched on top of the legs. Nauvoo stopped, only a hundred feet out from the shore. She wasn't even close to the midpoint of the river.

Bennie bit her lip as she watched. Her eyes misted behind the lenses of her flying goggles. *It's okay, Nauvoo,* she thought. *I know you're trying so hard, but you can't cross the Mississippi.*

This wasn't strictly true. Nauvoo had crossed the Mississippi once before. But that had been nearly four decades ago in the dead of winter during a rare ice gorge when the river froze completely solid. It was summer now. There was no ice. No place for Nauvoo to cross.

The 'thopter clanked and sighed around Bennie as she directed it down towards the temple. It was now or never.

Landing on Nauvoo in the middle of the night was a very bad idea. Nauvoo's ungainly gait caused her roof to pitch, yaw, and roll in a complex pattern. If she'd had daylight to work with, Bennie could have orbited Nauvoo until she figured out the pattern.

She'd done the same thing when she had to land on other striders for the first time. Other 'thopter jockeys waited until they could articulate the pattern exactly, but not Bennie. Many of the most important things in her life were things she understood without being able to put them into words. Why should flying be any different? Given a little time and a little light, she had no doubt she'd be able to touch lightly down and secure the 'thopter easily.

Problem was, she didn't have either.

Sure, the temple was illuminated, but that only meant the arched windows along the side were lit up. There were no lights on the roof, and the moonlight wasn't bright enough for precise observation.

Time was short, too. Her 'thopter's mainspring was nearly unwound. The machine already responded sluggishly to her controls. In a few more minutes—five, maybe ten at the very most depending on what updrafts she could find—she wouldn't be able to keep it aloft at all.

Ordinarily the solution would be simple: land on the *land*. But this was Missouri, not the Salt Lake Valley. Folks down there were far more likely to shoot her than help wind the mainspring. Especially since, as far as she knew, Executive Order 44 was still in force. They didn't even have to hate Mormons in particular. They just had to want her 'thopter.

Bennie had to take her chances with a night landing. On a moving temple. At night.

And as long as she was doing that, might as well do it now, while the temple was still in the river. At least then she'd have *some* chance of survival if she missed. As for the 'thopter ending up at the bottom of the Mississippi, well, out here there was no one else Bennie would rather have it after she was gone.

If she was gone.

Come on, Benevolence, she thought to herself. *Keep it together.*

The closer she got to the temple's roof, the more it seemed to move. Every step Nauvoo took turned the roof into a precipitous slide in a different direction.

With a jarring crash, the roof of the temple suddenly rose up to collide with the 'thopter. The temple must have stepped up onto a barely-submerged towhead.

Bennie flew forward over the 'thopter and crashed onto the back of the temple. She lay for a moment, watching the stars spin dizzily around the sky overhead.

I should probably get up.

The 'thopter's wings beat feebly, sending gusts of wind that seemed strong enough to blow Bennie off the roof all on their own. Not that it would take much. One of the things that made Bennie a good 'thopter jockey was her tiny size. She was not quite five feet tall and rail thin. When she was on her 'thopter she was the master of the wind. On her own, it didn't take more than a stiff breeze to blow her off her feet.

Bennie doggedly rolled onto her stomach and got to her knees, reaching out for the tie-downs that she could use to secure her 'thopter to... something.

She pulled herself to her feet, and nearly fell again as the roof lurched. The 'thopter screeched as it slid towards the edge.

Bennie searched the roof frantically, looking for something to tie the 'thopter to. She'd landed in the middle, and there were a couple of small pillars at the edge. That was *not* the direction she wanted to go in, but she lurched toward them anyway. She was pretty sure she had enough length to loop once or twice, and that would be enough to get the 'thopter secured for the moment.

She stumbled to the little pillar—it came up to her shoulder—and tugged at the rope to get enough slack. She reached up and looped the rope around it. The roof kept rocking, but so far the 'thopter had not slid again. Bennie leaned back and put a foot against the pillar, ready to pull the line tight, but the Nauvoo lurched.

The 'thopter didn't so much slide off the roof as hop directly off of it. The tip of one wing sliced across Bennie's cheek as it passed her, opening a shallow cut from her ear to her mouth.

Bennie had a moment to stand there, feeling vaguely betrayed, before the line she'd only half-looped around the pillar yanked taut and dragged her over the edge after her 'thopter.

She let go of the rope much, much too late. The smooth walls of the temple slid upward and away from her. She had one bizarrely clear impression of a sunstone frowning at her in disappointment as she fell past it. The gaudy surface of the Mississippi pin-wheeled up to meet her, and everything went dark.

∞

"Well, well, well," said a stranger's voice. "You're not dead after all. That's nice."

Bennie groaned. She lay on her back on something hard. Opening her eyes didn't seem like a good idea. Her head pounded. She ran a hand over it, expecting the leather of her flight cap. Her hand felt only the rough stubble of her shaved head.

"Surprised?" said the voice. "So was I. Never seen a lady with a shaved head before. Is that something you did yourself? Or was it done to you?"

Bennie tried to speak, but her stomach lurched. She turned to the side and vomited. She heaved again and again. It felt like she was throwing up the entire Mississippi.

"You *are* a lady, right?"

"I am," said Bennie. She braced herself before opening her eyes. It was still dark. She was in a small, single-room cabin. The walls were log and the floor was rough wood plank. The room was crowded with an unlit wood-burning stove, a rough table and two benches, and a few cots.

Bennie hadn't been laid on any of the cots. She'd been dumped on the floor between them. A small lamp hissed on top of the cold stove, and no other illumination. The room smelled stale and reeked of body odor at the same time, as though it had stood unused for a long time until recently and then been occupied by a team of hard-working laborers.

Bennie slowly sat up and scooted back to lean against the log wall.

"You fished me out?"

"Didn't take much," said the stranger. "I've landed catfish that could swallow you whole."

He was the only other person in the room. He looked about forty, double Bennie's age, and he sat on the cot farthest from her. He wore a wide hat; a voluminous coat; dusty, nondescript clothes; and a thick, gray mustache that completely hid his mouth. It made his expression hard to read.

He also wore a gun-belt. The bullet casings caught the meager light of the little lamp and reflected it into Bennie's eyes. It wasn't much, but it still hurt.

"You didn't happen to fish out my 'thopter too, did you?"

"As a matter of fact," said the man. "I did."

He leaned back on the cot, stuck his hands in his pockets, and stretched his legs out in front of him. "I'm no expert, but I'd say it's flight-worthy, still." He smiled. Bennie could tell from the way the skin crinkled around his eyes.

"Not without winding the mainspring," she said.

"Oh, that's something I reckon we could manage," said the man.

Bennie glanced at him suspiciously. "Where am I?"

"The Kentucky side, if that's your worry."

Bennie mulled that over. She'd been on the Missouri side when she fell, and the river wasn't narrow here. No one would have taken her to the Kentucky side without good reason. But that would mean he knew she was Mormon. And him telling her? That meant he wanted her to *know* that he knew. That sounded like a threat. Subtle enough to be polite, as threats went, but a threat nonetheless.

What would you prefer, Benevolence? Implied threats or explicit gunshot wounds?

Bennie massaged her nose, which still stung from throwing up the river water. Maybe she was being paranoid.

"My name's Clive Streeter," he said.

"I'm Benevolence Browning," Bennie replied. "Nice to meet you." She coughed and wiped the corners of her mouth. It was mostly just water she'd thrown up, but the bile left a savage taste.

"It's okay to meet you, too," said Clive.

Well, that's an odd thing to say, Bennie thought.

He squinted at her for a moment, then spoke again. "Who's steering that temple of yours?"

"Nobody. That's the problem."

"Nobody? You expect me to believe that?"

"We built it to steer on its own," she said. "It uses the sun, the moon, even a couple of the stars to navigate. Can also determine pitch and incline, that sort of thing."

"And detect water?"

"That, too."

"So, where's it going?"

"Hard to say," Bennie lied. "But we'd really like to get it back."

"How would you do that?"

Bennie reached into her soaking wet blouse. This wasn't a problem, socially speaking, since her blouse was under a stiff leather vest. On top of that she still had her leather flying coat. It was hot down here at ground level on the Kentucky-Missouri border, but Bennie spent as little time as possible at ground level. Or, come to think of it, anywhere near Missouri.

She pulled out a large, complicated key. It had teeth coming out in all three dimensions instead of just along one line. That made it fiercely uncomfortable to wear, and it was actually a relief to pull it out from under the tight-fitting vest.

"With this." She held the key in front of her. "I can take control and set in a manual course."

She hefted the key in one hand, trying to keep Clive's focus on it. With her other hand, she slowly reached back and felt for the throwing knife at the small of her back. She didn't intend to stab anyone just yet, but it'd be a familiar comfort.

"Knife's not there," said Clive. His eyes hadn't flickered off the key for a moment.

"It's okay." He picked up Bennie's knife from where it had been laying out of her view on the cot next to him. "I just wanted to be sure we had a moment to talk before we considered anything... drastic."

"Alright," she said as evenly as she could. "What did you want to talk about?"

"Can your 'thopter carry two?"

"It can. For a short hop."

"I'd like a lift."

"Where to?"

"Nauvoo."

Bennie frowned.

"The temple," Clive clarified unnecessarily. "Not the city."

"I got that."

"I know how you feel about your temples," he said. "You don't need to give me a full, guided tour or anything. Just a little peak. Enough to take a few photographs." He patted a large, canvas bag on the cot beside him.

Bennie was pretty sure that Clive did not, in fact, know how she felt about temples. Her father, Jonathan Browning, was a practicing polygamist. She loved her father ,and polygamy was all she'd known, but that didn't mean her feelings on the topic were uncomplicated. This ambivalence extended to the temples themselves.

But the Nauvoo Striding Temple? That temple in particular meant something to Bennie on a strictly personal level. Her father had spent his last months in Nauvoo working feverishly to finish the Nauvoo Striding Temple. At the time, it had been the largest striding building in the country, and even to this day it was the largest west of the Mississippi. Her father had poured his heart and soul into that building. He'd risked his life for it. That was enough reason for Bennie to risk hers.

"So, you want pictures?"

"Sure," said Clive. "I know folks. Newspapermen. They'll pay top dollar for a glimpse inside the Nauvoo Striding Temple. More than enough cash for me to buy my way back onto the tables."

Bennie considered.

"I saw you fly," he said. "Earlier tonight. I was watching you."

"Good thing," she said sarcastically.

Clive pressed past the sarcasm. "You're a natural. I can tell. I've seen plenty of 'thopter jockeys, but none like you."

Bennie couldn't remain unaffected by that comment. It wasn't the compliment. What would some card shark know about what made a great 'thopter jockey? It was just the reminder of how much she loved to fly.

It had only been a couple of hours—and she'd been unconscious for all of them—but she already missed flying. She loved every part of it. The view, of course. That was the first thing. Seeing the whole world spread out below you made you feel like you were out of the reach of all your problems and concerns. The speed, also. Even the smell was in Bennie's blood now. Oil and leather and metal and nothing else but empty sky.

Clive watched her with a knowing smile.

"It's the freedom," she said. She wanted to explain more. She'd ridden horses before, of course. There was power there, too. Power and speed. But something about riding on an animal felt restricting. She was always aware of the horse as another creature impinging on her solitude. That's probably why some people liked it. The companionship. But not Bennie. Riding a 'thopter didn't feel like sharing an experience with another being. The 'thopter was an extension of her own body. Up there, it was just her. Alone. She liked that conclusion, so she repeated it out loud.

"I'm alone up there," she said. "I like it."

"It's what you do, Benevolence," he said. "Well, cards are what I do. At that table, *I'm* alone."

That didn't really make sense to Bennie. Sitting at a table playing cards was like soaring among the clouds? Her brow furrowed. But then, who was she to judge?

"Okay, Mr. Streeter," she said. "If you can help me wind the mainspring, I'll take you to Nauvoo."

Clive smiled. "Let's go."

IT WAS MUCH EASIER in the daylight, but Bennie had to admit that what really made the difference the second time around was having an extra pair of hands.

Nauvoo was several miles farther south by the time they caught up with her again. She continued to plod along the bank of the Mississippi, and every now and then she'd veer into the water and wade until it got too deep, before wading back out again. Bennie had no trouble catching up, even with Clive and his packed camera.

So far, Bennie didn't see anyone else pursuing Nauvoo. They were in the middle of the wilderness along the Missouri-Kentucky border after all. Other than a few riverboats that stayed to the center of the river, they hardly saw anyone else at all.

Bennie let Clive know what she needed him to do. She came in for a hover over the Nauvoo on a flat stretch of land and dropped him off. She kept the 'thopter a foot or two above the roof until he got a rope loosely tied around one of the pillars. Then she landed the 'thopter while he pulled the rope taut.

As soon as the 'thopter was on the roof, she raced to a pillar on the opposite side and tied her own rope. They each ran another line, and the 'thopter was secure.

"Thank you, Mr. Streeter," she said as they met back up at the 'thopter in the center of the roof. Sweat dripped down the sides of her face, Bennie shrugged out of her coat and dropped her cap and goggles onto the 'thopter's seat. The air felt soothingly cool on her hairless scalp. She usually had a wig to put on when she wasn't flying, but she'd left in a hurry and hadn't remembered to take it with her.

"Well, I do appreciate the lift," said Clive.

He drew a small derringer from a coat pocket and shot Bennie in the sternum.

Bennie staggered against the 'thopter, holding out a hand to support herself. It didn't help. Her knees buckled and she sagged to the roof. She lay on her back, willing her lungs to start breathing again. They ignored her. The clouds in the sky swayed back and forth as the Nauvoo plodded on, heedless to the drama taking place.

A derringer? He had a six-shooter in his belt and he shot me with a derringer? Bennie was angry about that. It seemed disrespectful. Like Clive wasn't taking her seriously. But it made good sense. If he'd gone for the holstered gun, she'd have seen it coming. The derringer had been a surprise.

Clive's face came into view. He stood looking down at Bennie. "That was easier than I expected."

"Who are you?" Bennie gasped.

"Clive's my real name," he said. "That's all you need to know, isn't it?"

"You're not working alone."

"Of course I'm not. You think I could fish a 'thopter out of the river on my own? I'm amazed you didn't think of that. Good thing you're not too bright."

"Had sort of a lot on my mind," she rasped out. "Not dying and such."

This is what happens when you let good news in without thinking twice, Benevolence. This is what always happens.

He squatted down and roughly felt around Bennie's neck for the necklace that held the key. "Anyway, " he said, "you know what I'm really here for by now, don't you?"

"Yes," Bennie choked out. "I do."

She finally managed to draw a real breath. It hurt her ribs, but the air felt delicious as she sucked it into her lungs. "But you can't have her."

Clive jerked the key up from its place between her chest and her flying vest. Her *armored* flying vest. One did not grow up the daughter of a world-class gunsmith and arrive unprepared to a gunfight. The tiny derringer bullet, mashed beyond recognition where it had been stopped by the vest, fell out and tinkled across the roof.

"Oh dear," said Clive.

He jumped to his feet. The necklace and the key flew into the air as he leapt back just in time to escape Bennie's first knife slash.

She hauled herself up, pointed the knife at Clive, and... pulled the trigger. A tiny derringer of her own was embedded in the handle. The bullet went wild, but Bennie followed it up with a knife throw that did not. The blade buried itself in Clive's shoulder.

"I ought to thank you," she said. Her words came out in panting gasps as she continued to struggle to catch her wind. "I was feeling really conflicted about showing a gentile any part of our temple. Guess I don't have to worry about that now."

She reached into her boot and pulled out another gun. This one full-sized, at least by Bennie's diminutive standards. It was a custom 5-wheel her father had given to her when she turned sixteen. She pulled the hammer back, took careful aim, and pulled the trigger.

The hammer clicked down on an empty chamber.

Now how did you not notice there were no bullets in the cylinder, Benevolence? You almost deserve to get killed for that. Almost.

"About that," said Clive, his own teeth gritted. "I let you keep the gun, but I kept the bullets."

He drew his own revolver and managed to smirk despite the pain. "My turn."

Nauvoo swerved abruptly, making another turn towards the Mississippi. Clive stumbled and waved his arms in the air, firing uselessly into the sky. Bennie closed the distance before he could get his aim on target again, lowering her shoulder and colliding with him at full tilt. They both sprawled to the floor of the roof near the back of the temple, and Clive's gun went skittering across it. Bennie leapt after it.

It took her a moment to catch the gun. She whirled to face Clive again. He was right behind her, holding something strange. It looked like a wire-wrapped club, and it was trailing a line back to his canvas bag. The bag he'd said contained his camera.

Clive hit Bennie with the club before she could cock and fire the revolver. It wasn't a hard hit, but electricity leapt from the wires around the club and seized her in bands of iron. Every muscle in her body went rigid in a single, agonizing spasm, and she dropped to the floor.

Clive stood over her again, blocking out the sun. He mopped his brow and bounced the club menacingly in one hand.

Bennie's jaw was clamped so tight she was afraid her teeth might shatter. She tried to calm her breathing, but her muscles were still uselessly cramped.

"Phew-ee," said Clive with exaggerated cheer. "You Mormon gals certainly know how to keep things sporting."

He turned around, scanning the roof. "Now, where's that key?"

He spotted it a few paces away. He negligently tapped Bennie with the club again. While she arched her back and writhed, he went to retrieve the key. He turned around and held it up with a look of triumph.

Bennie still held Clive's gun. Her arm shook violently and her hands were locked into barely controllable claws, but she hadn't let go. She had the gun in her right hand, but she couldn't uncurl her index finger to get it inside the trigger and fire the weapon.

That was no matter. She used the blade of her left hand to pull the hammer back and jammed her left index finger in the trigger guard. She couldn't flex that finger, so she just pulled her whole left arm back.

The gun bucked, and a bright red stain appeared on Clive's dull gray shirt. He looked at the wound in shock. Bennie was shocked, too. She was ordinarily a good shot—how could she not be, given her family's business?—but this one had been complete luck.

Clive looked down at the lightning club he held in one hand.

"They said the effect... would last at least five minutes."

He let it fall to the roof.

He looked at the necklace clutched in his other hand. He looked back at Bennie and tried to spit at her. The spittle clung to his weathered skin and dribbled slowly down his jaw. He took a step back, toward the railing.

"No, no, no," said Bennie. She stepped toward him, gun held to the side as non-threateningly as she could.

Clive took another step back. He waggled the necklace at her, leered, then took one more step and toppled over the edge.

Bennie sprinted to the side and slid to a stop at the edge. She looked over. Nauvoo was back in the Mississippi again. The muddy river rushed past the temple's legs, just under the first floor of the temple itself. There was no sign of Clive or the key he had taken with him.

Bennie rolled back away from the edge and lay flat on her back, stunned. She held her curled hands against her chest to hold in the sobs.

She had no way to steer Nauvoo back home.

⚥

RODERICK GODBE almost died in the first minutes after he hijacked the nearly-complete Salt Lake Cloud Temple from the Salt Lake airworks. He'd been told the ballast was fully loaded. He'd been told wrong. After faking an emergency to clear the working crews and then cutting off all the moorings, he passed out while the temple rapidly ascended a mile straight up.

He'd woken with dried blood crusting his face from nostrils to chin. He had painfully pulled his face off the ice-cold bare metal flooring of the temple's engineering room, thinking that it was only the dried blood sticking him to the floor. It hadn't been only the dried blood. The metal was so cold his skin had frozen to it.

If he'd been more alert he would have figured that out before ripping away strips of skin from his face and hands. All in all, though, it was probably better that he'd done it in a semi-conscious daze. He might very well not have had the courage to rip himself free if he'd realized what was happening.

Roderick almost died again the next day. He'd been told that the engine and propellers had been installed and tested. He'd been told right in this case. What he hadn't been told was that the battery necessary to start the engine had been moved back groundside for more testing. He had no power, and that meant no way to steer.

So Roderick just sat and watched the jagged peaks of the Wasatch Front draw closer and closer as a westerly wind drove the cloud temple east across the Valley. Luck was with him again, however, and the wind funneling through a high pass tugged the derelict cloud temple along with it.

The mountainsides passed so close to the cloud temple that Roderick thought about trying to leap to them and make his way down. He'd suppressed the urge. For one, he was pretty sure even if he made it to the mountainside without dying, he'd never be able to climb back to the valley floor. For another, Roderick was formulating a new plan.

The new plan was the same as the old plan in its bare essentials: steal the Salt Lake Cloud Temple and vindicate his father. William Godbe had traveled to New York City in 1868. While there, he'd employed some of the world's foremost mediums to contact the spirits of Joseph and Hyrum Smith. They had explained how Brigham Young was getting everything wrong and perverting the Restoration.

But when William had returned to Salt Lake to spread this revelation, they'd *laughed* at him. Then they'd excommunicated him. Roderick had sworn then and there to not rest until his family was avenged.

Not everyone had laughed, of course. Some had listened. And when William Godbe founded the Church of Zion, they joined. But the more William taught the truth about communing with spirits, the more of them left. Roderick hated these cowards even more than the Mormons who'd never listened to his father in the first place.

Originally, he'd planned to take control of the Salt Lake Cloud Temple and give it to his father to rejuvenate the Church of Zion. Since he had no power, he couldn't do that anymore. But Roderick decided it was for the best.

He watched through the glass-tiled floor as the land passed below him. From almost two miles up, he could see everything. The sky around him was empty and silent.

But it wouldn't stay that way. There were major airship hubs in the East. None serviced ships quite as big as the Salt Lake Cloud Temple, but the intercontinental airships that plied the skyways between Europe and the East Coast were almost as large. Eventually, he'd drift close enough that they would send someone up to rescue him.

There was even some chance, if he talked fast and understood the basic laws correctly, that he'd be able to claim the entire cloud temple as salvage.

It wasn't what he'd originally intended, but those cowards who'd quit the Church of Zion and crawled back to Brigham Young didn't deserve anything from him anyway.

Roderick was going to be *rich*, and the Brighamites would never see their precious cloud temple again.

It wasn't exactly the revenge he'd wanted, but it was close.

◦§

BENNIE SAT UP. There was something winking near the top of Nauvoo's tower. It must be the lens of the telescope. Nauvoo was searching the sky again. That was unusual. She usually only used the telescope at night, since the sun was simple to track during the day without the telescope.

The last time Bennie had seen Nauvoo use her telescope during the day had been two weeks ago near Fort Kearney. Nauvoo had been assisting another band of pioneers across the Mormon Trail. The striding temple allowed the Saints to worship as they traveled, helped carry emergency supplies, and was big enough to keep the plains mastodons away from the wagons without hurting them. And, unless you wanted a raid from Cheyenne war 'thopters, you did *not* harm the plains mastodons.

On that day, Bennie had had no idea what Nauvoo was tracking, but the striding temple had abruptly left the pioneers and headed south. Bennie had followed it to the border of Cheyenne territory, then turned back. When she rejoined the pioneers, she learned that someone had cut the Salt Lake Cloud Temple free weeks ago, and it had been drifting eastward ever since.

Bennie had no idea what made the Nauvoo tick. Her father had built the engines and perfected the legs, but the autonomous driving had been installed by a newly arrived convert from England, Prevost Babbage. How Nauvoo could recognize the cloud temple, let alone decide to follow it, she had no idea. But that's what it had done.

And now it was scanning the sky again.

Bennie squinted in the direction the telescope presently pointed. There was something up there, alright. Hard to tell at this range, especially because the sun was nearby in the sky. But what else could it be?

And if the Nauvoo had followed Salt Lake this far east, why shouldn't she follow the cloud temple back west? All it took was someone to start the engine.

Bennie's eyes fell on the lightning club Clive had used on her. She followed the cable back to the sack and opened it. There was no camera inside. Just something that looked an awful lot like a powerful battery.

Well, Benevolence, I do believe this might work.

Bennie yanked the cord leading to the lightning club out, then curled it up and tossed the club and its cord into the sack. She threw the sack onto her 'thopter, untied the ropes, and took off.

Nauvoo seemed frantic now. Salt Lake was already on the other side of the Mississippi, and the striding temple paced rapidly back and forth on the riverbank, surging into the water again and again but always stopping when the water threatened to swamp over the legs and flood the temple proper.

Hang on, Nauvoo. Benevolence is going to take care of this.

⁛

BENNIE HAD NEVER FLOWN this high. The air was frigid. Her eyeballs felt like they would freeze solid where the cold snuck in around her goggles. The goggles frosted almost to the point of total blindness. Despite her warm flight gear, her teeth chattered and her lungs ached with every insufficient gasp of too-thin air.

She pressed on.

The 'thopter's power drained rapidly as it had to beat harder and faster for less and less lift. She already knew she didn't have enough power left for a safe landing if she turned back. She just hoped she had enough to make it to one of the landing platforms on Salt Lake.

She came level with the cloud temple. The sight took what little breath she had away. Inverted towers and downward-pointing steeples hung from two enormous gasbags that provided most of the lift. Some of the incomplete temple was still open to the elements, and Bennie could see the stairways and walls inside.

She forced herself to keep going. The landing pads, engineering, and other utilitarian portions of the cloud temple were all on top, where they would be hidden from view of anyone on the ground.

Bennie found one of the landing pads—the only part of this plan that had been easier than her original plan to manually steer Nauvoo home—and coaxed her tired 'thopter onto the pad with its last reserves of energy. She stumbled off the 'thopter and used her numb hands to tie it down to one of the dedicated anchors. That was all she could do before limping towards the door, dragging the canvas sack behind her.

Og

RODERICK WOKE to a strange thumping sound overhead. He rolled out of the sleeping nest he had made from piling all of the cold-weather gear into a single heap and looked out a window. He could still see the Mississippi below.

He stood quietly and listened. Steps and the sound of something dragging came from above. Someone had definitely landed a 'thopter on the cloud temple.

Roderick wracked his brains. Who could it be? There were a couple of big cities along the Mississippi that might support 'thopters, but as best he'd been able to track the cloud temple's meandering progress, they were in the middle of nowhere between Missouri and Kentucky. He didn't expect anyone to attempt to contact him until they were further east.

He heard the sound of an external door opening, then clanging closed.

It didn't really matter who it was, he decided. Either way it was a gift from heaven. The weakest part in his claim to have salvaged Salt Lake after finding her adrift had always been his lack of a 'thopter. He had some story made up about having lost his 'thopter in a storm, but it would be much more believable if he had an actual 'thopter on board. Otherwise, they might mistake him for a thief.

Now he just needed to get rid of his intrusive guest.

The warm glow of pride blossomed in his chest. He'd gotten through the hard parts. Just a little longer now, and he'd enjoy the fruits of his travails.

Og

IT FELT WARMER INSIDE Salt Lake, but only just. Bennie dimly noticed that the cold-weather stowage just inside the landing pad was empty. If her mind had been clearer, she would have stopped to wonder where it had gone, since it was something the workers would have used during construction.

But her mind wasn't clearer, and irrelevant details distracted her. Like the overwhelming metallic smell of the Salt Lake. Except for the lack of gunpowder, it smelled like her father's workshop.

She could only keep one goal safe from the vagaries of her oxygen-deprived haze. Find the engine. Find a way to connect this giant battery. Start the engine.

Something came after that, but she couldn't remember what. It didn't really matter. Engines made heat. Right now, that was more than sufficient reason for Bennie to keep plodding on. She'd figure the rest out after she was warm.

Come on, Benevolence. Dad told you all about his design work for Salt Lake. You know where the engine is. Just think.

Bennie couldn't think. But she could keep walking, barely. So she did, barely.

◦◦

RODERICK THOUGHT about taking off his boots to sneak up on whoever had boarded his ship, but he discarded the idea as a quick path to frostbite. He just focused on stepping as quietly as possible and hoped that would be adequate to sneak up on the pirate undetected.

It came naturally for Roderick to think of the cloud temple as just another airship. And to think of it as *his* airship. And from that it followed just as naturally that anyone on board without his permission was a pirate.

Roderick kept his thickly gloved right hand on the revolver in his pocket. He hadn't had to use the gun when he took possession of his ship, so it was still fully loaded.

The plan was to sneak up on the intruder and then force them back to their own 'thopter. Roderick would pretend to simply want them off his ship. But when their back was turned and before they had a chance to take off, he would strike.

Afterward, it would be a simple matter to roll the body off the landing platform, go back inside, and huddle down until real authorities showed up.

And if there were blood stains? Well, even that would help his story. After all, *somebody* should have been up here before him. Roderick rehearsed his ever-improving story.

"I don't know what happened to the crew, officers. It was as empty as a tomb when I landed. But look at this bloodstain here, officer. Something dark happened here, but what else would you expect from Brighamites?"

He would even throw his revolver over the side after he'd disposed of the pirate. How could he possibly look more blameless? Well, no. That was probably too far. After all, if there was one pirate, there could be two.

Roderick muttered to himself as he tried to work out what to do with the revolver. Of course muttering was not a good way to sneak up on a person, but Roderick had been alone in the cloud temple for weeks now. He'd gotten so used to talking out loud that he didn't even realize he was doing it.

"If I throw it away now, I'll be vulnerable if someone else comes on board."

Bennie tilted her head to the side to listen to the muttered conversation, but didn't really think much of it. She'd been down four different hallways already. Every door was unlocked, but none of them led to an engine.

"If I throw it away when I see the authorities coming, they might see it and get suspicious. What if I just hide it?"

I wonder what he's thinking of throwing away, Bennie wondered.

She opened another door. It was full of some kind of machinery, but it was all pipes and valves. Probably very important for running the cloud temple in some way, but not what Bennie needed. And nothing she could figure out in her present state.

"And then if they find it? Oh, well I can just say it wasn't mine! I can just say it belonged to... whoever. I don't have to make up a story at all. Let them guess at what happened here before I found it!"

Bennie stopped walking and frowned.

Benevolence, you fool, if you're hearing someone talk, it's because there's someone else on board!

This seemed like an important idea. She squatted and sat on the sack like a stool. It was uncomfortable, but better than the frigid bare metal everywhere else.

You didn't see any other 'thopters, did you, Benevolence? So that must mean whoever's on board now, came on board before the cloud temple was cut free. Come to think of it, they never did say they knew who had set Salt Lake adrift, did they?

ᦙ

RODERICK ROUNDED A CORNER AND STOPPED. There, in the middle of the hallway, was a 'thopter jockey sitting on a canvas sack.

This was perfect. He had it all worked out.

"Stand up," Roderick commanded.

The jockey turned around, stood, and then sagged against the wall.

"Roderick?" said the jockey in a slurred voice.

Roderick recognized the voice in spite of the slur. "Bennie?"

"Hi, Roderick."

"Hmm," he said. "Well, that's going to make this a little awkward."

ᦙ

"MAKE WHAT AWKWARD?" asked Bennie. She squinted at Roderick.

She didn't know him very well, but they'd seen each other around Salt Lake City. They were almost the same age, after all. She had the feeling Roderick had been interested in her, but then she'd gone and ostentatiously shaved her head. Yes, it was practical for the close-fitting 'thopter cap. It was also an obvious but deniable statement of her intentions with regards to courtship and marriage. Which was to say: none for me just now, thanks.

"Oh, just a plan I've been working on," said Roderick. He looked shifty. This made Bennie suspicious, but only a little. Roderick had small beady eyes, narrow features, and furtive mannerisms. He looked shifty even when he was just standing still. On top of that, he was always scheming. Which meant he often had things to look shifty about. So it wasn't unusual for him to look that way now. It was just how Roderick always looked.

"I think I heard that plan," said Bennie. "Getting rid of something?"

"Oh," said Roderick. "Was I talking out loud?" He looked into the distance for a moment. "I suppose I was. That's embarrassing. Well, on the bright side, I guess you know how this has to end. I am sorry, but you did bring this on yourself."

Bennie was confused. She knew it ended with hiding something somewhere, but she wasn't sure what. Or where. Or why he'd be sorry about it.

Roderick drew the gun from his pocket and aimed it at Bennie.

Oh, she thought. *That's why.*

Bennie sighed with exhaustion. *This would all be so much easier to keep up with if I could just take a breath of real air. Just one breath, and I could catch up.*

She watched in fascination as Roderick tried to pull back the hammer of the revolver, but he couldn't manage it with his gloves on. He held the gun to the side with one hand and then tried to use all the pressure of his other hand, but the hammer wouldn't budge.

"It's probably frozen," Bennie said helpfully.

"Oh," said Roderick.

"Let me take a look at it." She approached Roderick with a hand extended. Roderick stared at her in disbelief, but her face betrayed nothing but earnest helpfulness.

"Are you crazy?" he said, jerking the gun out of her reach.

"Roderick, are you the one that set her adrift?" Bennie asked. She was standing very close to him now. Her brown eyes looked directly into his pale green ones. The mist of their breaths intermingled in the cold air between them.

Roderick shook his head in confusion. "What?"

"Salt Lake." She gestured feebly around with her gloved right hand.

"Oh," said Roderick. "I did. To teach you a lesson. When my father came back from New York City—"

Bennie brought the lightning club up between them and poked Roderick in the chest with it. She didn't hit him hard, but she shoved him enough that he fell back away from her as the current surged through his body.

"I've heard that story before," she said. "It's boring."

She slumped back against the wall in exhaustion.

"If this battery doesn't have enough juice yet to start her, I'm going to use whatever's left on you."

She kicked Roderick in the boot. He moaned. She stepped over and pried the gun from his hand. Leaving him on the floor, she stumbled off to find the engine room.

⚙

THE BATTERY HAD enough juice to start Salt Lake's engine. Thereafter, Bennie basked in the radiated heat of the hand-built brass and steel behemoth until the painful prickles of numbness receded from her arms, legs, and face. By the time she felt appropriately defrosted, the revolver was, too.

She didn't find Roderick. She did a cursory search first, but then an idea struck her. She went to the landing pad. Her 'thopter was gone. That meant she was going to have to come back east *again* to find Roderick, beat him senseless, and take back her 'thopter.

Now that's just plain discourteous, she thought to herself. On the other hand, she could also try to find out who Clive had been working for. If he'd had a whole support team helping fish her 'thopter out of the river, there would be a trail to follow.

She set her planning aside. She could worry about all of that later.

With power restored, Bennie was able to get Salt Lake's massive propellers started. She turned the cloud temple in a wide, ponderous arc through the sky and headed west. Once she had some forward velocity, she was even able to bring the Salt Lake down to a reasonable altitude using the stubby wings attached to the gas bags.

She crossed the Mississippi back into Missouri directly over Nauvoo. The striding temple stood motionless on the bank of the river, but Bennie caught the glint of the telescope swiveling to track Salt Lake.

After the cloud temple passed overhead, the striding temple backed out of the river. Nauvoo rotated 180 degrees in place, then set off after Salt Lake. Following her sister temple and the setting sun.

Bennie kept the speed as low as she could to ensure Nauvoo could keep pace. She wasn't in a hurry. There were plenty of rations left on board.

"You did good, Nauvoo," she whispered. "Now it's time to go home."

ABOUT THE AUTHOR

NATE LIVES with his wife and family in Ashland, VA. He is a data analyst and tech entrepreneur by day and a space magic writer by night. Follow him on Twitter @WriteNateWrite or check out his webpage: www.nategivens.com.

The Robot Baptism

Carl Duzett

*Except a man be born of water and of the Spirit, he cannot enter into
the kingdom of God.*
   --John 3:5

Abigail was both conspicuously old to have no children and conspicuously young to use a cane. And yet, for once, she wasn't the most conspicuous being to be walking the Salt Lake temple construction yard.

"Mind yourself, Caleb!" she snapped to her companion. While the whole temple yard was aware of Caleb, Abigail had found that he was less aware of them, and had nearly tromped on more than a few scrambling water boys.

To his credit, he halted immediately with a screech of pistons and a puff of chalkboard smoke from his boiler. The robot turned his steel face and gas lamp eyes to the small boy frozen in shock before him, and sounded an apologetic note from somewhere within his chassis.

"Quit gawking, Will!" Abigail said, rapping the boy's leg with her cane. "Or I'll tell Sister Clementine about this and she won't let you set foot in the yard until you're a high priest."

The boy scrambled to his feet, still staring at Caleb.

"Sorry, Mother," Will said, brushing off crumbs of dirt.

Abigail told herself she'd tended the boy enough as an infant that she'd earned the title, and let him scamper off to the stonecutters or whoever he was apprenticing with this week. She'd already told

Clementine the boy needed to be more focused, but that had gone as well as serving sour milk.

A high-pitched whistle rang from Caleb—a question.

"Yes, Caleb, back to work," she said. "They want us moving blocks again today, see if you'll overheat or if your tin arms will snap after doing it several days in a row."

Another puff of smoke, and Caleb's four legs pistoned again, carrying the automaton forward while Abigail hobbled behind. It was a blessing he didn't move too fast for her; although perhaps he knew she couldn't keep up, and moved more slowly on purpose? Abigail shook the thought from her head. Caleb's inventor had been quite clear that his Babbage engine brain could only process the most basic of concepts, such as direct instructions. And with no children of her own, Abigail was full of direct instructions and low on people to give them to—or so she imagined the decision-making had gone when the Brethren had decided who would mind the prototype.

A screech sounded and Abigail almost bumped into Caleb's backside. She staggered, rebalanced with her cane, and peered around his metal frame to see a seagull walking slowly in Caleb's path. She arched her brow; had she missed someone else yelling for him to stop, or had he done that on his own?

"Well, Caleb," she said, "you might be slow, but you are learning."

After another full day of laborious, specific instructions to Caleb on how to move enormous granite blocks around safely, Abigail sat on a bench and cleaned Caleb as he held dutifully still. The sun had plummeted just behind the highest point of the half-built temple, shining a vibrant orange light across Caleb as she wiped off the granite dust and dirt.

A man in a long leather coat stepped in front of their light. Abigail squinted with a scowl; the man's silhouette featured a top hat with goggles perched on the brim.

"You're two days late," she said.

Ives Billingsley smiled and patted Caleb on his metallic shoulder.

"One's not late as long as one is making progress, right Caleb?" Caleb looked up at his creator and sounded a weak whistle.

"You were supposed to be back from the Great Salt Lake two days ago," Abigail continued. "I can't be minding Caleb every day of the week."

Ives removed his hat and gave a half-bow of apology. "But he's served your people well, I presume?"

"He's an enormous distraction to all the workers." Abigail crossed her arms. "But he can lift anything we put in front of him, so long as we tell him clearly how. Nothing's broken, and he's never overheated."

Ives waved a hand in dismissal. "Of course he hasn't overheated. It's impossible with my design." He stepped back and examined Caleb, who stared back blankly. He ran a finger along Caleb's shoulder. "You've been keeping him clean?"

"Clean as a baby."

Ives' face darkened. "You haven't opened him up to clean the inside, have you?"

Abigail snorted. "How much time do you think we have? If you haven't noticed, Brother Billingsley, we are at the business of building Zion here."

Ives smiled. "Of course, my lady. It's just that his internal components are especially unique—what sets him apart from the half-rate automatons my colleagues have built out east. The engineering is both sensitive and, well, a trade secret."

Abigail used her cane to stand. "I am more than happy to avoid cleaning Caleb's insides so long as you return from your... excursions on the date agreed upon. I have my own matters to attend to in building Zion." She didn't know exactly what those matters were at the moment, but she pushed the thought aside.

Ives sighed. "Should your prophet find Caleb pleasing and purchase a full order of my automatons, I must have the technology ready. Trust that my work out by the lake is vital for the future of your Zion. Or in these parts, is 'faith' the term you prefer?"

Abigail turned and began her arduous walk home. "I put my faith in a God who doesn't show up two days late, Brother Billingsley."

Abigail came home just in time to help her sister-wives set the table and needle the children into their seats. Clementine had made a barley stew, and Agnes had baked some kind of Swedish crisp bread. Their shared husband, Edward, came down the stairs and sat at the head of the table. He'd had no beard when he and Abigail had first embarked west to Zion eight years ago, and he certainly hadn't had that belly, Abigail thought to herself as she ladled stew into the children's bowls. Of course, she hadn't had a cane, either.

Edward smiled at each of his children—Will, Harriet, and Edna, all Clementine's; and then at Owen, Agnes's little one, although in Abigail's estimation her second was due to burst forth in a matter of weeks. Then he smiled at Clementine, Agnes, and Abigail in turn. The smile seemed worn to her, but he'd probably had a long day of tiresome work.

He said a prayer over the food, and then the room filled with the noises of a large family eating.

"How is your education coming, children?" Edward asked between spoonfuls.

Clementine looked down at her daughters. "Yes, what did we learn today?"

"Letters!" Harriet said. Edna nodded solemnly as she nibbled at a piece of bread.

"A fine thing to learn," Edward said. "And you, Will? How goes the temple?"

Will opened his mouth, then looked at Abigail and closed it. "Umm..."

"You'll have to do better than 'umm,'" Edward said with a smirk. "Come, what do they have you doing now?"

"I, well..."

Abigail sighed. "He was with the stonecutters today, dear."

"Let him speak for himself," Clementine said from across the table, smiling in that sweetly combative way of hers.

Edward waved a hand. "No matter. Will, it's good you're learning to help build the temple. You work hard, and one day soon we'll all go be sealed there, become an eternal family."

Will nodded and shrunk into his seat.

"Will's too young to be running around the construction yard," Clementine said. "I wish you'd forbid him. He's not even baptized yet, and it's a dangerous place, with all those heavy stones and... strange machinery." She eyed Abigail.

Edward laughed. "Hah! Strange machinery indeed." He wiped his mouth. "How comes the automaton, Abigail? Brother Woodruff asked me about it today at the office."

"Caleb's operating fine," she said. "No overheating, obeys every instruction, and can even communicate a little bit."

"Caleb?" Clementine asked, her face the perfect picture of confusion. "It has a name?"

Abigail pursed her lips. Sometimes she wished she hadn't helped Edward pick his other wives.

"Yes, Sister, his inventor gave him the name Caleb," she said. "Speaking of whom, Brother Billingsley finally returned from the Great Salt Lake and I should be free again to help with the children."

Clementine smiled. "What a blessing."

After dinner, she and Clementine washed the dishes while Agnes readied the children for bed, coaching them in her broken English.

"I'll be talking with Edward tonight about Will," Clementine said as she rinsed a bowl. "He's much too young to be running around the construction."

Abigail sighed, grabbed the bowl and dried it with a rag. "I'm afraid I must pull rank on you tonight," she said. "I need to talk with him about Caleb so he can report back to Brother Woodruff."

"I believe that I outrank you by three, dear sister," Clementine said.

Abigail fumbled the bowl she was drying. "Excuse me?"

Clementine sighed and relaxed her shoulders. "I'm sorry, Abigail," she said, looking ahead. "Please forgive me."

"Of course," Abigail replied automatically. She turned to see Clementine scrubbing a bowl furiously. "Be careful with that. That was Edward's mother's. We brought it all the way—"

"Yes, I know, you and Edward brought it all the way here." She handed the soaking bowl to Abigail, who took it with an arched brow. "I may not have rode the wagon with him, but I still know. Thank you." With that, Clementine stormed away, leaving Abigail with the remaining dishes.

Abigail should've felt poorly for taking Clementine's night with Edward, but after Clementine's comment, she couldn't work her conscience up to the task. After finishing the dishes, she hobbled up to the main bedroom and prepared herself for bed.

A while later, Edward came into the room. "Clementine," he began. "Oh."

Abigail sighed, hoping that wasn't disappointment in Edward's voice. "I needed to speak with you tonight," she said. "If that's all right."

"Always," Edward said, and Abigail helped him undress and prepare for bed. She noted the small scars across his body, marks of their trek west eight years ago. He was a different man now; better in some ways, and... strange to her in others. Or was he much the same, and he just seemed different because she had less time with him?

"Is everything okay?" he asked.

"I'm fine," she said. "I just thought I'd report on Caleb, so you could tell Brother Woodruff."

Edward smirked. "Oh, that? Well, Brother Woodruff doesn't need a full report for another couple weeks. The brethren are willing to give it time to see how Caleb goes before they make a decision."

"Well, I think Caleb's probably too inefficient," she said. "He's slow, and is always almost stepping where he shouldn't, and requires someone to be telling him what to do all day."

Edward grunted. "And?"

"I think he's learning," she said. "He's supposed to have some limited Babbage machine in his head, so it's all just mechanical, but how can that be if he's learning?"

Edward frowned. "What are you saying?"

Abigail sighed. "I don't know, Edward. I don't know." She turned over in the bed. "Did you think Zion would be like this? That you'd have three wives, and I wouldn't have any children, and there'd be walking steel automatons?"

He chuckled and put his arm around her. "I knew it's where God wanted us to be. And that you'd be there. That was enough for me."

Abigail shifted closer to him. "Sometimes I think we still have a long ways to go in building Zion."

❦

IVES BILLINGSLEY DIDN'T STAY in the city for long; just a few days later, he announced that he desperately needed to return to his workshop at the Great Salt Lake, and that he wouldn't return until the following Monday.

"Why couldn't you have set up shop here?" Abigail demanded as Caleb looked on, his metal face swiveling between her and Ives as they spoke.

Ives bowed apologetically. "Sweet Sister Abigail, if I may use the term, everyone seems to love saying 'Brother' and 'Sister,' that would just simply be impossible for the work I need to do in preparation for constructing more machines like Caleb."

"What am I supposed to do with him on the Sabbath?" she asked.

Ives shrugged. "Keep building your temple?"

Abigail's eyes narrowed. "We keep the Sabbath day holy here, Brother Billingsley."

"Then take him to church, I suppose. Whatever it is you do. I'll be sure to return on Monday." And with that, he departed.

Abigail looked at Caleb, who looked back at her with his gaslamp eyes and sounded a low note. "Looks like we have another full week ahead of us, Caleb."

It was a second full week of giving explicit directions to Caleb, using his strength to move heavy granite blocks, even spotting oxen at times. The workers got over their initial discomfort with such a strange piece of machinery involving itself in their work, and came to appreciate his strength. Whenever they congratulated him on a job well done, Caleb whistled appreciatively.

Abigail found that as the week went on, she needed to guide and direct him less and less. She was able to give more general instructions, such as "Help Brother Nielsen with that block," and he was often able to complete the task without further direction.

One day, Abigail tripped on a mislaid stone and sprawled toward the ground but never met it as Caleb reached out and grabbed her first. She hung there in his grip, confused, as Caleb looked down at her, emitting a high-pitched whine.

"I'm fine, Caleb," she finally said. "Thank you." When Caleb didn't move, she continued, "Please put me down." Caleb gently set her on the ground, and she grabbed her cane and stood herself back up.

His general awareness had increased as well. It was rare that he was in danger anymore of stepping on a small animal or water boy; he often stopped to let others pass in front of him or around him. And he'd taken to nodding and pivoting his head in answer to yes or no questions.

At night, Abigail would clean Caleb's exterior and leave him in the equipment shed. It felt strange to leave him there, knowing he would simply look around at the other tools in the darkness all night. She wondered what he thought about. She certainly couldn't take him home with her; first of all, there was hardly any room.

Instead, she found herself asking Caleb during the workdays what kind of things he wanted to do, what his favorite task was. Getting clear answers was difficult, and she ended up going through a gauntlet of yes-or-no questions, but she was getting better at interpreting the sounds Caleb made.

One evening while scrubbing at a particularly stubborn patch of dirt on Caleb's back, Abigail accidentally sprung the opening to a panel. She considered closing it, remembering Ives' warning; but curiosity got the better of her, and she opened the panel door wide. Inside was a confusing array of spiraling metal tubes, thrumming with the energy of something coursing through them. A thick wave of heat emanated from inside Caleb's body, hitting her full in the face like a furnace. She recoiled and closed the door, surprised it was cool to the touch.

Whatever Ives wanted hidden might as well have stayed hidden; she didn't know nearly enough to understand how Caleb was built. In some ways she wished it had been some simple contraption, so she could see Caleb more as a machine, instead of as the complex being she was coming to know.

When Sunday came around, she didn't know what to do. She couldn't bring herself to leave him in the equipment shed for an entire day, but knew he wouldn't be welcome in an actual chapel. It was her responsibility to mind him, but it was also her responsibility to take the sacrament. She compromised and decided she'd take him with her to sacrament meeting, but keep him just outside the door to listen in.

Their arrival made for quite the reaction, not the least of which was Clementine's unbelieving glare from the pews. She instructed Caleb to stay just outside, and made her way down the aisles of onlookers and sat down right next to Edward. The services were otherwise normal, with a pair of talks on repentance and baptism respectively, save for the constant craning of the congregation's necks as they checked to verify that Abigail had, in fact, brought an automaton to church, and that it was still there, its metal face peering through the doorway.

Afterwards, Abigail walked Caleb back to his shed. He kept making the high-pitched whistle noise that was his questioning sound, but nothing Abigail said seemed to satisfy him, until she began asking her own questions.

"Caleb," she asked, "did you enjoy coming to church with me?"

Nod.

"Did you enjoy hearing the speakers?"

Nod.

"Did you like what they said?"

Pause, then nod.

"Would you like to come again?"

Pause, then nod. Then shaking of the head.

Abigail frowned. She'd learned a lot about communicating with Caleb, but he'd never contradicted himself before.

"Do you... want to do more than just come to church?"

Emphatic nod.

Abigail sighed. "You want to join with the rest of us inside."

Caleb paused, then nodded.

She bit her lip. "I'm sorry, Caleb, but you're... different from the rest of us. It would be difficult to get others to..." She shook her head. "You know what, Caleb? You want to learn more about the gospel? I can teach you."

As she still had her scriptures with her, Abigail spent that afternoon reading the Book of Mormon to Caleb, skipping through to find her favorite verses and explain them. Caleb occasionally interrupted with questioning sounds, and she did her best to try to explain what she thought he was asking.

Ives returned the following evening. Abigail hadn't cleaned Caleb yet; she was reading him more verses from the Book of Mormon, as she'd done during their breaks all that day.

"Are you reading to my invention?" Ives demanded as he pulled up, adjusting the goggles perched on his hat.

Abigail arched her brow. "I'm reading the scriptures to Caleb," she said. "He seems to have quite the liking for them."

Ives threw his hands up. "Well, wonderful. I bring my greatest invention to the land of the Mormons, and of course they try to convert it. I hope you don't think the next batch will be as pliable; I've had Caleb a long while, and his operations are a bit loose."

Abigail set down her scriptures. "How long have you had Caleb, Brother Billingsley?"

Ives frowned, his eyes up in his head as he did some quick math. "Well, I started working on him about eight, nine years ago. But this version..."

Abigail stood up. "That's all I needed to know, thank you. Have a nice day."

That night, she co-opted Agnes' time with Edward to discuss Caleb with him.

"He's learning the gospel," she said excitedly as they laid down for bed. "And I think he's understanding it. He was excited by what he learned at church on Sunday, and wanted to come back... or at least I think he did."

Edward let his head flop back on the pillow and he stared upwards and sighed. "Abigail, he's... not human. He's not a real person."

Abigail caught herself. "I know that," she said flatly. "It's just—"

"Then don't treat him like one. This was just supposed to be an assignment to see if the church wanted to order more automatons for building the temple, not some kind of conversion effort."

Abigail bit her tongue until it nearly bled. She didn't feel the pain.

"Look, I know it's been hard for you," Edward continued, his eyes closed. "Everything... all of it. I just don't think this machine is going to fill the void for you."

Abigail turned to face him. "What void?"

Edward opened his eyes and sat up, putting an arm around her. "The accident eight years ago, on the trail. Your injured leg, your broken... womb."

"You think that's why I'm doing this? I was *assigned* to Caleb, and I've a suspicion you even volunteered me for it to keep me busy."

Edward shook his head. "No, it was the brethren's idea. I'm just saying, be practical here. Caleb is a machine."

"He's more than that," Abigail said immediately. "He can learn, he can think, he wants things, he looks out for others—"

"Be that as it may," Edward continued. "I just don't want you to think Caleb is some kind of replacement for what you're missing. He's not yours, and there's a lot we don't know about Caleb or Mr. Billingsley. We don't even know what he's doing out at the Great Salt Lake, really. Just... don't put too much emotion into this."

Abigail reached for her cane at the side of the bed, ignored Edward's protests, and left the room in her nightgown to retire elsewhere.

∞

THE NEXT DAY, Abigail found Caleb yoked to the front of the quarry wagon.

"Brethren want to see if he's useful at the quarry," Brother Allred explained. "If he can help these quarry trips go any faster or more smoothly, that would be a great advantage."

"But that can take days," Abigail said.

Brother Allred looked from side to side. "Uh, exactly correct, Sister. We're testing his capabilities to see if we can make it take any less time."

Abigail blew out a heavy breath. "Well, I can have my things packed in—"

Brother Allred shook his head. "I'm sorry, but you can't come. The quarry is not a suitable place for a woman of your condition."

Abigail scowled. "My condition?"

Brother Allred pointed at her cane. "Very uneven ground there in the quarry. And it'll be good for Caleb to be with some of the other workers for a few days, see how he does getting direction from others."

Abigail frowned. It made sense. But that was most of the week he'd be gone, and she'd planned on reading more scriptures with him. She looked at the workers who were set up on the wagon, and only then did she see little Will in the back.

She pointed at him. "You're taking Will?"

Brother Allred shrugged. "He's already seen as much as he can at the temple site, and they could use an extra water boy at the quarry. Edward gave his blessing," he added.

"Good luck, Will," she said, waving. "You mind Caleb, you hear?"

Will nodded, and Abigail sighed. Clementine was going to be even worse this week.

The week was just as bad as Abigail expected. Dinners were showcases of Clementine's passive aggressive remarks, and she spent all day complaining about how young Will was and the unnecessary danger he was in, and how unfortunate it was that he had to spend all that time with a reckless, unsupervised *machine*. Even Agnes couldn't bear it, and she once muttered a litany in Swedish and excused herself from the room while Clementine was complaining.

Clementine and Abigail waited at the temple site together on Saturday afternoon, the day they were expected to return from the quarry.

"I am sorry, you know," Clementine said quietly as they waited together.

Abigail poked at the ground with her cane. "Sorry about what?"

Clementine waved at all of Abigail. "About what happened to you. How you can't have children."

Abigail was ready to stoke the flames of indignation when she saw that Clementine wasn't being condescending, but actually seemed sincere.

"I shouldn't have said what I did that day," Clementine continued. "I just... I'm so jealous sometimes."

Abigail's mouth fell open. "Jealous?"

Clementine nodded. "You were Edward's first wife. His... real wife, I suppose. His choice when he thought he'd only have one choice ever. You have so much history together—well, more than me, and certainly more than Agnes. I just wish I had that kind of connection with Edward sometimes."

Abigail put her arm around Clementine's shoulder. "I'm jealous of you every day. You've borne children, and get to raise them. They're wonderful children, and I know how happy they make Edward. And how happy you make Edward," she added.

Clementine smiled and patted Abigail's hand. "Thank you, sister."

Soon after, the quarry cart rolled into view. At its front was Caleb, looking much dirtier than before, pulling the whole thing by himself, even with enormous blocks of granite on board. As the cart came closer, Abigail could see that Caleb wasn't just dirty, but that there were dents and scratches all over his exterior.

Clementine and Abigail rushed to the cart as they began unloading. Will jumped off the back of the cart looking like he'd slept in mud all week, and Clementine gave him a fierce hug. Caleb made a sound of recognition as Abigail approached and strode over to her as soon as he was unyoked. From up close, the dents looked almost intentional, as though he'd been struck by a tool over and over again.

"Did they treat you right?" Abigail asked. Caleb looked up at her and made a mournful, low noise, and nodded his head slowly.

"Will!" Abigail called. Will broke from his mother's grasp and came to stand before Abigail. "I told you to mind Caleb. What happened here?"

Will looked back at Brother Allred and the other workers, who were busy managing the unloading of the enormous granite blocks. "They... made a game," Will said quietly. "To see how much Caleb could take if you told him to stay still."

Abigail breathed deeply. "And you... *let* them do this?"

"He's a child!" Clementine protested.

"I told them not to!" Will said. "Honest."

Abigail sighed. "Thank you, Will. This isn't your fault." She looked for Brother Allred, but he and the other workers were still moving the granite blocks. "Come on, Caleb. Let's try to clean you up."

Abigail scrubbed away at Caleb for hours. She couldn't fix the dents and scratches, but at least had him looking closer to normal otherwise. Caleb was silent throughout the whole process.

"Caleb," she asked, "do you understand what you did?"

He responded with a questioning whistle.

"You lied to me," she said. "I asked if they treated you well, and you lied."

Caleb hung his head.

"Lying is a sin," she continued. "It's one of the Ten Commandments, even. Do you remember what sin is?"

Caleb nodded.

"You need to repent of that," she added, trying to dig some encrusted mud out of a scratch. "To be truly clean of your sin."

Caleb made a series of noises that she couldn't quite string together. She shook her head, Caleb repeated the noises, and then indicated, with his arm, a descent, and then an ascension.

"Caleb, do you want to be baptized?"

He nodded.

⚜

EDWARD EMBRACED her as she came home. "I heard what happened at the quarry; Clementine told me all about it," he said. "I'm so sorry."

Abigail pulled from the embrace. "Doesn't matter; they're small men, with small understanding. Look, I need to talk to you about something else."

After they closed the door to the bedroom, Abigail sat down on the edge of the bed, and Edward sat next to her.

"Caleb wants to be baptized," she said quietly.

Edward didn't respond at first. Finally, he said, "Well."

"I know this seems strange to you," she said. "It's strange to me, too. But I really think he's a person. And this gospel is for everyone, right? So if he says he wants to get baptized, who are we to say no?"

Edward cleared his throat. "Well, baptisms have to be cleared by priesthood authority."

"I know."

"And even if he is a person, he's not eight years old, right?"

"He actually is," Abigail said. "Billingsley said he's had him for over eight years."

Edward frowned. "The point of baptism is to be cleansed of sins, and to make a covenant. Caleb is like... a tree, or an animal. Even if he's alive, he doesn't sin."

Abigail shook her head. "He lied to me this afternoon. He said the men didn't do anything to him, but Will knew the truth. He didn't want anyone else to get in trouble."

Edward scratched his beard. "Huh." He sighed. "I'm sorry for what I told you the other night. I shouldn't have been so dismissive. This is just..."

"It is strange," she said. "And maybe you were right. Maybe this is just me wanting to fill that void, to make up for what happened to me. But maybe there aren't mistakes. Maybe Zion is big enough to fit a crippled barren woman and an automaton."

Edward embraced her and shook his head. "Of course there is." He breathed deeply. "I'll do it tomorrow morning."

Abigail pulled back. "Do what? Talk to the brethren?"

He shook his head. "No, I'll perform the baptism. The brethren won't agree, and neither will the bishop, or anyone else, really. But if what you say is true, knowing what you know, we can't deny him membership in Zion."

Abigail looked at her husband. "Are you sure?"

He smiled wanly. "I'm sure."

Early the next morning, they stole to the temple site and greeted Caleb.

"This is my husband, Edward," Abigail explained. "He has the priesthood and is going to baptize you."

Caleb nodded and emitted a sound of appreciation.

Edward looked at Abigail. "Is that good?"

"He's grateful," she explained. "Look, we need to get going now before everyone wakes up. Come on, Caleb."

They hiked to a nearby creek that Edward suspected would be free from prying eyes. On the way, they explained the logistics to Caleb, and how they'd have to achieve immersion.

"He can go under the water, right?" Edward asked Abigail quietly.

"I should think so," she said. "He's fine in the rain."

A few early risers noted their travel down to the creek—after all, it was hard to hide a large automaton that spit smoke out its back— but they just seemed to be curious onlookers and didn't follow. Once they reached the edge of the creek, Edward changed into his whites and led Caleb into the stream. They waded deep to a point where Caleb could actually become completely immersed, and reiterated how Caleb would need to get on his knees and then bend backwards —which was something Abigail knew he could do.

Abigail watched from the bank as Caleb raised his right arm. But before he could begin, she heard noises behind her and turned. She'd been wrong; several people had followed them down to the creek in curiosity, and now the number was increasing as more people were waking up for the workday and wanted to see the reason for the growing gathering.

"Are you going to baptize that machine?" a woman yelled incredulously.

Edward gritted his teeth. Abigail knew he hadn't wanted an audience for this. Now the brethren would know.

"That's misuse of the holy priesthood of God!" said a man. A murmur of assent spread through the crowd.

A figure pushed to the front of the group. It was Clementine. Had she seen them get up early and was the one to gather everyone to stop the baptism?

"Be quiet," Clementine said to the group. "Caleb wants to be baptized. If God doesn't want him to be baptized, well then, that's up to Him. For myself, I don't see the point of getting between." This was followed by some murmurs, but at least no one was yelling anymore or rushing the creek to stop the baptism.

Abigail looked at Edward, who looked back at her and took a deep breath. He raised his right arm.

"Having been commissioned of Jesus Christ," he said, "I baptize you in the name of the Father, and of the Son, and of the Holy Ghost. Amen."

Caleb lowered his metal chassis into the creek, articulating his back so the water swallowed him completely. Edward tried to pull him back up, which of course did nothing. After a terrifying pause, Caleb sprang forth out of the water, standing upright once again, glistening. He turned toward Abigail and hooted a happy sound, and Abigail smiled. They'd actually made it happen; they'd really found a place for Caleb in Zion.

Caleb took a step towards her but then lurched and froze. Smoke started streaming from his boiler, and he sounded a low note of confusion. Edward stepped back from him as Abigail rushed towards him.

"You idiots!" yelled a familiar voice. "What have you done?"

Abigail turned to see Ives Billingsley charging through the crowd.

"He can't go underwater!" he yelled. "He's full of liquid sodium!"

Abigail froze, confused.

"It makes an exothermic—he's going to explode!" Ives explained, turning to the crowd. "Run!"

Caleb looked to Abigail and made a terrified metallic shriek as more smoke streamed from him. Edward was wading as fast as he could out of the creek, but he was still so close—

"I'm sorry," she yelled to Caleb. "I'm so sorry."

Caleb made a mournful low noise and covered his head with his arms. He looked at Edward, still so close to him, and began descending again into the water. Abigail knew she should run, that this wasn't safe, but she stayed stuck to the spot as she watched Caleb submerge himself to mute his own explosion. His metal turned red with heat even under the water. Then the creek erupted into a massive geyser, launching steaming pieces of machinery into the air in all directions. A piece of a leg landed in front of her, and she saw his head fly nearly straight up and land just on the edge of the creek.

More parts landed, still steaming with heat, warped and shredded from the explosion. The creek settled into a rippling foam, and the air stilled. Edward sat up from covering himself and came to Abigail, holding her as she wept.

THE BRETHREN DISCIPLINED EDWARD, which heaped even more humiliation upon the family. He kept his priesthood but was now seen by the whole church as the man who'd unworthily attempted to baptize a machine. Ives Billingsley was furious with Abigail and with the church entirely.

"That's why I was at the Great Salt Lake!" he shouted for emphasis as he and Abigail picked up parts of Caleb. "I'm processing the sodium from the lake for the cooling system! It would have been the future of automata!"

"You should have told me," Abigail said. "I didn't want him to explode either." She picked up Caleb's head from the shore, which was both surprisingly heavy and surprisingly intact.

"Bah," Ives said. "Eight years wasted."

"You mean he's gone, then?" Abigail asked. "There's no putting him back together?"

Ives frowned. "I don't know why you'd want to do that. The

parts are all in complete disrepair. And I'm sure his Babbage engine is completely destroyed—"

Abigail hefted Caleb's head and showed it to him. "It's in here, right?"

Ives stopped. "Well, it's possible..."

He stayed in Salt Lake only long enough to help Abigail put Caleb's parts back together. His frame was more warped and beat up than before, and he only had three working legs, which meant that he would hobble even more slowly. Abigail decided that would only make them a better pair. Finally, Ives installed a new liquid sodium cooling system inside, with a strict injunction against future immersion.

"He can stay here if he decides to," Ives said begrudgingly. "If his Babbage engine even still works. He's of no real use to me like this, and I already have the materials to build the next generation anyway."

Abigail thanked him profusely, and they fueled him and powered him up. Caleb's gaslamp eyes lit up, and he looked immediately at Abigail and made a hoot of recognition.

After months of tinkering with Caleb and pleas to the brethren, Caleb was finally allowed back at the temple site, where he was no longer strong enough to lift the same heavy blocks, but still wanted to do what he could to help.

She was embarrassed and even felt foolish at times, but she found she didn't regret it, as difficult as it had made everything. It had certainly been a memorable baptism. Abigail had forgotten something about baptism, she realized. There was the baptism by water, but also the baptism by fire.

She and Caleb hobbled toward the temple construction site, and looked up to where its spires might one day reach.

"Let's get to building Zion," she said, and Caleb whistled with agreement.

ABOUT THE AUTHOR

Carl Duzett is the newest Defense Against the Dark Arts professor at a private British institution of witchcraft and wizardry. He's looking forward to an uneventful first year, and many more to come! When he's not pulling aside headstrong-but-brave teenagers after class, Carl writes science fiction and fantasy. Find his half-baked thoughts at carlduzett.net, and his quarter-baked thoughts at twitter.com/cduzett.

Can Such Things Be?

Lee Allred

I. THE SECRET OF MACARGER'S GULCH

March 12, 1888
Macarger's Gulch Mine
Price City, Republic of Deseret

Mormon Apostle and First Vice President of the Republic of Deseret George Q. Cannon carefully stepped down from the steam buckboard into coal-dirty snow. The shift in weight caused the wagon to flex on its springs, shattering the thin rime of ice formed from the dense fog. Shattered ice tinkled like tiny wind chimes.

Cannon stamped his half-frozen feet in an attempt to warm up. The ride from Price's train depot to the mining camp had been a long, cold one. Even his graying beard had started to form its own rime of ice.

His eyes and throat burned. Much of the heavy fog was coal, thick enough in the air to taste. Chimney smoke from the town, coal dust from the mine, from the tailings, from the mountains of heaped coal waiting along the rail lines for shipment.

If he hadn't had an audience, he might have spat some of that acrid taste from his mouth, but an audience he did have.

Besides a second wagon of government agents, there were two local men. The locals came up to greet him: Jean Pierre Arceneaux, the local bishop, and Tom Williams, representing the mine. Both men carried lever-action repeating Ogden-Browning rifles. They looked dead on their feet. White bandages swaddled Williams' head above his bruised and cut face.

Of the miners themselves, none had shown up, although Cannon could feel them staring at him from the putative safety of their tarpaper shanties.

Cannon couldn't blame them, if only because of the bitter cold.

Blizzard of '88, they were calling it Back East. Out here in the West, folks' teeth were chattering too hard to call it anything but cold. Frosts early, crop season cut short, granaries emptying rapidly—much of Deseret would be a mite hungry by and by.

Cannon already had a long list of things to worry about. He didn't need *things* like what had happened added to that list as well, and yet—if he didn't take care of it, who would? Deseret had nobody else to do it.

Bishop Arceneaux stepped up and offered a hand in greeting. Cannon's own hands were so cold, he couldn't pull his glove off. He had to bite the finger of it to pull it free. Arceneaux pumped the apostle's hand in the usual over-vigorous Mormon handshake.

"Don't know whether to call you Elder Cannon, Brother Cannon, or Mr. Vice-President," the French convert said with a weary attempt at a smile. The man had his own list of local worries.

"Vice President will do," Cannon said. "This falls more under my wheelhouse in Home Office than my ecclesiastical duties."

"You'd rethink that, if you'd seen 'em," Williams muttered. Williams had a face like a squoze lemon and a voice with all the dulcet tones of a wood rasp. "Straight from the fiery pits of Hell they were—"

"Tom," Arceneaux gently chided his companion. "What happened was bad enough, no need to embellish it."

Williams fell into a sullen silence.

Behind Cannon, his government men clambered down from the stake-bed wagon. They shrugged on curious overalls, rubberized like gum boots.

"You received my cable?" Cannon asked.

Arceneaux nodded. "We left one of them lay so you could get a look at it like you wanted."

Williams eyed the government unloading ropes and tackle and huge canvas tarps. "More than a look, I'd wager." He jutted a chin at the stake-bed wagon with its large, flat bed. "Plan on hauling it back with you, ain'tcha?"

"Back to town in the wagon, then from there by train back to Salt Lake."

Williams snorted. "You're gonna need a bigger wagon."

"We'll see. If need be they can cut it up." Cannon's men had also brought a couple steam saws along. "Now where—?"

"The mine head." Arceneaux took Cannon by the elbow. "This way."

Cannon let himself be led. The fog was thick, the snow-packed ground treacherous, and Cannon knew he was not a young man anymore.

The walk to the mine head didn't take long. Arceneaux stopped next to the office shack that sat at the mouth of the mine. "Here." He pointed.

Arceneaux needn't have bothered.

Fog or no, nobody could miss the monstrous giant rattlesnake coiled and curved across the cold, cold snow.

A rattlesnake Mother Nature never conceived.

A hundred feet long if it was an inch. Its tail forked out into a brace of rattles, each the size of a nail keg. And as for the head...

Heads, plural.

The foul thing had two heads, spade shaped and fanged. Dear heaven, how they were fanged. Its poison must also have been an acid of some sort. The red-brown dirt under its jaws boiled and sizzled under the still-dripping venom.

A true cold-blooded reptile could never have functioned in this temperature, but the snake hadn't frozen to death, that was for sure. Scores of holes pockmarked the entire length of the corpse. The locals must have shot bullet after bullet into the creature in an attempt to bring it down.

Worst of all—worst because it proved beyond a shadow of a doubt what Cannon and Deseret faced here with these monsters—the snake's corpse had begun to revert back to its original form—a ribboned seam of black, bituminous coal.

Cannon toed it gingerly with his boot. "Hard to believe this thing was ever truly alive."

"Alive enough to kill six men," the dour-face Williams snapped.

Arceneaux sighed. "Easy, Tom."

To Cannon, the Frenchman said, "Williams was down with the men when it happened, you understand. He's still a little shaken."

Cannon smiled, a smile as cold as the frosted air. "Myself, I'd be *more* than merely 'shaken.' Please tell me what happened down there."

Williams gave Arceneaux a sideways glance, as if expecting another reprimand, then began to relate his tale. "Like your bishop said, I was down there with them Greeks—"

"Miners, Tom," Arceneaux gently chided. "Miners."

Like most mining towns in Deseret, Price was predominately Gentile. And, like most such towns, that caused friction. That the miners here happened to be mostly Greek and the local Mormons mostly French didn't help matters. Nor did the fact that Williams, judging from the interplay between the two locals, furnished much of that friction personally.

Williams sullenly continued. "Like I said, I was down there with the *miners*. They'd ran into a coal seam so rich, the way they described it, it didn't sound possible."

"Tom's a mining engineer," Arceneaux said, "So—"

"Will you let me tell it?" Williams snapped. "Yeah, mining engineer—as if that made them Greeks ever listen to me. So anyhows, old man Macarger, he's the mine owner, he sends me down to check things myself, see if them Greeks were making things up or lying or maybe just drunk."

Williams' voice trailed off as his gaze wandered over to the government spreading the rubberized tarp on the ground next to the monster. "You really gonna try shiftin' that thing, ain'tcha?"

"Please, Mr. Williams," Cannon said, "my time is limited. Pray continue. And remember, I'm more interested in snakes than ethnicities."

"Oh, snake. Right. Of course," Williams said. He rubbed the white bandage around his head. "Anyhows, so me and half of first shift, we're standing there at the rock face of number one shaft, staring at the richest coal seam I've ever seen—richest one in the entire world—when all of a sudden, bang, it happens!"

"Bang, *what* happened?" Cannon asked.

White breath curled in the cold as Williams struggled to find words to explain it. "Gonna sound crazy, I know, but that coal seam began shimmying and shaking, just like a live snake, and started shining brighter than the morning star."

He made an undulating motion with his hand. "And then all of a sudden like, that coal seam just slithered right out of the rock face. Right out. Just like a living snake. It *was* a living snake." His voiced faltered. "Fanged two of us before we could bat an eye."

Williams wiped his brow. Sweat dripped down his face and neck just remembering it. "Me and the Greeks, we hightail it for the surface, that thing just a slitherin' right behind us. Lost four more before we made it topside. I rang the alarm—" he pointed at the rusty steel triangle dangling on a rope tied to the eaves of the shack "— and grabbed me a rifle." He scuffed his foot in the snow. "Me an' the pit bosses, see, we sorta keep some rifles in the shack in case the miners ever have a difference of opinion with old man Macarger."

Cannon frowned. He spent a growing amount of his time trying to keep a lid on disputes between miners and mine owners. That they needed each other—and that Deseret needed them both—was something Cannon had had great difficulty in persuading them.

"Where is Mr. Macarger now, by the way?" Cannon asked.

Williams clammed up.

For once, Arceneaux looked as sour-faced as Williams. "Mr. Macarger felt the best way to handle the situation was to leave on the first train out of Price."

"Naw, that ain't it." Williams scowled. "Macarger didn't light out, he just hopped a train to San Francisco so as to bring in Chinamen for the mine." He hooked his thumb in the direction of the tarpaper shanties. "On account of them Greeks refusing to go back down."

"Mr. Macarger needn't have bothered," Cannon said. "Nobody's going back down. I'm ordering the mine dynamited in the interests of public safety."

Williams sucked air through his crooked teeth in a breathy near-whistle. Arceneaux's face blanched, then turned lemon-sour.

"Macarger's not going to like that much," Arceneaux said with clear understatement.

"I don't know *I* likes it much," Williams said. "Maybe Arceneaux here," he pointed at his companion, "he might not care. He's still set with his dry goods store down there in town and all, but me? Means *I'm* out a job—right alongside them Greeks."

"Might be a blessing in disguise, Tom," Arceneaux said. "The Fisk brothers have been hounding you to go work for them anyway. I'd rather take their money than Macarger's any day."

"They're down Emery way, though. Not sure I want to pull up stakes."

"Better stakes than snakes."

Williams grimaced. "You got that right."

Simpson, the lead government man, walked over to Cannon, his awkward rubber boots *scrunching* in the snow. "We're ready to start bundling it up, sir, any time you say."

"Just a few more minutes, Simpson," Cannon said.

Simpson shrugged. "Getting dark soon. I'd prefer doing this while we still have light, if you know what I mean."

Cannon knew what he meant. Strange things happened in the dark these days. "Just a few more minutes."

He turned back to the mining engineer. "Please continue, Mr. Williams. You just sounded the alarm and laid hands on a rifle—"

"Yeah, yeah," Williams said. "I'd stopped running and grabbed me my rifle. Them Greeks, though," he turned his head and spat in the snow, "they just kept running."

"That isn't fair, and you know it, Tom," Arceneaux said softly. "Most of them came back after they'd seen to their wives and kids. You know they did."

"Okay, so some of them did," Williams said. "Some of them even had the mother-wit to bring their own guns." He spat again. "Not like that did a whole lot of good. Here, let me show you."

Williams held up his repeating rifle. With a quick back-and-forth levering of its handle— *chak-chak*—Williams ejected a round. He caught the ejected round in his hand and held it out for view.

Just a common .40 caliber lead slug. *Lead.*

Williams fed the round back into the receiver.

"We musta pumped a hundred lead rounds into that thing," he said. "All that did was put a lot of fool holes in it. Lead didn't hurt it one bit. Not one iota." The rasp of his voice softened. "If it hadn't've been for your bishop here..."

Arceneaux shrugged. "I just happened to be in camp at the time. Besides my main store in town, I run a small cash store here in camp maybe one day a week." He pointed off in the fog where the cash store must lay.

He continued. "I heard the alarm, we all did. First I thought it was a cave in, but then I heard the fleeing miners shouting about a monster."

The Frenchman shrugged again in that Gallic way of his. "Then I remembered those crazy instructions the Brethren sent last month —" Arceneaux's face suddenly flushed, realizing who he was talking to.

One corner of Cannon's mouth turned up slightly. He'd written the letter himself. "Not so crazy sounding now, I'd wager."

"I'd fight any man who tried to say it was," Arceneaux said, with an exhausted attempt at a smile. "Anyway, I grabbed that carton of cartridges that came with the letter—"

"The copper-jacketed slugs," Williams put in.

"The copper ones, like Tom says," Arceneaux agreed. "Well, they seemed to do the trick."

Williams snorted. "'Seemed to do the trick.' Let me tell you, after me and the Greeks shootin' the barrels off our rifles with no effect, your Bishop here walks up and calmly as you please puts a single copper slug into that snake and it immediately keels over and dies."

Arceneaux's face clouded with the memory. "That's when—"

"That's when them others all slithered out," Williams finished. "The baby snakes." He snorted. "If you can call thirty-foot snakes 'babies.' Over a dozen of 'em."

"We counted fourteen of the smaller snakes later after it was all over," Arceneaux supplied.

"Evidently you stirred up a nest of them," Cannon said. That wasn't good. Wasn't good at all.

Williams spat. "You ain't foolin'! And them Greeks? When the smaller ones showed up, them Greeks all run off a *second* time."

"Georgiadis stayed."

"Okay, Georgie stayed," Williams admitted. "And maybe the Kokolakis kid, too."

"Did lead bullets have any effect on the smaller ones?" Cannon asked.

Both men shook their heads.

"Like spittin' into a furnace." Williams said. The mining engineer tapped the receiver of his rifle. "Now, I may be slow but I ain't stupid. I shucked out my lead bullets fast as I could lever and reloaded with those magic copper ones of yours. Got them two Greeks to do likewise. "

Williams shook, and not from the cold. "Twenty cartridges in a carton don't go all that far among four shooters, especially when you're so skeered you couldn't hit a barn door. W-we were down to our very last copper slug when we managed to put the last of them down."

Bishop Arceneaux laid a comforting hand on Williams's shoulder. "We did it, though. We killed them all."

He turned to Cannon. "But could you please tell me *what* we killed?"

Cannon looked at the two local men. Hurt, tired, but proud of what they'd done. And scared they'd have to do it all again.

Nests of them.

And neither the Brethren nor the government had the answers as to how such things could be—why the law of nature and reality were suddenly shifting and breaking.

He could, however, answer at least one thing.

"Coal Rattlers," Cannon said softly. "That's what we've taken to calling them."

"Taken to—? Sweet heaven above," Arceneaux breathed. "You mean this wasn't the only—"

Cannon shook his head. "Park City and Coalville confirmed. Rumors of other places."

The locals fell silent and stared at each other. The mountains around Price were lousy with coal mines.

The Apostle toed the snake again. "You burn those other snake corpses?"

Both men nodded.

"Just like you cabled," Williams said. "Ground's too cold to bury 'em, so we just threw 'em down an abandoned shaft. Poured kerosene and quicklime on 'em and set 'em ablaze. Burned them down to ashes, that did. They was mostly back to being coal again by then, anyways. They burnt up real nice."

"Good. But I'd like to make sure. Before we dynamite the mine, I want you to pour salt on those ashes."

"Salt?"

Cannon tilted his head in the direction of the wagons. "We brought some fifty-pound sacks with us. Seems to work like copper does on them." Salt taken from the Great Salt Lake, at least. "We don't know why, exactly."

Salting the very ground. Maybe those ancient Romans knew more than they put down in their histories. The evils of ancient Carthage never came back, that was for sure.

Arceneaux cleared his throat. Concern lined his face.

"President Cannon," he said, "we were lucky this time, but what do we do if there's more of them?"

Williams nodded. "Yeah, sure, maybe you're dynamiting *this* mine, but we got a heap load of other coal mines around here."

"Your letter—this policy of having the local ward leaders handle these things," Arceneaux said, "it won't work. Maybe once, maybe twice. Not in the long run. We're just plain folk, family men. We're not soldiers. We're not gunmen."

And that, Cannon knew, was a very good point.

Yet, who else did Deseret have?

Cannon had no answer.

II. THE REALM OF THE UNREAL

That evening
Deseret Pacific depot yard
Price City, Utah

The vice presidential train sat on the rail siding, its engine chuffing steam in great clouds of white that drifted upwards to join the lingering fog. Gas lamps lit the dark fog-shrouded night in fragile cones of white-wisped light.

George Q. Cannon stood on the end platform of his private saloon car watching the government men tie down that giant snake carcass to the flatbed hooked between his car and the caboose.

Engine, coal car, saloon, flatbed, caboose. All for just one person: him.

Cannon still felt a bunch of foolishness, an entire train just to haul him around, but he didn't begrudge the extravagance this time. Time had been of the essence.

The government men had tightly wrapped the snake in that rubberized tarp back at the mine head. They'd had to chop it into sections with their steam chainsaws after all. Now the men, finally out of their rubberized overalls, were lashing a second tarp over it, securing the cover tarp to the flatbed railcar.

Simpson, their leader, jumped the distance between flatbed and saloon.

Must be nice to be young.

"Just about got it secured, sir," Simpson said, white breath pluming with every word. The temperature must have dropped another ten degrees since they arrived back at the station. "Why don't you go inside and warm yourself up. You can't help anything by standing out here watching and fretting."

Cannon chuckled sourly. "I'm in your road, is that what you're trying to say?"

"I wouldn't say that, sir," Simpson said, "but the Good Lord provided Franklin stoves and warm railway cars for a reason."

"Alright, alright," Cannon sighed. "I'll go inside and get out of your hair."

Simpson sighed. "All due respect, Mr. Vice President, but you've said that before." Simpson opened the door into the railcar and gently chivvied Cannon into the car's small entry hallway, closing the door firmly behind them both.

After being in the bitter cold so long, the cherry warmth of the car near staggered him. Simpson began to peel layers of clothing off Cannon. His heavy outer jacket and the woolen muffler around his neck were rimed with ice.

Cannon pushed away Simpson's hands. "I'm not decrepit yet. Quite capable of removing my own coat."

Simpson smiled, ducked his head in a clumsy bow, and exited the car to resume supervising his men.

Cannon, coat and scarf over his arm, stepped into the car's main parlor.

The furnished compartment was much too ostentatious for Cannon's tastes. Gilt metal fixtures, red velvet wallpaper, overstuffed chairs—but that expected pomposity came with a Vice President's high office. Cannon preferred working while he traveled rather than luxuriating, so he'd had a desk dragged in as well.

The man who oversaw Vice Presidential security felt the same way about work. He'd had a second, smaller desk brought in.

He sat behind that second desk now, a withered shell of a man in a high-backed wheelchair writing with an almost clockwork precision.

The working surface of the desk was as Spartan-sparse as its owner: a pad of telegraph forms, a pen holder, an electric buzzer. Only one decorative item sat upon the desk, a wood carving of the Three Wise Monkeys, each monkey in turn covering eyes, ears, and mouth.

See no evil, hear no evil, speak no evil.

Without even looking up from his writing, the crippled man asked Cannon, "Simpson finally chuck you inside where you belong?"

"Your men are far too cheeky, Samuel." Cannon held his hands over the compartment's Franklin stove to warm them.

"My men are doers, not crawlers," Samuel Peck said, making one last scrawl on a pad of telegraph forms. He pressed an electric button on his desk, sounding a bell, and a fresh-faced young man—boy, really —popped in from one of the back compartments.

Peck tore the top sheet from the pad and gave it to his runner. "Get these code groups off," he snapped.

The young man immediately dashed out of the saloon. Seconds later his head streaked past the saloon's window as he headed for the train station's telegraph office at a dead run.

Peck set down his Waterman fountain pen. "Wanted to get that off before we pull out of the station. Confederates are stirring the pot again. Running guns to the Cleburnites this time."

Cannon winced. Deseret's southeastern region was rife with disgruntled Gentiles who thought the Mormon's northern half of New Mexico should really belong to the Texas Republic. What the Confederates had to gain from it, heaven knew.

"It never ends, does it?"

"No," said Peck. "It never does." Peck looked far, far older than his actual sixty years. Ravaged as much by the crushing strain his job as head of Deseret's intelligence service brought him as by his injuries.

The train's whistle blew a warning. It was ready to leave. Evidently Simpson's boys had finished tying down their tarp.

As if in echo, the steam kettle on the stove whistled, too. Peck spun his wheelchair around and rolled it from behind his desk over to the pot-bellied stove.

"Sit down, Mr. Vice President. I'll fix some chicory to warm us up."

Peck carried the kettle to a little side table where he spooned a roasted mixture of ground sugar beets, rye, and chicory root into a couple of mugs, then poured in the scalding water. He carried the cups in a lap tray over to where Cannon sat in his favorite overstuffed chair.

The train whistle blasted again, the engine started chuffing and puffing. The train slowly pulled out of the station.

Cannon spoon-stirred his hot drink. "Bishop Arceneaux is right, you know." He took a sip. The warmth felt good, even if it tasted nasty. "We can't just keep relying on the local congregations to handle these... *things*." The incidents were growing more frequent. And more deadly.

"No, you surely can't," Peck agreed, sipping his own chicory. "So, what do you plan to do?"

Cannon finished off the last of his drink. He'd never cottoned to the coffee substitute, but he'd drunk his share of it in winter. This winter, well, this winter Deseret ought to be using every sugar beet and grain of rye for *food*.

What to do, indeed.

Soldiers weren't the answer. The Nauvoo Legion didn't have enough troops to guard every coal mine, and even if they did, posting soldiers in the powder keg of a mining town wasn't a viable solution.

Only one path open that he could see.

"Hand it over to your Beehive 5," he told Peck. "Increase your appropriations, have you recruit up some—"

"No," Peck said.

"—more men—"

"No."

"— more teams—"

"*No.*"

Peck put aside his mug of chicory. "No, Mr. Vice President. It won't work."

The crippled man angrily wheeled his chair back around behind his desk. "That telegraph I just sent? Do you know what it says? Do you know what it means? It means the traitor Jim Bowie Cleburn won't live past the week. *I* sent that in a cable. *Me.*"

Cannon's mouth hung open. "You ordered a cold-blooded *assassination*—? That's *monstrous*."

"Yes, it is. And that's my point," Peck said.

He picked up the pen he'd written the telegraph with, then set it down again.

"Oh, I didn't order *my* men to kill him. Merely made it look like Cleburn was double-crossing the Rebs so they shoot him themselves. But he had to die one way or another to protect the Republic."

The clatter of the moving train filled the silence.

"As you say, 'monstrous,'" Peck said at last. "That's what this job is. That's what I am, that's what my men are."

He sighed. "You need men who fight monsters, Vice President. Not men who *are* monsters."

Cᴀɴɴᴏɴ ᴀʀᴏsᴇ from his chair and placed his hand over Peck's, patted it. "You're not a monster, my friend."

After another silence, Peck picked up the carving of the three monkeys. His finger ran along the carving's rightmost edge, jagged and knife-hacked.

"There used to be a fourth monkey," Peck said, "sitting with his hands in his lap. 'Do no evil.'"

He set the carving back down. "I keep him in my safe where his idealism won't be tainted."

Peck rolled his chair to the window. He watched the sandstone canyons roll by.

"The hardest battle," Peck whispered over the clatter of the rails, "the hardest battle I fight behind this desk is preserving my last shred of decency still doing the job this desk requires."

He spun his chair around. "And you want to give me *more* power? *More* authority? You know what happens when you give a man even just a *little* authority!"

Cannon knew all too well. "Then what should we do?"

"Not that. It's all my men can do not to think of our flesh-and-blood enemies as inhuman monsters. Training them to fight *actual* monsters... they soon won't make any distinction."

Cannon frowned. "I repeat, then—what should we do? These unnatural incidents grow in number and strength. Not just coal snakes but the Meadow revenants, the hungerers at Donner Pass, that lake creature high in the Uintahs..."

Peck wheeled back to his desk and took up his pen.

"What's needed is a new organization," he said. "One parallel to Beehive 5, one a mirror opposite of Beehive 5. Instead of spies—and, yes, assassins—composed of shining knights and dragon slayers instead."

On the back of a telegraph form Peck sketched out an organization table of sorts.

"You'll need scholars to master the old forgotten alchemies; engineers and scientists, the steam power and the sciences. Inventors to combine them both into new tools, new weapons. Field agents to wield them."

The pen nib came to a halt, then resumed writing one last line with a flourish.

"And to lead your new dragon slayers, a St. George."

He handed Cannon the piece of paper.

Cannon frowned.

The organizational structure was there in the chart, alright. But the neatly labeled boxes were empty. No names, no particulars, not even where or how to find them.

Even the organization's name had been left blank.

Only one box had been filled in. In the topmost box, signifying the head of this new bureau, Peck had penned in: "Our new St. George."

"And where shall I find this St. George?" He looked at Peck. "Where shall I find this other you?"

Peck leaned against the high wicker back of his chair. "Not me. My talent lies in rooting out dishonest men, not honest ones. But if and when you do find him, tell him I have a monkey for his brand new desk."

Cannon stared at the chart.

He'd start putting what he could in place, do all he could, but—it would all be meaningless without the right man at the top. Cannon knew in his gut he could comb the whole of Deseret and not find his St. George.

Some say the Lord will provide, but mostly what the Lord provided was two hands, a brain, and a strong back to pull the handcarts, to dig the irrigation ditches, to dig out the coal, to build the steam engines, to carve an independent Mormon nation out of a barren desert.

Cannon would do all he could, even if it was hopeless. For Deseret, for the men of the mines like Arceneaux and Williams and the Greeks. He'd do all he could, and maybe then the Lord would provide.

But if the Lord planned on providing, he'd better do it soon.

III. THE MOONLIT ROAD

April 5, 1888
Near Mount Shasta
Upper California, United States of America

Four newspapermen sat around the hunting cabin's roaring fireplace. The cheap booze and the cheap talk flowed freely. There was one from each of the Four Americas—Ramon Gallegos from Texas, William Shaw from Dixie, George W. Kent from the original United States, and drunken Barry Davis, a Jack Mormon from Deseret.

The four traveled with US President Grover Cleveland on his nationwide tour of a proposed Continental Park system that encompassed scenic sites of all four nations, but even the most determined scribbler could only write "Fat Man Looks at Local Scenery" so many times before ennui set in.

So here they were, the four of them, up in an old hunting cabin on the foot of the Shasta slope rather than down in the main lodge with presidents and potentates and their hangers-on.

The four newspapermen preferred it that way, to be honest. The company was better, after all, for they were with their own: a fifth reporter of the group and the second most newsworthy personage in the travelling caravan, the celebrated author, poet, and columnist Ambrose Bierce.

Bierce stood, elbow resting on the fireplace mantle, the center of their attention, warming himself as much in that adulatory glow as that of the fire's. Ambrose Bierce in the flesh was the same Ambrose Bierce of the penny postcards: a leonine head atop a leonine body.

An unruly mass of dark hair, a bristling moustache, a set of bushy brows perched above a Jovian glower. At rest or in animated conversation, Bierce's face inevitably took on a misanthropic mien of utter contempt for the human race.

In short, he looked like this year's model of a new Mark Twain.

In fact, one of the company mentioned that; Shaw, it was, from the *Picayune-Democrat* out of New Orleans. "Heard tell some folks say it's not only his looks you're trying for, you're trying to *be* the next Mark Twain."

Bierce only laughed, a hearty chuckle that tapered into an asthmatic wheeze. "Back when I was younger—and a bit more foolish —I once thought to myself, why not? Why not be another Mark Twain? Alas, I realized I lacked the most essential ingredient of a Mark Twain—a cracking good pseudonym."

He struck a lucifer against a fireplace brick and lit his cigar with it, a foul-smelling five-center. "Oh, I tried on every name I could think of in my attempt to come up with a good Twainish pseudonym. Even tried anagrams made out of my own name."

He puffed long and hard and blew out a greasy blue cloud of smoke. "Only anagram I could come up with that wasn't pure gibberish was 'Creameries Bob'."

The circle of newspapermen laughed, even the ones who'd heard it before.

"No, gentlemen, I could never be a Mark Twain—or even want to be one. And why's that you ask?"

Bierce hooked a thumb in his vest pocket. "Because Mr. Clemens has achieved his goal—fame and fortune. And, having achieved that modest goal, he has now settled back into a long, comfortable semi-somnambulance to await eventual expiry. A wait he affects with the least possible effort expended. I wish him and his porch swing well."

Bierce extracted the cigar from his mouth and examined its smoldering end as if it held the secrets of existence. "As for myself, I desire far, far more. I seek a cause worthy of my talents." He stubbed his cigar out with quick, angry stabs. "So far I haven't found it."

Reaching for his overcoat, for the night was windy and chill, he said, "And now if you gentlemen will excuse me for a moment, I must see a dog about a horse."

And with that, Ambrose Bierce stepped off stage and through the door of the cabin.

AWAY FROM THE CABIN, hidden in a copse of evergreens that Bierce made double sure was out of earshot, Ambrose Bierce, the great man, bent over double, hacking and wheezing, trying to draw in his breath in long, agonizing asthmatic gasps.

The cold, clear night air bit like burning daggers in his lungs.

Those infernal cigars. They'd be the death of him yet.

He checked the white cloth of the handkerchief he'd coughed into. No blood. No TB, at least. At least he was spared of that.

Somewhere in the struggle for breath, Bierce had shot out a hand against the rough bark of a tall pine for support. The crackled bark stabbed his palm. Astringent resins smeared his fingers.

He pushed himself away from the tree and stood on his own two feet.

He scooped up a handful of snow and washed as best he could his pitch-sticky hand.

The night wind soughed high in the trees. Bierce looked up at the sound and saw the glories of the night sky. The bright twinkling stars, the pale of the moon, the glow of the snow-capped cone of legend-shrouded Mt. Shasta.

For the mountain did glow.

Not just a reflection of the feeble, friable light of moon and stars, but a true glow—a glow blue-white and eerie, a glow that seemed to pulsate in time with his now-calm breath.

"Balderdash," he wheezed at the glow. "Poppycock."

A trick of the light. An aurora borealis. Or an undigested lump of potato, as Dickens might say.

But only a potato and no Marley, for the world as Bierce knew it held no chain-dragging ghosts or admonishing holly-wreathed spirits Yet To Come.

And no glowing mountains.

Breath regained, reality reimposed, Ambrose Bierce, the great man, stomped his way though the crusted snow back towards the hunting cabin.

That the mountain, as if not to be denied, started calling Bierce by name in the moan of the soughing night wind was something Bierce deliberately paid no mind.

WHEN BIERCE RETURNED, the cabin's candles, none too tall to begin with, had all guttered out. The only remaining light source lay in the flickering red flame of the fireplace.

The other reporters sat around it, their backs against fitful pools of shadow capering across the room. Savages huddled against the ancient terrors of the night. Children clustered around a campfire trading spooky tales. Middle-aged men picking apart the rumors and legends surrounding Mt. Shasta out of boredom and malice.

That last was the last thing Bierce wanted to discuss—that brooding mountain outside—but he was chilled to the bone and the lambent warmth of the fire too inviting to resist. He pulled up a chair and joined them.

Fat-bellied Kent of the *New York Telegraph-Sun* spoke of the old Klamath Indian legends, about the sacred mountain being home to both the mighty Spirit-Above-Ground and the Spirit-Below.

The southerner Shaw spoke in his characteristic drawl of dead men walking its slopes the way they do in the hoodoo camps of the Louisiana bayous.

The aristocratic Gallegos of the *Austin Star Courier* lectured them in that dismissive, high-and-mighty *hidalgo* tone of his. He spoke of the writings of modern so-called alchemists, of the Shasta mountain being the last abandoned outpost of sunken Lemuria, of it being a nexus of ley lines, lines of force from the unseen worlds rubbing up against our reality.

But Davis of Salt Lake's *Gentile Vedette* said nothing, only slowly and methodically consumed the last third of the bottle cradled in his tremoring hands. Yet it was Davis who turned to Bierce and asked, "And what does our i'lushtrush...illustriush...our eshteemed celebrity think on the matter?"

"I think you've had enough, friend," Bierce said with a knowing smile, and reached over and plucked the bottle from Davis.

Davis made a clumsy grab and snatched it back.

Gallegos laughed. That condescending patrician laugh of his. "Don't you know, Davis? Mr. Bierce, here, doesn't believe in such things. He is the world's leading agnostic."

"'Agnostic,'" Kent quoted, fingers clasped together atop his sizable paunch, "'is what an atheist calls himself in polite company.'"

Bierce reached in his pocket for another cigar. "Did I really say that? If not, I shall have to steal it and use it."

"But surely," Shaw said, "you cannot deny the veritable storm of recent strange events. Monstrous winged cuttlefish off the shores of your Massachusetts, your own Yankee army fighting off hordes of fishlike men in Kingsport!"

"I can and I do deny such things," Bierce said.

"But the affidavits, the photographs—great heavens, man! I *myself* have seen *zuvembie* shambling through the moonlit bayous!"

"After which, you sat down with them and shared Davis's bottle," scoffed Bierce.

Bierce rose from his chair and once again took center stage, leaning against the fireplace mantle, for he felt an oration coming on.

"As for photographs and affidavits," Bierce said, settling into his subject matter, "didn't that old fraud P.T. Barnum have plenty of both testifying to the veracity of his Cardiff Giant? Yet this one truth remains: a concrete statue is still only a concrete statue and will always remain but a concrete statue."

Bierce lit his cigar. He waved the sulfur-tipped match to extinction. "Oh, I don't deny we may have recently encountered heretofore unknown specimens of flora and fauna—this is still a vast, virgin continent, in the main, uncharted even— but to assign mere heretofore unknown cryptozoological specimens some supernatural or infernal attribute—this I do categorically deny."

Gallegos sniffed. "You Yankees! You don't believe in anything you can't jingle in your coin purse."

Bierce fixed upon him a haughty stare. "If by that you mean I admit only in the rational, the tangible, the provable, then you surmise correctly. We live in an age of science, gentlemen. With every turn of a locomotive's wheel, every revolution of its engine, we travel further down the track to rationality, leaving further and further behind the old ignorances and superstitions."

Davis looked up owlishly from his bottle. "You don't believe in God, then."

A long, blue cloud of cigar smoke streamed from Bierce's mouth. "I hold the question of God's existence in abeyance. Mortal senses cannot detect Him, who if He does exist, seems hell-bent on using His Omnipotence solely to hide from us."

Bierce held up his hand to quell the inevitable uproar.

"As for religion itself," he continued, "I need only point to Davis, here, to show the value of *that* flummery. Behold the fruits of dime-store prophets and do-it-yourself gold Bibles."

Davis set aside his bottle and made to stand. When he realized he couldn't, he clutched his bottle again. "My—my failings don't mean the Church isn't true." His voice lowered to near inaudibility. "Only means *I'm* not."

Bierce blew another cloud of smoke. "Hear how he phrases it? His church is 'true.' How can any form of Christianity be 'true,' predicated as it is, on untruth."

He swept his hand at the circle of men before him. "You all are newspapermen and a newspaperman is the greatest student of human nature this world has ever produced.

"It is our stock in trade to know the high and the might, the poor and the destitute. To tear the public masks off presidents and popes and ploughmen and expose what's underneath. Have you ever once —once—encountered a man who became his utter and exact opposite in the space of a single heartbeat like the supposed Saul of Tarsus on his road to Damascus? Can sinner become saint, persecutor become protector, all in the flash of a blinding epiphany? Can such things be?"

Bierce exhaled a wreath of smoke that swirled around his head.

"No, by thunder! They cannot! And your own lifetimes of experience tell you so. No such Saul—and thus no such Paul—ever could or ever did exist. That story is no more real than dead men walking the slopes of Shasta. No Saul ever traveled down any moonlit road."

Gallegos snorted. "It was broad daylight."

"See?" smiled Bierce. "The falsehood doesn't even make good fiction."

Silence fell over the cabin, the only sounds that of crackling pine logs burning.

Bierce lost himself in a creative reverie, composing in his mind the column he would write on tonight's discussion. He thus was only dimly aware of the scrape of Davis's chair against the floor as the man pushed back and stood.

The drunken Deseretan stepped over to the larder cupboard and uncorked a new bottle of hooch with his teeth. He brought the lip of the bottle to his mouth, then slowly lowered it and recorked the bottle.

It was that motion, so uncharacteristic of the man, of human nature, that caught Bierce's attention.

"You talk a lot, Bierce," Davis slurred, "but I don't see you doing anything to prove what you say."

Bierce took the cigar out of his mouth. "Eh? What's that? The drunk speaks?"

Davis swept his hand in the direction of the mountain outside. "I mean, here we are on the slopes of Mt. Shasta where from all accounts you can't take ten steps without running into the preternatural, and you can't be bothered to get up off your duff and take those ten steps to prove it or not."

Davis pointed the neck of the bottle at him like Gabriel's fiery sword. "You say such things do not exist. Well, walk up that mountain and prove it!"

Shaw chuckled. "He's got you there, Ambrose."

Bierce bristled, stung as much from an inferior—and a southerner—taking the liberty of addressing him by has Christian name as by Davis's drunken challenge.

He thought of pointing out the absurdity of trying to prove a negative, then realized the others would see it as cowardice.

Bierce threw the stub of his cigar in the fire. "Very well. I'll leave right now." Far from entrapping him, a hike up Shasta would put the perfect cap to his column.

Portly Kent struggled to his feet. "Now hold on, A. B.," he said, "it must be after midnight now. You can't go out in the snow and cold at night. Why, your lungs would never stand it."

Bierce shrugged on his heavy coat. "The devil take my lungs, sir, not that my lungs are any of your business. As for it being night, aren't those the normal business hours for ghosts and ghoulies?"

He gathered a few things from the hunting cabin, a few slices of cheese and some hardtack wrapped in a bandana, a canteen of water, a small knapsack to put them in, and a heavy hardwood walking stick.

He made Gallegos dig out the alchemist's book he carried and dutifully marked with an 'X' on his trail map the confluence of the dozens of supposed ley lines that intersected on Shasta.

Packed up and ready, Bierce stepped out of the cabin and into the moonlight. The four others followed him out.

"At least let us accompany you, Bierce," Shaw pleaded, shivering in the cold. "You can't go out there alone."

Bierce waved them off. "These things only seem to show

themselves if a man's alone. The supernatural must have a visceral dislike for corroborating witlessness."

Bierce settled his pack strap and gazed up the moonlit trail. "Adieu, gentlemen. Save a chair at breakfast for me."

The four reporters watched him round the first curve of the trail and disappear behind the snow-covered pines.

❦

AND THAT WAS the last the world ever saw of Ambrose Bierce.

Search parties the next day quickly found the spot on the map Bierce had marked. The spot turned out to be a small hollow ringed by lava boulders. They found his walking stick and knapsack neatly placed against the rock face.

Searchers swore that only one track of footsteps in the deep snow led into the hollow. None led out.

Afterwards, for years and years, reports came in that Bierce had been sighted here or sighted there: Bierce walking arm-in-arm with the Mormons' prophet on the grounds of their Temple Square; Bierce manning a steam harpoon aboard a whaler off Kingsport, Massachusetts; Bierce deep in the voodoo-ridden swamps of the Louisiana bayous; Bierce walking the moonlit roads of Appalachian coal country carrying bags of salt upon his shoulders.

These reports were all dismissed as testimony of cranks and crackpots.

No, Ambrose Bierce died that morning. However, the remains of his body had managed to vanish, one thing was certain: the man known as Ambrose Bierce died upon the slopes of Mount Shasta.

On that, even Ambrose Bierce could agree.

IV. POSTSCRIPT

April 6, 1888

Salt Lake City,
Republic of Deseret

George Q. Cannon sat straight up in bed, gasping for breath. A *skritch* of a match revealed not quite five in the morning on the hands of his bedside clock.

His wife Charlotte murmured, "George?"

"Go back to sleep, dear," he told her. "I'm just going into the office early. General Conference this weekend."

She murmured again and rolled over, back asleep before he finished speaking.

He stroked her long braided hair in apology. While perhaps not a lie, his words had been a prevarication. Work was not the reason he quickly dressed and climbed aboard his steam buckboard and motored it onto the dark, deserted streets of the city.

Cannon was the practical one of the Council. The doer, the organizer, the administrator. Let the Wilford Woodruffs of the Twelve dream their dreams. Cannon was the feet-on-the-ground one.

He didn't dream dreams.

But he'd awoken from one.

In truth, not a dream, though, a nightmare.

He dreamt he had been a monkey trapped inside an airless box, pounding and pounding on cold steel walls to get free, gasping for breath.

Cannon spent his drive deep in thought. When at last he slid his buckboard to the curb, he found he'd driven, not to his Church office on South Temple, but his Vice-President's office at Council Hall on First South.

Quickly climbing the stairs to his office, the first thing Cannon did was spin the dial on the heavy document safe in the corner.

There inside the cold steel walls sat Peck's fourth monkey statuette, given Cannon "for safe keeping," Peck had insisted. The little fellow still had his paws folded snugly in his lap. The bland expression carved on his face showed no sign of ever gasping for breath or desperately pounding to be free.

For no reason Cannon could think of, he took out the monkey and turned to place it on his desk.

That's when Cannon saw the stranger.

Shock white hair on a leonine head, white eyebrows, white moustache. The stranger's face somehow seemed to glow, and his facial features were slowly shifting as if a new face was settling into place.

The man wore a heavy coat and had snow upon his boots.

The stranger espied the one sheet of paper that never left Cannon's desk these days, the organizational chart Peck had scribbled that night on the train. Cannon had made no progress on fleshing it out.

"Quickly," the stranger said, "a pen."

Cannon handed him the one from his pocket.

Taking it, the stranger hastily began to fill in the chart. At the very top of the page, the stranger wrote "Correlation Department" and then proceeded to fill in the empty boxes. Precise names of agents to hire, precise names of scholars to recruit, precise items of equipment to design and build.

The stranger scribbled furiously, racing as if to finish before the glow about him faded, before the virtue had gone out of him and the vision of what he saw dimmed.

Finished at last, save the topmost box, the stranger paused. His newly shaped face had dimmed of all epiphanic glow.

He thought for a moment, then in the box where Peck had facetiously written "Our St. George" as leader of Deseret's new legions of dragon slayers, Ambrose Bierce—given at last a cause worthy of his talents—scratched that out and penned his New Name.

ABOUT THE AUTHOR

Lee Allred has sold dozens of short fiction stories to Asimov's Science Fiction Magazine, Pulphouse Magazine, Fiction River, and numerous anthologies. Lee also scripts comic books for Marvel and DC, including such titles as Fantastic Four, Batman Black and White, Batman '66, the DC Young Animals miniseries BUG! The Adventures of Forager, and most recently IDW Comic's Dick Tracy Dead or Alive.

"Can Such Things Be?" is set in the same fictive Mormon steampunk universe as his earlier story "Tracting Out Cthulhu" published in the previous Immortal Works volume All Made of Hinges. Lee is currently working on more Correlation Department tales. Lee currently resides on the beautiful Oregon Coast.

You can find him on Twitter at @lee_allred or on the web at www.leeallred.com.

Breaking O'er the Purple East

Justin Riley

I stood my ground before a triumvirate of steam-spewing, demoniacal beasts. Nerves steeled by an old battle-born proclivity, I hummed the familiar lines of the Reformer's Hymn, took in a deep breath of cold night air, and brought my Model 1855 Colt revolving carbine up to bear. Then, I aimed each .56 caliber bullet between a set of glowing red eyes, and shot them down, one-by-one.

A mighty fortress...

Click, BOOM!

...is our God,...

Click, BOOM!

A tower of strength...

Click, BOOM!

...ne'er failing.

Dove-like, the gun smoke drifted heavenward.

I was mournful that the percussive explosions from the short-barreled rifle may have awakened my neighbors and kin. But the good Lord be praised, it was only the middle of the night. There was no telling what kind of harm would have come to folks, especially young children, caught strolling up North Temple in their Sunday finery with three rampaging and flame-belching oxen running amok. For that matter, it was pure chance that I'd been working this late in the smithy getting things ready for Conference Sunday the next morning —an Easter one at that.

As an eerie silence settled over the street, the receding blast-echoes were accompanied only by the occasional drip of water falling from the thatched corner of the smithy roof into the collection barrel.

For the past three days, a deluge of Spring rains had poured down, turning the street into a fen of mud and excrement.

An involuntary shudder wracked my body as I realized that, in the rush of leaving my shop to find out what had been making such an infernal racket, I hadn't thought to throw anything over my leather apron and bare chest. I slapped my shoulders and shook some warmth into my limbs. Grateful for clear skies, I moved forward to look over the fallen corpses of the erstwhile-crazed oxen.

Jane Ellen, my fourteen-year-old daughter, knelt at the side of a fallen ox. Inquisitive as ever, she poked at its stomach with a spare rod of iron. My oldest child, she had been assisting me in the smithy when the unholy racket of the bellowing oxen sounded from without. Apparently, she had refused my command to stay put and had followed me outside. I shook my head, taking note to address her dogged resolution at a more convenient time.

The appalling affront of burning hair and rotten flesh filled my nostrils. Senses overwhelmed, my stomach threatened to turn, which caused me to bend over, hands-to-knees. The memories and horrors I'd witnessed in my fighting days as a seaman for the Royal Navy returned to the forefront of my memory. That was well before my conversion to the Mormon faith and subsequent immigration to the States. Nonetheless, it was a pestilent weakness I had been forced to suffer since.

My retching was interrupted by an enigmatic whirring of gears accompanied by the burst of a rush of flames that arose of a sudden from behind me. I stood up straight and turned to find one of the oxen miraculously reanimated, struggling to free itself from the marshy ground. The beast bellowed an awful and uncharacteristically lion-like roar toward me. I raised my carbine, and the final line of the hymn I'd been humming returned to calm my mind before I fired a second .56 bullet into its black-horned head.

Click, BOOM!

...And he shall reign for evermore.

After a few moments of struggle, the pitiable creature remained low.

I released my breath and offered a silent prayer of thanks to my dearly departed mother for teaching me the soul-securing songs of the Lord. Mother was a former governess and tutor to the Duke of Bridgewater's estate at Worsley. She had bestowed on me an educated and cultured upbringing in the land of my nativity—Little Leaver, near Bolton, Lancashire, England. Well, that in addition to an illegitimate claim to the British throne borne from a passionate dalliance she'd had with then Prince William IV, later the *Sailor King*.

I was christened John Spencer Haslam after my mother's people. Without a doting father, especially a royal one, I worked my way from the coal mines to the high seas. After the short-lived reign of my King father, I turned to the blacksmith trade. With those skills, I was later appointed to serve my fellow brothers and sisters as a wagon builder in the ever-expanding American territories. After nearly dying in the harsh winters of Far West, my young family and I led the last of the pioneer wagon trains and handcart companies heading toward Zion. Since then, I'd served as the chief blacksmith to the Church and a personal confidant of the Prophet.

"Father!" Jane Ellen called out, interrupting my reverie.

"Yes, Jane Ellen," I replied.

"You'll want to see this," she advised.

Wondering what had caught her attention, I turned to walk back to the place where she was conducting her field examination of the fallen ox.

"What have you found, Jane Ellen?" I solicited, still anxious from what we had just experienced. Soul weary, I used the butt of my carbine to help me sit on my heels.

"Look here," she instructed, pointing the rod of iron toward the well-placed bullet hole I had located in the center of the beast's forehead. "There's no bleeding!"

"Well, isn't that something," I commented, nonplussed. Like Jane

Ellen, the fact that there was no blood anywhere struck me as terribly odd.

I was no stranger to the circumstances of death. I'd witnessed bloodshed not only in my navy days but while fighting hostiles to our faith since joining the Saints and being forced from home-to-meager-home across the disconsolate plains. I'd even stood guard with some of Porter's boys over the bloodied bodies of Joseph and his dear brother, Hyrum, the very night of their murders at Carthage while men painted-up and dressed as Indians sought to mutilate their corpses.

Why isn't *it bleeding?* I wondered to myself.

Hoping this ox just an anomaly, I turned on my heels to look at the others. Sure enough, they weren't bleeding either. Despite my efforts, I was unable to come up with an immediate explanation for what I was seeing.

"And take a look at this..." Jane Ellen reached out to grasp and pull back a brittle and ashen flap of dry skin hanging from the beast's neck. To my alarm, it tore free, too easily, like a piece of painted papier-mâché, down along its throat to uncover its breast.

I sucked in my breath while taking in the abomination lying before me. I reached out with my own tremulous hand to tear away a large swath of the mottled hide from the creature's side just above its shoulder. It was apparent that the creature's skin had originally belonged to the animal. Somehow, it had been removed and reattached to cover up the alien viscera disguised within.

What kind of damnable blasphemy is this? I questioned.

Assuredly, someone had been playing at God. And although I suspected that I was wrong, I held hope that these were the only creatures of their kind. I resolved to get these things out of the public way before they were discovered by anyone else, and then find some answers.

I stood.

"Jane Ellen..."

"Yes, Father?" She turned her head to look up into my face while dropping her hand and the tip of the iron rod into the cold mud.

"Help me get these *things* inside. Then," I said, failing to stop a quaver that took over my voice. "Run as fast as you can to wake up Brother Brigham!"

◦§

WITH THE HELP of a make-shift sledge, we extricated the remarkably-lightweight carcasses and dragged them through the mud into the smithy. After we laid them in a line on their sides near the back, Jane Ellen ran out the door to get help. I pumped the bellows of the forge to stoke the fire and heat up the shop. I took off my apron, threw on a long-sleeved homespun shirt, and carried a lantern over to the table near the dead animals.

Nose plugged, I knelt by the oxen and continued to remove what number of layers of the reattached hides I could from their frames. I discovered that, except for their bleached-bone skulls and black horns, hidden beneath the leathered exterior of their bodies was nothing I'd ever seen in all my days as a blacksmith. Where bones should have been, there was a strata of shiny metal rods and girders held together at moveable joints with bolts and pins beyond our current industry. In between them was constructed a complex network of bronze gears, sinew-lined pulleys, and leather-drawn bellows in a variety of shapes and sizes. And at the literal heart of it, there had been placed a blast furnace the size of a breadbox covered in levers, valves, and glass-domed windows. Within the windows, I could behold the still-smoldering, coal-fueled fires within.

Eager to find out how this technology worked, I took hold of the large rods comprising one ox's foreleg to move them back-and-forth and up-and-down, to replicate the running and pawing locomotion of the once-enlivened animal. As I did so, the brazen gears along its side rotated and whirred. Pulleys wheeled and bellows opened and shut.

This caused the back leg on its opposite side to shadow the front's movement.

If I had not witnessed the fluidity with which the interconnected parts worked together, I would never have believed such art was possible. Although I was sure the animal was now truly dead, the fires within the glass domes of the blast furnace, and even those which substituted for its normally dull-brown eyes, were awakened to a bright red glow. Smoke shot from the ox's mouth as a yellowish fuel flowed up through a tube running along its neck and into its mouth from a large bladder attached between its joisted ribs.

So, that's how it can breathe fire!

It was alarming to me that someone had intentionally disturbed and reanimated the corpses of these animals. Who was to say that their inventor didn't just kill them only to take from them their mortal flesh?

And where are the rest of their bones?

These questions were left to grapple in my mind against a growing excitement for the possibilities this newfound machinery could have on the economy of my people. They were endless and most astonishing.

Are these otherworldly creatures ordained of God or somehow aligned with the Father of Lies, himself? Could they be a sign, or even a warning, from either?

I contemplated the various arguments for each side. But something gnawed at my memory as I began to recollect what I had been taught by my mother in my Sunday school studies as a child. One of John's revelations. Even a revelation concerning *resurrected* animals. In it, multitudes of resurrected beings, including animals both great and small, came together to praise the Messiah.

And I beheld, and I heard the voice of many angels round about the throne and the beasts and the elders: and the number of them was ten thousand times ten thousand, and thousands of thousands;

Saying with a loud voice, Worthy is the Lamb that was slain to receive power, and riches, and wisdom, and strength, and honour, and glory, and blessing...

And the four beasts *said, Amen.*

I couldn't argue away the fact that the maker of these mechanical oxen had, in his own way, truly brought them back to life. But mechanical beasts donned with the skins and skulls of their God-created forebears hardly fit within my religious concept of a resurrected being. Composed now of mostly insentient materials, I knew these creatures would not rise to sing or praise anything. I refused to acknowledge that what I had shot down in the street could be a sign of the Second Coming. Nevertheless, it gave me pause. I wanted to run and get as far away from the blasted creatures as I could.

Frazzled by these ill-bred omens, I nearly jumped out of my own skin as the smithy door creaked open. Thinking not to find Jane Ellen returned so quickly, I was startled when a deep voice called out from behind me, "Good evening, John Spencer!"

My heart took courage knowing to whom it belonged. I turned to find the Prophet, Brigham Young, leaning on his cane just inside the doorway. Behind him, a perspiring and flushed Jane Ellen panted at his heel.

To my astonishment, Brigham was dressed in his Sunday-best black suit, white collared shirt, and silk string tie. He stood at just over five feet tall and yet still managed to cut an imposing figure. But he wasn't called "The Lion of the Lord" for nothing. His voice and presence shook the souls of men, not to mention the very foundations of the earth. I knew from his attire that Jane Ellen must have found him awake. He would not have had time to be roused from his sleep and don such a formal array in the short time since she had been gone.

Despite my agitated state, I managed to bring forward a warm smile. "Good evening to you as well, Brother Brigham. I'm sorry to have bothered you at this late hour. Especially with tomorrow's Conference details in which to attend."

"Not at all, John Spencer." He waived off my apology with a reciprocated, yet tired-looking smile. Then he said with a look over his shoulder, "Jane Ellen caught up to me as I was returning home from an urgently called meeting with the Brethren."

Always timid in front of the Prophet, Jane Ellen gave us a small, brief nod of confirmation.

With the aid of his black cane, Brigham walked forward to clasp my hand.

"I was assured that you have something exceedingly important to share with me," he said. And although his tone was bright, a badgered concern lumbered across his furrowed brow.

"Of course, President. Just over here," I acknowledged.

Leaving Jane Ellen behind to tend to her work, I led Brother Brigham to the back of the shop where he came to a halting stop at my side when the three sprawling mechanized oxen came into view.

"Our Mighty God, there *are* more of them!" he exclaimed under his breath.

"What do you mean, President?" I turned to him. "More of *what*?"

He looked behind us to make sure Jane Ellen could not hear our conversation from where she worked near the doorway. Content, he cleared his throat, leaned toward me, and whispered, "Mechanical creatures—even ones raised from the *dead*!"

His declaration sent shivers down my arms and spine. Maybe my theory regarding the portent of these animals made newly alive had not been shot so far from center.

Marking my distress, Brigham proceeded to give me his account.

"Earlier this week, we received information that a number of oxen had disappeared from a farm near the southern end of the valley."

"Indians?" I was quick to enquire.

"That's who we suspected," he agreed. "What with the severe winter we experienced this past season, they may have needed the food. We sent several parties out to investigate and trace the herd.

But other than what we're now seeing here," he waved his cane over the oxen on the ground. "There hasn't been any sign of the missing oxen. No hoof prints leading outside the corrals or the valley. Nothing. It's like they were just spirited away."

I had to agree, that was truly unusual. Both settler and Indian alike understood the near-priceless value of livestock in these arid plainlands. Stealing such precious resources was an absolute crime.

Whoever did this should be hung from the tree until dead, I prejudged.

"And you think these to be some of those missing oxen?" I examined him.

"I suspect they are," he admitted. "In fact, that was the crux of the meeting I just held with the Brethren. Reports reached us this evening that fire-breathing oxen were harassing parts of the city. But thank the heavens, all of them were taken down without injury or incident.

"Because of the late hour, I had resolved to look in on the matter tomorrow afternoon following Conference services. I didn't think to find any of them here. I'm sure glad I agreed to see what Jane Ellen had been fussing about." He poked an ox in its metal shank with his black cane.

"Where were the other oxen found?" I asked.

"Well, let's see." He lowered his bearded chin to rest against his chest. "I believe three were discovered near the park on the west side of the city; three more, five blocks south of here along West Temple; and of course, another three oxen were dispatched near the cemetery." He looked back up to me.

Something he'd said about the number of oxen, and where they'd been discovered bothered me. I tried mapping out in my head the locations. With the realization that the cemetery lay to the *east* side of town, I was struck with a peculiar thought.

"So, the other three sets of oxen were found on different sides of the city—east, south, and west?" I asked.

Brigham nodded.

"And I shot these oxen down on North Temple." I pointed down at the beasts lying on the ground before us. "On the *north* side of the city."

"Yes, I believe that's true," Brother Brigham scratched his head, showing me that he hadn't made this connection before I had pointed it out.

"How many oxen were reported to have been lost earlier this week?" I asked.

"Oh, I think about a dozen," he answered. "Why do you ask?"

"You'll have to excuse my impertinence, President. But, don't you think it curious that the number of prodigal oxen once missing and now found, is *twelve*? Or that the skulls and hides of those very twelve oxen have now been discovered this evening in a miraculous state of mechanical reanimation set upon the city at the four points of the compass as if they had appeared from the *four quarters of the earth*?"

He forgave my discourteousness with a patient nod. "Yes, John Spencer, I do find that unsettling. But I must admit," he pulled at his beard, "there have been a lot of strange events as of late that may have occupied my thoughts."

"Like what, would you say?"

"For one," Brother Brigham rummaged in his coat pocket, "a bunch of these little *devils* showed up in the Lion House garden a few days ago."

After a brief, one-handed struggle with his pocket, Brigham managed to pull out a wadded handkerchief. With a grimace, he placed the pitiful mass in my hand.

Carefully, I unwrapped the soiled bundle. When the contents were finally unveiled, my wonder was accentuated by a gasp from behind me.

Apparently, Jane Ellen had sneaked up to eavesdrop on our private council. I looked down my nose in censure, but Jane Ellen ignored me as she stepped around Brigham to take the handkerchief and its burden from me into her own cupped hands.

"What is that thing?" I insisted.

"It's a *mechanical* frog!" she proclaimed. Then, as she did with her examination of the ox on the ground, she poked the bladder suspended between the bowed metal rods serving for its abdomen.

Except for a jeweler's attention to the exquisite detail of its finer parts, like the oxen, the *frog*'s creator had endowed it with life-simulating mechanisms. But in the case of this metal amphibian, there was no morbid exoskeleton or bone structure to prove that the animal once held claim to a former, swamp-filled life.

"They were menacing our seedlings," Brigham chimed in, shaking his head. "Luckily for me, what with all that rain we just received, they all began to spark, convulse, and then lay still."

Incredulous, I looked up to see if he was being earnest.

Noting my exasperation with a nod, he continued. "There has also been a rash of disease among the local livestock—a pestilence of boils—I've been told. Our fishermen complain they've found the river bottoms of the Jordan teeming with mosquitos in numbers never observed before. Not that it would matter anyway. There is a species of reddish-brown algae that has overgrown the surface waters that also appears to be killing our fish."

He shook his head, his short-lived joviality gone. "I have to confess, John Spencer," he sighed and pulled the fingers of his free hand through his gray hair, "sometimes I plead for the Lord to appear and redeem His Zion. I, for one, am ready to enjoy a paradisiacal glory!"

I didn't have anything to offer in consolation to my dear Prophet. The Lord had asked more of him that anyone still alive in leading the Saints to this desert valley where he'd orchestrated a remarkable work in establishing an ensign to the nations in the Rocky Mountains. It was too bad that work paled in comparison to the creations we were now studying.

Standing at my side, Jane Ellen turned the frog over in her hand to set it upright on its tiny metal legs. This caused its hinged-mouth to drop open, and something fell from out of the frog's mouth down to the dirt floor.

I bent over to pick it up and discovered a small packet wrapped in cowhide. I unloosed the binding and opened it up to find the feather of a red-tailed hawk hidden within. Wrapped around the quill of the feather were tiny wooden beads held fast with a string of catgut.

Jane Ellen bent over and opened the jaw of one of the oxen lying on the ground. With her small hand, she reached into its open mouth and pulled out a larger, but in every other way, similar leather packet. This packet had been attached to the hollowed-out roof of the poor creature's braincase and covered with an unusual film that had protected it from the fires that once issued from its snout. She produced two more packets from the skulls of its brothers.

She handed them to me. The packets found in the oxen yielded the brown and white feathers of a bald eagle, similarly adorned to that of the hawk feather found in the frog. Now, there was no doubt in my mind that the creator of these mechanical marvels had to be none other than one of our long-lost Lamanite brethren. And the revelation that the heathen nations were savvy to such incredible technology beyond anything we recognized was earth-shattering.

But why would they be sending these creatures to harass us? I had to ask myself. *How could they know anything of the scriptures or the signs of the Savior's return?*

Following Brigham's recitation of the abnormal happenings as of late, something tugged at my memory from biblical history. These events didn't sound much like those I'd originally considered to be precursors to the Second Coming even if the *return* of twelve oxen seemed comparable to some of the markers of the gathering of the twelve tribes. In spite of that, I couldn't get past the fact that they had to signify something familiar, yet terrible.

"Were the Brethren able to come to a consensus of why the local tribes might be behind all of this?" I asked.

"Not quite yet," he admitted. "Some have suggested that there could be any number of tribes upset with either the Church's settlement of their holy lands or simply with the territorial government. Brother Taylor even suggested that since the frogs were found on my property, maybe I might be the recipient of these spiteful messages."

"Is there any reason they may be upset with us?"

"Oh, it may be any number of reasons."

"Like what?" I asked.

"Well, tensions have been high between the southern tribes and settlers ever since soldiers of the territorial government captured a handful of squaws and their young children found gathering food near Manti. The Governor has refused to release them."

"Well," I offered. "I'm not sure what any of this means, but we have to figure it out before it gets any worse."

It was then that my ever-studious daughter, educated by my dear wife in the history of the Gospel and the holy scriptures, offered us the answer to the puzzle we'd been trying to solve all morning.

"Father," she interjected, pulling at my sleeve.

"Yes, Jane Ellen?" I asked, a little too tersely.

"I know what these signs are."

"And *what* could they possibly be?" I implored, trying to humor her.

"It's the curse of Moses—the plagues of Egypt!" she declared.

You could have bowled me over with those feathers. She was right. It made complete sense. Whichever tribe those squaws and children belonged to were sending us a biblical command. Let their people go. Until we did, I suspected the plagues would continue.

The clarity I now felt could be seen clearly in Brigham's eyes.

"If that is true John Spencer," he said, "then you know what we may expect to find next."

"Yes, I do, President. Fiery hail. A plague of darkness. The death of firstborn sons!"

A pang of sadness mixed with relief swept through me. I didn't need to fear the final plague. I had already buried my firstborn son in a shallow, frozen grave somewhere in the meridian of the punitive plains. Nonetheless, I was remiss that my reprieve would be unlike so many others, for I would not have to mark a lamb's blood above my own door against the destroying angel.

A grave frown settled on Brigham's mouth. The weight of our people, and the fate of the world as its divinely-called prophet, was clearly etched in every line of his aged face.

Unable to withstand his regard, I looked out the nearby window, half expecting to find the skies filled with a thunderstorm of fiery stones, or that an unnatural or swallowing darkness had settled in while we had been talking. But, to my delight, the subtle glow of dawn's illuminating light announced the arrival of the Easter morning. The night was far spent, and the approach of the Sabbath day filled me with great hope. My heart longed to sing out in praise the refrains of Parley's Hymn.

> The morning breaks, the shadows flee;
> Lo, Zion's standard is unfurled!
> The dawning of a brighter day,
> The dawning of a brighter day
> Majestic rises on the world.

I turned back to share my joy with Brother Brigham but failed to speak when a strange cacophony from outside the front door reached my ears.

President Young asked, "What's wrong John Spencer?"

"Can you hear that?" I asked him.

"Hear what, Father?" Jane Ellen placed her small hand on my arm, voice tremulous.

What I now took as the shouting of people and the pounding of feet grew louder.

"Wait here," I instructed.

I shouldered past Brigham and grabbed my rifle from off the table along with a handful of .56 shells. I loaded four, threw the bolt to open the smithy door, and ran out into the middle of the street. I found myself within a river of my fellow Saints, fleeing down the muddy street toward the temple site.

From amidst the maddening crowd, I grasped the suspenders of a young boy rushing past me.

"Let me go!" he demanded.

"What is going on?" I inquired.

With horror-filled eyes, he cried, "They've returned!"

I looked about me in the street but saw nothing but the bedlam to be amiss.

"*Who* has returned?"

He pointed east toward the mountains while trying to free himself from my grip. "The *crickets!*"

Even before looking, I knew he was wrong.

It's a plague of unhallowed locusts! I wanted to correct him.

Looking toward the east, I held witness to the arrival of the eighth plague—hordes of black, metallic locusts—swarming toward the city from the dawn-crested shadows of the Wasatch peaks.

If we didn't find those squaws and Indian children to set them free, we would soon meet our Maker.

For what I resolved not to be the last time, I brought the stock of my Model 1855 Colt revolving carbine up to my shoulder, pulled back the horned hammer, and began to hum to myself.

> Come with high and holy hymning;
> Chant our Lord's triumphant lay.
> Not one darksome cloud is dimming
> Yonder glorious morning ray,
> Breaking o'er the purple east,
> Symbol of our Easter feast.

ABOUT THE AUTHOR

A self-proclaimed Renaissance Man and Skald (Norse mythology expert and warrior-poet), Justin Riley has been reading voraciously and writing stories since his early, formative years. He's the author of the middle grade novel, The Runesongs (yep, Norse mythology and really cool Vikings). He received an honor from the SouthWest Writers Association for a short story, and is a practicing attorney and a published legal author. He lives in a house on the side of a mountain in a beautiful city called Bountiful with his amazing wife, three girls, a son, and their lazy English bulldog, named Odin. This is his first published work of speculative fiction and his first foray into the wonder-filled world of Steampunk.

Joined in Silence

John D. Payne

By flickering candlelight, Hans Henry skimmed over the neatly penned lyrics in peevish silence. Well, silence on his part. Snowy crickets chirped in the aspens outside, Julia Maria sang while the baby fussed in the bedroom, and a mouse scratched around somewhere under the floorboards.

And of course, there were the quiet whirs and clicks of gears turning inside the clockwork man sitting patiently on the other side of Hans Henry's kitchen table. As well it might be patient. Nobody had come knocking on its door in the middle of the night, interrupting its sleep. Not that it needed sleep.

Hans Henry stifled a yawn. "You want me to set this to music, yes?"

"Yes." The words that came out of the automaton's voice box had a cheery, pleasant tone. But a bit tinny, and a trifle muffled, or distant—as if from the bottom of a well. "If you please."

"It would please me," Hans Henry said, "to have this discussion in the daytime."

"I apologize for the inconvenience of the hour," it said, not for the first time. "But it is the only way to maintain anonymity." It lifted one heavy iron arm to gesture at its massive metal frame. "I am rather noticeable in the daytime."

"You are hard to ignore at any hour." He sighed and pushed the pages back across the table. "I don't understand. Why don't you just publish the verses yourself, Mr. Pilgrim?"

"Please," the mechanical man said. "Call me Brother Pilgrim."

Hans Henry smiled as politely as he could manage, which was a bit strained. He tried to show Christian hospitality to any guest that entered his home, but he was not accustomed to receiving them at this hour of the night. "As I said before, we call each other brother and sister because we are all children of the same Heavenly Father.""Exactly. You and I, and..." The automaton extended one shining metal arm to gesture toward the unseen mouse. "Every living thing. All part of the same divine plan. All created by the same loving Father."

Hans Henry folded his arms in irritation. "Well, if you will forgive me for speaking plain, I see more kinship between you and the stove than between you and me. Or even Brother Mouse."

The clockwork man turned to regard the Pennsylvania fireplace. "As both of us can thank the esteemed Doctor Franklin for our existence, I am proud to say that the stove and I are indeed kin. Hello, cousin. Thank you for warming this fine home and all of us."

The mouse scratched its assent.

"An ingenious contrivance, to be sure." Hans Henry stroked his goatee. "And like yourself, a creation of Man. Not of God."

The mechanical man's face remained fixed in a calm, mildly pleasant expression. Because that was its *only* expression. "True, my body was created by human beings. But so was yours. After a fashion."

Hans Henry shook his head vigorously. "You cannot compare the sacred act of procreation between man and wife to, to..." he spluttered with indignation, "factory workers assembling a machine, no matter how sophisticated."

"The process is very different, I will admit. The result, less so."

Hans Henry's face flushed with anger, and he did his best to tamp it down. "The infant child my darling wife is rocking to sleep–" *Back* to sleep, he did not add. Because *you* woke the baby, and all the rest of us, with your loud banging on the door, he did not add. "–is more than flesh and blood. That tiny body, that tabernacle of clay, is inhabited by an immortal spirit created by the very hand of God."

"As was my spirit."

"A gnomus is not a soul!"

A shocked silence followed his impassioned outburst. Shocked, and complete. No crickets this time. No mouse. Hans Henry did not remember rising to stand, but he was on his feet, hands curled into fists. Without a word he took his seat, face now red more with embarrassment than with anger. In the bedroom, the baby began to cry again.

"Perhaps not," said Mr. Pilgrim, still wearing the same faint smile. Because it was painted on. "But a gnomus is a spirit, and it is not created by the hand of man."

Hans Henry took a deep breath and made sure this time to keep his voice low. "But they are found by men. Found and captured and entombed in walking, talking metal coffins by alchemical engineers. In their natural state, they are simple earth spirits, mindlessly grubbing around in the dirt like..."

Once again he heard a faint scratching from underneath the floorboards.

"Like mice," he continued. "And like mice, or beetles, or worms, they are their own creatures, such as they are. If they are souls, then they are their *own* souls. Yours was stolen for you, not created."

"The book of Abraham," the machine monotoned, "teaches us that the spirits of men are not created, but organized from existing intelligences. Do you know what an intelligence is? What it looks like, where it is found? Neither do I, but I think it possible that one might be something not too different from a gnomus. Spirits of lava, perhaps, incubating in the stone womb of their mother earth."

"Blasphemy." Hans Henry shook his head.

"Speculation." The clockwork man raised its heavy iron shoulders in a facsimile of a shrug. "We may never be able to get close enough to the molten rock to know its inhabitants, if any there be. The same is true for the depths of the ocean, the heights of the skies. And above that, the vastness of space and uncountable stars. What unfathomable, fiery angels might dwell in those celestial spheres? Heaven only knows."

"Fiery angels?" Hans Henry muttered. "The Revelation of John teaches of an angel that fell into everlasting fire. And that terrible old dragon took a great many stars with him, as I recall."

"Yes. A third of the host of heaven, the scripture says."

Hans Henry tapped his fingers on the table. "You know that some say a gnomus is a fallen angel, escaped from its infernal prison in our planet's core. They say that Helvetic machines are the work of the devil and that any who employ them are accursed."

"Thankfully," the machine said, "the heresies of Captain Ludd have found little purchase among the Saints."

"Thanks to you, in no small part. What you write. What you teach." He leaned back and stroked his goatee. "And what you did. On the plains."

Pilgrim said nothing for a long moment. "I did only what any in the company would have done."

"*Would* have, but not *could* have." Julia Maria closed the bedroom door behind her slowly and gently, careful not to disturb the baby. "Hello, my love."

"Hello, my darling." Hans Henry stood and pulled out a chair for her.

She took the proffered seat with a grateful smile. And then frowned, cocking her head and squinting faintly in concentration. She pointed at the floor. "Do you hear that?"

He nodded. "A mouse. I will set out a trap tomorrow." He gave her hand a reassuring squeeze. "You were saying?"

She sighed. "Only that I hate to think what would have happened had we not had our very own steel Sampson with us when the juggernaut foundered."

Hans Henry snorted. "There were hundreds of us. We would have pulled it out of the river."

"With what? The ropes were in the cargo hold, and the hatch was underwater." She placed her hand over his in gentle remonstration. "No, if we had been on our own, we should surely have lost the juggernaut."

"A useful device, but replaceable," the machine said, without a touch of–*Ha!*– irony.

Julia Maria shook her head. "And in that desolate wilderness, where should we have found a replacement, Brother Pilgrim?"

At this appellation, the clockwork man's yellow eye-lights brightened. And a cantankerous grumble rose up in Hans Henry's throat, but he kept his peace.

The automaton's gaze fell to the floor, as if humbly embarrassed by the praise. Hans Henry wondered how long it had taken the mechanical man to observe and practice such a human behavior. "You are too kind, dear sister," it said.

"Indeed," Hans Henry muttered to himself.

"Not at all," Julia Maria said. "Rather, I am ashamed that I have never sought you out to thank you before."

"For the juggernaut?"

"For my husband."

Hans Henry stared at her in disbelief and opened his mouth to dispel this ridiculous notion, but his own wife interrupted him before he could form the words.

"If he–" she pointed to the mechanical man "–had not been there, would you not have rushed down into that river, my husband?"

As captain of the company, he would not have let any of the other men face a danger he had not faced himself, first.

"I would," he admitted.

"And would you not have been swept away in the current?"

"I would not."

"Drowned, then. Frozen. Or slipped in the mud and cracked your head on the iron walls of that monstrous juggernaut."

Hans Henry shook his head. "Perhaps, my love. Heaven only knows."

"Speculation," the mechanical man said, wearing a smug smile, an idiot's smile. The same smile it always wore. Because it had no more choice in the matter than a weathervane. Still, Hans Henry gave it a good glare.

"Tell me," the mother of his children said quietly, "that you would not have lost a toe in that icy river."

Hans Henry's eyebrows drew together in confusion and consternation. What was the point of this? And why was she taking the machine's side? It made no sense to him. As well thank a train or a boat. Better, since trains and boats were not pushing the country to the brink of a second civil war in which men–good men–would kill and die, fighting over the supposed rights of machines.

It was not that Julia Maria could not see this bigger picture. But for her, the immediate consideration was always to tend to the needs of those who the Lord had placed in her path, the strangers within their gates. It did not always make sense to him, but in the six years they had been married he could not think of a time he had 'safely trusted' in her heart's more charitable impulses and been sorry.

He took a deep breath. "I would have lost a toe."

With a smile and a squeeze of the hand for him, she turned to the clockwork man. "Then, good brother, I thank you for my husband's toes, if nothing else."

"You are welcome."

"Now, can you tell us why you are here?"

Mr. Pilgrim leaned forward and, with a kind of delicate reverence, plucked up the manuscript pages with his thick metal fingers and handed them to Julia Maria. "I wanted to share this with you. It is a song. Or poem, perhaps. The music is not yet written."

"A song? How wonderful!" Julia Maria eagerly devoured the pages. "I don't know if you knew this, but my husband is not just the city recorder. He's also an accomplished lyricist and composer, with several hymns in print in Europe and America."

"I did know that," the clockwork man confessed. "The company sang some of his hymns on our journey west. I found them quite moving. As did the rest of the company, as anyone could see. You have an amazing gift."

"How perfectly sweet," said Julia Maria, reaching across the table to pat the automaton's massive hand.

"Yes. Thank you, sir," Hans Henry said, a bit more stiffly than he intended. It was a kind sentiment, to be certain, but he wasn't sure how to take a compliment on music from a machine. "As you say, we all did our part."

"Yes, we *do*," said Julia Maria. "We do our part. Thank you, Brother Pilgrim, for sharing your song with us. We will certainly do whatever we can to help you with it."

"Will we?" said Hans Henry, turning to regard his wife with raised eyebrows.

"We will."

The automaton made a clanking sound somewhere inside its barrel chest, which almost resembled a man clearing his throat. "I should clear up a misconception. I did not–"

"Think of it!" she interrupted. "There are Helvetic machines built to play instruments in an orchestra, or to recite poems and speeches, but I have never heard of one that could create such works. Will this be the first?"

"No," said the clockwork man. "Because I did not write it. This was given to me by... a friend, who is shy."

Despite his best intentions, Hans Henry was unable to entirely contain his snort of derision.

"And what is that supposed to mean?" Julia Maria asked coolly. And when he made no reply, she raised her eyebrows in a wordless reiteration of the question.

So he answered. "Only that he has no friend."

Julia Maria's eyes opened wider in rebuke, and even the scratches of the mouse under the floorboards sounded accusatory, somehow.

"I do not mean to say that he has no friends at all," Hans Henry continued, reasonably. "Only that this song was not written by a friend."

"I assure you," Pilgrim said, "that the writer of this song is, indeed, a very old and dear friend. Oldest and dearest, perhaps."

"There is no friend so old as one's own dear self, I suppose." Hans Henry chuckled, but from the stony silence in the room, no one else seemed to find his little witticism amusing. With the possible exception of the crickets and the mouse.

"It's perfectly obvious. Look." He stabbed an accusing finger at the first verse. "The opening words are 'I'm a pilgrim.' He can't even be bothered to keep up the ruse all the way to the end of the first line."

"Perhaps because it is not a ruse," she said. "Brother Pilgrim, did you write this?"

"No."

Julia Maria shot Hans Henry a look that said this settled the matter completely as far as she was concerned.

Hans Henry shrugged. He found the denial unconvincing, but he supposed the metal man had his reasons. After all, he was something of a – *Ha! Ha!*– lightning rod in the territory, and perhaps he simply didn't want his politics to get in the way of the song's message.

"Tell me," he said, "about your friend. Why does he wish to remain..." He searched for the right word. "Underground, so to speak?"

"Indeed. Is he an automaton like yourself?"

"No." The clockwork man looked down at the floor rather than meeting Hans Henry's gaze. "But he has similar... challenges in terms of legal standing. For example, he would not be able to register a copyright."

"Then how would he secure his royalties?" Hans Henry asked.

"He would like you to have them, such as they may be. A gift to your growing family."

"And how does he know our family?" Hans Henry asked, at the same time that Julia Maria exclaimed, "How very generous!"

The mechanical man spread his hands. "The laborer is worthy of his hire. In hymn writing as in any other craft. My friend is proud of his words, and wants to ensure that the music you create will be a fitting complement."

Hans Henry nodded and leaned back in his chair, stroking his goatee. It would not be easy. The lyrics were bold, dramatic, unusual.

It would make for a very strange sort of hymn– more Lord Byron than Charles Wesley. Not at all his typical style.

"If anyone can do these words justice," Julia Maria said, "it will be my husband." With a look of love and pride, she took his hand and squeezed it fiercely. "He writes music for the very angels."

Hans Henry was not so sure, but he squeezed her hand back. "I will do my best."

"Thank you." With a series of clicks, creaks, and metallic groans, the mechanical man rose to his feet. "It is all we can ask."

In happy haste, Hans Henry rushed to open the door and usher their visitor out into the night. "Safe travels to you, Brother Pilgrim. And a good evening."

Evening? Closer to morning by now, surely. Perhaps because of the ungodly hour, the massive iron man made his way to the door with a surprising lack of noise, his footfalls no louder than a cat's. He was so quiet, in fact, that Hans Henry was able to hear the mouse scratching about under the floorboards again. Shocking boldness! Hans Henry would have expected such a small creature to be as shy as the automaton's unseen friend.

Lost in thought, he nearly bumped into the automaton, who had paused in the doorway. His blunt iron head rotating almost directly backward to face Julia Maria.

"There was one other thing my friend wanted me to mention to you."

"Yes?"

"Oatmeal," said the machine.

She looked as puzzled as Hans Henry felt.

"With butter on top." The machine did its imitation of a shrug again. "He says this is the only payment he desires in return for the work he has been doing. Oatmeal, with butter on top. He said you would know what that meant." He stepped out of the doorway and left.

"How very odd," Hans Henry muttered, closing the door. "Maybe it's all that talk earlier about a gnomus, but it almost sounds as if he were talking about an elf or spirit. I thought we had left all that pagan nonsense back in Denmark. How strange to hear it now from a mechanical man, of all people, don't you think...? He trailed off upon seeing her face–pale as a ghost's.

"My darling—" he began.

She let out a tiny squeak and fled to the bedroom, slamming the door behind her. At which sound, of course, the baby began to cry once more. And once more, Julia Maria began to sing, which–despite all the bizarre disturbances of the evening– brought a smile to his face. He did love to hear her sing.

Hans Henry thought about snuffing the candle and following her into the bedroom. It was late, and he was certainly more than ready to lay his weary bones down on the featherbed. But the manner of her departure left no doubt that his wife did not want to talk to him about buttered oatmeal and why it upset her. He would not press her. She would tell him when she was ready. Perhaps in the morning, in the light of a new day.

Meanwhile, Hans Henry had other things to occupy his attention. He had already started musing on a possible melody or two for the new hymn. And in the past he had found it best to act quickly when the inspiration was upon him.

So he fetched a few clean sheets of paper, along with ink, quill pen, and sander. Sitting down at the kitchen table, he placed Brother Pilgrim's manuscript where he could easily refer to it, and then drew quick, straight staves on the new pages, marking them with alternating treble and bass clefs.

Closing his eyes, he took a deep breath and shut out the few extraneous sounds remaining in the deepening night. Chirping crickets, scratching mice, even his sweet wife's lullaby, he gently pushed out of his awareness until he could hear nothing but the faint beginnings of a song to fit the words.

He picked up his quill and noted the melody as it emerged, hearing it in his mind in Julia Maria's clear soprano. On the second verse, her solo became a duet as he added a tenor part, which he actually sang out loud (not loud enough to keep anyone else awake, he hoped). And of course he needed a foundation for these chords, so he chuckled to himself and imagined the automaton joining them on the third verse to rumble out a bass line.

"A fine trio," Hans Henry murmured to himself, sprinkling a pinch of sand on the paper to blot the drying ink. "But we need a fourth to sing alto. Who shall it be? The baby?" He gently blew away the sand. "She's a coloratura, if anything."

A sudden scratch beneath the floorboards caught his attention, and he laughed. "Very well, Brother Mouse. I am not sure it is in your register, but since you are the only one to audition, the part is yours."

Picking up the quill again, he made his way through the staff one last time, marking down the alto part. And as he did, he could not help but picture an odd quartet—two pairs, really. Himself and his wife, standing close, holding hands. Behind them, the bulky iron form of the labor automaton, cradling a fuzzy little white mouse in his own powerful hands.

Each of them, one of God's wondrous creations, contributing a unique voice to the choir. All of them, together, united in perfect harmony, engaged in the act of creation themselves as they joined in song. A new, and beautiful song.

"I'm a pilgrim, I'm a stranger, cast upon the rocky shore..."

ABOUT THE AUTHOR

JOHN D. PAYNE grew up in the American Midwest, watching the lightning flash outside his window and imagining himself as everything from a leaf in the wind to the god of thunder. Today, he lives with his wife and family in the shadow of the Organ Mountains in New Mexico, where he imagines that with enough concentration he might be able to rustle up a little cloud cover for some shade.

His debut novel, The Crown and the Dragon, is now a major

motion picture produced by Arrowstorm Entertainment. A lover of all kinds of books, John also publishes short stories in various speculative fiction genres as well as literary fiction. His work can also be found in anthologies such as Dragon Writers, edited by Lisa Mangum, and Tides of Impossibility, edited by K.J. Russell and C. Stuart Hardwick.

For updates and exclusive content, visit: https://www.patreon.com/johndpayne.

The Reach of Mercy

Sean Smith

Midnight. The soft, almost silent tread of clothbound shoes stirred up tiny curtains of dust from the broken stones of the road. The rustle of leaves scattering over broken cobblestones split the night's silence, a dry scraping over rocks long since abandoned. The full moon hung low in the sky, illuminating the deserted countryside and the roadway that led to the squat shapes of decaying buildings, dark against the horizon.

Gaping windows with jagged teeth of glass looked out into the night. On some houses there still lingered black streaks of soot; others bore strange jagged marks where the wood had splintered as if struck from some force within. Here and there, shapeless piles of fallen timbers and stone lay where buildings had once stood. Then a sound, a low moaning like that of a wounded animal, stopped Jessimina as she crept through the deserted street.

She paused, her hand dropping to the butt of the pistol she carried at her side, cool metal and wood against her palm. She waited, listening, wondering if the sound would repeat itself. It hadn't lasted long enough for her to think she could pinpoint it with any accuracy. It seemed like it had come from the southeast, but she wasn't certain. She slowly counted to one hundred, but only heard the susurrus of the withered and brown leaves continuing unabated.

She resumed her walk, perhaps a bit more deliberate and cautious than before. The town she traversed no longer had a name and showed up on no survey maps; for a decade it had sat, empty and void of life, a sullen monument to one man's hubris in thinking he and he alone could reform the world. In that time, seemingly so far away now, it had been called Hope.

The final houses and buildings took a year to build, fueled by the determination of fifty or more families who had felt the words of Ammon Harris held prophetical vision. It had only been a mere five years after that for those who'd chosen to hear his words, for those who had given up everything for a different chance at salvation, to abandon the town in an exodus of fire and noise. They were, perhaps, the lucky ones, though they would forever bear the memory of that terrible night. They were only twenty-seven in number, the rest having been caught up in Ammon Harris' madness, fed into the great machine he'd built.

Those ten years felt like a lifetime, and memories had scarred over. None dared to investigate immediately, and over time the events at Hope had been relegated to the deeper recesses of things best left forgotten. The involvement of aethyr had prompted some initial inquiry among the Elders, but to all outward appearances, they considered the matter closed.

Those who had escaped scattered to various communities around Utah, rarely making their homes in the same place as anyone else who had followed Ammon, to avoid painful reminders of that time. "Ammon Harris" and "Hope" became rarely uttered words among them.

But there was value in what they knew. Jessimina had petitioned the Sisters to permit her to interview the survivors, to determine if there was cause to at least return to the ruined town and make sure that whatever hellish project Ammon Harris had been working on was truly gone.

It had taken several years and much pleading to even get a grudging nod of assent; it had taken even more time to seek out those survivors and gain their trust sufficiently to where they would be willing to relate what they had seen in the final days of Hope's existence.

She'd spoken with nearly all of the twenty-seven souls who'd managed to escape the horrors of that final night. Though there'd been a few things they hadn't revealed and moments where their stories defied reality, the weight of their words and their intensity had resonated with her. None had offered up a coherent explanation of what had happened to Ammon Harris. Each one—man, woman, and child—had maintained that Ammon was simply gone. That there was nothing more to it than that. That he had found his own grace within the machine he'd created.

She, and many others, suspected that the survivors had enacted their own brand of justice, and their own penances had reflected that, but without other witnesses, and in part because of the crimes of Ammon himself, there had been nothing to prove their stories otherwise.

One among them had barely spoken, though—Ammon's only son, Parley, whose fifteen-year-old eyes were darting and haunted, as if at any moment he expected to be snatched away by the hand of some dark force. He steadfastly resisted any and all attempts to elicit information about his father and what had happened. It was for him she'd solidified her own determination to uncover the truth of Ammon's misguided dream of Hope.

Over that time, other obligations had intervened, though, and she'd had to do what she could in-between her other duties which had taken her far afield over the past decade. But upon her recent return from a mission to the East Coast, she found that Parley had left Pahreah like a man possessed, or a man fleeing demons he could no longer grapple with. The years had not been kind to Parley, who'd slipped into drink and had been barred from fellowship several times already, just barely managing to meet his conditions for penance before falling back into the same black pit as before.

Right before that, he'd been teetotaling for months, she was told, and his moods and passions were even more unpredictable, so much so that those around him would have preferred him to seek the devil in the bottle once more. One afternoon he'd simply stood and announced he was to seek a greater penance, one that would redeem him. "A baptism in the fires of heaven," he'd proclaimed. And he'd gathered some supplies, his rifle, and his horse and rode off in the same fateful direction his father had gone, years before.

There'd been no other choice at hearing this news. After taking a night's rest, she set off to find Parley and hopefully catch him before he made it back to the town that had plagued every moment of his life since. With nearly a week's lead on her, though, she knew she wouldn't arrive before he did, even had she pressed her own horse to the limits of its endurance. So she made her way steadily toward where she believed Parley was headed, taking care to watch for any changes in his trail.

And now, here she stood, making her way quietly through what seemed to be a peaceful, if disconcertingly empty, town that had fallen on hard times, seeking answers to fill in the gaps of what had happened, and bring some peace to everyone who had known or followed Ammon Harris to a promised land of Hope.

She had to. She felt an obligation; after all, Parley was her only brother, and Ammon Harris had been her father.

⚬

THE DIRTY AND nearly naked figure on the floor writhed in almost silent agony as the memories took hold. *Another seven went in, unsuspecting—a man, two women, and four children of varying ages, all dressed in white cotton shifts, unsullied by any other use. They seemed familiar, but there was no longer any reason to pay attention to the faces and names. It didn't matter. The noise and light always ended with the same result—an emptiness in the chamber, devoid of any remnants of those who had entered, and the ever-increasing internal glow of the machine from within, a deepening of the colors in the fasbra latticework surrounding the machine and chamber.*

There had been promises. He didn't know if those promises had been a mistake. But all who had passed into that chamber had done so certain in the knowledge they would be closer to salvation than anyone else, that the transformation from the mortal to the celestial simply required passage through this portal and a firm belief that what they'd been told was true.

He still hoped it was.

Ammon Harris had been a stern man, unrelenting in his beliefs. He had ambition and was quick to seize any opportunity to make something more of himself. But time and again he'd been passed over, deemed "of insufficient temperament" to serve the Church in ways he believed he was best suited. His bitterness knew no boundaries.

His children lived and suffered his bitterness. They had borne the brunt of his wrath, the fiery eyes filled with madness every time he raised the wooden rod, as thick as his own fleshy thumb, the rod he called Charity—and who would withhold charity from his own children? Not he, he swore. No, the children of Ammon Harris would be humble, would be contrite, and then they could join him in his personal kingdom of glory.

He'd searched for answers, some way to move himself closer to the exaltation he so craved. And he had found it, he thought, in the newly discovered aethyr, a source of energy, a power none understood but none could deny its transformative essence.

As aethyr slowly broke down the tenets of faith and belief across the world, as it powered more and more devices and homes, little consideration had been given to its nature initially. It had been the Revelationists who'd given Ammon the first clue. There was something about aethyr that pulled at the soul, that felt different than any other source of power previously.

But their approach had seemed foolish to Ammon. Breaking fellowship with the rest of the Church had been their first mistake, he felt. It was better to operate within the given structures that already existed.

Or so he thought. The Elders believed differently about the

matter, and had forbade any further experimentation or interaction with aethyr for any purpose other than to provide power to the growing towns and cities. But he was determined. He was certain the Elders had their own investigations going on, but he wasn't able to find anything out.

Ammon's skills as a craftsman, though, served him in this instance. He'd spent his entire life working with metals, an artist who was often in demand. He began experimenting with fasbra, the phosphorus and bronze alloy used to contain and direct aethyr, as a new way to express his art.

And as a way to direct his own studies into the strange nature of aethyr. The Elders suspected what he was doing, but he fulfilled all of his contracts and, for several years, did nothing they could act upon.

In his basement workshop, though, on the edge of Pahreah, he'd found something and made his move.

☙

JESSIMINA HAD PREPARED herself for the worst—Parley's struggle with the demon of drink was leading to only one outcome. She just hoped he had not taken matters into his own hands.

She should have traveled to the site of her father's folly and sin long before this; perhaps then Parley wouldn't have taken it upon himself to do so now. But her duties had left little time, if any, to devote attention to her father's transgressions. There was still so much to be learned, and perhaps feared, about the effect aethyr was having on the Church and, more compellingly, society at large. It was no longer something that could be ignored.

She had only been newly come to her endowment when her father had left; since then, the Sisters had dispatched her and others to places around the States to listen, to see, to gather whatever they could on this mysterious source of energy. The apostasy of her father, coupled with other incidents involving those who had gone astray from the Church's teachings, had lent impetus to the Sisters' mission.

Besides, the Elders had considered the matter of Ammon Harris as closed—to their knowledge, the apostate had not survived that fateful July night, and his teachings had not arisen elsewhere, so what cause was there for further concern? The town of Hope was an abandoned shell; no one from the Church would willingly set foot there.

She had thought she'd be the first, but she now trailed in the footsteps of her younger brother. She knew her father's house still stood in the town, though damaged and likely in a greater state of disrepair. Those who had fled had set fires in the town but none had lingered to see the results of their handiwork, fearing, perhaps, to share some similar fate as to that of the wife of Lot. Reports from gentile wanderers, though, had maintained there were sections of the town that had survived, including a large building in the center which made anyone approaching it uneasy. Beyond that, she did not know if his machine had succumbed to the passage of time or if it had somehow avoided that fate, but the eerie feelings lingering around the town suggested it might have survived.

Still, those who had fled there a decade ago maintained they had buried the machine to where none could reach it. They had feared to destroy it themselves—its terrible and delicate beauty had stayed their hands and hammers. The pulsing glow it gave off, too, made them stop, for they didn't know what the release of the aethyric energy contained within might do.

None of the wanderers had entered the town proper over the years, skirting its edges. They'd observed that even animals shunned its periphery, unwilling to approach more closely. So Jess was confident that anything still there remained undisturbed except by time and the elements.

And now her brother had presumably crossed that threshold, passing over the streets she now trod, whipping up the dust and dirt that had settled in over a decade's time.

She just hoped he hadn't stirred up anything else.

⚬⚬

FINGERNAILS DUG INTO DIRT, finding stone beneath. The nails themselves were worn down by the repeated motions, and the fingertips were slowly beginning to bloody.

He still tried to avoid looking at the faces—especially after that first time he'd taken a moment to look more closely.

He'd always watched the looks of rapture and ecstasy as they had entered the chamber, watching from his hidden perch on the other side. The switch was thrown, the click reverberated, and then only the hum of the machine remained.

This time, he'd watched those inside the chamber as the switch made contact. The look of expected ecstasy was instead a silent expression of horror, dissolving into a golden light that left nothing in its wake.

⚬⚬

"YOU DARE DEFY *ME*, GIRL?" Her father's voice roared in her ears.

"I told you, I told you time and again. You. Are. Not. Worthy." He spat each word out in disgust as he looked Jessimina over, newly clad in the grey and green of her chosen calling, the Sisters of Heaven. "AND," his voice rose to a furious pitch, "It is nothing more than *obscene* for a girl to wear such things."

He reached out toward where Charity, the wooden symbol of his household rule, rested against the wall nearest his desk. "I shall make you understand as you must, that my word here is as law and you defy me at the risk of your very soul!"

His long fingers pulled the leather-wound end that served as his grip toward him, as Jessimina took a step back. She had known he'd disapprove, but she was an adult, a woman already married, and no longer subject to her father's whims.

"Father, is everything ok?" The door opened, and her younger brother, Parley, walked in, his nine-year-old eyes wide from hearing his father's loud voice resonate through the door to the study and out into the long hallway. He seemed surprised to see his older sister here; he apparently hadn't known she'd come home to visit this day.

"Bear witness, boy. Bear witness to the calumny that is your sister and your own fate should you fail to believe in your father, to heed his words." He raised the rod, expecting Jessimina to submit, as she had done for years as a child, to receive the punishment her father felt she deserved.

She simply shook her head. "No Father. This is where it ends." She closed her eyes briefly to shut out the livid red face that stared at her, uncomprehending, took a breath, and strode out of the room.

She almost turned back when she heard the wailing cries of her brother, but she knew there was little she could do. Under his roof, her father was lord and master of all, whether she agreed with it or not. And she could do little to bring Parley out from that house. She could only pray her father's rage would subside or that Parley would manage to play the role her father expected until he reached his majority and could make his own path.

She also prayed that today did signify the end of things between her and her father. She had her husband and her own children yet to come; surely there would eventually be a reckoning or a reconciliation. Such things were always part of the Lord's plan, were they not?

∞

FINDING her father's house really hadn't been that difficult—situated in the center of the town, it loomed over the rest of the buildings like a sharply upraised finger of warning to all those around. Hundreds of feet beyond it, she could see the rising swell of the hill where his workshop was said to be located, its entrance blocked by a dynamite-induced rockfall. As the reports had said, the house was damaged, but so much was still intact that it almost seemed like someone could just move back into it with little effort at all.

Jessimina shuddered. She wasn't sure what she might find here, but she hoped at least it would be her brother. The wind and light rain of a few nights ago had erased any signs he might have left in coming to this place, but where else might he have gone?

As she approached the building, she could feel something deep in the pit of her stomach, an uneasy sensation she'd expected to feel much further out, at least based on what others had said about the town over the years. It didn't quite make her nauseated, but heightened her senses to where she was acutely aware of her own breathing, the small pops of muscle as she moved, the grinding of bone over joints. It was disconcerting, but she pressed forward toward the front door, which hung partly off of its frame at the top of a series of broken white steps.

Inside, the feeling grew stronger, but not overwhelming. From the pack at her side, she pulled out one of the Thyrlumens she'd bought during her time out east. Far more dependable than a lantern, and requiring no other fuel than drawing aethyr from wherever it came from, the small tubular devices had started to proliferate in places like New York and Boston, and were slowly working their way out west.

The tight, focused beam revealed dust and dirt strewn everywhere, but most of the windows had remained intact with the shutters all tightly latched, and the contents of the house seemed relatively undisturbed. Those who had fled had been more interested in getting as far away as possible, rather than spending any time going through Ammon's things. They'd simply hoped the fires that had started would consume everything, but it was evident those hopes had been in vain.

Still, Jessimina had her first confirmation Parley had made it at least this far. In one corner near a large wooden wardrobe lay a half-open pack, and against the wall leaned a newer Winchester rifle, untouched by the detritus that covered everything else.

THE STEADY STREAM of wagons departing Pahreah over the past few weeks was dwindling to a trickle. Occasionally, wagons filled with those who'd chosen to follow Ammon had come from other towns further away, stopping in Pahreah for additional supplies and information, but the vast majority were those who had found Pahreah no longer tolerable once Ammon had been found wanting by the disciplinary council, though the Elders had only sought to have him removed from fellowship until he had repented and made atonement.

But Ammon, haughty and unmoved, had rejected that avenue to reinstatement and instead quit the Church entirely. And to the surprise of many, over half of those who lived in Pahreah had done the same, determined to follow the man who had swayed them with his powerful words that he was the instrument of the Lord and the Lord's salvation.

His own family were not among those who left, all except for Parley, whom he took, calling the boy his only true son, and Jessimina's husband, to whom Ammon told lies to get him to abandon his new bride in favor of wild promises of celestial glory. Their parting had been angry, as Gideon accused her of breaking her vows to him in joining the Sisters, that her own calling was to serve only as his wife, even though the Elders themselves has chosen her to serve with the Sisters.

In the end, Gideon had left with her father and the other families who had chosen to embrace Ammon Harris's path.

Parley had been among the twenty-seven who had returned, scarred and broken spiritually, ill-treated for who he was even as he was beheld with a certain amount of pity—the child who had witnessed his own father's damnation.

Gideon had not been so lucky. He had been among the first victims of her father's infernal machine.

ornament

THEIR VOICES GROW LOUDER, *more numerous. They clamor for release, to be led to the salvation they were promised. But the one who should have guided them did not trust in his own words. The nightly struggles, the mutterings—they consumed him, drove him to greater experimentation. The chamber grew larger, the fasbra lattice surrounding the machine became more intricate, more elaborate, a rainbow-hued filigree that kept the aethyr contained and perhaps even more. The sheer beauty of the machine belied its terrible purpose, its hunger used to sate Ammon's own soul.*

There was a guilt, a fear that somehow there was a chance Ammon had been wrong. But that questioning, that guilt was a long time in coming. Convincing everyone of his sincerity, his belief, had been easy at first, for did he not graciously allow his own son-in-law to be among the first to enter into the machine and attain glory? The son-in-law he had chosen over his own daughter, his own flesh and blood who had defied him?

In time, it felt like the machine began to speak, to whisper its own promises. Ammon muttered about them in his sleep. He longed for the relief waiting in the darkness, but he could see the cage rising around his own soul, a blackening tracery invading his mind and heart.

ornament

SHE SEARCHED THE HOUSE, or at least what she could, and found nothing. There was simply no trace of Parley she could see anywhere, aside from the two fraught relics of his presence, the pack and rifle.

A search of her father's study had yielded nothing about the machine he'd built or anything else, really. She'd expected at least some notes, some reference to his project—he'd been very meticulous about documenting the things he'd done in the past, so it was unusual to find nothing at all. Since his desk showed no signs of being searched, carefully or otherwise, she had to assume either he'd abandoned his prior habits or had kept those notes elsewhere.

She sat down near the pack and rifle. Both had the appearance of waiting for Parley's eventual return, as if he hadn't gone far or intended to be too long away, rather than being carelessly tossed aside or otherwise discarded. But he hadn't come back. Where would he have gone without them? It was a puzzle that demanded an answer, but Jess had no idea where she might begin looking. If she found nothing else here, she'd have to go looking for the cave where the machine was buried, in the hill she'd seen as she approached her father's former home.

The flickering of the Thyrlumen brought her out of her reverie. Its glowing beam had been strangely erratic as she searched. It wasn't supposed to waver, but here and there it had grown dimmer or brighter, seemingly of its own accord.

It seemed to pulse now, like a deep, slow heartbeat of light, and the feeling she'd had upon entering the house started to come back, making her more uneasy with every passing moment. She considered turning it off, but she wasn't sure she wanted to be alone in the darkness of the decaying house. Before long she would need to make a decision. It was at least three in the morning now, and exhaustion was starting to take its toll. She could wait out the remainder of the night and seek rest in the morning, or she could take the risk that little had changed in the abandoned town and that nothing, human or animal, lurked in the shadows waiting for her to fall asleep.

A loud, hollow groaning rose from somewhere near her, startling her and causing her to draw her revolver, though she had no idea where she might need to aim it. It lasted for several seconds, with a resonating echo to accompany it. There were two tones to it, one which seemed distant and deeper, while the other was almost a hissing echo far, far closer.

A minute passed, then two. Her breathing was shallow as she strained to limit the distracting sounds of her own heartbeat, her own lungs, as she listened intently. The light of the Thyrlumen had become steady once more, she noted.

She stood, and another low moan started up. She held her breath and waited. The light began to pulse once more and she turned toward the large wardrobe near her brother's things. Unless she was mistaken...

No, there was no doubt. One of the sound's tones was clearly emanating from the depths of the closed wardrobe. Yet it still didn't seem that close. It was a thin sound, one far from its origin.

Gripping her pistol, she approached the ornate wooden doors, playing the light from the Thyrlumen over the carved wooden surfaces. If anything lurked within, it already knew she was here. Curiosity mixed with apprehension propelled her forward, and she hooked a finger around one of the metal handles and pulled.

∞

EVEN BEFORE AMMON HARRIS had left his family and his home in Pahreah, he gave them a promise: "*A promise of hope,*" he'd said. He had spent months away from his household, carting materials and supplies to a destination none of them knew.

His meaning became clear when he announced his own split with the church and called others to his own fellowship. He had laid the seeds for the gateway to the kingdoms of Heaven, sown them in the wilderness of Utah, a holy place whose sole purpose would be to purify and prepare those brave and pious souls who were worthy enough to approach the throne of God directly from this mortal existence, and to do so without suffering or death.

For aethyr was the key and Ammon the locksmith who would forge that key and open the gates. All that remained was to believe and follow.

∞

THE WARDROBE WAS NEARLY EMPTY. None of its contents hung from the wooden bar within; instead, they lay piled up at the bottom, two mounds of clothing pushed to either side of the boards, leaving a two-foot gap of space between them.

The reason was quickly obvious. At the back of the wardrobe a panel stood open, beyond which the top of a ladder descended into a hole. She had no doubt she knew where it would lead—her father would have wanted more than one way into the cave where he'd done his work. One that he alone knew of.

But apparently Parley had known of it, too. Why? How? She tried to imagine his life at ten years of age here, growing up under the shadow of a brilliant, if terrible, man. Would he have been that disobedient, to let his curiosity take him into the hidden secrets of the house? Had he merely watched their father use this portal but never had himself until recently?

Those answers lay in wait through the passage below. She slung her own pack over her shoulder once more, holstered her pistol, and started to descend the ladder into the yawning darkness, the flickering light of her Thyrlumen barely penetrating a few feet into the inky blackness.

The passageway didn't seem to be wholly manmade, though there was ample evidence of where it had been widened and raised, with heavy oaken beams for supports. Her father must have found a natural tunnel and simply reinforced it. The area around Hope was pocketed with systems of caves and tunnels formed over the slow march of time; she supposed he must have found it before the other settlers had come to Hope. His home had been the first one built; it stood to reason he had taken measures to conceal this tunnel's existence from everyone else to afford himself a private entrance and egress from where he kept his machine.

After ten minutes of slowly making her way through the tunnel, it started to narrow until the rough earthen walls were barely a foot from her shoulders on either side. As she walked, the Thyrlumen grew somewhat in intensity, as if it was able to draw more aethyr current than usual. This increased brightness allowed her to see a narrow wooden door standing at the terminus, hewn from a single piece of oak.

Set into it, near the top, was what appeared to be a small sliding panel of wood. She cautiously approached and her Thyrlumen went out. She drew her pistol once more and listened in the darkness. She knew of nothing that should affect an aethyric lamp like this, save certain interactions with electricity, which wasn't very likely at all here.

In a few moments, though, she realized there was still the pulsing glow of aethyr—an incomplete rectangular outline of light that could only be coming from the other side of the small panel in the door. She moved toward it, her fingers fumbling to softly and slowly push the panel to one side, revealing the tiny window beneath that let her look into the next room. The perspective seemed wrong. It was almost as if she were looking slightly upward into the cave.

She tried to take in its size as best she could through the small opening, but all she was able to focus on was the pulsating latticework of energy near the center of the cave, an intricate design that could only be the fasbra cage surrounding the machine her father had built. Its beauty was both natural and unnatural. Though she could not directly see the metal itself because of the light that suffused and enveloped it, the muted rainbow sheen still somehow stood out to her as she gazed upon the wonder she now beheld. The aethyric current running along the lengths of wire twinkled like constellations in the night sky, tiny motes of light that pulsed and brightened as they reached points where two or more of the wires intersected and crossed one another.

But she had been told the machine had gone dim, that her father's final action had been somehow to shut it down, rather than see it destroyed. Either they had lied or someone else—her brother, most likely—had restarted the machine, creating this unsettling tapestry like a dark field filled with summertime fireflies in the depths of the cave.

She pulled open the door, and the reason for the odd perspective became clear. The bottom of the door itself was a little over three feet below the level of the cave floor. Set into the stone were two flat pieces of steel, carefully hammered into the rock, forming a steep pair of steps, with a sharply bent steel bar on either side secured at the top for balance.

Pistol at the ready, she moved up the steps and into the cave proper, wishing she still had the use of her Thyrlumen. While the light from the machine was more than enough to provide illumination to all corners of the cave, the pulsating light was unnerving. Something didn't seem right about it.

She glanced around, letting her eyes adjust to the shifting shadows that created a sense of disorientation in the room. The machine dominated every aspect of the cave, but she could just make out additional wire running from the latticework to what had to be controls of some sort on the other side of the cavern.

She heard the watery sound of labored breathing, shallow and erratic, and another groan. At the sound, the light of the machine dimmed somewhat, though she still could see well enough to look further.

And there, in a dark recessed corner near the machine, lay a writhing figure on the rough stone, barely clad in rags and covered in dirt and blood.

Her hand trembled and she took a moment to calm herself and make sure she had a firm grip on her revolver. She carefully moved forward as the tableau unfolded in front of her. She took in the details —a knife, a battered bowl, and some other supplies lay near the figure —a man, she could tell as she got closer. He didn't seem to notice her presence at all.

He twisted again and she caught a glimpse of his face in the light from the machine. It was Parley; the cracked shell of the man he had been. From the jagged cuts in his clothing, she could tell he'd torn at the fabric, shredding it until it was mere strips of cloth that barely concealed his body. Something must have driven him to that, but she had no idea what it might have been. The presence of small cuts on his arms and legs revealed his efforts to cut away his clothing had not been without injury; none seemed deep enough to be worrisome, but the sum total of Parley's condition placed him on the cusp of danger and infection.

She knelt beside him, and her presence finally seemed to register. Parley opened his eyes and looked up at her with a baffled stare that shifted to something akin to anger, then slipped back into confusion.

"Y-you? I didn't think that..." There was a pause and a deep breath. "I came... I came to get away. But I know too much, now, more... more than I knew then."

∘₈

THAT FINAL DAY. The day they had dared... had so arrogantly and ignorantly confronted him. Questioning him. Doubting the salvation of those who had gone before them.

Quelling his own doubts, birthed from the faces he'd seen in the chamber, the ones he tried so hard to blot from his memory, he had assured them all that salvation merely required obedience to him and entering the machine.

The accusations began from those who had already lost family members to the machine standing near the center of the cave, who'd been denied the chance to see them as they left, who were coming to believe Ammon had merely murdered them in some blasphemous ritual for his own gain.

He'd tried to explain, to demonstrate that here was a mystery not to be shared with all but until they were ready, until they were pure enough to step through and be translated into the celestial. But the absence of over one hundred of their own left them unrelenting, unhearing as Ammon spoke.

He remembered watching detachedly as Wilford Beckstead and his sons moved forward with grasping hands, seeking purchase on the limbs of the man who tried to flee before them; the tense circle of faces of those who still remained in Hope as they watched the ensuing struggle and futile fight to get away; the silent determination as they pushed that single figure into the waiting chamber; and the final click of the switch that activated the lattice in a spray of multi-colored light.

And the darkness that consumed his eyes and being, the blackness that he drowned in for a decade.

Waiting.

∞

"BUT NOW YOU'RE here to help, aren't you, Jessimina?" Parley's voice was hoarse and rasping, but something else tinged it, a tone that made her uncomfortable. He had rarely called her by her full name, but she supposed in his current state it was understandable. "I need you to help me destroy that contraption. To set those souls free."

He had spent nearly an hour haltingly telling her what all he'd found out and things he hadn't told her before at all. A decade of silence was eroding before her, and she tensely waited for each new revelation about her father and his mad plans.

"He truly believes... believed it takes those who are worthy directly to the next kingdom. Body and soul. I watched him do it. Every time. I lied to him, didn't tell him I'd seen him head into the tunnel the night before the first worthy ones were sent here... that I explored it and saw him send the first ones through." He told her of their father's feelings of guilt, how he'd taken to talking in his sleep and shouting during nightmares, and Parley had overheard, night after night, Ammon's terrible fear he might have been wrong.

"And they... they took that from him. I know he was... wrong," the final hesitant word seemed to cause Parley pain, "but they trapped him, trapped him and everyone else within the machine. They didn't have the courage to do what needed to be done. Their bodies may be gone, but their souls are eternal. And at the last, father realized... accepted that this machine made them spirit, but also bound them here."

The words kept repeating inside her mind. *I need you to help me destroy that contraption. To set those souls free.*

She looked over at the machine, the soul-wrenchingly beautiful monstrosity squatting next to where Parley lay. It seemed easy enough; there was a logic to it all that made sense. But the machine was powered by aethyr—how could it possibly be a trap like Parley claimed? What unholy thing had her father done?

Even if the souls were bound to it, what would destroying the machine do? Would it be enough to let them pass on to whatever judgment they had incurred? Did she have the right to make that decision?

She glanced down at her brother's recumbent form. There was something in Parley's eyes that didn't register correctly. They stared almost blankly at a point in space beyond her, dull and disengaged from the passion in the voice speaking to her.

And beneath that, deep inside the pupils—fear.

Something clicked into place. Back east, she'd encountered many theories about aethyr and its origins, its properties and powers. Most agreed it was a fuel and energy that existed all around; the fasbra machines merely directed and contained it in a usable form for everyone. But how could it capture and hold souls? She'd never understood her father's wild claims and ravings about the power he had harnessed, that it could transform life and soul to a state befitting the truly Elect. But it couldn't just be "turned off."

"But how do you know that? Everyone said he never turned it off. How do you know that those souls will…"

"M-m-m-m… m… The notes. I found notes about the machine. And they said… they told about what he realized was happening." Her brother's voice shifted from moment to moment, cold and calculating, almost inhuman, to then being on the verge of terror and hysteria, with something unspoken beneath the words themselves. "It's the only way to release them. You can do it. You can save 'em. Even… e-even Gideon." There was a visible and perplexing struggle within Parley, and she didn't understand it.

But the mention of her husband's name gave her pause as she sifted through memories and feelings. She felt no obligation to him now, at least not as his wife. He'd passed beyond or, if Parley was right, had passed into the machine and was in some sort of stasis of the soul.

But he was still a good man, despite what he had done. She believed that. And the others, the innocents who had accepted her father's path... at the very least the children, anyway... while all were far from blameless, didn't they deserve this chance?

Something about it still didn't seem right. "I don't know. I should consult with the Sisters. We should get you back to Pahreah, and..."

"The Sisters?" The familiar and old contempt rattled her coming from her brother, for he'd never said a word against the Sisters.

"And again, you dare defy me girl? Foul daughter." The voice of her father spilled forth from Parley, and she could barely fathom what damnable union had taken place. She sat, horrified and immobile, listening as her brother's lips moved at the will of someone else. "Perdition awaits you and yours, as well as this pathetic vessel." He struggled to rise, and she stood and took a step backward, moving closer to the brilliant latticework around the machine.

Deep down, she knew it was Ammon, that somehow her father's soul had become wedded to her brother's corporeal form, something she had heard of in passing during her travels but had scarcely believed. Parley's body shuddered and his face twisted as Ammon attempted to assert control. But neither seemed to emerge victorious, and the cacophony of two voices assaulted her ears.

"Jess, please! He lied! It'll destroy them all, set them outside o'..."

"Boy, you are no better than her! Hold your tongue! You will obey..." Parley's expression twisted again and again, shifting back and forth between contempt and terror.

"Please?" There were tears in Parley's eyes despite the smoldering glare within them. "He has me. I can't fight it forever. I..."

"Son of perdition! I showed you the plan, I was going to give you the divine and you have rejected it. Son and daughter of perdition!

You shall be denied the light and grace, to dwell in pits of sulfur and fire... you shall..."

"I may be beyond mercy now, but so is he..."

Her brother's voice was fading, getting weaker as his body started to stand, Ammon assuming control by sheer force of will. He slowly rose up before her as he spoke, reopening some of the cuts on Parley's arms and legs. "Mercy is only mine to give now. And in my judgment I find you wanting." He took a lurching step toward her.

There are no daughters of perdition, only sons, she thought. And Parley was no son of perdition, despite what he may have thought. He'd been deceived by his own father, never seeing the light of the intended plan for him until these final moments. Parley had thought himself beyond the reach of mercy, but she stretched out her left hand and fingers, brushed away the caked sweat and blood on Parley's chin... Her father's smile took over Parley's face as he grabbed at her wrist, pulling her to him... she raised her right hand... and...

Mercy. All she could deliver was mercy.

The smile turned to hatred and horror as her father realized what she had done. Parley's legs were weak, starting to give out, and his head turned once more toward the machine and the glowing traceries of metal that continued to pulse more and more violently as the conflict had escalated. With a calculated smile, Parley's body leaned toward the fragile lattice, toward an opening that led to a small chamber within the machine, arms extended in a parody of an embrace.

"NO!" Parley's voice screamed out, and a twisted dance played out in front of Jessimina as her brother and father wrestled for control of Parley's dying body, finally collapsing in a heap just inches away from the opening. The light from the machine grew steady, no longer pulsing, and her Thyrlumen began to glow once more. She shook her head, unsure as to what was happening. The perpetual hum of the machine grew louder until she could almost hear... something, a whispered word, a nearly silent request for...

She moved closer to the machine—careful to avoid her brother's body—and the entrance to the chamber inside of it. As she did so, the whispers resolved into a hundred soft voices, some familiar, some unknown, but all gently pleading for release. They spoke of their lives, their fates, and she knew their stories as intimately as they did. And they told her what they knew had to be done.

For there had been some truth to Ammon's words. The more than hundred wretches whom he had deceived were still caught in the aethyric web of the machine. But listening to them, she knew their salvation did not rest in destroying the deadly and intricate device just the barest breath away from her fingertips.

To do so would be to lose all of them to the aethyr itself, rather than to judgment. They would be forever outside of time and grace, barred from the light itself.

She wept, for there were few choices she could make. She wept for the families who would never know the terrible decision she had to make, and she had to think of her own soul in the bargain. Would this save her or damn her?

The machine's humming was now silent. Instead, she felt it inside her, the thrumming heartbeat of the souls she carried within. She had reached out and touched the mesh of wire and light, bringing forth the souls of those whom Ammon Harris would have surely otherwise damned. She didn't know if she would be able to contain the burden herself; but they were free of her father's machine. She could feel them longing to move onward, yet the barrier of her flesh kept them anchored here. She knew Gideon was among them and wondered if he would understand.

∞

As Parley felt the world dissolve from a brief moment of pain, through the final struggle with his father, and finally into a cold warmth that suffused his entire body, he contemplated his final moments and the worth of his own soul. He had, at least for himself, been redeemed in one respect. He could rest more easily, even if he were confined to the outer darkness for eternity.

For in those final moments when his sister set the souls free from their aethyric prison, when she had touched the delicate metal work surrounding the machine, he had made sure he held on to the one soul which should not be her burden to bear. Had Ammon succeeded in getting Parley's body into the chamber, he and Parley both would have been trapped with all the others, leaving Jessimina with the untenable choice to redeem the others at the cost of hosting her own father's soul as well, or condemning them all to either a perpetual state of flux or place them past the point of salvation. He had fought, and years of frustration, pain, and horror had fueled his efforts, and he had won. Parley would take his father into the darkness with him and only the final grace would determine whether father, son, or both were truly beyond the reach of mercy.

ABOUT THE AUTHOR

Sean Christian Smith is an English professor and a native of Indiana. He is purveyor of all things strange and creative, moonlighting as a musician, actor, writer, cosplayer, and artist in his spare time. On occasion, he adds gears to various things "just because," and his front hallway is wallpapered with maps. He is the servant to five cats, none of whom really appreciate anything he does unless it involves food.

The Many Wives of Solomon King

Christopher McAfee

Solomon King believed one wife was better than none, but no wives was better than two. Even when Joseph Smith told him to take a second wife, he refused. But in the end, Solomon King left eighteen wives behind.

Most who knew Solomon described him as a quiet man. Those who knew him well described him as a difficult man. His wife, Stella, knew him best of all, and she called him a selfish man, which is why she left that summer day.

Stella King left Nauvoo the same day Jacob Pennywell disappeared. Though not directly connected, the confluence of these two events provided the mental environment that led Solomon down an aberrant path. His wife's departure left a hole in his heart and a dent in his ego, which twisted into the dark idea that a wife, his wife, should be more submissive, more easily controlled, than Stella. The disappearance of Jacob, Nauvoo's most brilliant individual, left an abandoned workshop filled with books, notes, tools, and devices of curious workmanship. The opportunity provided by these details came to Solomon as a clearly spoken idea—perhaps he could *build* the wife he deserved.

After dark, Solomon stole into Jacob Pennywell's vacant workshop and found several books to aid in his undertaking. He found books on mechanics such as *The Book of Hydrolic Elegancies* by Shui Shi Tu Jing and *The Book of Knowledge of Ingenious Mechanical Devices* by Ismail al-Jazari. He discovered anatomy books like *On the Fabric of the Human Body* by Andreas Vesalius. He dug up several of Jacob's notebooks containing ideas, plans, and ruminations including a highly annotated copy of Mary Shelley's *Frankenstein*. Writings regarding the nature of the soul were also there, such as *On the Soul* by Aristotle, *City of God* by Saint Augustine, and "The Immortality of the Body" by Parley Pratt, all of which Solomon took for good measure. At the end of his perusal, he found a copy of a book called *The Grimoire of Solomon*, a book of spells attributed to King Solomon, which Solomon took as a sign that Providence approved of his plan. He procured all of these and more from Jacob Pennywell's collection, but perhaps most importantly, Solomon found Jacob's plans for building a portable power source called a "battery," the key to making an independently mobile being.

Because he preferred agriculture over academics, Solomon had an intellect that went unnoticed, but he had a large capacity for learning. Though he hadn't applied his abilities to science or invention, he certainly had the capability to do so. He read all night, the entire next day, and late into the following evening. On the third day he awoke still hunched over his reading desk with the conviction that creating a conscious automatous human body could be done. Perhaps not in the same way God created Adam and Eve, but combining mechanics, science, and magic, Solomon believed he could simulate God's work.

Having now spent some time in Jacob's workshop, he realized that while he had all or most of the required tools, he didn't have nearly enough of the right materials. He also needed a more private place to work, somewhere away from his Nauvoo neighbors who might get overly curious. As if a voice was speaking in his ear, Solomon was reminded of the factory in Kirtland, Ohio. When the majority of Saints left Kirtland, they left the factory, too. They had no way to transport their equipment, and they left the bulk of their raw materials behind. Surely there would be enough and more for him to work with.

He loaded his cart with all of Jacob's notes, the most relevant books, some tools, a fair amount of money, and as many survival essentials as he could carry. At sundown, he harnessed his horse to the cart, strapped a rifle to his back, and rode the horse out of Nauvoo.

The trip took fifty-one days, which brought Solomon to the factory in early autumn. The factory lay a short distance to the southeast of the Kirtland temple. It rested on a north-facing hill and spanned a river, which allowed the factory to gain power from waterwheels placed at intervals along the stream. The Saints fabricated every commodity they might need in the factory, and the building contained raw materials and equipment of every kind. Solomon found lumber, wool, fabric, leather, glass, stone, and metal—including copper, zinc, steel—and some prefabricated sheets, rods, and gears. The sawmill, looms, and tannery appeared in good working order, as well as the metal-working machines for smelting, forming, forging, and welding. And the greenhouse still extended from the north side of the factory, glass intact.

Before getting to work, Solomon took time to prepare for winter. Not knowing how long the process of building a wife might take, he patiently took his time preparing to provide for himself the most basic necessities of life. He planted a garden in the greenhouse, hunted rabbits to make rabbit jerky, and purchased other supplies in Kirtland. He set up basic living quarters within the factory, which consisted of a table, a chair, a bed, and nothing else. He made a schedule for tending to the garden, hunting as needed, and generally maintaining his life, budgeting time for the work to come.

The water wheels stood to the side of the river where sluices were constructed. When Solomon opened the sluice gate, river water ran through the sluice and under the wheel, putting the wheel in motion. The turning wheels gave Solomon power for light, heat, and machines.

While he knew he could build a wife, he still had much to learn about how. He spent the winter on a more in-depth study of the books he'd brought. He read all the books, some of them twice, and internalized the information therein. When he tired of reading, he took time to learn the use of the factory machinery. He built several small models of the different body parts, applying electricity to make them functional, leaving him with an interesting assortment of kinetic sculptures. Following Jacob's notes, he built a battery half the size of a breadbox, which could be recharged by attachment to any power source. By spring, he was ready to start constructing a body.

He began with the skeleton, which he made of metal parts, with gears, pistons, wires, and springs to get the skeleton moving. He next worked on a brain capable of understanding rudimentary commands, as well as performing simple actions such as walking or picking up a cup. After wiring the brain to the body, Solomon attached the battery and tested his automaton with simple commands. Stand up. Sit down. Walk forward. The skeleton performed as commanded, though a bit awkwardly. Solomon loosened joints, tightened springs, and lubricated rods until the skeleton moved more gracefully, if only a bit more. To smooth out the body's shape, Solomon carved from wood the shapes of calves, shoulders, and the other rounded body parts. These he fitted to the skeleton. He used leather for skin, binding it to the wood and metal, and shaping it as well as he could. For hair, he made a wig from his horse's mane and gave her a dress from a store in Kirtland. Throughout the work, Solomon's inner voice prodded, comforted, and guided him.

The final step in this process came from the *Grimoire of Solomon*, a spell called "The Breath of Life" for binding spirits to corpses. The rudimentary brain would control actions that normal living humans perform without thought, but such a brain could not provide complex thinking or dictate personality. Solomon believed a sentient spirit inhabiting this body could become the control center for the mechanical brain. What the spirit commanded, the body would do, with the caveat that it could not go against Solomon's wishes; the wife would be submissive to her husband. Solomon couldn't choose what spirit would inhabit the body, but it would nevertheless bring personality and intellect, making the automaton a unique individual, someone a man could love. Solomon cast the spell and the automaton became a living being.

He named her Chloe, and feeling the euphoria of success, he was blind to her imperfections. They lived as man and wife for a time, working side by side and getting to know each other. Chloe prepared meals, cleaned house, and beautified their living quarters while Solomon tended the garden, hunted, and read his books. But as time wore on, her face became an irritant. Solomon lacked the skills of a sculptor, and Chloe's face showed it. It appeared roughly human, but more masklike. The leather had the proper shape, but the round black eyes never closed. The nose folded outward as it should, but with a triangular opening at the bottom instead of two holes. The slit for a mouth barely moved when she spoke. The uncanniness disturbed Solomon, and he came to avoid looking at her face. Rejected, Chloe continued to serve her husband in silence, resembling an obedient house servant rather than a submissive wife.

As Solomon brooded over his failure, that familiar inner voice whispered to him that he could build another, even better, wife, but he knew that would mean defying his credo against multiple wives. He could destroy Chloe, but that felt too much like murder, and he had no disposition for that. Instead, that inner voice made an argument for polygamy, and he began to open his mind to the idea. Two wives might be better than one, at least in an unusual situation like this.

He set to work on a second automaton. He followed the same process as before, making a few improvements that came naturally as a result of doing something twice. This time, he took more care in molding the leather to her body. He wrapped it around the wooden carapace of her legs, arms, and torso, stitching it together tightly in the back. Her face contained only metal, but Solomon had crafted it so it bore the rough shape of a female skull. To this he molded the leather, forming it to the forehead, eyes, cheeks, and chin. The eyelids, lips, and nose he sewed with fine thread to the wire frame of the face, forming them with his fingers to a nearly exquisite shape. He cast the "Breath of Life" spell and she awoke. He named her Rachel.

While Chloe continued to cook and clean, Solomon spent many

days with Rachel taking walks, reading books to her, and staying up late into the night talking. But he soon became disturbed by the way her properly shaped black eyes never closed—never blinking, ever staring like drill bits boring into his mind and soul. He found himself avoiding her gaze, and eventually avoiding her altogether.

Once again, the inner voice whispered, and once again Solomon built a new body. He named her Mary and enjoyed her company, until the uncanniness of her appearance pushed him away. This time the sharp metal cheekbones beneath the leather broke through, giving her cheeks the appearance of dark and twisted roses.

Solomon's work continued this way, the inner voice speaking to him, driving him onward. He came to rely on the voice, listening more intently, recognizing more quickly. The voice became his muse. It became for him a Voice rather than a voice, more a name than a simple noun. The Voice guided Solomon to the relevant pages of the relevant texts, and Solomon's skills improved, each wife becoming more beautiful, more graceful than the last. Where no relevant text existed, the Voice inspired new ideas, which led to new discoveries, which led to new and better forms. As Solomon strove for quality, he also improved his efficiency, and the creation of each new automaton moved quicker than the last. Additionally, he learned that the other wives could be skilled mechanics. They seemed eager to help build more friends for themselves, despite the jealousy they seemed to hold for each other.

His next wife, Rebekah, had eyelids that blinked, but the rest of her face stayed motionless. Priscilla's face could change with her emotions, but her legs moved haltingly. Martha's body moved fluidly, if not completely gracefully. By the time Candace came to be, Solomon had advanced from using leather to growing skin from his own skin cells. He grew the skin onto Candace's body, but the skin became infested with warts. Leah had the first moving eyeballs, though still carved from wood. Before Naomi, he made the vocals to project from the spinning of a rough-edged wheel over a small horsehair bow, the vowels and consonants being formed by mechanical means inside the head. Naomi, on the other hand, articulated vowels and consonants with the movements of her lips and tongue. Elisabeth's voice came from her ability to breathe and push air through taut cords for a more human sounding voice. By the time he made Dinah, Solomon had perfected skin growth. She had skin as smooth as any man could wish for. For hair, Solomon had tried sewing in horsehair or making wigs, but Julia could grow her own hair, even the downy hair of the neck and arms. Karen had the first glass eyes, though Solomon's skills as a glassblower could still be improved. Joanna had perfectly articulating fingers and Deborah had the first finger- and toenails. Hannah's ears had proper shapes rather than just smooth, somewhat convex flaps.

Again and again, year after year, Solomon continued to build new wives, each different from the last. Every body shape and every face made different, each more beautiful, more perfect, more graceful than the last. Even their personalities differed. Chloe had a good work ethic, Julia made work fun, Martha shared unique insights, Deborah showed physical affection, and Karen could be mean. Well, all of them were spiteful or venomous at times, and none of them truly loved him, but Solomon could ignore that as long as they continued progressing. But even after seventeen wives (if we also count Stella), Solomon hadn't achieved full satisfaction, and he was losing his will to continue.

But the Voice whispered to him one last time. Number eighteen would be the one.

This time Solomon took greater care than ever before. He took more time with her ankles, knees, elbows, and wrists so her movement would be graceful. He built her neck to just the right length with just the right curvature. He configured the gears and rods in her face for full expression of sadness, joy, pain, and pleasure. He gave her tear ducts and a way to replenish them through drink. He made her so she could eat and socialize over food. He controlled the growth of her skin and it grew smooth and without blemish. He made perfect eyes of glass with just the right shade of blue. He made sure her eyelids could blink and flutter. He worked on the hair until it would grow a deep and glossy brown. Her breath would pass through his most perfectly crafted vocal cords. He included every tiny detail of human movement. For the first time, Solomon was creating for love and not out of selfishness, and he loved her before she breathed life.

He gently laid her body on a bed and cast the "Breath of Life" spell. When she sat up and spoke, Solomon's heart beat faster and his hands grew cold with confusion and fear. The sound coming from her mouth didn't match the voice he had designed. The voice he designed was light and lilting, but this voice was deep and smooth. Impossibly, his muse was speaking through the mouth of his eighteenth wife. The Voice had inhabited this body and she named herself—Jezebel.

Solomon had been tricked! The Voice was not helping him but herself. Jezebel's spirit had used Solomon as a tool to create her perfect form, allowing her to return so she could enact vengeance on the world. And Solomon had created an army for her. His loyal wives had not been loyal at all, but only biding their time until Jezebel returned. At Jezebel's command, they converged upon Solomon and smothered him to death.

As he was dying, Solomon's credo, no wives are better than two, passed through his mind, and he remembered the one wife who was better than them all. Stella. But Solomon had been blinded by his own selfish wants and had mistreated her. Now he was paying for it with his life, and because of his actions, others would also be made to pay the price for his sins because, now, there were monsters in the hills of Kirtland.

ABOUT THE AUTHOR

CHRISTOPHER MCAFEE MAKES BOOKS, which is not a fancy way to say he writes books. No, he literally makes books using the same machines and techniques used during the Victorian age. In the last two years, he has made two steampunk books and written two steampunk stories. He also built and plays a steampunk ukulele that he plugs into a steampunk amp.

To see some of his work, go to http://christophermcafee.com.

The Tunnel

Jay Barnson

The mechanical hand attached to Eloise White's left forearm tapped its fingertips together in response to Ellie's nervousness. She hated it when it did that. It tempted her to disconnect the linkage pipe, but if she was nervous enough to cause the involuntary ticking, then she was probably in a situation where she might need to call upon its other features. Sloane Square in central London wasn't particularly dangerous after dark these days, even for a lone woman of her particular talents. Privately owned electric lights supplemented the gas lamps to provide adequate illumination to see anyone coming. In the event of an opportunistic attack, the concealed revolver and knife—not to mention the hand— would provide her with ample protection.

Her contact was late, and they were dealing with kidnappers. That was an ugly business, and it wasn't a random masher or mugger she worried about. The kidnappers had covered their tracks well, meaning they were smart and organized. Smart and organized enough to get rid of someone poking around their affairs.

The click of a woman's boots caught her attention. Ellie turned to note the figure approaching in the shadows between the pools of lamplight. No man's footfalls accompanied the woman, and as far as Ellie could tell, she was not followed. Ellie's hand ceased its tapping.

"Vivian! What happened? I saw you leave the meeting thirty minutes ago."

The woman—a widow at age twenty-two—smiled weakly. She wore a homemade red-and-black dress with a wool shawl appropriate for the late spring evening. "I'm sorry. After I convinced several young men I did not need them to escort me home, I meant to come straight here. Then I met one of the missionaries... a Brother Smith. He'd missed the meeting, but offered to take me home in his steam carriage."

"He wasn't in your last report."

"He said he was new."

"Were you introduced by Mr. Stokes?"

"No. But he said Brother Stokes informed him of my upcoming baptism and had paperwork to go over before that happens."

Ellie's metal hand clanged shut in a fist. "Your what?"

"Oh. I'm sorry. I meant to tell you." She opened her purse and pulled out the derringer Ellie had given her two weeks earlier. She handed the weapon to Ellie. "I'm done, Ellie. I have found nothing of this conspiracy the papers spoke of. More importantly, I believe what they teach. I am joining the Mormon church, and as soon as I can afford it, I plan to go with a group to Deseret. Via steamship or airship, not some secret tunnel running under the ocean like the rumors say."

Ellie held up her hand, refusing the weapon. "The rumors are undoubtedly a wild exaggeration. But what about the missing girls? Finding them is of paramount importance, far more than this story."

"I want to help find them, but I am convinced the church is not responsible. They are as concerned as everyone else, and the police have already investigated them thoroughly."

Vivian returned the tiny pistol to her hand-purse.

Ellie sighed and willed her left hand to unclench. Never as responsive as her living hand, it took some mental coaxing. The engineers who worked for her brother were brilliant, but the replacement hand still didn't feel like a natural part of her. Most of the time, it didn't feel like anything at all, other than a weight strapped onto the stump where the real hand used to be.

"Vivian, I learned the hard way that great evil can wear a

pleasant face." She held up her left hand. "These people may still be dangerous. We have done these stories before. You know the police do anything but a thorough job. You must be cautious."

"I am. I will be."

"So tell me more about this missionary. Could he be our real culprit?"

Vivian shrugged. "I don't know. Perhaps. I will attempt to gain more information on him. I'll ask Brother Stokes if he knows anything of this person. I will also demand that Brother Smith meet me by appointment, so you can follow us."

"Did I not just say something about being careful?"

"We also just spoke of saving those five missing girls, if they can still be saved. If I learn anything new, or see this missionary again, I'll be sure to let you know. Otherwise, I am afraid I have nothing else to contribute to your story."

They said their goodbyes, and Ellie watched over Vivian until she was completely out of sight. It was almost too late before she became alerted to the soft footsteps approaching her.

The man changed his pace as soon as she turned, attempting to make his stealthy approach seem casual. "Evenin', miss." He touched the brim of his hat, but his eyes swept over her entire body. He didn't conceal his leer, full of yellowed and rotting teeth. His loose, worn work-clothes covered the wiry muscles of a man accustomed to physical labor. She found that an admirable attribute, when it wasn't looking at her like a roasted mutton leg.

"Good evening," she responded, not meeting his gaze. "Do keep walking."

"Now miss, a young lady ought not be left alone in the city at night. It might be dangerous." He reached forward to take her arm. Instead, she caught hold of his wrist with her mechanical hand. His eyes bugged out for a brief moment at the sight of the complex work of brass and steel before she let the accumulated charge surge. Even insulated from the discharge, a sting of pain shot through the linkage pipe that made the hand obey her commands. The man accosting her stiffened, emitting a short squeal of pain before she loosened her grasp and let him drop to the ground.

She winced as his head cracked against the cobblestones. "A gentleman never takes a woman's arm until she offers it," she commented as she walked away. He groaned in response.

08

ELLIE DIDN'T HOLD much stock in the wild rumors of Mormons abducting young girls, shipping them off through a tunnel that went all the way under the ocean and the United States to the contested land of Deseret, and marrying them off to lecherous old polygamists. Nevertheless, five girls who had joined or expressed interest in the church were missing, and two local "branches" of the church were at the center of things. Ellie still suspected them, in spite of Vivian's assurances, and held her friend's sudden conversion with even more suspicion. It was this last part that made sleep difficult that night.

Ellie and Vivian had been friends since finishing school. While she'd always been a bit adventurous, Vivian hadn't been so rash since the day she'd been swept off her feet by the handsome Lieutenant Thorington. She attended church on Sundays, but she'd never been particularly devout, even when in mourning after receiving news of her new husband's death in an airship en route to Egypt in 1880. Vivian had been a widow for two years, nearly six months longer than she'd been married. She had regained most of her adventurous spirit in that time, offering to help Ellie in her journalistic "capers." Her keen eye and lack of noticeable features—such as the burn scar and a mechanical hand that Ellie possessed—made her a formidable ally when Ellie needed an "inside woman."

Now, Vivian had discovered religion anew and planned to leave forever to a remote desert. As much as Ellie tried to concentrate on the kidnappings, this element nagged her. What hold had they found over her friend?

The next morning, Ellie arrived in her "office," the parlor of her brother's house that he'd graciously offered for her use. Filled with paintings, plants, and thickly padded chairs, it was a far nicer place than a tiny third-floor room she'd otherwise have been able to afford. Her brother still considered her investigations for the paper (under the pseudonym, "Eli Whittaker") a safe and innocent hobby, a presumption she took pains to preserve.

Forrest Buckley was already waiting for her. "Rather a late start to the day, Miss White," he commented.

"Of course, Mr. Buckley. Stories don't keep business hours. What can I do for you?"

"Have you completed the story on the Mormon kidnappings yet?"

"If I had, it would be in your hands by now. It is my top priority. Surely you didn't come all the way here simply to ask about it."

"No. I came to give you warning. Mr. Reginald Baxter recently contacted the families of the missing young women. He informed them that he has already dispatched a team into Deseret to rescue the girls, using whatever force is necessary. They plan to uncover the tunnel at its source, if they can find it."

"The Reginald Baxter of Baxter Holdings? He was one of my brother's investors."

"The same. He lost a son to those Mormons, too."

"As I understand it, his son willingly abdicated his position and moved to Deseret over his father's protests. In any event, I find it highly unlikely that the girls would have arrived in Deseret already."

"Unless there really is a tunnel."

"You and I both know that is all but impossible, Mr. Buckley."

"Modern technology has created a great number of new marvels, Miss White. You of all people should know that. And the people of Deseret are no strangers to turning their considerable resources and technology to industry."

"Don't tell me you believe that story!"

"No, but apparently Baxter believes it, and he's Cambridge

educated. So do a lot of our readers. I came here to let you know that in a short time, your story will no longer be relevant... or of interest to the Journal."

"I'm more concerned about the rescue of the missing girls and bringing the real villains to justice."

"Of course. Naturally, I give you this news under the strictest confidence until the rescue is secured."

"Naturally."

With that, Buckley took his leave. Ellie raised her metal hand and stared at the clenched fist. Rather than force it open, she uncoupled the tubing. It would take it a full minute to unclench and return to its neutral state, but in the meantime she could continue to brood without losing control of it. She felt like brooding. Baxter was on a wild goose chase if he was sending men into Deseret, regardless of whether the Mormons were responsible or not. Even if the girls had been taken to Deseret, it was a huge territory with a population approaching a quarter million.

He had to realize this. What was Baxter's angle?. Publicity was the obvious motive, as he sought attention and limelight at every opportunity. But could this have something to do with his son?

A rap at the parlor door interrupted her thoughts. Her brother's maid opened the door, handing Ellie a card. "Pardon me, ma'am, but this just arrived for you." Ellie immediately recognized the card as one of Vivian's. On the back, a hastily scrawled note stated, "Smith noon Sloane S."

The grandfather clock in the hall struck eleven. There was little time to spare!

⚙

LESS THAN AN HOUR LATER, Ellie stared through specialized opera glasses out the window of the steam carriage. The overcast sky cast dim, flat light almost devoid of shadows around the square. Since leaving her brother's house, the sky had only grown darker. Vivian stood on the north side, just outside the great hotel, patiently awaiting her missionary. She carried an umbrella in her white-gloved hands, a smart precaution against rain and a potential weapon against an attacker.

A lone missionary seemed an oddity, as in Ellie's research the missionaries were normally found in pairs. Her mechanical hand, plugged back into her nervous system, clicked fingers and thumb together in an uneven rhythm that matched her anxiety. She was torn between desperately wanting this young man to be the real kidnapper and wanting him to be an innocent that presented no risk to Vivian.

The opera glasses allowed her to slide in cartridges containing different lenses for different kinds of magnification. They currently let her view Vivian and the street before her as if she was only a quarter of the distance away. When the steam carriage pulled up, Ellie could readily make out the features of the young man who stepped out.

He appeared to be in his mid-20s, clean-shaven with short reddish-brown hair beneath his hat. After speaking with Vivian for several minutes, he opened the door to his carriage. With a quick glance in Ellie's direction, Vivian stepped into the carriage. The young man, presumably Smith, glanced suspiciously in the same direction. It was unclear if he noted her, but he leaped onto the driver's bench and engaged his engine.

Speaking into the tube to the driver on the bench outside the cabin, Ellie said, "See that steam-carriage leaving the hotel?"

"Aye, miss," her driver called back.

"Follow that carriage!"

"Aye, miss."

They followed Smith's carriage west along King's Road for some distance. At a crowded intersection, Smith turned and looked at them. Ellie spoke into the tube. "We're too close. Don't follow them so closely."

"Aye, miss."

Six intersections later, after stopping for pedestrians and an extremely slow wagon, their quarry had vanished.

"I'm sorry, miss," the driver said through the tube. "You want what we should keep going?"

"Yes, please. A little further."

"Aye, miss."

Once again, her thumb and fingers clicked together. Had she failed Vivian? She knelt backward on the front seat and peered through her opera glasses out the front window, past the driver's shoulder. There was little on the road ahead. After two more blocks she said, "Turn back around, please. Let's backtrack."

"Aye, miss."

Searching along every intersection on the return drive, she spotted the missing carriage parked along the side of Smith road. In her glasses, she could see no one in the vehicle. "Park here," she ordered, and the driver complied without his usual response of "Aye, miss."

She stepped out of the carriage and looked around the street. The traffic was reduced along this road, especially at this time of day and with an increasingly angry-looking sky threatening to unleash a torrent with scant notice. The steam engine of Smith's carriage was silent except for the last hisses of escaping steam. He would have to take some time to restart it and get the pressure built up again.

But where had he and Vivian gone? Had they switched carriages? Gone into one of the buildings?

A speck of white on the ground near one building caught Ellie's attention. She opened her opera glasses to get a better look. It was a white glove, much like the ones Vivian had been wearing.

Absently, Ellie opened her purse and paid the driver more money than he demanded. "Thanks, miss. Need me to stay around a bit?"

She shook her head. "Thank you. I think that will be all for today."

He saluted her and steamed off. Ellie made her way to the fallen glove and reached down to pick it up. It was Vivian's size and, aside from a little bit of new dirt, clean. It couldn't have been here long.

"Good thinking, Vivian," Ellie remarked to the empty air. The only building nearby was what looked like some sort of concrete storage shed to the side of a warehouse. Ellie tried the door, and with some surprise, found it unlocked. With care, she opened it, and discovered a set of stairs descending within. A sign on the wall read, "Smith Street Station" with an arrow pointing diagonally down. It was very official and in the style of all the tube stations. But there was no railway, underground or otherwise, along King's Road.

With a last look around, spying no one, she unholstered her revolver and descended the stairs. Several early efforts to build the underground railway had failed, due to flooded or collapsed tunnels. This certainly went deeper than many of those prior excavations but could easily have been one such aborted station.

At the bottom of the stairs, a left turn led her deeper into darkness. As her eyes adjusted, she noted a pinpoint of light ahead. Keeping the revolver trained in front of her, she put one foot in front of the other, unsure of her footing on a floor slowly being reclaimed by the earth.

As she drew closer to the light, her eyes adjusted and the ghosts of shapes took form around her. Supporting columns flanked her path on either side. Her slowly returning vision wasn't enough to help her spot the one dark shadow that separated from a column beside her. Her brain registered the presence and the sudden whoosh of air too late, and her first true realization of danger came as a lead pipe crashed down on her hand—the good hand—knocking the revolver from her grasp.

Ellie cried out in fear and pain, reeling to one side as the pipe whooshed through the air again. This time, she saw the wielder, a man about the stature of "Brother Smith." Her back touched the wall, and the man took a step forward, raising the pipe.

She warded off the blow with her metal hand. Pipe struck the brass and steel with the crunching sound of a small fortune in damaged one-of-a-kind mechanisms. The man hesitated at the sound, but after a moment, cocked his arm back to swing again.

This time, she was ready. When the pipe struck her hand again, it landed solidly in the palm, denting the metal structure and jarring the straps that attached it to her wrist. But this time, she clamped her hand around the pipe. It wouldn't take her attacker more than a few seconds to yank it free from the low-friction of her artificial hand, but she wasn't giving him seconds.

The hand discharged into the pipe. She didn't let up even after a shriek strangled in his throat and he stiffened, unable to let go of the pipe until the last bit of current had run its course.

He dropped to the ground without another sound.

Ellie felt around for the fallen revolver but couldn't find it. She couldn't hear her attacker's breathing, either, but was too terrified to care. She found the pipe, but it hurt to hold it in her real hand. Her mechanical hand hung dead at the end of her wrist. It would take several minutes of motion for it to build up enough charge to function again, assuming the charging mechanism was undamaged.

Ellie stumbled toward the light. It turned out to be both larger and more distant than she'd expected. The rear of the station had been excavated more recently than the rest, a tunnel that sloped down from the original station and curved off to the left. The shorings of this new tunnel were of steel girders rather than stone. The light came from around the bend, splaying on the wall.

Silently, she followed the passage down and to the left. At the bottom, several lanterns lit the tunnel, and a set of small railroad tracks came to an end. Voices echoed distantly off the walls. Ellie pressed herself into the last bit of shadows in an uneven corner to stay hidden, peeking with one eye to make out what was happening.

The tunnel seemed to stretch forever, sloping gently deeper into the earth. Besides the lanterns illuminating the tunnel, a brilliant electric light shone from the front of a train engine. The train wasn't turned directly at her, or it would have completely illuminated the curve of the tunnel where she now stood.

She repressed a gasp. The tunnel was real. The Mormons had excavated an actual tunnel to Deseret, stretching under the Atlantic. Anyone capable of something like that would be a threat to any country on Earth! But something about this scene seemed wrong.

Six cars followed the engine, terminating in another engine facing the other direction. It, too, projected a beam of light behind it, down the tunnel, illuminating three men coming up from the other side. Two carried a giant spool of wire between them, un-reeling it slowly as they moved. Behind and below them, the tunnel shrank in size, only widening enough to accommodate a new pair of shoring girders, then shrinking again to less than the size of the train. At the furthest end, only enough rock had been excavated to allow placement of tracks, and a set of shoring girders were left horizontally on the floor. One side chamber had been excavated, through which Ellie glimpsed a giant, dirt-covered metal contraption. The tunnel, as extensive as it was, was unfinished.

Judging by the amount of dynamite packed along the walls, they had no intention of completing the tunnel.

A voice, concealed on the other side of the train, called out, "You'll never get away with this, you know. The truth will be discovered."

One of the three men, the one not carrying the spool, laughed and turned to face the other side of the tunnel, speaking through the coupling between the rear car and the second locomotive. "I've gotten away with worse, Mr. Stokes. The newspapers love me. The people believe the papers. I can do no wrong in their eyes."

Ellie recognized the voice: Reginald Baxter, the wealthy industrialist. The one who footed a significant portion of the bill for the prototype hand she wore. The one who had helped secure a great number of patents and helped her brother turn their modest inheritance into a technology industry empire—while building an even greater one for himself.

From the rear car, the muffled voices of girls echoed through the tunnel. "Let us go! We won't tell!" one of them cried plaintively. Reginald tapped one of the men on the shoulder and pointed to a steel pin holding the door of the car in place. The man nodded, and for one hopeful moment, Ellie thought he might relent and let the girls go free. Instead, the man stepped back around the train and returned with a stick of dynamite, which he tied to the pin. When it exploded, it would remove the evidence that the girls had been locked inside the car.

While their attention was diverted, Ellie slipped from her hiding place, ducking low to avoid casting a shadow on the wall as she approached the front locomotive.

She failed.

"What was that?" a man asked as she flitted over to the opposite side of the engine.

"Did you see something?" Baxter asked.

The first man shouted, "Hey, Smitty, is that you?"

"Smitty?" Baxter asked.

"Smith is the name Lew is going by these days, posin' as a Mormon. We've been calling him Smitty just to get his goat. He hates it."

"He's supposed to be keeping watch, not playing games."

Ellie tiptoed along the opposite side of the train, shadowed by all the lanterns on Baxter's side. She found Vivian and a middle-aged man roped together on the ground next to one of the cars. She held her finger to her lips, her living hand hurting just by the gesture. Something was broken.

Gritting through the pain, she drew her knife from her boot. She tried to cut their bonds, but her injured hand couldn't hold the knife with much strength. Her mechanical hand was barely beginning to function again, without enough charge to hold a knife securely or to shock someone with anything more than a barely noticeable tickle.

As Vivian and the man watched, eyes wide, she held the knife between her palms and made rapid sawing motions. As the rope began to fray and give, the knife slipped and fell on the ground.

"What are you two doing back there?" Baxter called. There was no time to even attempt to pick up the knife. There was just enough room for Ellie to roll under the undercarriage onto the tracks, taking care to cover her metal hand so it did not clank against anything. Vivian pushed herself around by two inches, spreading her legs slightly in a most unladylike fashion, but successfully hiding the knife from view with her skirt as Baxter climbed over the couplings to check on them.

"I'd recommend against doing anything rash," he said.

"Why not?" asked Vivian. "You are just going to kill us anyway."

"There are many ways to die. Some quick and painless. Others very, very painful. We can make it very painful and make sure there is nothing of you that will ever be found."

"Why are you doing this?" she asked. "We've done nothing to you!"

"You chose poorly, young lady, and it's regrettable. My son made the same choice. When I am done, the Mormons will be ejected not only from Britain, but from all civilized nations anywhere. The uproar over the kidnappings and violent destruction of the rescue party and the wronged women might even force the United States to finally invade and annex Deseret. Even if the truth is eventually learned, decades from now, you people will be nothing more than a footnote in the history books."

Stokes spoke. "Is that what you want your son to be? A footnote? A criminal?"

"Don't try me, old man. He made his choice. As I am now. Whatever we do to you, they won't be able to tell the difference when they discover your remains and determine that you were the one who detonated the tunnel, killing several innocents and rescuers."

"What rescuers?"

"The ones whose bodies are too far buried to ever be recovered. They'll never be able to excavate fully, because the Thames itself is going to fill in what's left." Baxter hopped over the train coupling and returned to supervising the placement of the demolitions.

Ellie carefully crawled back out from under the train. She experimented with the mechanical hand. The fingers now moved well enough to grip the knife. With quick movements, she cut the ropes.

Vivian whispered, "We have to free the other girls."

Ellie and Stokes nodded. Stokes pointed to Ellie and said, "You get the girls. I'll distract the villains."

"How?"

Stokes shrugged and moved to the back of the train. Ellie followed. At the last car, she slipped quietly under it again, her slight frame just enough to wiggle between the track and the undercarriage. She maneuvered under the door, unsure of how to remove the dynamite and the pin without being spotted by the men on that side.

The brilliant lamp on the rear locomotive shut off.

"Hey, Smitty, that had better not be you fooling around," one of the men called. All three rushed past Ellie, guns raised. While their backs were turned to her, Ellie slipped out and used her metal hand, with some guidance from her living hand, to work the stick of dynamite free. After setting it carefully beside her, she took hold of the pin and slowly pulled it loose.

A lantern flew across the back of the tunnel. The oil sprayed and caught fire, the flames quickly drawing close to one of the emplacements of dynamite. The three men raced to stamp and scuff dirt over the flames. Ellie carefully slid the door open in the commotion, holding her metal finger to her lips and pointing toward the exit to the tunnel. Five terrified faces looked back at her, but one of them nodded. One by one, they quietly exited the car and tiptoed along the tunnel to the exit.

Baxter roared. "You? How did you get loose?" For a moment, Ellie froze, thinking she'd been discovered. A moment later, Baxter opened fire. Stokes cried out and collapsed on the other side of the locomotive. Ellie stood and began following the five girls along the train, but Baxter shouted, "The other one! She's going to try to free the girls! Stop them!"

"Run!" Ellie called, and the girls abandoned stealth for haste.

A gunshot fired behind her, the shot striking the wall very near where another lantern hung. Ellie grabbed the lantern with her living hand as she raced past it, wrenching more agony from her wound. She cast the lantern behind her. It broke and caught fire in a pool of flame, but as she ran the heat followed her. She stopped and looked behind her, ignoring another gunshot that struck the front locomotive beside her.

Smoke rose from her skirt, and a tiny fire trickled along the hem where burning oil had splashed. She yanked at the fasteners, using the building strength of her hand to tear away at them so she could run free, abandoning the smoldering skirt behind her. Immodesty was preferable to burning to death.

Baxter caught her by her arm—the undamaged arm—before she could continue her flight. "Ellie White? I'm so sorry you got mixed up in this. Your death might send your brother over the edge."

Ellie wiggled and turned, but couldn't break free from his grasp. It was almost as firm as her own when her hand was fully charged. Even if it had enough power, shocking him would only shock herself as well.

A gunshot echoed through the chamber, and one of the men beside Baxter collapsed, blood staining his shirt. Vivian stood at the mouth of the curved incline; Ellie's revolver in her hand. "My late husband taught me to be an expert marksman during our brief time together. Very un-British of us both, I'm sure, but I'm pretty sure I can kill you both without getting anywhere near Ellie."

Baxter whirled behind Ellie, aiming his gun at Vivian. "Are you sure of that?"

Ellie grabbed Baxter's gun hand with her metal one and jerked his aim clear. She squeezed, and his trigger finger cracked.

Vivian calmly pointed the gun at Baxter's henchman. He

hesitated for the space of two heartbeats, and then dropped his gun on the ground. "Smart," Vivian said. "Now get in that first rail car."

The man obeyed, pulling the pin and climbing into the car. "Now you," she hissed at Baxter.

"I'd rather die."

"Slowly and in a lot of pain, or quickly at the end of a rope?" Ellie squeezed again, even harder. Baxter cried out this time and let go of her arm. "Into the car, now."

Head lowered, Baxter climbed into the railcar with Vivian keeping the revolver trained on him the entire time. Ellie fumbled the pin while attempting to slide it closed and lock the door. The lack of feeling in her fingers was still a hindrance, and the hand was no longer behaving exactly right. But perhaps it had saved her life.

"We should go and get the police," Ellie said.

Vivian shrugged. "No, you do it. I'll make certain they don't escape. Or that the gentleman on the floor doesn't get any ideas."

"There's a chance the fires may reach the dynamite."

Vivian shook her head. "No, they have all but burned out. We shall be fine."

"I think Stokes is…"

"Dead? I think so. I shall mourn with his poor family. But at least there will be justice. Thank you, Ellie. Now go and get the police. After all, this is your story."

ABOUT THE AUTHOR

JAY IS AN AUTHOR, game developer, and software engineer. A steady diet of Star Trek, Star Wars, and The Twilight Zone as a child, mixed with an addiction to the words and worlds of Robert E. Howard, Lovecraft, Heinlein, and of course Tolkien produced a mixed-up young man who went on to corrupt the youth making console and PC video games, and writing stories that grow out of bizarre questions that begin with the words, "What if...?" While he tries to keep up on the newest speculative fiction by established and new authors, he'll often be found with his nose in pages of seventy-year-old pulp magazines. Usually digital versions, because those old pulp magazines are delicate! Jay is the winner of the 2016 DragonComet award for science fiction and fantasy.

The Tears of Nephi

David J. West

Ticking seconds warped into eons. The fragile hands of the pocket watch beat like war drums as the father waited to speak to President Young. Stinging sweat ran down his neck in this warm Dixie October.

"He will see you now," said the secretary as he opened the door.

"President Young, my daughter has been taken! Kidnapped!" shouted William Tullidge as he was ushered inside the office.

"Calm down. By whom, Brother Tullidge?" Brigham furrowed a weary brow. "Do you know why?"

"Some carpet-bagging drifters came into town last week, said they needed to do a little work on their machine, an airship. I let 'em do the work at my place. Don't know why they took little Virginia, but we need to get a posse together and go get them before anything happens." He looked away from Brigham's powerful gaze.

Tullidge stared out the window toward the Temple then back to the floor. "If anything happens to her, I'll never forgive myself."

"Your daughter, the blind one?"

"Yes, Virginia. Brother Kimball blessed her, but she's still blind."

"We have trials for a reason, blessings don't take away agency, even from choices in the preexistence. Virginia asked for this opportunity before she came here," answered Brigham.

"She did not ask for this one," said Tullidge.

"Does this have anything to do with your rather large promissory tithing receipts lately?"

"No, President. What do you mean?"

"You have been promising that you will turn in some rather large tithing settlements of late, are you about to come into something special? Is there something else behind the kidnapping?" asked Brigham. "Have you been gambling?"

"No, sir. I have been working real hard on my land, the cotton's going well, so are the vineyards," said Tullidge, looking away. "Sacramental wine will be ready soon."

Brigham bore holes through Tullidge's soul, but he didn't crack as so many others had. "Very well, you want me to tell you what to do?"

"Yes, President. We need a posse."

"Get Porter."

"I can't ask him," said Tullidge.

"Can't or won't, Brother Tullidge?"

Tullidge avoided the question. "Why not Brother Hamblin?"

"If it's desperadoes, you need a man that will deal with them in a way they'll understand. You need Porter," said Brigham. "I believe he's down at the mercantile getting his new horse shod."

"I won't ask him, he's a drunk. He's no Saint as far as I'm concerned. I saw him carousing with some of the army last week and speaking to some of Madame Flint's hussy's up in Salt Lake last time I was up there," said Tullidge. "Besides, these men took off in an airship. There is nothing to track."

Brigham frowned at the mention of Madame Flint as it was a near futile war to get the prostitutes out of the Territory since he was no longer governor. "Porter can track a raven through the sky. Get him. Good day."

"No, you listen to me," shouted Tullidge.

Brigham stood abruptly, glowering at the other man, but calmly said, "You asked me for assistance, and I told you. If you want your daughter back, you will get Brother Rockwell."

"But I saw him drunk as a skunk not a week ago. He's no better than those rogues that took her. I need Brother Hamblin," pleaded Tullidge.

"You can't have him." Brigham returned to scanning some

paperwork spread on the desk before him. "He is out beyond the Colorado with Chief Tuba."

Tullidge visibly darkened and slumped into the chair opposite the president. "Then there is no hope."

"Brother Tullidge, time is of the essence. Go and do as I commanded you. Far be it from me to deny any man enough rope to hang himself with, but for the sake of your daughter you will ask Brother Rockwell to retrieve her. If he can't fetch her back, then no man can."

"Yes, President Young. I'm sorry," Tullidge muttered.

"It's alright, get going," he too glanced out the window at the gathering charcoal clouds, "a storm is coming."

⚭

WILLIAM TULLIDGE WENT NORTH UP to the mercantile and then across to the blacksmith's. Porter was brushing down his pale buckskin horse.

"Porter," shouted Tullidge, almost sounding like an accusation.

"Yeah?" came the unconcerned reply.

Tullidge's face reddened when Porter didn't even bother to turn around and face him. He just kept brushing his horse down. "Porter. President Young said you have to help me get my daughter, Virginia, back. She has been kidnapped."

"That so? By who?" asked Porter, still casually brushing the horse down.

"Some odd desperadoes. Must be at least four or five of them. I didn't get a good look at any but two. Only had them at my place for a couple of days," said Tullidge.

"How old is your daughter? Seventeen, eighteen? It happens." He shrugged.

"I told you they kidnapped her. She is only eight, just got baptized a month ago in the Santa Clara," said Tullidge. Port turned to look at him as he plead before him. "She is blind and scared. I don't know why they would take her."

"Yeah," said Port. "Well, what's the last place they had her, and how long ago?"

"My property, out past Snow Canyon, past Jacob Hamblin's, towards the Red Mountain," said Tullidge, now holding his hat in hand.

"I'll be ready right quick."

"No, now," insisted Tullidge.

Porter turned and got in Tullidge's face. "Brother, I don't even know your name, so before you go and get all riled at me preparing to help you out, I suggest you show a few manners or I'm gonna knock your teeth in." Porter shoved him back and proceeded to put the horse blanket and saddle on his pale dappled mount.

"President Young said that you'd help me," muttered Tullidge, as tears came unwillingly to his eyes. "She's my only daughter."

"He didn't say nothing 'bout me being ordered around by you. Probably told ya to ask me and you're a poor asker." Port hefted himself onto the saddle.

Tullidge frowned and lowered his head.

"I'll do it, but you watch your mouth. Go get your horse."

Tullidge retrieved his horse and met Porter at the edge of town.

"What's your name anyway?" asked Port.

"Charles William Tullidge. Call me Bill Tullidge, my daughter is Virginia."

"You're one of the vineyard owners—I've heard of ya. Heard you struck it rich here-bouts lately," said Port coolly, as he cocked a grin at Tullidge.

"No."

"Yeah, I heard about some kind of mother-lode."

"No, I never found anything."

"Look Tullidge, you are a powerful poor liar. You must have found something and then sampled a bit too much of the sacramental wine, just like everyone else that grows it, and you talked, you bragged to the wrong people about what you found. And they took your daughter for ransom. Now you're too scared to admit that to Brigham. You want my help? You might as well come clean. Nothing wrong with giving old Port a little cut for helping out."

"I told you," said Tullidge, giving spurs to his horse to get a little ahead of Port's big Buckskin. "I never found anything."

"Alright, be like that, but you aren't fooling this old wolf," said Port.

"Don't know why I'm even trying this with you. You can't get these men anymore than I can," complained Tullidge.

Port stopped his horse. "You got a powerful strange way of asking for help."

Tullidge pointed up at the sky. "Well, they plum got away in an airship. Don't know how we'll ever catch them, since we don't even know which way they went."

"How about you start off by telling me a direction then?" asked Porter rolling his eyes.

"It was night, well past midnight. Dark and cloudy too, when they took her. I know the airship lifted up and went beyond Snow Canyon, but I couldn't tell which direction they went, there were no stars."

"You got a world of excuses, don't cha?" Porter spat then took a flask from his vest and drained it in one mighty gulp.

"Alcohol—and you call yourself a saint?"

"And do you call yourself a pharisee?" Port chuckled. "Cuz you sure as hell act like one."

"What's that supposed to mean?" argued Tullidge.

"You're awful judgmental for a man that dips into the sacramental wine as much as I've heard you do, and for a man that has a number of unpaid debts all over the territory. Don't think I don't know about folks with vices. Everybody talks."

"How dare you!" Tullidge fumbled for his gun.

"Don't even think about it." Porter's six-gun was already leveled at Tullidge. "I'll say it again. I'm here for the girl, not you. So, you can just keep your trap shut unlessen I ask you something."

Tullidge gulped and nodded.

"Now put that piece in your saddle bag and don't get any other ideas or I'm gonna have to go find an orphan. Got it?"

Tullidge nodded.

"Say it!" barked Porter.

"I got it," said Tullidge with a cough, before depositing his pistol in the saddle bag.

⁂

THEY RODE on in silence for some time. The homes grew sparser along the trail and Porter finally asked, "Whereabouts is your place anyway?"

Tullidge gestured toward the red-brown waters of the Santa Clara river. "All my vineyards and such are down by the river, along with the two families that help me work them. But I bought a homestead for the wife farther up into the hills, about a mile that way. She had consumption and wanted to be well away from folks. She passed away six years ago."

"Sorry to hear that. But, you stay up there?"

"Yes. Little Virginia was familiar with it, so we stayed on, and I ride on down to the vineyards every day to work."

They traversed a steep embankment of a road. The agitated caw of carrion birds caught their attention. Black wings flocked and jabbered over a dirty patch of brown and white.

Porter urged his horse to canter over there and he shot once to scatter the crows. Tullidge followed and gasped.

A dead man lay upon the ground with his arms and legs flung wide. He was bloody and broken as if beaten severely. His head lolled to the side in an unnatural position.

"You know him?" asked Porter as he dismounted.

Tullidge doffed his hat, clutching it to his chest. "Yes, that's

Arthur Gaskell. He settled here years ago, and I bought my homestead from him. He kept trying to get me to sell it back to him, but I didn't want to sell since Virginia loved it. He got pretty agitated years ago about it, but then we never spoke again."

"You argued with him?"

"Well yeah, sometimes rather heatedly, but I didn't kill him! What are you trying to lay on me?"

Porter tipped his own hat back. "Easy Chuck, I know you didn't kill him."

"How?" Tullidge flushed, realizing the way he had spoken.

"No bullet wounds, hell not even anywhere somebody struck him with a club or anything."

"He sure looks beaten up to me," said Tullidge.

"Are you confessing?" Porter grinned.

"No!"

"I'm just joshing you. Look here, no tracks anywhere around, and he ain't been dead for more than a day, half day even. I think this happened last night."

"How can you tell?"

"Look at them flies. He's still pretty fresh."

"But his body. Those legs look broke."

"Oh, they are, and his neck too."

"Who did this?"

Porter pointed round about the area. "Only our tracks have broken ground here. Not a blade of grass is bent, nor stone overturned, not even a mark in the dust."

Tullidge scratched his head and looked around.

Porter asked pointedly, "You said those fellers had an airship?"

"Yeah, so?"

Porter pointed skyward. "So, my guess is somebody dropped him from a good long way up."

"But why Gaskell? He didn't know them."

The wind moaned mournfully across the rusty hills. "That is the puzzle, isn't it?" Porter took a long pull from his flask.

❧

Later that afternoon they rode to Tullidge's ranch house and took care of the weary horses in his stables. While they brushed down the animals, Porter asked, "So, they had an airship and said they needed to do some repairs on it here at your place? Why not fly just the few more miles to get into St. George where there would be more supplies and such? Did they ride into town for anything?"

"No, they never did. What are you driving at?"

Porter rubbed at his beard, then signaled for Tullidge to follow him out of the stables. "You say they needed to work on an airship, but they never needed anything more from you or town?"

"They had everything they needed on board they said. Lotta brass and gears, you know, steam gadgets. They just needed water and a forge."

"Did you see them work the forge?"

"I saw them heating up some metal, and they went through an awful lot of water too. They didn't have much in the way of tanks on board, near as I could tell. All of them new-fangled gimzo's need a lot of steam to power the contraption, and they run low in the desert I suppose."

"Now we're getting somewhere," said Porter, as he glanced out across the red desert.

"That's what they said, though I didn't understand their meaning at the time. They used my blacksmithing shop yonder. They had most of their own tools. I never did see much of anything they worked on. They wouldn't even let me talk to the pilot. Queer folk."

"So, they might have been faking the repairs and just taking an inventory on you?"

"I don't see how or why they would. I already told you that I don't have any discoveries or what not."

Porter chuckled. "And I've heard tell you did find some kind of treasure. Some gold in a mine or cave. Something ancient. Maybe

Lamanite. You still don't want to tell me about it, even when it comes to finding your daughter?"

Tullidge tore at his hair and stamped his foot. "I don't have any treasure!"

"But you know where it is?" Porter prodded.

"No! Why do I have to answer these ridiculous questions?"

"Because," shouted Porter, "they took your daughter for a reason. What is that reason? I suspect they are trying to get a ransom outta you."

Tullidge didn't say anything, but his bulging eyes and ferocious cynicism wavered as a tear rolled down his cheek. "I don't know anything. I just want my daughter back."

"Tell me the truth, ya puke!" Porter slammed Tullidge up against the barn door and slammed his bowie knife in the plank beside his right ear. The blade quivered in the gray slats.

"All right! But the angel said if I told anyone, I wouldn't be able to get the gold," lamented Tullidge.

"Angel? But you already bragged to a few of your local friends."

"I did," sobbed Tullidge. "I did. At first, I was so excited. I saw an angel. I even tested him, and I felt his hand! He was made of flesh and blood! He was resurrected! I told my brother-in-law, Miles and then Winston and Splain too."

"And then?" urged Porter.

"I went back to the cave. The angel met me there. Told me the gold could be mine by rights since it was on my land. I just had to wait until the time was right, and then in due time I would use it to lift both myself and the church up."

"When would that be?"

Tullidge shook his head. "I'm not sure. It's been two, almost three years. Sometimes he was there when I would go back and sometimes he wasn't. Usually he isn't."

Porter pulled at his beard. "He? What's his name?"

"Lucius. He was a Nephite warrior who was called to guard the treasure until the time is right. He is a resurrected being, with a body, kinda like the Three Nephites."

"Mmm hmm," mumbled Porter.

"You don't believe me?" said Tullidge, wiping away his tears. "I shouldn't have told you anything. Your savage kind can't understand having that level of spiritual experience."

Porter folded his bear-like arms across his chest. "Pound sand Chuck, my best friend in all the world was the Prophet Joseph Smith. I know righteous men, and I have had spiritual experiences, but it still sounds to me like you've been sold a bill of goods."

Tullidge shook his head adamantly. "No, that's not possible. I felt a burning in my bosom over this." He placed his hand over his heart.

"Here's what I think," offered Porter. "You discovered a lode with some good ore. Someone found out about it and gave you this cock and bull story, they pretended to be a spirit waiting for when the time was right *for them*, then they came back to get it."

"No, you can't understand unless you saw him. He was such a beautiful man."

Porter squinted, asking, "Did he come to you first or did you find the gold first?"

"He came to me first. He showed me where the mine is. I never would have found it otherwise. There was a hidden door in the rock. That's how I know it's true. He appeared wreathed in light. He is a resurrected being! I've seen him ascend into heaven!"

Porter screwed up his face in puzzlement. "You better just show me the mine."

"It's a cave," corrected Tullidge, "but the angel Lucius revealed to me that it was a Nephite mine far back in the ancient times."

"Lucius?"

"Yes. It means Light bringer."

"So does Lucifer."

Tullidge scowled. "I was not deceived. I felt his hand. He is a resurrected being."

"An angel?" Porter scoffed. "Did you tell President Young about him?"

Tullidge balked. "Well… no, because the angel Lucius told me not to. He said it was my own privilege. That's why I quit telling people, after he rebuked me for my iniquity and flagging tongue."

"Uh huh."

"Don't mock the heavenly powers, Porter!"

"I ain't. But I also don't think what you experienced was heavenly."

Tullidge threw up his hands, shouting, "Well I felt the hands. Not you! I saw the gold. Not you! I'm telling you it's all real!"

"So then, why would these men take your daughter? So they could demand the gold from you?"

Tullidge shook his head. "I never told them about it. They were filthy gentiles."

"But they knew, didn't they?"

Tullidge bit his lip and muttered, "Not that I'm aware of."

"So, what did they want? What demands have they given you for little Virginia?"

"Nothing yet. They just took her and flew away like birds."

"Like birds," mused Porter as he glanced up at a trio of vultures. The scavengers circled high over a nearby mesa.

"Where is the cave?" asked Porter.

Tullidge balked. "I ain't telling you! You'll steal my gold."

"So, it's all yours now?" asked Porter with a chuckle. "Thought you said it would help the church in due time."

"The church, not you!"

"For a man that needs help fetching his daughter and was told by the president to ask my help, you sure are skittish about things."

Tullidge dug his toes into the red dirt. "It's just over yonder. Ain't never showed anyone the door except little Virginia, and she's blind, you know. She knows her way in there just as good without a lamp. Sometimes I've let her lead me down with the lamp turned down low to save on oil. She knows the way real good."

"There we have it," exclaimed Porter.

"What?"

"That's why they wanted her."

Tullidge shook his head. "But I never told them about any of that."

"Face it, Chuck, there are folks that know things you don't think they do. Mysteries are just secrets you don't know yet."

"No, that's not possible. Only me, the angel, and Virginia knew about the mine."

"You talked."

Tullidge put his hands to his ears and shook his head. "No. Well I did, but only to friends, and I never told them where or anything."

"What about Gaskell? Why would he want the property back so bad?"

"That was years before the angel."

Porter chuckled to himself. "Mighty fine coincidence, if you ask me."

"I didn't ask you!"

"Easy, Chuck. Why don't you show me that mine so I know what to watch out for. Them kidnappers are surely coming back for it. They're just trying to run you off by taking the girl, even using her as a guide or hostage I suspect."

"It's there." Tullidge pointed at the nearby red hills.

"Beyond that mesa?"

"No. It's right at the foot of the mesa. There is a stone doorway. I never would have found it without the angel Lucius showing me the way. You could see it from right here if the door was open. Just to the left of that bush. You push and the door will open. It's ingenious, really."

Porter scanned the mesa and looked to the top again at the circling vultures.

"Seems to me we ought to see what them buzzards up there are watching. Could very well be that the pukes are up there waiting on what you're gonna do before they make their move."

"What if you're wrong and they're not up there? What if it's just a dead deer or something?"

"Life is all about taking risks, Chuck. 'Sides I don't think a deer could get up that sheer slope and they wouldn't be circling unless something was there that could give them a fine meal."

"I don't want to risk my daughter's life fooling around on chances."

"You're not, them bastards are, and we are gonna make them pay for it in spades." Porter strode to his saddle bags and proceeded to place a second belt of ammunition on, and grabbed a few spare chambers for his six-gun.

"You think its gonna come to that?"

"In my experience. Yes."

Tullidge scrunched his eyebrows together.

"I like to be prepared." Porter dropped a couple more into the pouch in his vest.

The pounding of rapidly approaching hooves made both men move to the door to investigate. A rider approached, waving his hat.

"It's all right," said Tullidge, "that's Ammon Price. I know him."

Ammon was a young man wearing buckskin pants and a bleached white shirt. He put his hat on as he slid from the saddle. "I was hoping I'd find both of you. An airship was seen up above Snow Canyon halfway to Mountain Meadows by the Swensons. Brother Swenson said they made quite a racket early in the morning shooting at his livestock. He shot at them, but they flew away. It's gotta be them same fellers who took Virginia! Marshal Ricks already has a posse together to go after them. I was sent to fetch you two right away."

Tullidge put his hat on. "Let's go!"

"Hold on," said Porter. "They must have dropped Gaskell early this morning, then headed up that way when they were spotted."

"So what?" asked Tullidge.

Porter explained, "I think they wanted to be spotted to lead us on a wild goose chase. It wouldn't have been that hard for them to circle back in the night."

"Well, that's our best guess so far. They probably are up that way trying to make a getaway north," offered Ammon. "We need to hurry."

"I doubt it," said Porter.

"What do you mean?" asked Ammon.

"He's right, Porter," said Tullidge. "We need to get a move on, catching up to an airship is tough. Our best bet is to hurry and ride all night and catch them making camp maybe halfway to Reno."

"That's exactly what they want you to think, but I ain't buying it," said Porter.

"Are you a coward?" accused Ammon.

"Pull your reins back kid, you don't know the half of it."

"I heard tell you was something special, maybe that's all a lie!" shouted Ammon.

"You best lay off the accusations afore you get hurt kid. Now how big is that posse the marshal has?"

"Fifteen men," he answered sourly.

"That's more than enough without me, if you're right, but I got a feeling that the kidnapping airmen are gonna be sticking around and may be watching us even now. Tullidge, I want you to ride with the kid, wearing my hat and coat. I want them to think that you're sticking around by yourself."

Tullidge shook his head. "You're crazy. And I'm not about to leave you here by yourself with my..."

Ammon looked at him suspiciously.

"You still don't trust me enough to get your daughter back and you think I'll rob you? You have a remarkable sense of morality."

Ammon glared at Porter.

"You best ease up on that stare, son, or someone is liable to knock it off your face. You swing on back this way real quiet like after dark if you're worried about me, Chuck, but I think soon as they see you two ride away, they're gonna make their move and we'll get to the bottom of things and get Virginia back."

"But the posse," protested Ammon.

"Ain't gonna find anything, but ride with them if you like" Porter took Tullidge's hat and placed his own on the man's head. "We want them to think I'm leaving and you're staying. Get going."

"All right, but I'm coming back soon as it's dark," muttered Tullidge.

"Take my horse," said Porter. "This trick has to fool them but good."

Tullidge mounted Porter's big buckskin and he and Ammon rode away.

OͦͦOͦ

PORTER SAW them off then showed himself into the home as if he owned it. He got something to drink but swiftly prepared for the worst, checking out the windows and camping himself where he could watch the mesa as dusk set in.

All was still for another hour as the sky bruised red and purple. He saw no more movement nor any other sign of life. Even the vultures seemed to have vanished.

Soon as the darkness hid the landscape, he lit a lamp in the front room but slid out a side door and eased his way, hugging the shadows, ever watchful of where he believed his enemies lurked. Still, there was no sign of them.

Stalking past the sage and cactus, he moved abreast a Joshua tree and made his way for the hidden door. "Just left of the bush," Tullidge had said. Porter could see nothing out of the ordinary against the side of the craggy hillside. He felt along the warm stone until he found a near invisible vertical crack. He followed it until it turned abruptly and ran horizontal for three feet then turned down again. This had to be the hidden door, but how to open it?

He pushed and nothing happened, it didn't budge or even flex.

He may as well have been pushing against the mountain. No matter, he could see that as long as he had been there, no one else had tried to enter it either. He would try to traverse the mesa and spot what had caught his attention earlier.

Not far from the doorway, an eroded gouge in the mesa twisted up the side like a staircase made of cracks. Part of it folded in on itself and Porter had little trouble ascending half the height. From there it did become more precarious and the handholds were necessary to climb. He inched his way up the red and tan surface. Looking back down, the ranch house in the moonlight looked miniature.

The sky was nearly as dark and red as the land itself now.

Right before getting to the top, he heard voices.

"Almost time," said one.

"Everybody up. We'll move on down soon."

"No posse?"

"Nope. Looks like the bait worked, even with dropping off Gaskell in the wrong place."

"That sumbitch got what was coming to him," said another with an eerie guffaw.

"Keep your voice down, Tullidge is still down there and we don't want to give him no warning."

Porter crept to the edge of the mesa and looked over. Far back against the rocks in a slight depression was the airship. It was far enough from the edge that there was no way anyone could see it from below. The envelope of the thing was perhaps fifty feet long and more than a bulbous fifteen feet high above the gondola which was itself as large as three wagons and all made of brass. It had been positioned in such a way to just barely hide it from anyone down on the ground. A strange engine towards the rear, Porter guessed, must control its steering and such. A slew of equipment was spread about as if the men were in the process of making room for new cargo. Four men huddled about a small campfire nearby, a fifth skirted along the edge of the mesa, but at the moment he was the farthest one away from Porter. He had a spyglass and seemed to be watching the house. Good news, they must believe that he, as Tullidge, was still inside.

A slight muffled sound caught his ears. Just inside the gondola of the airship was a small blonde girl. Her white eyes stared blankly ahead.

Porter moved like a pantherish shadow, scaling over the lip of black basalt as if he were one with the very forces of nature. Not a one of the men heard him, but the girl did. Her blind eyes saw nothing, but she cocked her head, obviously aware of the faint trace of sound that was Porter's boots, scuffing ever so softly on the black rock.

"Who's there?" she queried.

"Be quiet," snarled one of the men.

But the more wary of them glanced about with a lantern, just in time to spot his own death warrant.

"Drop it." Porter leveled both pistols at his foes.

The men scrambled, rocking back on their heels. "Who are you?" challenged the leader.

"Porter Rockwell, Federal Marshal. You're all under arrest for kidnapping and one murder at the least, though I'm sure there are some other unsavory goings-on, too."

The man furthest out in the shadows took a shot at Porter. Porter's hat flew from his head and sailed off the edge of the cliff.

The rest of the men jumped into action. Shots rang out like the thunder of hell, and red flashing gunfire lit the top of the mesa up like a fuming volcano.

How the men missed Porter is one of those things that a body just cannot understand, but he was blessed years ago by his friend, the prophet Joseph Smith, that if he should not cut his hair, no bullet nor blade could harm him. Still, Porter didn't just walk into a hailstorm of lead. He took cover behind a nearby boulder as he returned fire.

One of the kidnappers cried out, clutching his fat chest as two of Porter's slugs tore through him. Another, wounded in the arm, fell forward and hid in the gondola of the airship.

The wounded kidnapper jumped up with the girl held before him and the barrel of his gun at her temple. "You best lay down your arms, Marshal or we end this right now!"

"You're not gonna do that," returned Porter from behind his cover.

"You don't think I've got the sand for it?" challenged the kidnapper.

"Sure, you do. But *if* you hurt her, I've got no reason to go easy on any of you. Right now, you can still surrender peaceably."

"We outnumber you five to one," growled one.

"Four to one," corrected Porter. "Fatty ain't ever getting up again. You got nowhere to go."

"That's what he thinks" One of the men rushed into the gondola. He ran toward the back and started firing up the engine.

The two men outside the airship waved their guns suspiciously at the darkness where they thought Porter hid.

"We're gonna get in the airship, and you're gonna let us walk Marshal, or the girl gets it."

"I can't let you leave with her," answered Porter.

"You got no choice. We fly off or she dies."

An engine groaned to life at the rear of the gondola and a faint red spark erupted into a balefire of orange energy, howling like the damned.

"Get in," shouted the lead kidnapper.

The airship pitched forward ever so slightly as it lifted off the ground.

Porter shot a few holes into the envelope, but this accomplished nothing.

The two remaining kidnappers rushed to the open door of the gondola, firing wildly in Porter's general direction.

Porter shot one in the leg, shattering his calf. The cripple smashed into the ground, cracking his head open. His companion rushed past and dove into the gondola.

The kidnappers rained gunfire at Porter. He ran and leapt off the side of the mesa to avoid being hit.

The airship rose and turned about as the engines roared, fully alive. Venting jets of flame acted as a rudder, propelling the thing forward. The pilot took them over the lip of the mesa to better see where Porter had gone.

He hung on to the side of the mesa and shot up at them with a remaining pistol. His six-gun could not penetrate the bottom of the gondola, neither could the kidnappers get a good bead on him while they remained overhead. They shouted to the pilot to bank across from Porter to kill him.

A sudden down draft caused the airship to move farther down than the pilot had meant, and Porter took the chance and leapt atop the envelope. Rigging provided a sure grip as he held to the web-like ropes.

Pulling out his bowie knife, he slashed a long gash across the envelope and the airship buckled and began to lose altitude. It careened downward at an alarming rate.

As the airship hit the ground, it bounced twice and skidded to a stop. The envelope buckled and sent Porter flying up and back down to the ground. He landed hard, the wind whooshing out of his lungs. His vision faded and all went black as he lay amongst a tangle of boulders.

∞

PORTER AWOKE to a bit of daylight teasing in at the corner of his vision. It was still very early, but the dawn was coming. His body ached and he wondered a long moment if anything was broken. No, everything could still move, sore as he was. Poking his head up over the boulders, he saw the broken airship a short distance away. The envelope was fully deflated, and no one appeared to be anywhere nearby.

He heard something at the ranch house a short way off, and he glanced about for his gun and knife. Not seeing the gun anywhere, he was grateful at least that the knife was close by. He slipped it into his belt and trotted silent as he could toward the ranch house. One of the kidnappers was trying to secure horses inside the stable.

Porter crept up behind him and clocked him on the head with the butt of his bowie. He gagged and hog-tied the man and tossed him into the corner of the stable. He took the kidnapper's pistol and put it into his own belt.

Searching about, he saw no sign of the others. He slapped the bound kidnapper awake and yanked the gag free.

"Where are they?"

The man snapped, "I ain't telling you nothing!"

Porter drew his bowie knife and let the edge shear off a section of the man's whiskers. "You might want to rethink your position."

"They went into the mine. They're gonna get some treasure out and then come back and get the horses. You better skedaddle afore they get back or you're a dead man."

"Oh, I'm just a shaking in my boots at what some low-life kidnappers can do. Where's the girl?"

"They took her with them, for insurance in case you came back, we thought you fled the coop."

"Why all the sneaking around? Why not just take the gold earlier?"

"We had to have a way to get it out quick before you Mormons knew about it. That was what the airship was for."

"And Gaskell?"

"He's the one that told the boss in the first place. It just took some time to come up with a surefire way to get it."

"Why the deception?"

"That was Gaskell's doing, he didn't want to alert anyone local that he was a party to it, was afraid Brigham would claim it, but we were done with him and threw him out the other night to cut down on the shares. But he lied, and we couldn't find the opening, and Tullidge refused to talk until we took his daughter. Turned out she was the one who was supposed to know where the door is, but we didn't know she was blind. You Mormons sure are a dirty bunch, what with your own trickery."

Porter chuckled. "Sounds like you all got what was coming to you, but I'm a gonna finish the job."

Porter gagged the man again and made sure he was trussed up real good. He went to the hidden door of the mine. It was slightly ajar, and he carefully swung it open. If they were inside, they were a long ways in. He couldn't see or hear anything. He was aware that by opening the door, the pressure change could alert the enemy of his coming, but that couldn't be helped now. He turned the wick on his lamp as low as he dared and proceeded inside.

The lava tube was rough going and only a partial trail was easily passable. Some places looked worn smooth and Porter found those especially curious, considering Tullidge couldn't have worn them smooth by his own passage even if he had come down every day.

The tunnel wound deeper and deeper into the earth. The air was stuffy and warmer than outside. At one point, Porter thought he heard something, so he cautiously crept around every corner expecting to hear the thunder of guns.

Echoes carried from further below, and he wondered as he walked past numerous false turns if the way out would be difficult to remember. It was enough of a concern that he marked a few stones with the butt end of his knife.

An orange glow ahead signaled he had caught up to the ruffians. They bickered and cast long, creeping shadows on the walls.

"Where is the treasure?"

"We're almost there, I swear it," answered the girl.

"Either I'm as blind as she is, or there is nothing here and Gaskell lied to us. None of this rock denotes gold ore," said one.

"It's here, please let me and my daddy go," begged Virginia.

They laughed. "Not until we have that gold we heard about."

"It's on the other side of the Tears of Nephi."

"What is that?"

"Through the waters," she said.

"You're in for a hard lesson, girly. There's something here all right, we just got to find it."

They moved beyond a wide chamber and stopped. As Porter followed a short way behind, he heard the continual drum of dripping water. A vent in the rock above had a cascade of dripping water that clung to long stone pikes that gleamed like sabers as the lamps cast their light upon them. Crystal clear pools of water caught the falling drips, the sound magnified in the cavern.

They stepped through a curtain of falling water, and the girl said, "Feel that? We are at the Tears of Nephi. The treasure room is just beyond. Let me and my daddy go now, please."

"Har, har, har. Ain't you in for a surprise," said one. "But your daddy turned tail and ran when we took you. We don't have him. But we needed you to find this, and now, we'll take the treasure and leave you down here to rot!"

The girl sat down on a flat stone.

Porter crept closer, and though the girl's pale white eyes stared blankly ahead, she turned her head slightly toward his approach.

The men hooted and hollered just beyond Porter's line of sight. He inched closer and reached the girl. He whispered urgently, "I'm Porter. I'm here to help you and your pa. Keep silent and I'll get you out of this."

The girl stood.

"Hang on. I'm gonna cut you loose." His knife sheared through the ropes about her hands. He led her back the way they had come. She was as sure footed as any mountain goat.

"You all right, little missy?"

"I know the way just fine. I've come down here with my pa enough times."

Porter pondered that, then was disrupted by a rude echo of a gunshot that caused tiny bits of rock and dust to fall upon his hat. The bullet ricocheted angrily just above him like a hornet gone mad.

"Hey you guys! That marshal is down here and he's a trying to get away with that there girl!"

"She can name us!"

"*He* can name us!" shouted another.

"Kill him! Kill them both!" ordered their boss as they emerged from beyond the edge of the tunnel, shooting toward Porter and Virginia.

Bullets whizzed by with the stifling choke of fetid gun smoke.

Virginia screamed as the deafening gunshots echoed in the cavern like a storm rolling across the canyons.

Porter shot the lamp in the lead ruffian's hand. Dragon fire engulfed the figure, ravenous orange flames licked over the flailing man. He screamed and ran headlong into a stalactite before dropping, silent as the grave.

A cascade of bullets chipped away at the stones near Porter. He returned fire while Virginia clutched at his feet. She cried out as a bullet grazed her calf. Porter knew there was no cover for her, none but himself, sooner or later the barrage would strike her. As the flames licking over the dead man faded, Porter was struck with an idea.

He threw his lamp at the attackers' boulder.

Oil and broken glass again flared orange in the deep murk before returning the cave to stifling darkness.

Tearing a strip of his shirt off, Porter bound Virginia's grazed wound. "That should staunch the flow until I can do better in a safe spot."

Virginia squeezed his hand.

"We gotta get going, little sister," he said. "Can you lead us out?"

"Yes, sir." She whimpered slightly as he tightened the cloth.

Shielding her body, Porter urged her up and back toward the way they'd come. They passed beyond the dripping water she called the Tears of Nephi, splashed with the cool water and plunged into darkness as the last vestige of light behind them was snuffed out.

Something lurked in the gloom up ahead. The gleam of a dying lantern shone upon a raised knife. A body pounced upon Porter and Virginia.

Ripping and tearing, Porter fended off the brutal attack, striking the man senseless with the butt of his empty pistol.

Virginia cried out in pain.

"You okay?" Porter asked.

"I'll be alright, he just hit my shoulder is all," she said.

A few stray bullets whistled through the chamber as the killers chased after them, shooting wildly. None of their chaotic shots touched them as they reached the crook in the cavern.

Porter clasped Virginia's cold, clammy hand. She led him on through twisting tunnels he never would have known were there in the palpable dark.

"We're almost out," she said, before collapsing.

Porter reached and picked up her limp body. The wet from the tears was almost gone, but warm fluid ran down her shoulder and chest. The bandit's knife must have got her bad.

He pressed a hand against the wound and cried out, "Dear Lord, take me, not her."

Her breathing came in hoarse, feeble gasps.

Holding her in his arms, he struggled down the tunnel which now had the barest hint of light revealed ahead.

Morning shone through the cracks of a doorway, and Porter kicked it open as he struggled out the door, his hands drenched in blood.

A posse rode up, Tullidge at the fore, shouting. Porter couldn't understand a word.

Tullidge leapt from his horse and tried to take Virginia into his arms. Porter shoved him away.

"He is her pa," said a deputy.

"Then he should'a taken better care of her," snarled Porter.

"She is his daughter," said the deputy.

Porter let Tullidge take her and he looked back into the tunnel. "Get me another lantern. I'm gonna finish this."

"You sure? You look wounded," said the deputy.

"Ain't my blood," said Porter over his shoulder as he went back into the mine.

"This is all your fault!" accused Tullidge.

"Is it?" Porter challenged.

Tullidge swore and ran back toward the ranch house, carrying Virginia.

"Is she gonna make it?" asked someone.

Porter shook his head.

"How many are down there?" asked the deputy.

"Least two more, maybe a third is still alive. I aim to take them in alive."

Back toward the ranch house a black buggy approached. Tullidge charged from the house, running toward them.

Tullidge ran toward Porter, shouting. He held something in his hand, like a candle.

"What is he doing?" asked the deputy. "Has he got candles?"

Porter squinted and cocked his head, curious at the screaming man's demeanor.

When Tullidge was about thirty feet from Porter, he threw the sparkling stick. Porter stood stone still and, as the candle stick neared, he casually brought his arm up and deflected it, sending it reeling away toward the mine entrance.

The candle stick fell just inside the threshold, and a terrific explosion followed. Great chunks of stone fell, a calamitous boom rang out, and a big section of ground suddenly slumped and fell in, creating a ditch beside them. Smoke and dust rose into the cool morning air like a specter rising from the grave.

"Didn't expect that," mused Porter. "Looks like I won't be needing that lamp."

Tullidge fell to his knees, dumbfounded. "My gold mine and my daughter all lost, and it's all your fault."

"Perhaps not," came a new voice.

There stood President Young with Virginia beside him. She was alive.

"It's a miracle," said the deputy.

"Virginia?" cried Tullidge. "Thank you for healing her, President Young."

"It wasn't me," said President Young. "I had a feeling I should come out and see about this fine mess. An angel was attending your daughter and she opened her eyes to look upon me as I entered your home."

"Then why am I still alive?" asked Porter. "I said I'd trade my life for hers."

"We don't always get to choose such things, but I imagine you have saved up some bargaining power with the other side and it was called in."

"Good to have credit," Porter mused.

ABOUT THE AUTHOR

DAVID J. West writes dark fantasy and weird westerns because the voices in his head won't quiet until someone else can hear them. He is a great fan of sword & sorcery, ghosts and lost ruins, so of course he lives in Utah with his wife and children.

About the Editor

Holli Anderson grew up in a small town in Utah where she read anything she could get her hands on-- mostly from the scant selection offered by the BookMobile that came around once a week. Her love of books grew from there and often became a means of escape from the real world. During an especially difficult time in her life (it involved teenaged sons...), reading was no longer giving her the escape she longed for, so she decided to write her own stories in order to visit different worlds when the real world was in too much chaos.

Holli is the author of the FIVE trilogy, a young adult urban fantasy/paranormal; and Saved, an adult romantic suspense; and Myrikal, a YA dystopian/superhero. She has many other projects in the works. She is the Chief Editor for Immortal Works, a Registered Nurse, wife of a very supportive husband named Steve, and the mother of four boys.

This has been an
Immortal Production